THE
SPECTACULAR

ALSO BY FIONA DAVIS

The Dollhouse
The Address
The Masterpiece
The Chelsea Girls
The Lions of Fifth Avenue
The Magnolia Palace

THE SPECTACULAR

A NOVEL

FIONA DAVIS

DUTTON

DUTTON

An imprint of Penguin Random House LLC
penguinrandomhouse.com

LIBRARY OF CONGRESS CATALOGING-IN-PUBLICATION DATA

Names: Davis, Fiona, 1966– author.
Title: The Spectacular: a novel / Fiona Davis.
Description: 1. | New York : Dutton, [2023]
Identifiers: LCCN 2022059177 (print) | LCCN 2022059178 (ebook) |
ISBN 9780593184042 (hardcover) | ISBN 9780593184059 (ebook)
Subjects: LCGFT: Novels.
Classification: LCC PS3604.A95695 S64 2023 (print) | LCC PS3604.A95695 (ebook) |
DDC 813/.6—dc23/20221212
LC record available at https://lccn.loc.gov/2022059177
LC ebook record available at https://lccn.loc.gov/2022059178

Printed in the United States of America

1st Printing

For Greg Wands

THE
SPECTACULAR

CHAPTER ONE

DECEMBER 1992

I still dance in my dreams.

But not in my life. In my life, I shuffle around this too-large house, tossing whatever is within reach into the nearest cardboard box, not bothering to wrap anything in newspaper or to make sure the box labeled *living room* actually contains items from the living room.

The movers are far more worried about my belongings than I am. As I've hit my fifties, I've found that the stuff that surrounds me every day has lost its charm. Like the clock on the fireplace mantel that I pick up, surprised at its heft. The darn thing hasn't worked in a decade. Or the cast-iron Le Creuset pot that sits in a drawer doing absolutely nothing. I haven't given a dinner party in ages, and I'm not about to start now. Some people end up hoarding their possessions, unable to get rid of the plastic bags that the groceries came in, but that's not me. To be honest, I'm getting a kick out of seeing box after box go out the door, like a snake shedding its skin. Out the door and into the big truck, to be dropped off at the Salvation Army. The few pieces that are left, including my antique bed and my favorite armchair, will be delivered to a sunny one-bedroom with high ceilings in Sutton Gardens, an independent-living community for the fifty-five-and-over set, where you can mind your own business in the comfort of your room or join in on a water-aerobics class, depending on the day.

You would think that after independent living comes dependent living, but instead it's "assisted," which brings to mind someone delicately holding your elbow as you cross the street in the best of circumstances or offering extra leverage as you rise from the commode in the worst. Having been the assistant myself for many years, I know full well what's involved. Finally, there's the memory-care floor, which is a laugh because for most folks behind those locked doors, there aren't that many memories left to be careful about.

That's not me, though. Not by a long shot. At fifty-five, I still have all my memories intact, thank you very much. There are days when I wouldn't mind blocking out the more painful ones, but I have nothing to complain about, not yet. I'm aware of my limitations, but I'm not defined by them.

My new lodgings are just down the road from this house, so I'm not venturing very far. Even though Bronxville is only eighteen miles from Midtown Manhattan, it's an oasis of green, renowned for its "stockbroker Tudor" houses, the term coined after the newly rich snapped them up in the 1920s and '30s. People like my father, who was looking for a home that was close to the city but not too close, a place that showed he had good taste and a good job. My father never got tired of pointing out the slate roof and lead glass windows to visitors. He may not have been a stockbroker, but he was a company man and proud of it.

I look about my living room, almost expecting to see him drinking a scotch in his favorite armchair, and my throat tightens.

"Let me help you with that."

One of the movers, a skinny kid with freckles whom the others have teased all afternoon, puts the box he was carrying on the coffee table and comes toward me, eyes wide. He gently takes the clock from my hands.

"It doesn't work," I say, wiping the dust from my palms. "You can have it, if you like. Maybe it can be fixed."

"We're not allowed to take anything," he says. "But thanks."

He looks like he's barely sixteen and is more tentative in his actions than his cohorts, who move about the house like they own it. "You're new at this," I say.

"It's my first day."

"That's why they're making you do all the hard work, like climbing up into the attic. You better not take that kind of guff from them. They'll never stop."

"I don't mind." He pauses. "I found some things in the attic that I thought you might want to sift through, maybe give a last look."

I wave my hand. "No one's been up there in decades—whatever it is, I don't need it."

He turns to the large box sitting on the coffee table and opens it. "Well, this almost split open when I was upstairs. I'll have to take everything out and tape up the bottom anyway." He lifts out a pair of pointe shoes from when I took ballet class as a teenager, the ribbons fluttering loose like silk ringlets. "You were a dancer?"

I wish I had taken a moment, just one moment, back when I was dancing, to stop and appreciate what it felt like to lift my leg effort-lessly high, what it was like when my limbs and mind were rich with music and my body snapped into place. When my arms and legs did exactly what I told them to do. In my dreams, I stretch like a rubber band and my body is nineteen again. And then I wake up stiff and sore and realize it's only getting worse.

He places the shoes carefully on the coffee table, as if they were made of glass. Reaching back into the box, he pulls out a program for the Radio City Music Hall *Christmas Spectacular* of 1956. Then a pair of worn Capezio character shoes. I remember exactly what it felt like to buckle them up and dash out of the dressing room, how they eventually molded to my feet after hours dancing onstage. When I see those shoes, the voices of the other dancers fill my ears, along with the strains of the orchestra warming up.

But some memories are not as welcome. Screams of fear, the smell of smoke. Bloodstains on my dance tights, a lone red ribbon.

A combination of terror and regret wraps around me like a straitjacket.

The boy is about to dig deeper, but I stop him. "Enough."

The doorbell rings and I leave him so I can answer it. He can decide what to do with that box. I don't want it.

A young girl with raindrops in her hair stands on my porch.

"Yes?" I ask.

"Ms. Brooks? I'm Piper Grace Cole. You can call me Piper. I'm here to pick you up."

"For what?"

She blinks. "Um. The Radio City Music Hall anniversary? It starts at seven P.M. Sorry I'm early, I didn't want us to run into rush hour traffic." Behind her, a black sedan with a driver sits idling at the curb.

The Rockette alumni group is always sending me newsletters with chipper reports of grandchildren and moves to Florida. I usually give it a quick scan for any familiar names and then toss it in the bin. I don't remember ever saying that I'd attend the anniversary celebration.

"Do you mind if I come in?" Piper asks. The wind has picked up and the rain is getting both of us wet now.

I let her inside and she follows me to the kitchen. There, on the refrigerator, is the invitation, held in place with a small magnet: *Radio City Music Hall Invites You to the 60th Anniversary of the Rockettes.* A couple of weeks ago a woman called to confirm I was coming. Ann

Burris was her name. I said I couldn't because I don't drive or take the train anymore. She told me she'd take care of that, and apparently Piper is the result.

"Are you a Rockette?" I ask.

"Gosh, no." She says it with a rush of air, as if I asked if she were the Queen of England. "I'm an assistant to the events coordinator, Ms. Burris. I was told that you were precious cargo and to make sure you made it to the theater in one piece."

"Precious cargo." What a strange phrase. "I'm sorry to make you come all this way, but it's not a good day. I'm moving, you see."

"Oh." Her face is crestfallen. "Ms. Burris will be very upset. She'll think I did or said something wrong." She digs into her bag, hands shaking. "I brought the program for you, so you can see that it's going to be terrific. Won't you reconsider?" She looks like she might cry.

I take it from her without looking at it. "I'm sure you'll have a bevy of current and former dancers in attendance. Why do I have to go?"

"It's because of the book. I hope you won't think me insensitive— I mean, I still can't believe what you went through—but the book is the reason they want you there. Everyone is so eager to know more about what happened when you were a Rockette."

Right. A recent nonfiction account of the events of 1956, published a couple of months ago, has stirred up interest in a time I'd rather not dwell on. Since it came out, I've had all kinds of former friends and foes resurface, not to mention reporters who looked up my address and stopped by unannounced, hoping for an interview. It was a time when I was at my best as a dancer, yet the worst happened.

I haven't been in that theater, that beautiful, majestic space, since.

"That was long ago. I don't wish to talk about it. Or think about it."

"Oh." Her eyes flit to the windowsill, where several family photos sit in silver frames. "Of course." She pauses. "I just need to call and let Ms. Burris know. Do you mind if I use your phone?"

I show her into the hallway, where it sits on a narrow table.

As she murmurs into the phone, I go back into the living room, where the young mover has left another box on the coffee table, this one marked with my mother's handwriting. Inside are her treasures, objects that she touched and worried over, pages she leafed through and scribbled on in pencil. I remember the time when, as far as I was concerned, the programs and diaries might as well have been dusted with cyanide.

Piper comes back into the room, tucking a loose strand of hair behind one ear. Her chin trembles. "Ms. Burris is so disappointed. And I'm sorry to have wasted your time. I'll excuse myself now and head back."

Just then, the young mover bounds down the stairs carrying a dress on a hanger across his arms as if it were a sleeping maiden. "Do you want to keep this, Ms. Brooks? Or donate?" He holds the hanger up high to better display it.

"Oh my gosh!" Piper says. "How beautiful!"

It's one of my favorite frocks, sapphire blue with a high neck and long sleeves. I haven't seen it in years, but I know it would still fit.

I wore it one of the last times I saw my first love.

The mover is only doing his job, but I don't want to engage with these questions—or these objects—anymore. The slow drip-drip of memories feels lethal, or at least dangerous enough to drive me from the house. I could stay here and have my heart torn open or I could go into the city and lose myself in the bright lights and the constant swirl of people. I could mix in with the crowd and disappear for a while, and when I return, all this detritus will be gone for good.

I stand there, unsure, and notice that I'm still holding the program in my hand. I open it and quickly scan the run of show: some speeches, a couple of dance performances, a popular singer. And then a familiar name catches my eye. For a minute I'm thrown back to a different time, when I was silly and young and had no idea what the world had in store for me. What suffering, and what bliss.

Well, it appears I have no choice. I take the hanger from the mover and sweep up the fabric with my free hand so it doesn't touch the floor.

"I've changed my mind," I reply. "I'm going after all."

CHAPTER TWO

OCTOBER 1956

D ottie, we do not lick the mirror during ballet class, remember?"
Marion dashed to the front of the dance studio, where five-year-old Dottie stood flush against the floor-to-ceiling mirror, fingers splayed against the glass, staring intently at her reflection. Her tiny pink tongue darted out once more before she turned and threw a mischievous smile Marion's way.

"That's enough. Please get back in line with the other girls." Marion took her hand and led her back to her place among the class of ten, clad in pink tights and leotards, with ballet slippers no bigger than parrot tulips on all twenty feet.

Make that nineteen.

Tabitha had taken one shoe off and was batting her neighbor's behind with it.

Marion glanced at the clock. Forty-five more minutes to go. She'd been working as an instructor at the Broadway Ballet and Dance Studio for two years now, after having studied here herself since the age of five. Miss Stanwich, the kindly owner and founder, had asked her to teach the beginners part-time when Marion was a senior in high school, and most days she had a knack for corralling even the feistiest of children. The studio was like her second home, and if anyone asked, she'd say that she enjoyed her job immensely.

Although, to be honest, she'd enjoyed it much more before Miss Stanwich retired and moved to North Carolina. Marion had been asked to stay on by the studio's new owner, Miss Beaumont, who, unfortunately, was difficult to please on the best of days.

Marion put her fingers into her mouth and let out a whistle loud enough that the taxis gliding on Broadway three floors below might have pulled over in hope of a fare. It also served to bring Tabitha's mother to the glass viewing window that connected the studio to the waiting room, where she stood peering with disapproval over her reading glasses, a copy of *Woman's Day* clutched to her chest.

At the sound of Marion's whistle, all ten girls miraculously fell into place, making two rows of five. Marion signaled for the accompanist to begin playing and led her tiny dancers through another round of pliés.

"Imagine you're surrounded by marshmallows." Marion faced them, demonstrating. "Use your knees to gently push the marshmallows out, and then they gently push back, until your legs are straight. Necks long, like you're wearing a dangly pair of earrings and want to show them off."

For a glorious few minutes, she had their rapt attention, until Tabitha plunked down on the floor. "I want a marshmallow," she demanded.

"Me too!" chimed in Dottie.

Whenever her students became fidgety, Marion couldn't bring herself to resort to what some of the newly hired instructors did, namely, snap at them and scare them back into focusing on her. While the other teachers had no problem wrenching a student's feet into the proper turnout with a forceful hand or humiliating a struggling dancer in front of her classmates, Marion vowed to never stoop to such behaviors. After all, dancing was supposed to be joyful.

Although right then no one in the room was feeling much joy at all, including Marion.

She walked over to the accompanist and whispered in her ear. The students, sensing that something was up, quieted, and even Tabitha rose to her feet, curious.

"It's time for freestyle," said Marion, and was rewarded with cheers.

The accompanist broke into Carl Perkins's "Blue Suede Shoes" as the girls assembled against the side wall in a line.

Marion pointed at the first dancer, who sailed across the studio floor, performing a mad jumble of moves that involved a great deal of shimmying, jumping, and twirling. One child rolled around on the floor, finishing off with a crablike scuttle, while the next skipped gaily, flinging her arms as if she were tossing confetti into the air. Each student earned praise for her originality and effort.

After two rounds of freestyle, it was back to business, and the rest of the hour went off without a hitch.

Marion dismissed the girls and thanked the accompanist. As she turned to go, she noticed that the whisper-thin Miss Beaumont had joined Tabitha's mother at the window, their lipsticked mouths wearing matching frowns. Out in the waiting room, Miss Beaumont asked Marion to see her in her office before she left for the day.

The Broadway Ballet and Dance Studio was considered one of the best in New York, where former ballerinas from national companies taught master classes after they'd retired, and Marion knew she was lucky to be teaching and taking classes here, having no professional experience herself. One of the perks of teaching meant she could slip into any classroom she fancied, focusing on lyrical jazz one day and modern dance another.

She still remembered the moment she fell in love with dance. When Marion was five and her sister, Judy, eight, their mother took them to see a children's performance in the city. The way the dancers crossed the stage mesmerized Marion, their arms like jelly, as if there were no bones inside, rising high on their toes, where they stayed for what seemed like whole minutes at a time. Marion wanted to move like that, to spin until it seemed like there was no way she could possibly remain upright, and then freeze in place, one leg outstretched. She'd told her mother that evening as she was tucked into bed that she wanted to be a ballerina, and her mother had kissed her nose and said, "Of course," with a satisfied smile, as if that were the most natural thing in the world.

Marion collected her things from the locker room and passed through the waiting area on her way to Miss Beaumont's office. Two of the advanced students had gathered in front of the bulletin board. Marion recognized one—Vanessa—as they'd been in the same ballet class several times. The girl had landed a job as an extra in the film *Seven Brides for Seven Brothers* a few years ago and spoke of it incessantly.

"Who knows? Maybe this time next week, I'll be a Rockette," Vanessa said loudly as Marion walked by.

Marion glanced up at the bulletin board. A notice that read *Join the Rockettes!* was pinned next to the studio's class schedule. The auditions were to be held at Radio City Music Hall the next day.

Marion had seen the Rockettes many years ago, when her father's company bought a block of tickets for employees and their families. The dancers moved as one, with every arm position, every tilt of the head, exactly on cue. When they lined up in a long row and began kicking for the big finale, a shiver had run down Marion's spine and then she'd burst into tears. Judy had looked at her like she was mad, but when Marion had tried to explain how magical it all was, she found herself unable to find the words. At home, she'd tried duplicating the kicks in front of the mirror in her room until her father yelled up at her to knock it off, that the chandelier in the living room was shaking from all the jumping around.

The student next to Vanessa turned to Marion. Pauline was her name, Marion remembered. "Miss Brooks, did you hear that Vanessa's going to audition for the Rockettes? Isn't that brave? I know two girls who auditioned and never even got a callback."

Vanessa gave a not-so-modest shrug. "They need good tap dancers, which is my specialty. It's an honor to be invited to audition."

"But it says here it's an open call." Pauline pointed to the notice. "Anyone can show up."

Vanessa looked annoyed. "Michael talked to them beforehand. He mentioned my name. It helps to have industry connections."

Marion couldn't help herself. "Michael who?"

"Michael Kidd. He was my choreographer for *Seven Brides*," Vanessa said with a proud huff.

"Right, I forgot you were in it."

Pauline giggled but stopped when Vanessa cut her a sharp look. "Trust me, auditioning for the Rockettes is not for amateurs. You must be proficient in ballet, tap, and jazz. It helps that I have a professional credit."

The girl certainly had no lack of confidence. "Well, good luck," offered Marion.

"*You* should audition," said Pauline, looking at Marion. "I saw your grand battement in class last week, you'd be a natural."

"Oh, no," said Marion. "I'm happy teaching."

She could only imagine her father's expression if she ever did something as audacious as audition for the Rockettes. He'd be livid; steam would come out of every pore on his face. Simon Brooks was born into a working-class family on the Lower East Side and went from slogging around the city in work boots to pushing papers in a corner office as a salaried executive, an incredible feat. At work, she knew, he could be charming and smooth, but at home his rough side emerged whenever he felt crossed. Or blindsided. "You and your sister have two choices, as far as I'm concerned," he'd said when they were young girls. "You can either get married or you can take up a reputable, secure job that's fit for a lady."

Marion knew already what that meant.

Nurse, teacher, or secretary.

So she became a dance teacher. For Marion, coming to the studio every day—teaching or taking class, consulting with the parents, choreographing the year-end performances—was enough to fill her creative soul.

In some ways it had been easier for her since Miss Stanwich had retired. When Marion was eleven, her former teacher had tried to get Simon's permission for Marion to audition for the School of American Ballet and been summarily shut down. Marion had begged and pleaded with her father that night, hoping she could change his mind, but despite her tearstained face and repeated promises to be the best daughter in the world if he just said yes, he remained unyielding. Long after, Marion would catch Miss Stanwich staring wistfully her way during class, muttering under her breath about what a beautiful soloist she would have made, which always left Marion with the uneasy feeling that she'd disappointed her mentor.

No, she was happy the way things were. Marion would let the Vanessas of the world have the spotlight and concentrate on bringing up the next generation of dancers, even the ones who liked to lick the mirror occasionally.

Miss Beaumont sat behind her desk, her forehead wrinkled. When

Miss Stanwich was in charge, the office was a welcoming place, smelling of crushed rosin and coffee. Miss Beaumont had replaced the scratched-up oak desk with a stark, modern one, and now the small room reeked of cigarette smoke.

She began speaking before Marion had even sat down. "I'm getting more complaints, Marion. You're not giving the young ones enough structure. You know what I'm saying, right? We've had this conversation before."

"The freestyle was only for a few minutes of class. It helps them shake off the fidgets and get back on track." She was about to add that Miss Stanwich used to encourage a sense of play during class but thought better of it. Miss Beaumont had little patience for what she considered the lax methods of the previous owner.

"They're sent here to learn discipline and grace," said Miss Beaumont. "They can run about like hooligans at home; that's not why they come to my dance studio."

"I'll stick with the standard program from now on," conceded Marion.

"You said that last time. You seem to have a hard time obeying the rules."

"Sorry. I promise. No more freestyle."

Miss Beaumont let out a dramatic sigh. "No. I can't do this anymore. It's not working out, I'm afraid." She paused.

"I'm sorry, what?" Marion's heart raced. There was a finality to Miss Beaumont's tone that frightened her. *Not working out?*

"There are a number of teachers with storied professional careers in the dance world who are eager to join our faculty, and I've been putting off the inevitable out of respect for your long association with Miss Stanwich. But enough's enough. Your services are no longer needed here at Broadway Ballet and Dance Studio."

She picked up the cigarette that was smoldering in the ashtray and took a long drag, aiming her exhale at the open window. "Effective immediately."

*

"What are you doing home so early?"

Marion's sister, Judy, sat at the antique rolltop desk in the living room of the house in Bronxville, paying bills, and from the sour look on her face, she wasn't pleased at the interruption.

Marion dumped her dance bag on the floor and plopped on the couch, legs wide, arms flung out. Judy was the last person she wanted to share her day with.

Yet that hadn't always been the case. When Marion was a little girl, Judy had been her entire world. It was Judy's idea to put on a variety show for the neighbors and charge admission. She rode her bike around, pasting flyers up on the telephone poles, cut out paper tickets, and collected the coins in a coffee can. Marion happily danced about the stage in her leotard and tights for a good fifteen minutes before an older boy who juggled shoved her off. At the end of the show, the parents in attendance praised Marion for her lovely performance while Judy sat counting their riches at the bridge table that served as a ticket booth. Judy paid Marion ten cents, which seemed like an enormous sum at the time.

Their father doted on Judy, whose affinity for order and logic matched his own, while their mother, Lucille, demonstrated a flair for glamour that aligned more with Marion's nature. When Lucille was preparing for a night out, she never minded if Marion rummaged through her closet and tried on her too-big high heels or draped herself with layers of long silk scarves; once she'd even dabbed her favorite perfume on Marion's tiny wrist. Marion would watch as her mother transformed into a veritable movie star, lining her eyes with kohl and spraying her strawberry-blonde hair into a tower of curls before stepping out for a night at the theater or a jazz club.

After the shock of Lucille's death when Judy was ten and Marion seven, the sisters were left grieving, confused, and angry, but for their father's sake they sublimated their misery. He went back to work the day after the funeral and they were expected to return to school, carry on with their lives. Each night, Marion would crawl into Judy's bed and listen as her older sister made up stories about dancing monkeys and singing turtles until sleep finally came. For a time, they were inseparable. But as Marion filled out in all the right places and slid through adolescence without a hitch, Judy battled shiny skin dotted with pimples and hair that always seemed greasy, and soon their relationship began to splinter. If Marion had milk with her cereal, Judy ate it dry. As Marion's wardrobe became more colorful and stylish, Judy dressed in gray and black. Marion's social circle widened, while Judy preferred to stay at home with a book.

When Judy began working as Simon's assistant not long after graduating from secretarial school, the tectonic plates of allegiance slid solidly into place. Without her mother around as a counterbalance, Marion was now on the outside, listening at the dinner table as Simon and Judy discussed people she didn't know and delved into minutiae she didn't understand about the life of a busy executive.

"My day was awful," answered Marion finally.

"Huh." Judy pushed her cat's-eye glasses up the bridge of her nose.

She seemed about to inquire further, but Mrs. Hornsby, their housekeeper, trundled into the living room, buttoning up her overcoat. She was a stout woman with dark-brown eyes whiskered by deep wrinkles who had been in the family's employ ever since Judy was born. After Lucille's death, Mrs. Hornsby had quietly taken up the role of caretaker to the children without ever presuming to replace her.

"You're back early." She gave Marion a kiss on the top of her head and did the same for Judy. "I'm off, dinner's in the oven. Make sure your father eats some of those string beans. There's leftover pie in the fridge and I'll pick up the dry cleaning on my way in tomorrow. Oh, and you have a surprise visitor, Marion," she added with a mischievous smile.

Mrs. Hornsby was out the door before Marion could ask who, but then she heard voices: her father's and another man's. She recognized it immediately.

"Nathaniel's back?"

Judy nodded. "He flew in this morning."

Marion jumped to her feet as the two men entered the room.

Her father stepped inside first. Simon Brooks scared most people upon first impression. He was an imposing man with a shiny bald head and a massive torso, his hands still callused from his early days working for Met Power, climbing around buildings and helping to provide electricity to the entire city of New York. Marion and Judy used to crawl all over him when they were young, and at bedtime he would tuck each of them under an arm and carry them up the stairs to bed as they cackled with delight. The bulldog effect of his head and thick neck was softened by blue eyes and high cheekbones.

Marion's boyfriend, Nathaniel, seemed lithe in comparison, although his wide shoulders and large hands had carried the high school football team to a championship twice. He sported thick hair the same dark brown as his eyes, and Marion joked that his only flaw was the white scar on his chin he'd gotten from horsing around with his brothers as a boy.

Marion and Nathaniel had dated for the past few years, although much of that time he'd been away at Dartmouth or, most recently, on a European tour that his parents had surprised him with after graduation. She hadn't expected him back so soon and only now realized how comforting it would be to have a sympathetic ear to share her day with.

"Nathaniel, you're back! How was Europe? I can't believe you're here!" She ran into his arms and he pulled her close but gave her just a quick peck on the lips, no doubt because Simon was standing only two feet away.

"I figured I'd surprise you." He was wearing a sumptuous leather jacket, one she hadn't seen before, but it suited him and made him seem worldly and sophisticated. "What are you doing home so early from work?" he asked.

An odd question, when they hadn't seen each other in months. How best to answer?

"I got fired."

There, she'd said it.

"What?" Nathaniel pulled back, his eyebrows arched in surprise. From across the room Judy let out a soft gasp.

"What happened?" asked Simon.

"Miss Beaumont didn't like the way I taught my students. She thinks I'm too easy on them."

"You're a terrific teacher," said Nathaniel. "Your students all love you. She sounds like an unreasonable woman."

"I couldn't agree more. She said I'm not good at following her instructions."

Marion glanced in Simon's direction, wondering how he'd react. He'd never been all that happy with the fact that she was still involved in the dance world, even if it was a paying job.

Simon walked over and cupped her cheek with his hand. "My dear, you've been at that place for ages. It must be a shock, and I'm sorry to hear it."

"Thanks, Dad." His unexpected sympathy, along with the sudden reappearance of Nathaniel right when she most needed him, made her a little weepy.

"But there are protocols in place for a reason, even in a small business like that one—" And Simon was off, launching into a lecture on effective personnel management.

"That's enough, Dad." Marion tried to keep her tone breezy; Simon didn't like to be interrupted.

She turned back to Nathaniel. On their first date, Marion had returned from dance class late and reluctantly left him alone with Judy in the living room while she showered and dressed. Their father had been out at a business dinner, and Marion hoped Nathaniel wouldn't be put off by her sister's nerdiness. But when she came downstairs, she found the two of them sitting around the coffee table working on a jigsaw puzzle, comparing teachers and complaining about the ones who were too full of themselves. Nathaniel had refused to head out until they had all four edges of the puzzle completed, and his genuine show of interest in her weird sister had pleased Marion. He was a sweetheart, through and through. "Can we go out to dinner tonight? It would be nice to catch up."

"Dinner?" Nathaniel glanced over at Simon, as if they shared some secret. "Um, maybe not tonight."

"Why not?"

"Well, I'm sort of in a rush right now."

Something was up. "What's going on?" she asked. "If you knew I wouldn't be home this early, why are you here?"

"I was excited to see you, I guess." He was hiding something from her, she was sure of it. There was a moment of silence as the two men exchanged looks again.

"Now I'm getting worried," said Marion. "What are you not telling me?"

Judy spoke up. "For goodness' sake, stop being dense. He was asking Dad for your hand in marriage."

"Judy!" Simon was trying to be stern, but a smile broke through. Nathaniel was beaming as well.

"My hand?"

Nathaniel was going to propose. She hadn't expected it quite so soon. They'd been apart for so long, with Nathaniel off at college followed by this summer's European tour, that although they'd officially been together for three years now, it was a little like dating a mirage. Marion had figured they'd get to know each other again over the next year or so, as Nathaniel looked for a full-time job. But he was ready to make the leap.

He lifted her hand to his lips and kissed it. "I wanted to catch your dad when you weren't home. Sorry to ruin the surprise, but I didn't expect you to be here. Although it's wonderful to see you," he added quickly. "I know it's been hard being away from each other all this time, but I promise I'll make it up to you."

"Maybe getting fired was a sign, Marion," said Simon. "Now you can throw yourself into the wedding plans instead."

Things were moving awfully fast. On the train ride home, she'd already begun compiling a list of other New York dance studios where she could apply for a teaching position and take classes. She'd been either taking classes or teaching them forever; it was part of her identity. Was she ready to turn in her pointe shoes for good? "I can't imagine not dancing," she said. "It would be like giving up air." Even saying so made her feel like she was suffocating. She put one hand to her throat.

Simon grinned, oblivious to her distress. "Before you know it, you'll be a married woman with kids, so you won't have time for that kind of thing."

"I'm not sure how I feel about that." Her tone came out petulant, which was not what she intended.

"Your mother was content to settle down as a wife and mother. I don't see why that's not good enough for you, young lady."

At times like this, Marion wished more than ever that her mother hadn't died, so that she could turn to her for advice and guidance. She looked back and forth between her father and Nathaniel, at a loss for words.

Nathaniel snapped his fingers. "I know, I promise I'll take you out dancing once a week. Problem solved."

Although she appreciated the effort, doing the samba at the country club wouldn't be enough to satisfy Marion's creative itch, not by a long shot. "Why don't we take a walk? We can talk more about all this."

Nathaniel shook his head. "I'm afraid I can't, not tonight. I leave for Florida in a few hours, but I'll be back on Saturday and I promise we'll do dinner, dancing, whatever you like."

"You're going away? Again?" The day's events had whipsawed Marion, and she wasn't sure which end was up anymore.

"Only for a few days." He looked over at Simon once more, as if asking for backup.

Simon nodded sagely. "Nothing wrong with a quick golf trip. After all, you haven't seen your buddies all summer, right?"

"He went to Europe with his buddies," said Marion. "What are you not telling me?"

Judy, who'd been silent all this time, not even offering up a word of congratulations, piped up from the corner. "You're ruining everything, Marion. Just be quiet."

"How? I don't understand." The three of them were ganging up on her, gaslighting her; something was afoot and she wanted to be in on the joke. Maybe she was overreacting, but she'd just lost her job and was now being almost proposed to by her almost-fiancé, and she didn't know whether to laugh or cry. "Tell me."

"Nathaniel is going to see his grandmother in Florida to collect your engagement ring," Judy said, clearly thrilled to spill the beans once again.

For the second time that day, Marion had ruined the big surprise. She wanted to crawl under the rug and disappear. "I'm so sorry."

Nathaniel gave a helpless shrug. "Don't worry. It's not exactly the way I planned it, but the important thing is that we're in each other's lives again. You know how much I adore you, my beautiful girl, don't you?"

He was a good man, she was lucky to have him.

Then why did Marion feel like she wanted to scream?

CHAPTER THREE

After Nathaniel left, Marion, her father, and Judy ate dinner and then settled in the living room. Simon eased into his leather armchair and opened a biography of Henry Ford while Judy did a crossword at the desk. For some reason this scene of domestic tranquility set Marion's teeth on edge. It was as if they were an old married couple and Marion the sullen teenager. She was always the third wheel.

"What is it, Marion?" Simon asked.

She hadn't realized she'd let out a long sigh. "Nothing. I guess I'm a little overwhelmed."

In a few days, Marion would be getting engaged. There would be a guest list to draw up, invitations to order, meetings with florists. It was a lot of work ahead. Her heart felt heavy at the thought of it for some reason.

"I remember your mother was overwhelmed at first as well," said Simon. "That's perfectly normal. I'll tell you what, though, I can't wait to walk my little girl down the aisle." Her normally stoic father was about to cry, which, in turn, made Marion's eyes well up.

All her annoyance dissipated. She walked over to her father and gave him a peck on the cheek. "Tell us again how you and Mom met."

A soft smile crossed his face. "I've told you that before."

Judy piped up. "She was reading a play, right?" The two sisters shared a quiet glance, united in their thirst for details about their lost parent.

"That's right. I was still getting used to working in an office, after years of running around town. Around midday, I'd go to Madison Square Park, take off my suit jacket, and roll up my sleeves. Breathe in the fresh air. I didn't realize how loudly I'd been breathing, in and out, in and out, until the woman sitting on the other side of the bench said, 'If you're about to faint, please let me know so I can get out of the way.'

"I looked over and there was the most gorgeous creature I'd ever laid eyes on. As pretty as a movie star, sitting three feet away from me. She wore red lipstick and, I swear, her legs went on for days. She was reading a play by Eugene O'Neill, and when I asked her about it, she started telling me about the Greek myths that inspired it. I nodded along, like I had any idea what she was talking about, until she realized I was an ignorant oaf and teased me, but I didn't mind. She was always gentle, in that way."

"And then you went for lunch at the Automat," said Judy.

"That's right, where she entertained me with stories about ancient gods wreaking havoc on men and women."

"What was the wedding like?" asked Marion.

"A simple affair. Her family and mine. Some friends. We put sunflowers in buckets on the tables for centerpieces, and she carried a single sunflower down the aisle. It was the Depression, so there were no frills, but that didn't matter. Not like your wedding's going to be, Marion. Whatever you want is fine with me. If you want a twenty-foot train and a honeymoon in Tahiti, it's yours."

"Thanks, Dad. Not sure about the train, but Tahiti sounds fun." Maybe getting married would be an adventure, as she and Nathaniel created a life together the way Simon and Lucille had. Maybe, to honor her mother, she'd carry a single sunflower down the aisle as well. She rose to her feet and yawned. "It's been a wild day. I'm going to turn in early," she said.

"You get your beauty sleep."

Upstairs, Marion stepped inside Simon's bedroom. On his bureau sat several framed photos of Marion and Judy when they were young, along with one of Lucille from her wedding day. She wore a bias-cut silk dress that skimmed her hips and fell to the floor. Simple and classic. Marion hadn't thought about wedding dresses just yet— Nathaniel's mother would probably want to take her into the city and help her shop for one—but she might be able to fit into her mother's dress, if it had been saved. It would be a way to pay tribute to her and would make her father proud.

She climbed into the attic and began sorting through the boxes and trunks stacked under the eaves. It had a peaked ceiling, so she could stand upright in the center but had to hunch over everywhere else. One of the trunks held some of her mother's evening gowns, and at the very bottom lay a long white dress. She'd found it.

But once she'd pulled it out and held it up to the bare lightbulb that lit the space, her heart sank. The years had slowly turned the white silk more of a tea color, and the fabric practically fell apart in her hands. If Lucille were alive, no doubt she would have made sure it was stored properly.

Most of the time, Marion's lack of a mother didn't figure into her day-to-day life, although sometimes she'd try to recall her voice or what her hands looked like. Marion had just turned seven when Lucille was summoned to the Boston bedside of a sick friend. Marion and Judy had happily carried on with their lives, with Mrs. Hornsby seamlessly taking over in the interim, until one day after school, when Simon sat them down and shakily explained that a driver had hit and killed Lucille the night before as she was crossing Boylston Street. The name of the street always stuck in Marion's head. Such an ugly name, like a boil.

Marion shook off the memory. As she closed the lid of the trunk, a box behind it caught her eye. The cardboard was dusty and wrinkled, her mother's handwriting on the front faded. *Mementos*, it read.

Marion pulled it over to where she could open it without hitting her head on the ceiling. Inside were what looked like dozens of thin paperback books, but on second glance she realized they were plays: Shaw, Williams, O'Neill, Odets. There were also a good number of playbills from Broadway and off-Broadway productions. She opened a crinkled envelope and gasped. Inside was an invitation from the American Academy of Dramatic Arts to study acting, dated 1931. She did the math in her head. Lucille would've been eighteen.

Marion's heart began to pound, as if she'd discovered a trove of her mother's love letters to another man. Lucille had delighted in going to the theater, but she'd never mentioned anything about attending drama school.

A daily calendar from 1932 was filled with entries for what appeared to be acting classes: *9am, Scene study; 1pm, Shakespeare; 4pm, Voice.*

Her mother didn't just enjoy theater, she'd pursued it. Why had Simon never mentioned any of this? Or why hadn't Lucille when she was alive?

Marion dug deeper.

The biggest surprise was a play at the very bottom of the box with a piece of paper tucked inside. The play was called *Wednesday's Child*, and the letter was one of congratulations for Lucille being offered a part in the Broadway production, to be mounted at the Longacre Theatre in January of 1934.

The same year that Lucille and Simon were married. The same year Judy was born.

Lucille clearly had a passion for acting as strong as Marion's for dance, and she had, for a time, followed through on her desire to pursue a career that was risky and creative. Marion had never even suspected, and the thought made her both giddy and apprehensive. It was as if the world had tilted slightly and now everything—past and present—had to be reevaluated with fresh eyes.

Her mother had been gone for so long that sometimes Marion forgot that she'd been a living, breathing creature, one who'd saved playbills and filled in days on a calendar in her flowery hand.

How tragic to think that all that was left of Lucille's burgeoning career had been packed into a box and hidden in an attic, untouched until now.

※

Downstairs, the living room was just as she'd left it, her father in his armchair, Judy studying the crossword. But to Marion it felt like she'd been gone for years.

"I thought you were going to bed," said Simon, rubbing his eyes. "I'm on my way myself."

"I found some of Mom's things in the attic."

"Is that right? I haven't been up there in ages."

Marion glanced over at Judy, wishing she didn't have to share this news in front of her sister but knowing that it would be impossible to keep inside. "There's a box there, full of playbills and letters and things."

Simon got up and poured himself a scotch, his back to Marion.

Marion wondered if he knew what was coming. "Your mother sure loved the theater."

"But it wasn't that she just loved the theater, is it? She had trained to be an actress. She went to acting school."

Judy put down her pen and stared at Marion. "What are you talking about?"

"She went to drama school, and on top of that, she was offered a role on Broadway. I found a letter saying so."

Simon surveyed his daughters and took a sip of his drink. "It was all so long ago."

"Why didn't she ever talk about it? Why didn't you ever mention it?"

Simon sat back down in his armchair. He leaned forward, arms on his knees, studying the drink in his hands. "It was in the past, that's why. Like any mother, she had her hands full raising you." He laughed. "How could she ever get a word in edgewise?"

Judy crossed her arms in front of her. "Tell us now, then."

Marion echoed her sister. It felt good to be on the same side as Judy, for the first time in ages.

Simon swirled the ice in his glass and began to speak. "When I met your mother, she wanted to be an actress. I figured it was a hobby, something that she'd try before settling down with me. We'd talked about a life together, of a house in the suburbs and having two kids. It was all planned out, I thought. So when she got cast in the show on Broadway, I was shocked. As was she, to be honest. She'd beaten out much more experienced actresses for the role. Anyway, I couldn't imagine how it would work, me toiling at an office job during the day, her gone nights and weekends. That was no way to start a life together. To me, it was a deal breaker. When she said she was going to accept the offer, it broke my heart."

"What made her change her mind?" asked Judy.

Marion already knew the answer. "Because she found out she was pregnant."

Simon gave a sheepish grin. "Exactly right. With our firstborn daughter, Miss Judy Brooks. And so, in a way, the decision was made for her, for us. She bowed out of the show and we married, had Judy and then you. She was happy. It worked out fine."

Judy looked slightly shell-shocked. "Really?"

"Yes, really. She doted on you both. The life of an actress wasn't for her after all."

"But she never really tried, so how could she know?" asked Marion. A sudden realization dawned, and her heart went to her throat. "Is this why you wouldn't let me audition for the School of American Ballet?"

"What? No. Those are two separate matters."

"But you stopped me from following my dreams just like you tried to stop Mom."

"It's not the same thing at all. Your mother was a grown woman who made the best decision for her family, one that gave her great joy. You were a child, and besides, there was no point in you trying to become a ballerina. There's no future in that, no security. I made the best decision for you, as your parent, and if your mother were around, she would have agreed."

Lucille's dreams may have been dashed, but she'd kept all those mementos, reminders that she was an artist. Deep down, Marion was certain that her mother would have encouraged her to dance. What if she'd overruled Simon and allowed Marion to study ballet? Marion might be a principal at American Ballet Theatre and touring across Europe by now. While she loved teaching, the loss of the opportunity to dance in front of an audience stung.

"You should have told us the truth," said Marion. "We deserve to understand who our mother really was, not some made-up version of her that suited you."

Simon's neck turned red and his fingers tightened around the drink in his hand. "Watch it, Marion."

"How could you have kept this a secret?"

"Stop fighting," said Judy. "It's all in the past, I don't want to hear any more."

Marion turned on Judy. "How can you not want to know more? I want to know everything."

Simon shook his head. "You got to teach dance, take classes. I really don't understand why you're so upset."

"How can you not see my point of view?" Marion said through gritted teeth. "You're not even trying."

"That's enough," warned Simon.

"Mom would have understood!"

Simon walked toward Marion, holding one palm out. "Hand them over."

Marion's hand flew up to the pearls around her neck. This was Simon's punishment whenever she disobeyed or disappointed, by staying out longer than curfew or getting a D on a physics test back in high school. The pearls would be taken away for seven days. He knew how much they meant to her, that they had once belonged to Lucille. "That's not fair."

"Marion."

Reluctantly, Marion unclasped the pearls and dropped them into his hand. She stepped back, trying not to cry. "None of this makes any sense. What would it matter if I had become a professional ballerina? It would be a paying job, just like Judy takes home a salary."

"Judy has a job that is serious, with benefits and long-term growth. Being a dancer would have provided neither of those things."

"But it would have made me happy."

His tone softened. "I know you don't understand now, but you will later, I promise. When you're married to Nathaniel and have a child of your own, you'll see that sometimes your wisdom trumps their wishes. That's the job of being a parent. I want more than anything to see you safe and taken care of." He held out his arms, expecting her to fall into them. "Trust me, my dear. I only wish your mother was here to explain it better."

Simon had never remarried—his devotion to his dead wife was that strong—and Marion knew he missed her terribly. Still, he couldn't keep Marion and Judy in a bubble, safe from harm, forever. That wasn't fair to them.

Marion ran upstairs, away from her father's searing compassion and the stricken look on her sister's face.

Her bed was covered with dance magazines and pointe shoe ribbons. She swept them off with one hand and threw herself facedown on the quilt, but the tears wouldn't come.

One of the magazines lay on the floor, splayed open. A photograph showed a row of dancers dressed in red. Marion recognized the Rockettes kick line instantly. She leaned out and grabbed it, turning onto her back to read the article. It was all about tomorrow's auditions: where to go, what to bring, what to expect.

Tomorrow, Nathaniel would be in Florida, and her father and Judy would be at work.

Meanwhile, Marion would be moping around her childhood bedroom, fretting over being fired and wondering what might have been. There was no way for her to travel back in time and audition for the School of American Ballet, but perhaps that didn't mean all was lost. What if, for one day, she pursued a path that she'd thought was closed—followed in her mother's footsteps and took a chance? Instead of tamping down her passion for dance, as her father and Nathaniel wanted, what if she struck out on her own and joined the hundreds of dancers hoping to become a Rockette at Radio City Music Hall?

If she failed and was laughed out of the room, she'd at least know that dancing professionally had never been an option after all.

There was only one way to find out.

CHAPTER FOUR

Marion rose with the sun and slipped a cotton day dress over a fresh pair of tights and a leotard. She put her hair up into a tight bun and brushed her teeth as quietly as she could in the bathroom. Her bag was by the door where she'd left it, holding her pointe shoes, a pair of tap shoes, and her well-worn character shoes. She had to be prepared for anything.

She was still angry at her dad for taking away the pearls like she was a child. Last night, after she'd stormed upstairs, she heard him go to his study and open the safe, where he would keep the necklace until her punishment was over. It was stupid, really. She and Judy knew where he kept the key: tucked under his "Employee of the Year" award on the bookshelf behind the desk. Deep down, she understood that he wanted to have control over his daughters as a way of keeping them free from harm, especially after losing his wife. That was why he blew up at them every so often. Blew up at Marion, was more like it. These days, Judy could do no wrong.

Marion slipped out of the house before Judy or her father was even awake and made the six fifty train to Grand Central just in time. From there, she zigzagged her way up Sixth Avenue, maneuvering around the men in overcoats and hats heading to their office jobs. A block away, she caught sight of the marquee for Radio City Music Hall, its neon lettering and sapphire-blue stripes curving gracefully around the corner of the limestone building, and felt a zing of excitement and nerves travel up her spine.

Underneath stood an army of young dancers who all looked like Marion: hair tied back in buns, a slash of red lipstick on their faces. The line stretched from the box office entrance up to Fifty-First Street, where it disappeared off to the right.

As Marion neared, she heard a voice call her name. Vanessa stood on the opposite corner of the street.

Marion crossed with the light. "Hi, Vanessa."

"What are you doing here?" Vanessa's eyes were narrow, suspicious.

The answer couldn't be easily explained. That this was Marion's way of reclaiming what had been lost? Not only her mother, but the chance to become a professional dancer, the opportunity to pursue what she loved. Or was it a petty rebellion against her father for taking away her pearls like she was a child, and not telling her and Judy the truth about Lucille, and against Nathaniel for the cavalier way he assumed she would abandon dance once she was married?

"I had the day off and figured, why not?" she finally ventured. "That's a really long line."

Vanessa studied Marion closely before turning away. "Someone said they're expecting around five hundred girls."

Together, they walked to the back of the queue, behind a high-spirited group of girls from Long Island, some of whom had auditioned the year before and were quick to share their horror stories.

"I did one combination and they sent me packing," said one of the dancers, a tall blonde. "One!"

"Even the dancers who get the job have to reaudition every year," answered another. "It's relentless."

A girl with big round eyes piped up. "I'm worried I'm too chunky. I've been dieting all week."

Vanessa rummaged around in her purse and pulled out a newspaper clipping. "I read this in the *New York Times* the other day, it's the measurements of the average Rockette."

Marion and the other girls leaned in close to read the clipping.

"Miss Average Rockette," read the headline. "There are 46 full-time Rockettes, with 36 of them in the line at any one time. Topographically, they average out like this—"

"'Topographically'?" said Marion, wrinkling her nose.

"Keep reading."

"Bust 34", Waist 24", Hips 34½", Wrist 6", Ht. 5'6½", Wt. 118–122 lbs."

It went on, and the level of detail was astonishing, including measurements for thighs, calves, ankles, necks, and heads.

"Luckily, I fit every one of them," crowed Vanessa.

Marion stifled a groan.

As the line grew even longer behind them, Marion realized how crazy this was. Her chances were slim to none—some of the girls had already worked on Broadway or on national tours of shows—*they* were the dance professionals, not Marion.

Eventually, Marion and Vanessa were ushered inside and led past a security guard at his desk. From there, they squeezed into an elevator that deposited them on the sixth floor and then walked up a set of stairs and along a narrow hallway, where they were told to get into their dance clothes and stretch. Marion and Vanessa peeled off their dresses and did as instructed.

A group of girls swarmed out of a door marked *Rehearsal Hall*, a few looking excited and others distraught. One was weeping openly.

The rehearsal hall was grander than any dance studio Marion had ever seen, with a vaulted ceiling painted a sharp white and a mirror covering one entire wall. Half a dozen official-looking people sat behind two long tables, each one with a notepad and a pencil in front of them.

Marion's heart skipped a beat. Auditioning for the Rockettes would expose the truth about her abilities, and there was a good chance the one thing she loved doing would be sullied by other people's opinions. This was madness, and she'd probably be cut in the first round. She sidled toward the door, wondering if she should make a break for it. Vanessa, meanwhile, had pushed herself to the front of the crowd of girls and stood with a hand on one hip, confident and strong.

One by one, they were called over to be measured, standing against a wall while an assistant checked that they were neither shorter than five four nor taller than five eight and a half. Three girls out of the forty assembled were dismissed right away. The rest were given a stiff white card with a number on it and a large black safety pin and told to pin the card to their leotard, just below their left shoulder. Marion got number 310. Vanessa was number 299.

A genial-looking man with a wide forehead and a narrow mustache stepped forward.

"Ladies." He clapped his hands. "You'll notice that there are numbers marked in tape on the floor. Please stand on one now."

They rushed into place while he waited. Vanessa got a good spot at the front, while Marion sought safety in the very back.

"I'm Russell Markert, the director for the Rockettes. We are looking for forty-six girls for this year, thirty-six to be performing at any one time while ten have the week off. I'm not going to lie, this job is not for the lazy or the vain. If you pass the audition, you will become part of a machine that operates day after day entertaining this great city. There will be times when we rehearse into the night, then you'll get up early and perform first thing the next day. If chosen, you will be exhausted, your body pushed beyond its limit. But in return, you will be part of a company that is the most supportive, wonderful dance troupe in the world." He paused. "Although maybe I'm a little biased."

The girls laughed.

"A little history for you first. I founded a precision women's dance company in 1925 in St. Louis, known as the Missouri Rockets. We came to New York and performed on Radio City's opening night, way back in 1932. And we're still going strong today, God help me." He put a hand to his forehead and pretended to faint, making the girls laugh again. Marion felt her muscles loosening.

Maybe this wouldn't be so bad after all.

Mr. Markert called for his assistant, a woman named Emily who had thick, short bangs and wore a jangle of charms on her wrist.

"Emily's going to show you a ballet routine, four measures, eight counts each. She'll demonstrate it twice, and then you'll do it on your own.

Emily ran through the combination, a simple petit allegro followed by an adagio with lots of arabesques. It was hard to see her through the rows of bodies in front of Marion, but she did her best. Ballet came easily to her, thank goodness, and the combination wasn't too difficult.

As Emily counted out the steps, the dancers mimicked her movements but kept them small, eyes glued to their leader, impressing the choreography into their muscle memory. After the second demonstration, Emily went and stood next to Mr. Markert. "Now with music. Beulah, hit it."

A woman sitting behind an upright piano in the corner of the room nodded and began to play. One of the girls next to Marion swayed dangerously close to her during an arabesque, but Marion stayed strong and focused. Next, one row of girls was brought forward to dance while the others watched from the side. Marion's row was last, giving her even more time to study the steps, and when it was her group's turn, she danced with confidence. Vanessa had as well, and they exchanged quick smiles.

The dancers changed their shoes and learned a tap combination before finally switching into character shoes for the jazz portion of the audition.

"Remember, ladies," Mr. Markert reminded them, "I don't want to see anything but a bright smile on your face, no matter what's going on with your feet."

Having to change dance styles every fifteen minutes was harder than taking a two-hour class in one. By the end of the jazz combination, Marion was beat. But they weren't done yet.

"Time for fan kicks," said Emily. "I want sixteen outside fan kicks, sixteen inside. Arms in second position. And begin."

Several of the girls stumbled, but Marion got a second wind and her kicks were strong, her toes tracing a large fan shape into the air. At one point, every judge turned to watch her. In that moment, it felt as if gravity had released its grasp, that Marion had risen into the air like a cloud, free from the constraints of mere mortals. She couldn't have wiped the smile off her face if she'd tried.

They were asked to execute the fan kicks line by line, then once again all together, as Emily and Mr. Markert whispered and pointed from the front of the room.

While the dancers caught their breath, hands on hips, exhausted, the judges gathered for a good three or four minutes. Marion's competitive juices were flowing; she wanted another chance. This was more fun than she'd expected.

At the end of the session, the numbers of the girls who made it to the next round were called out, and to Marion's delight, both she and

Vanessa were chosen. She ran over to Vanessa after the group was dismissed. "Congrats!"

"Yeah, thanks," Vanessa replied stiffly. "You too."

Emily clapped her hands, her bracelets clanging. "We'll see those whose numbers we've called at two o'clock. Don't be late."

Marion went with a few of the girls, including Vanessa, to grab lunch at an Automat. Marion managed to down a hard-boiled egg and some coffee, but Vanessa stuck with water. "You'll end up with a huge belly if you're not careful. They're judging us on looks as well as technique, remember."

Vanessa, always the charmer.

They were back at a quarter to two, their hair smoothed and new lipstick applied. There were around a hundred women who had made the second round, and they all seemed so glamorous to Marion, like gazelles. She couldn't help but wonder if it might have been better to be cut in the first round rather than be crushed by this graceful stampede.

Mr. Markert asked them to take their places. "Congratulations. You've made it through. I'm pleased to introduce you to our esteemed producer, Leon Leonidoff."

A small man with round wire glasses got up from the table and stood beside Mr. Markert. Where Mr. Markert was laconic and loose-limbed, Mr. Leonidoff was tightly wound, his fists clenched.

His voice was overly loud, even for the large rehearsal hall. "We have rules here at Radio City. You must be between eighteen and twenty-three years old. If you're younger or older than that, leave now." He waited, but no one left. "If you are chosen to be a Rockette, you'll make seventy dollars a week. You cannot change your weight, you cannot change your hair color, and you absolutely cannot get a tan or a sunburn. Am I clear?"

They answered in unison. "Yes."

"Back to you."

Emily and Mr. Markert worked the dancers through the same combinations as earlier in the day, but with only one demonstration, as a test of the dancers' memory. An additional sixteen counts were added, as Mr. Markert called out instructions. "We are pushing you to your limit because Rockettes need to not only have exquisite dance technique, they have to be smart. You'll be learning new routines every week, so I expect you to hit these combinations with even more energy than you did earlier today. I want precision, no less than perfection."

Marion's head felt like it might explode from everything she had to remember: chaîné and piqué turns, more fan kicks, and then on to the tap and jazz combinations. Every fifteen minutes, Mr. Markert pointed to a few of the dancers and asked them to step to the side, which they did, teary-eyed. The group became smaller and smaller, until only sixty were left.

Including Vanessa and Marion.

Marion was amazed she'd made it this far, but her legs were shaky and her heart was pumping madly. They were shown a kick-and-turn combo, then brought up to the front of the room one at a time to perform alone.

Vanessa strode to the center of the room when her number was called, a huge smile on her face. The music began, and she did the choreography perfectly, her kicks hitting eye height, exactly as they'd been directed. But on the final piano kick, she caught her heel on the side of her other shoe. It was a tiny bobble, hardly noticeable, but she grimaced before catching herself and smiling wide once more.

Hopefully they hadn't noticed, but several of the judges wrote something down on their pads as Vanessa ran back to her spot. She didn't meet Marion's eyes as she passed by.

"Next up, number 310."

Marion walked to the front of the room.

As the music began, she thought of her favorite dancer, Gwen Verdon. She'd seen her last month on Broadway in *Damn Yankees*. As the enchantress Lola, there were times her body seemed to be made of liquid, yet she also had an inherent strength, especially in her upper torso, that counteracted the wild freedom of movement in her limbs. She could seduce with a turn of an ankle or a flick of a wrist, yet underneath her performance was a childlike playfulness. The woman was the toast of Broadway, and for good reason.

But the choreography Marion had learned today was the exact opposite, all about precision and technique, and presented a different kind of challenge, one that Marion welcomed. She remembered her mother and her wasted dreams and used that energy to fuel every step, keeping each one sharp and taut. When she kicked, she imagined her mother's glee at finding out she'd been cast in a Broadway play. Same with every arm lift, each snap of the head. She felt her mother's spirit watching her, pushing her harder, urging her on.

And then it was over. Marion was dismissed and withdrew into the crowd of dancers. Vanessa stood on the other side of the room, her arms crossed.

A few more women performed, but Marion didn't bother watching. Now that her audition was over, she'd have to go back to her old life and figure out how to fix it. Figure out what would make her happy. The energy drained out of her at the very thought.

As Mr. Markert called out the numbers of those who'd made it, the lucky girls screamed with happiness and were congratulated by the dancers next to them.

"And finally, number 310."

Marion looked up.

"Sorry?" she said.

"That would be you," said Mr. Markert, pointing to her number and closing his notebook. "That's it, ladies. Thank you for coming. For those who didn't make it, please don't give up. There's a big dance world out there. For those who did, we'll see you tomorrow morning at nine o'clock for orientation and first rehearsal. Congratulations."

CHAPTER FIVE

t's not fair. If you hadn't auditioned, I might have gotten your spot."

Vanessa wiped her eyes and refused to look at Marion. They'd taken the elevator together down to the stage door, part of the scrum of girls who'd made the callbacks and were now divided into those who were giddy with excitement and those who were devastated. Marion wasn't sure how she felt. She'd made it through the entire day without being eliminated, and now she had the opportunity of a life- time: to dance on the stage of Radio City Music Hall as a Rockette. Her life had taken another sharp turn and her mind tumbled with questions: How would her father react, especially after their argu- ment last night? What about Nathaniel?

What on earth had she done?

But first, Vanessa was in pain, and even though it wasn't at all certain that Vanessa would've made the cut if Marion hadn't shown up—she'd fumbled her kicks, after all—Marion wouldn't have even considered auditioning if Vanessa hadn't been talking about it in the waiting room.

Marion pulled her into the corner of the small lobby. "I'm as sur- prised as you are. I'm sorry you didn't make it, but there's always next year." The words sounded hollow even to her own ears. Vanessa wasn't the nicest person in the world, but Marion hated to see her upset.

"You hadn't even considered doing this until I told you about it."

"That's true. I guess I was curious to see if I was up to the challenge. But remember what Mr. Markert said at the end, about it being a big dance world. The city is full of possibilities."

"Don't patronize me."

"I'm not. Look, my father is going to flip when he hears this. And not in a good way."

"Great. So you'll get the job, turn it down, and screw up everything for the rest of us. Nice going." She moved toward the door but put out a hand as Marion tried to follow. "I need to be alone right now."

Marion watched her go. Deep down, she knew Vanessa was angry at herself for not making the final cut, and Marion was an easy target to lash out at. At least Vanessa hadn't brought up *Seven Brides* since lunchtime. That had to be a record.

"You're really not going to accept the offer?"

Marion turned to see a girl leaning against a wall. Marion had noticed her in the auditions—she was one of the dancers who'd made the cut—although she'd simply smiled and shrugged when her name was called out. She was a stunner, with dark-brown hair and perfectly arched dark eyebrows against ivory skin.

"I want to do it, I really do."

The girl came closer and stuck out her hand. "I'm Bunny."

"Marion. Marion Brooks."

"Congratulations. I was watching you earlier today and you were terrific—not only gorgeous but also gifted. Your friend is way too full of herself. Don't let her get to you."

"She's not really my friend. We're at the same studio."

Bunny cocked her head. "Why wouldn't you take the job?"

Marion hadn't had time to process what had just happened. How to explain? "I'm absolutely over the moon at having been picked, it's not that I'm ungrateful, but there are some personal complications that I hadn't really considered."

"I've been a Rockette for two years now, and I remember the day I first got picked like it was yesterday. The best day of my life, and the best job I'll ever have." She hit the button for the elevator. "You should know what you're missing if you do decide to turn down the job. Follow me."

The elevator doors slid open, and Marion stepped inside.

"The Rockettes have been around for ages, starting back in the 1920s when Russell had the idea of doing a *Ziegfeld Follies*–style show featuring sixteen girls. It became a smash hit, traveling all around the country." Bunny spoke quickly as the elevator rose. "Eventually, the impresario S. L. Rothafel, a.k.a. Roxy, brought the troupe to his Roxy Theatre in New York and changed the name to the Roxyettes."

"That's a mouthful."

"Roxy joined up with Rockefeller when he built the Radio City Music Hall, and so then they became the Rockettes. On the second floor are the producers' and directors' offices. Here on the third floor you'll find the dressing rooms."

They walked down a hallway until Bunny opened a door to a huge room with long rows of mirrors flanked by white bulbs and makeup tables overflowing with cosmetics and brushes. The back of each chair was draped in striped fabric with deep pockets for shoes. As Marion glanced around the room, she found she could guess at the personality of each dancer by the state of their station. Some were bursting with bouquets from an admirer, the surfaces covered with spilled powder; others had lipstick tubes lined up perfectly in rows like shiny toy soldiers.

"Just wait," said Bunny. "In less than an hour, this will make

Grand Central look like a deserted island. There's never enough time and you can never find the right hat."

There couldn't be much room to maneuver when all thirty-six dancers were rushing to get ready.

Bunny shut the door and they returned to the elevator to continue their ascent.

"How many new girls does the troupe hire each year?" asked Marion.

"It all depends. There were around ten new hires this time around, who'll get worked in over the next week or so, right before the current dancers step down, so there's no break in the schedule. Some Rockettes leave to get married and have kids, others age out of the job. Some, but not many, don't make it when they reaudition, but that's rare." The elevator stopped on the sixth floor. "The fourth and fifth floors are for the production offices. Here on six are the electric shop and the poster department—they create all the billboards." They climbed a set of stairs and continued past the rehearsal halls and down a long hallway. "Check this out." Bunny opened a room to what appeared to be a small cinema. "We get to screen the movies before anyone else."

Another door led to a dormitory with around twenty beds, where the girls could sleep if they needed a nap or stay over if rehearsals went late. A small lounge had card tables with half-finished puzzles, and there was even a medical station where a nurse was always on-site, in case of accidents or injuries.

Around every corner, on every floor, Radio City hummed with life. In the costume shop, a long line of seamstresses worked on candy cane–striped smocks and jeweled gloves, the buzzing of the sewing machines filling the room like a giant beehive. One dancer stood on top of a wide table, being fitted into a short skirt by a woman with pins in her mouth.

"The shoe and hat department is just down the hall," said Bunny.

Marion was impressed. "Wow. The only thing missing is a restaurant."

"Basement level. We have a swell cafeteria that's great for grabbing a muffin when you arrive in the morning. They take good care of us here."

"I can see that."

"And now for the final stop on your tour." They'd reached the top of the stairs, and Bunny pushed open a heavy metal door.

Sunlight blinded Marion as she stepped out.

They were on a wide expanse of roof, about ten stories up, surrounded by the skyscrapers of Rockefeller Center. There were deck chairs scattered about, a net for some kind of ball game, and even a shuffleboard court.

"This is where we relax, although if you get a sunburn, Mr. Markert will ban you from the show until it fades. Do you play Wiffle ball?"

"No."

"It's a blast." She turned back to Marion. "I saw you dance. You're phenomenal. You should be up on that stage with us." Bunny was smiling, but there was a steeliness to her delivery.

Marion decided to own up to the truth. "My father will kill me. He disapproves of any job that's not secretary, nurse, or teacher. He barely tolerates that I teach dance. Taught dance, I mean. I got fired yesterday."

"Perfect timing, then. And don't worry about your dad. When my father came to see me the first time, he wept like a baby. Everyone does when they see the show. You can't help it, you get tingles up your spine and then you cry."

"That's exactly what happened to me when I came to see the Rockettes as a child."

"Mr. Markert says it's because we move as one, which is near to impossible for normal humans, and it triggers some primal response. It's like the entrance of the Shades in *La Bayadère*."

Marion had seen the ballet several times and knew the moment

Bunny was referring to. To the velvety sound of violins, a line of thirty-two dancers dressed in white slowly made their way down a ramp and onto the stage, repeating a simple series of steps punctuated by an arabesque. For four minutes, the hypnotic power of so many women moving in perfect unison was undeniable, and the audience never failed to burst into applause when they were finally assembled onstage.

Bunny walked to the door that led back into the building and held it open. "But then again, maybe you just had a good dance day. Keeping up that level of precision is not for the weak."

"You're trying some reverse psychology on me, aren't you?" said Marion with a grin. She liked Bunny's energy, her confidence. "I'm onto you."

"Just telling the truth."

"Thanks for the grand tour. I really appreciate it."

Down in the dressing room, the roar of sound took Marion by surprise. It was now filled with dancers brushing their hair or applying makeup, a crazy collage of legs and arms and sparkly costumes. Marion stared, overcome. They joked, preened, laughed, all the while transforming into beautiful dolls. Into Rockettes.

"I've got to join them," said Bunny. "You can take the elevator back down to the stage door. It was nice meeting you, Marion."

"Same here." Marion watched as Bunny made her way along one of the aisles and was swallowed up by the dancers. Then she slowly turned and found her way out into the street.

Bunny was right. This was a chance of a lifetime.

But did she have the courage to take it?

CHAPTER SIX

At dinner that evening Marion sat quietly, waiting for the right time to tell Simon her news. She'd rehearsed it in her head on the train ride home from the audition, but nothing she came up with seemed right. There was no way to gently slip into the conversation that she'd been offered a job as a professional dancer on a New York City stage. And not just any stage. Radio City. There was no way of phrasing it that didn't end with Simon upending the dining room table in a rage. What she'd done by auditioning went way beyond the pearl-withholding misdemeanors of the past. This was treachery.

Judy passed the bowl of peas to Simon. "We have two new secretaries starting next week, and I'm in charge of training them. Oh, and it looks like I'm going to join Beth and the others from accounting on a trip to the opera next week."

"Beth?" Simon scrunched up his face. He was known for being on a first-name basis with everyone who worked in the executive offices. "Is she the one with the curly hair?"

"That's exactly right." Judy nodded approvingly. "They're a lively group. We may even go to dinner beforehand."

Live daringly, thought Marion, then reprimanded herself for being churlish.

"Did you get the note about moving those files?" Judy asked. "Lorraine sent it out to the staff yesterday."

"The dead ones, right. Let's keep them on the same floor as where we are."

Judy made a face. "There's hardly any room. But I'll make it work."

"You always do."

"And don't forget that it's Mary's birthday tomorrow. I've ordered a cake and we'll be passing around a card in the morning."

Marion put down her silverware with a clatter.

"Marion?" said Simon. "Are you all right?"

"Yes. In fact, I'm doing very well."

Simon smoothed down his tie. "I've had some time to think after our discussion last night. I'm sorry if I come off like a tough guy, but I love you and I'm doing it for your own good. What happened between your mother and me in the past shouldn't be of any concern. We loved each other, we loved you both, and I still love you. If you want your pearls back, you can have them."

"It's not about the pearls," said Marion. "You see, I—"

"Besides, Nathaniel will be back from Florida before you know it and we'll be breaking out the champagne."

Nathaniel. She'd been so busy today that she'd barely thought of him. Meanwhile, he was in Florida procuring her engagement ring. The impulsivity of her actions scared her a little. Perhaps this was what her mother had felt like when she'd been cast in a Broadway show and then been forced to make a choice between her career and having a family. It was all a muddle.

"I suppose," said Marion.

Simon paused a moment, studying her, and she tried not to squirm. "Now, tell me, what exactly did you do with yourself today?"

It was almost as if he knew she'd been up to something. Luckily, before Marion could come up with a response, Mrs. Hornsby entered carrying a pitcher of water.

"What are you still doing here?" said Simon with mock outrage. "Go home already. We've got to get used to being without you eventually."

Mrs. Hornsby smiled serenely at him as she refilled his glass. "Mr. Brooks, I'm retiring on December 31, not a day before. Don't think you can push me out the door so fast."

"We're going to miss you terribly, Mrs. Hornsby," said Judy. "I'm not sure how Dad will manage without your apple turnovers."

"Are you kidding?" said Simon. "You'll have to pry my hands from around her ankles that day, or she'll be dragging me behind her the whole way home."

Mrs. Hornsby laughed and flicked her dishcloth at him. "Tommy's taking me to California for a vacation on the first of January, and he only bought two plane tickets, so you'll have to restrain yourself."

Her son, Tommy, was a New York policeman, and Mrs. Hornsby, a widow, was as devoted to him as he was to her.

Marion watched as they all joked and teased each other. She already felt excluded from her father's and Judy's lives. Meanwhile, her close friends from high school had either gone off to college or were married, and the other teachers at the dance studio lived in the city and led busy lives of their own. Her own choices—waiting around for Nathaniel and spending most of her time at the dance studio—had left her lonely and isolated.

She had no one to turn to for advice, right when she needed it most.

Marion woke up early and stared at the ceiling. What if Bunny was right, and she'd just shined for that one day, driven by her competitive nature and the need to prove everyone who doubted her wrong? Or what if it was her beauty that had gotten the judges' attention and landed her the job, not her dancing?

If she showed up at the first rehearsal today, she'd find out. And no one needed to know. She figured if Mr. Markert found her dancing subpar and fired her, she'd be able to move on with her life without wondering what might have been.

Before she could change her mind, she pulled on her dance clothes, threw a skirt and a sweater over them, and headed out the door.

She took the train to Grand Central and gave her name to the security guard at the stage door. The rehearsal was in the same room where they'd auditioned. Bunny squealed when she spotted Marion and ran over.

"I knew you'd show up. This is great, come meet the others."

But there was no time for socializing. Mr. Markert, or Russell, as he insisted they call him, clapped his hands together.

"All right, gather around, my dancing daughters. The new movie at Radio City opens in a week. It's called *The Wings of Eagles* and stars John Wayne and Maureen O'Hara. Our routine will feature a cowboy theme, complete with holsters, guns, and hats. The new Rockettes will rehearse with the old hands every day from ten to eleven thirty A.M. and then again from one thirty to two thirty P.M. The ones who are already performing will continue to do so, four shows a day, in between each film viewing, starting at noon, three, six, and nine. Are you exhausted yet?" He smiled. "Good. And don't forget to stop by the costume shop for a fitting today whenever you have a break."

The assistant, Emily, called out their names and told them where to stand. Marion hurried to her place and then they were off, learning one combination after another and stringing them together as Emily counted out the beats. Then Emily motioned for Beulah—who was positioned at the piano, peering at the sheet music through thick-framed glasses—to begin playing, and they did it all over again, this time to music. Everything moved so quickly Marion barely had time to breathe. But her technique, developed over years of dance training, kicked in once the panic calmed down.

"Right now about half of you look like you're in excruciating pain," said Emily. "We want to see smiles on your faces, even during rehearsals. Here's the secret: relax your jaw and tongue, lift your eyebrows, and breathe through your nose. No panting through your mouth. Your nose, ladies. Breathe through your nose."

Every slightest move and gesture was taken apart, examined, and then put back together. A flick of a wrist, a lift of an elbow, all had to be performed the exact same way, dancer after dancer. An hour later, Marion was dripping with sweat and her arms ached as if she'd been pushing boulders uphill. She hadn't worked like this in ages. Possibly never. But she loved the challenge of transforming words into motion. It was as if Emily and Russell spoke a secret language, one that Marion's body knew fluently and instantly translated into movement.

Or so she thought.

"You, Marion." Russell was pointing at her. "You're using too much hip during the cross. And when I say tilt your head back, I mean a slight tilt. You're throwing your head back too far."

She tried to get it right the next run-through, but again Russell addressed her. "The cross is better, but now your head's not tilted enough. All right, take a break. I think we all need a break."

Marion sought out Bunny. "I think Russell is regretting his decision to hire me." She was only half joking.

"You'll be fine. Here's the trick for the head tilt: think of it as 'sunshine head.'"

"What?"

"Tilt your head as if you're standing up on the roof of the theater and getting a touch of sun. Imagine the feeling of the sun on your face, and you'll nail it."

Marion understood exactly what she meant, and Russell gave her a quick nod after the next run-through, which felt like being awarded a gold medal at the Olympics.

But the longer the rehearsal wore on, the worse she danced. She could see in the mirror that she was slightly out of sync with the other girls, but she couldn't figure out how to fix it. She actually *was* going to get fired the first day, right as she was beginning to realize that this was what she wanted more than anything else in the world. Finally, Russell called out for the pianist to stop. He and Emily spoke in low voices to each other and then he addressed the dancers.

"We'll get there," said Russell, staring right at Marion. "This is different from what you learned in your tap or ballet class. You are not ballerinas, you are not hoofers on Broadway. What we do is about the art of synchronization, precision, which involves suppressing your individual dancing style. Not an easy thing to do, by any means. Now, it's time to learn the famous Rockette kick line."

They were told to stand side by side, with the taller girls in the middle, tapering down to the shortest ones at either end.

"When we kick, your arms are in a W shape, elbows bent, but they do not touch the girl next to you," said Russell. "I'll repeat that. They *do not touch* any part of the girl on either side of you. Not her arm, her back, her shoulder. From the audience, it's an optical illusion that you're all connected, but I don't want any connection at all. Why? Because if you wobble, I don't want the dancer next to you to wobble as well. No touching, no wobbling. Got it?"

They all nodded.

"Let's go over the individual kicks. A strut kick is level with your belly button. Eye-high kicks are exactly that. Piano kicks are eye height but your leg crosses over and touches the floor just outside of your standing foot. I'm not looking for some French cancan action when you kick." He directed the words at Marion and she cringed. "Your foot stays straight, with no turnout. And you always smile. You will be doing around one hundred and fifty kicks a show, four shows a day. This is what our audience expects, and it's got to be perfect."

He waited, looking around the room. "Any questions?"

No one dared ask, if they had them.

"All right, then. Emily, show them the combination."

"We'll start with a right bevel." All eyes were on Emily's reflection in the mirror. "Step one, stretch the leg out, hold three and four. Five, stretch six, hold seven and eight. Repeat this twice. Now, left kick for four, right for four, kick right, kick left, inside ronds de jambe. Four kicks to the diagonal, four to the front, four left diagonal."

"Your head snaps when you switch feet," added Russell.

Emily wrapped up the sequence. "Four piano kicks, looking across, cross over, piano and over, four times, and you're done. For that section."

Not touching another dancer was much harder than Marion expected. They were so close to each other. She held her torso stiff to support the movement, but her strut kicks were always too high. To her relief, she noticed several of the other new dancers struggling as well.

She wanted this job. She wanted to do well and please Russell, to be part of this legendary team.

She certainly wasn't lonely, for the first time in ages. The dancers who were already Rockettes, like Bunny, went out of their way to help the new girls, and by the final run-through Marion had relaxed enough to enjoy it, especially at the end, when they pulled pretend guns out of holsters and gave a tip of a hat to the girl on either side. Prop guns and cowboy hats would be added in the afternoon rehearsal. Maybe then she'd earn another nod from Russell.

"Don't worry, everyone has a tough time the first go-round," said Bunny as they gathered up their things. "Come with me to the dressing room while we get ready for the show. You should stay and watch it. What do you say?"

It wasn't as if Marion had anywhere else to be.

※

In the dressing room, she sat in the empty seat next to Bunny's station as Bunny pulled on her costume: a one-shouldered striped bodysuit with a big red corsage. A matching top hat also sported a corsage, and the final touches included gold dance shoes and long gloves that reached above the elbows.

In it, she was all legs and glamour.

"You look marvelous," Marion said.

Bunny searched around her messy dressing room table for the right lipstick. "I know today was probably overwhelming, but you'll see, we're only a small part of the show. There's the corps de ballet—their dressing rooms and entrance are on the other side of the building, so we rarely cross paths. They even have their own rehearsal hall. But they're all quite lovely and nice when we do run into each other. There's also a choral ensemble, a glee club, sometimes they add in a magician or a comedian. It's a team effort, and each show goes by really fast, once you know the number."

"All that, and then there's a movie?"

"Crazy, right? But folks eat it right up."

"I don't think Russell liked my dancing much."

"You stand out, no question."

"I'm not trying to."

"You'll get it, I promise. It's only been one day."

"He scares me a little," she confessed.

The girl on the other side of Bunny leaned over. "I remember feeling like that. Russell's tough in the rehearsal hall but a sweetie outside it.

Last year, when I was living in a terrible apartment with a horrible roommate, he found me a new one."

"Apartment or roommate?" asked Bunny.

"Both."

The girl who sat on the other side of Marion piped up. "When Dolores's father died last year, right before she got married, Russell stepped in and walked her down the aisle. He's there for you, no matter what. Better than my own dad, to be honest."

They all laughed.

"Speaking of, how did your father take it?" asked Bunny.

Marion didn't want to talk about it in front of the other girls. "He's fine," she lied. "He's happy for me."

She promised Bunny that she'd meet her in the cafeteria in the basement after the show and then made her way around the building to the front entrance of the theater on Sixth Avenue. She showed the ticket taker the Radio City employee pass that had been handed out at the end of rehearsal to all the new dancers and was ushered inside.

The last time she'd been here she'd been a little kid, yet even as an adult the scale of the grand foyer overwhelmed her. She could only imagine what it had been like in 1932 when it first opened. Most theaters in New York were like hoop-skirted maidens from the last century, overly ornamented and full of froth, with flamboyant chandeliers and rococo plasterwork. In contrast, Radio City resembled a Jazz Age siren wearing a silk slip, sleek and elegant.

The gold-leafed ceiling rose a good sixty feet up, with two chic cylindrical lighting fixtures that blended in nicely. Six oversized mirrors reflected the airiness of the space, but Marion's eye was drawn to the huge mural that covered the northern wall where a staircase rose to the mezzanine level. The mural depicted a man on a mountaintop looking up into the sky as cloud-like visions from his life floated by.

But the foyer was only the warm-up act. Inside the theater, a deep-red curtain hung from the half circle formed by the stage proscenium, like a burning sun, and from there the walls and ceiling swept out into a series of arches, illuminated in yellow and orange, traveling all the way up to the balcony like the rays of a sunrise. The mezzanine and balconies were shallow, which further accentuated the giant scale of the auditorium.

She found a seat and settled in as a merry melody boomed from two Wurlitzer organs that flanked the stage. After, a thirty-piece orchestra slid out of nowhere via some kind of hydraulic system and settled in at the foot of the stage. The show was as varied as Bunny had promised, with a magician doing tricks with a rabbit and a hat, followed by a song from the glee club and a short ballet. The curtain came down briefly and then rose again to the sight of the Rockettes as the audience cheered and clapped, even though they hadn't begun dancing yet. Marion surveyed the dancers and finally located Bunny stage left, but they all blended together so well that she found she lost sight of her with each new formation. The show was heart-stopping to watch, seamless, and she couldn't imagine becoming that proficient in only a week, when the new routine was set to premiere.

As the tempo picked up, the dancers moved into place and began a kick line that was even more complicated than the one Marion had learned that morning. The audience shouted and applauded and she found herself crying, as was the entire family sitting next to her. What was it about the synchronicity of movement that created a swell of emotion, one that couldn't be helped? It was a strange kind of alchemy.

Finally, the last note sounded and the Rockettes, smiling, hit their marks.

Only up close would anyone know how hard they were breathing.

CHAPTER SEVEN

Following the afternoon rehearsal, Marion took the subway downtown to Union Square. The Met Power offices were at Irving Place, in a stunning neoclassical building with a giant clock at the very top, which was lit up at night with colored lights.

The elevator ascended quickly to the eighteenth floor, where the top brass worked, and Marion followed the hallway to her father's corner office. As she neared, dread rose in her belly, the same queasy feeling she'd had when she'd confronted him about her mother's belongings in the attic.

Marion didn't mean to defy Simon's wishes, but this incredible opportunity to be a Rockette was too delicious to pass up. She hadn't realized until now what a passive participant she'd been in her own life, gliding along with everyone else's desires for her future. Nathaniel had walked up to Marion at a party her junior year of high school and claimed her as his girlfriend. Her father wanted her to marry Nathaniel, and so it was assumed she would. Even when sweet Miss Stanwich had told her she should teach, she hadn't thought twice about following her mentor's lead.

But the day's rehearsal at Radio City had changed all that. Finally, she was making a choice of her own. And there was no doubt in her mind that she wanted to be a Rockette.

Judy sat at a desk outside Simon's office door and was typing away with blinding speed, her eyes glued to a steno pad. Her tongue poked out the corner of her mouth, like it used to do when she was focused on a task as a kid. The memory made Marion smile.

Judy looked up and blinked twice. "What are you doing here?"

"I thought I'd stop by and say hello." Marion gave a weak wave of her hand, her courage already faltering. She pointed to the door. "Is he in?"

"He is, but his calendar is full."

Her dismissiveness wasn't new, but there was an added coldness to Judy's tone. Marion could only imagine what it must have been like for Judy to learn that she was the reason Lucille had given up her dream of acting. Even if their father insisted Lucille was happy to do so, it still had to make Judy wonder whether she'd been a welcome surprise. Marion lowered her voice. "Look, I'm sorry about the way we found out about Mom's decision the other night. To quit acting and raise a family instead."

"I really don't see why you had to dig up the past," said Judy quietly. "Hasn't Dad been through enough?"

Just then, the door opened. "Judy, I need the file on—" He caught sight of Marion and smiled widely. "There's my beautiful daughter!" Marion cringed at the adjective, knowing he'd never say such a thing to Judy. Her sister tended to get pegged with *capable* and *smart*.

Judy had risen from her desk, a file in hand. "Here you go, the Jones file."

"Thank you, my dear." Simon took it from Judy and put his free arm around Marion. "Come on in and tell me, to what do I owe the pleasure of your company?"

She stepped with him into his walnut-paneled office, where a drinks tray was parked next to a marigold-colored couch. Two matching chairs sat opposite a mahogany desk. Outside the windows, the Empire State Building needled up into the sky.

Marion settled into one of the chairs. She knew without looking that Judy was still standing in the doorway, curious as to what was going on.

The nameplate on Simon's desk gleamed, the words *Simon Brooks, Vice President of Personnel Administration* etched in brass.

Her father bragged to anyone who asked that he'd worked for the same company his entire life. He'd been hired right after graduating from high school on the Lower East Side, racing around Manhattan in dark-blue coveralls, going wherever a repair was needed. His natural affability had led him to get to know many of the other technicians, and he'd quickly realized that the way they were deployed made no sense. He might be called to Wall Street in the morning and up to Inwood two hours later, which involved a painful crawl from the southern tip of the island to the north through traffic-choked streets. He put together a map that gave each worker a territory as well as a system for appointments that saved time and money while increasing efficiency. Before he knew it, he was the boss of his team, then the boss of the whole repair division, and, eventually, vice president in charge of hiring, evaluating, and paying thousands of Met Power employees. This last promotion had come five years ago, with Simon Brooks heralded as a shining example of American ingenuity and grit. The three "Employee of the Year" awards on the bookshelf behind him—in addition to the one in his home study—were a testament to his standing in the company. He threw himself into his work and enjoyed it immensely.

"What's going on, then?" asked Simon.

He opened the file Judy had given him and smoothed it flat on his desk.

"I have something I wanted to tell you," she said.

His eyes went to her left hand. "Is Nathaniel back already?"

She covered her bare finger with the other hand, annoyed that was the only thing that ever came to his mind these days. She disliked being treated like chattel. No doubt Simon intended on giving away a few goats for her dowry as well. "No. It's not that. You see, yesterday I went to Radio City—"

"Simon! We have bad news."

She turned. Two men had charged into the office, concerned looks on their faces. Judy slipped in after them and closed the door behind her.

"What is it?" asked Simon.

One of the men caught sight of Marion and blushed. "Gosh, nice to see you, Marion."

Marion nodded back, unable to remember the man's name. She'd been introduced to him at last year's Christmas party, probably.

"There's been another bombing," said the other man. "That makes four just this year."

"Where?" Simon rubbed his face.

"The New York Public Library. In a phone booth."

"Anyone hurt?"

"Not this time. Luckily."

Her father rose from his chair. "We have to see the chairman. Girls, I'll be back. Don't go anywhere."

The men were gone as fast as they'd come in.

"How many does this make?" asked Marion.

"Thirty-one," answered Judy.

Both sisters knew the story well. For the past sixteen years, starting in 1940, someone had been planting pipe bombs around New York City, in subway stations, department stores, theaters, even Grand Central Terminal. The newspapers called the culprit the Big Apple Bomber, and so far, a dozen people had been injured, some seriously. The very first bomb was planted in a toolbox at a Met Power compound on Sixty-Fourth Street, with a note reading *Met Power crooks—this is for you.* That one hadn't gone off. But since then, the bomber had expanded his reach and his skill, setting off explosions in well-populated places like the Port Authority and Penn Station, sometimes repeating the same target years later. And now he'd hit the library. Even worse, the madman's pace was picking up.

After the very first bomb and note, the Big Apple Bomber had struck Met Power twice more, leaving one in a phone booth in this very building in 1951 and mailing another a few weeks later. Only the first had detonated, luckily with no injuries. The police figured he was probably a disgruntled customer or an employee, a description that in a city of millions made him hard to pin down. Simon had been helping the police with the investigation, which so far had gone nowhere.

"Maybe I'll head home," said Marion. She'd won a reprieve, for now. She'd talk to Simon back at home, after he'd had a drink and was more relaxed.

"He said to stay put," said Judy. "You can wait in the lounge."

"I'm fine here," said Marion, planting herself on the couch. "Although I could use a cup of coffee."

"I'm not your secretary." Judy turned and headed for the door. "You can get it yourself."

Marion helped herself to some coffee and brought a cup for Judy as well, standing like a dope in front of her desk as she waited for her to look up from her typing.

She wished they were closer. Nathaniel and his brothers teased each other mercilessly but also shared an easy camaraderie that Marion basked in when she went over for dinner. All four were popular in school, adored by teachers and students alike. Where Nathaniel excelled in sports, his brothers did the same in the student council, or on the debate team, or in the drama club.

Unlike Judy, who'd refused to join any teams or clubs at all.

That wasn't exactly true, Marion corrected herself. During Judy's second year of high school, she'd joined the math club, which consisted of all boys and Judy, and for a while her confidence had seemed to grow. She walked straighter and smiled more. She'd even invited one of the boys over to the house to study one afternoon. Marion had been up in her room the entire time, reading the latest issue of *Seventeen* and figuring out what outfit she was going to wear to the middle school sock hop that night, when she'd heard Judy yell and the front door slam shut. She ventured down, concerned, and asked her about it.

"Mind your own business," Judy answered. She sounded tough but Marion could tell she was near tears by the way the tip of her nose turned red.

"Judy, what happened?" Marion asked. "Did he hurt you?"

"Stop messing in my life. Just go away." Judy ran past her up the stairs, shoving her out of the way. Unprepared, Marion banged into the wall, hard, but Judy didn't care. She continued up the stairs to her room and didn't come down for dinner.

They'd already been living separate lives, but from then on, even the odd shared laugh at the expense of their father had died out.

Marion cleared her throat.

"Yes?" asked Judy.

"I brought you this." Marion placed the coffee on the one corner of the desk that wasn't covered with papers and files.

"I don't drink coffee in the afternoon."

"I know. It's decaf."

It was like trying to impress a rock. The girl wouldn't budge an inch.

"Fine," Judy finally said.

Only as Marion stepped through the doorway of her father's office did she hear a whispered "Thank you."

Finally, Simon returned. His phone rang at the same time and Judy stayed at her desk to answer it.

"What did Mr. Howell say?" Marion asked. Tom Howell was the company's chairman and often called their home on weekends to talk with Simon.

He rubbed his eyes with his fingers. "He's as frustrated as the rest of us. The police never seem to make an inch of headway. I mean, thirty-one bombs, and they have no better idea who's setting them than they did sixteen years ago. What's it going to take to catch this guy?"

Judy entered, looking somber.

"What is it?" Simon asked.

"A reporter from the *Herald Tribune* just called. The bomber mailed a letter to an editor there that arrived today."

"What does it say?"

She read out loud from her notepad. "'Bombs will continue until the Metropolitan Power Company is brought to justice for their dastardly acts against me. I have exhausted all other means. I intend with the bombs to cause others to cry out for justice for me. If I don't get justice, I will continue but with bigger bombs.'"

"Signed *F.P.*?"

"Yes. Same as all the other letters."

Every time a bomb went off, Simon went into overdrive, trying to manage the bad publicity that arose with each act of terror. Marion sympathized with his exasperation. "I'm sorry you have to deal with this, Dad."

"It's an unfortunate part of the job." He sighed. "Now we're going to have to comb through all of our employee files, once again, to satisfy the police, looking for similarities to his latest letter." He looked over at Judy. "Have the clerks pull a team together to start reviewing the files, past and present. We might as well get a jump on it, as I expect the police will be arriving any minute."

"Will do." Judy practically snapped her heels together, like the good soldier she was.

"I'll leave you to it, then," said Marion.

"Wait a minute, what made you decide to stop by? You said something about Radio City?"

Now was definitely not the time. "No, that's nothing. I wanted to apologize for upsetting you the other night. That's all."

"You're a good kid. I know that. Now scram on home and I'll see you there. You can have the pearls back."

It wasn't about the pearls, it was never about the pearls, but he didn't seem to get that.

"Sure."

She turned to go, and Judy did as well. Unfortunately, both refused to slow down as they neared the doorway, and they bumped into each other like Laurel and Hardy. Marion's handbag fell to the floor.

Marion's employee pass for Radio City landed faceup on the carpet. Judy snatched it up before Marion could and rose to her feet. "Why does this say that you're an employee at Radio City Music Hall?"

Marion grabbed it back and stuck it in her handbag, but it was too late.

"What's that about?" asked Simon.

"You have enough going on, we can talk later," said Marion.

"Huh. Now I'm curious. Let's see." Simon placed one elbow on his desk, the hand turned up, waiting.

Slowly, Marion withdrew the pass from her purse, walked over, and placed it in his palm.

He studied it. "Are you an usher at Radio City now? Do they allow lady ushers?"

"It's a long story, but I went to an audition there—someone from the dance studio told me about it—and I got the job."

"And what job is that?" His tone came off as teasing, but she knew he was dead serious.

She braced herself. "As a professional dancer, for the shows they do in between films. There were hundreds of girls and I was picked after a full day of auditions." She glanced back at Judy, whose mouth was open. "It's an honor. And it pays well."

"You're a chorus girl?" boomed Simon. "You're a dancing chorus girl?"

"No." She paused, gathering her courage, wanting to make herself heard. "I'm a Rockette," she said proudly.

The room fell silent.

When he finally spoke, Simon's voice came out as a low growl. "You're a Rockette, you say?"

Marion nodded.

"Over my dead body." He motioned to the door. "I don't have time to discuss this right now, but I assure you we'll talk more when I get home."

CHAPTER EIGHT

DECEMBER 1992

I start doubting my decision to go into New York City as soon as the car merges onto the highway. The dress still fits, but in it I feel like I'm an imposter from another time, traveling into the future. I watch the rain drip down the passenger window as the windshield wipers keep up their steady rhythm and wonder if it's not too late to turn back, have the driver pull off at the next exit. Piper sits primly next to me, hands in her lap. When we hit traffic going through Riverdale, she apologizes.

"It's not your fault," I say.

"I'm just so glad you're coming. It's going to be a terrific evening. Did you come back for any of the other anniversaries?"

"No. I've been too busy."

"Of course. I've been following your career since I started dancing. Your very first job was as a Rockette, right?"

I realize the best way to evade further questions is to ask them myself. I learn that Piper started dancing when she was five, somewhere in Florida, and she prefers ballet to tap, and modern above both. "Did you ever audition for the Rockettes?" I ask.

She looks down, cowed. "I went to the open call for auditions the first year I came to New York, in the hopes that I could sneak in. But

I'm too short. They measured me as soon as I walked in the door; I didn't even get a chance to dance."

"Did you end up dancing anywhere else?"

She shakes her head. "I was so embarrassed after being told to leave that I pretty much gave up trying."

"How old are you?"

"Twenty-one."

"You're still young. Audition for something else. Anything. A commercial, a national tour. If you want to dance, you can't let anyone stop you. I know that from experience."

"I'm fine working behind the scenes these days. Not long after my audition, I saw this job in the newspaper, as an assistant to the events coordinator, and it's been a lot of fun. The offices are right in Radio City, so I feel like I'm part of it all."

The words come out thin. She's miserable in this job, too sensitive. If she's this hesitant with me, I can only imagine what it's like when she's tasked with handling a demanding celebrity. I feel the need to cheer her up. "Have you seen Roxy's ghost around the theater yet?"

"Yes!" She claps her hands together. "Well, I didn't see him exactly. I was up in the viewing room giving some VIPs a tour just a couple of months ago. You know where that is, right?"

I squint, as if that will help me remember. But then I do. "Next door to the projector room, at the very back of the theater?"

"Yes. I was telling them all about Roxy, how he was this larger-than-life impresario who convinced Russell Markert to bring his dance troupe first to his Roxy Theatre and later to Radio City Music Hall, and suddenly all the lights in the room went out. I'm sure it was him, and I tell you, it was spooky. Did you ever encounter him?"

"I didn't, but my friend Bunny said one time she saw a man escorting a beautiful woman down one of the hallways. When she turned the corner, they'd completely disappeared." I warm to the memory of Bunny flying back to the dressing room, breathless with the news.

"I love that about old theaters, all the history and the ghosts." Piper's face goes red. "I'm sorry. I didn't mean—"

It takes me a moment to realize what she's referring to. "That's all right."

Now it's her turn to change the subject. "I was doing some research into the early days of Radio City for the event tonight," she says. "Did you know that the opening night for Radio City was an utter disaster? It dragged on until two thirty A.M., crammed full of vaudeville acts that bored the audience. Poor Roxy collapsed and had to be taken out of the theater on a stretcher."

"I had heard that, yes." Russell loved to share stories of the early days during rehearsal breaks. We'd gather around, eager to feel part of something historic. "Let's hope tonight goes a little smoother."

Even seated in the back of a sedan, Piper keeps her posture that of a ballerina, her neck long and shoulders back. To have her hidden away in some back office seems a shame. "What is it you love best about dancing?"

Piper's eyes go wide. "Gosh, everything. I love the thrill of performance, the moment when the curtain goes up and you distill all the hours of practice and repetition into one beautiful moment, on cue, with the music. And I really love the way it feels when you come home after a long day and your muscles are sore but your mind is still humming with the choreography. And then you drift off and have dreams of dancing."

I find myself moved to tears by her unexpected eloquence. "You're a dancer, not an assistant. I can tell by the way you speak about it."

"It means a lot, you saying that." She offers a shy smile. "Thank you."

CHAPTER NINE

OCTOBER 1956

B ack at home that evening, Marion was making herself a turkey sandwich as she waited for Simon to return when Judy drifted through and curtly informed her that their father would be pulling an all-nighter to deal with the latest bombing. "But I know he wants to discuss this matter with you," she added. "ASAP."

"I'll have my secretary schedule something right away," sneered Marion before retreating to her room to eat. Judy was probably thrilled that Marion and Simon were on the outs; that way she could have him all to herself.

But up in her room, Marion regretted her snideness, as she always did after one of their spats. It was as if they couldn't control themselves, fighting over limited resources like animals in the nature show that aired on Sundays. Scuffling over Simon's attention, Simon's approval. As they grew older, Marion could count on one hand the times they had really talked. Once, when Judy was about to graduate from secretarial school, she'd confided in Marion that she'd been offered a job as the secretary to an insurance executive who was based in San Francisco, but that she'd turned it down to work for their father instead. Marion had been aghast.

"Why wouldn't you go out west?" she'd said. "What a great

opportunity to see the world." They'd been sitting on the porch drinking lemonades on an unusually warm May day, trying to catch some semblance of a breeze. As little girls, they'd taken turns spraying each other with the garden hose on days like this, shrieking and laughing with glee at the shock of freezing-cold water on sweaty skin. That easygoing camaraderie was long gone.

"I don't need to see the world," Judy answered. "I'm fine where I am. Besides, Dad said he needs me. All his other secretaries have been complete duds, and I understand what he requires better than anyone else."

"Dad will manage, I promise you. He's made it this far without you."

Judy winced. "It's better this way."

"Is there something else you're not telling me?" Marion asked.

Judy pursed her lips. "I overheard the executive say something to the school administrator after my interview. He said his wife wouldn't let him have any pretty secretaries, but he figured she'd approve of me."

Marion's heart broke for her sister. "Then I'm glad you're staying put. He sounds like a jerk."

"What would you know about it?" Judy rose abruptly, spilling her lemonade across the table and onto the patio. The subject was never brought up again.

Marion wished she could do something to change their dynamic, but right now she had enough to deal with when it came to Simon and her new job. She made it through the morning and afternoon rehearsals at Radio City, keeping a bright smile on her face even as her father's ominous words echoed in her head, and then stayed on to catch the final performance and the late film to avoid going home.

She could hear Simon's snores when she crept up the steps to her room. Her reckoning would no doubt come the next day, a Sunday, when he'd be home from work and the new Rockettes were excused from rehearsal, which left an entire day with the two of them in the same house. But she couldn't keep on like this, sneaking in and out, as the trepidation and anxiety ate away at her.

※

The sound of plates clattering and people talking loudly downstairs woke her the next day. Someone else was in the house, and she poked her head out of her bedroom door to listen. She recognized Nathaniel's baritone immediately. She got dressed and put on some lipstick and powder before joining them. Thank goodness he'd stopped by, as his presence might keep her father's anger in check, make him more likely to hear what she had to say. Unlike her father, Nathaniel might show some excitement—or even pride—at her news.

She took a deep breath and then entered the kitchen breezily, giving Nathaniel a kiss on the cheek and pouring herself some coffee, as if this were any other day. Judy was buttering toast at her place at the table next to Simon, who took a sip of his coffee and glowered in Marion's direction without actually looking at her. It was amazing, really. Just as the force of his attention could make someone feel like they were the only person in a crowded room, his wrath was equally destructive and left one feeling all alone in the world.

But she wasn't alone. She had Nathaniel. He was back, and surely he'd listen to reason. She was a Rockette, which would make any boyfriend proud as could be.

She knew from experience that it was best to punch through her father's wall of silence sooner rather than later. "How are things with the bombing?" she asked him.

"Nothing yet."

At least he was speaking to her. That was progress.

"And, Nathaniel, how is your grandmother?"

"She's fine. Says to say hello." He glanced over at Simon and ducked his head.

So he knew.

The coffee left a burnt taste in Marion's mouth. Judy took a big bite of toast and somehow managed to chew with a smirk on her face.

"Nathaniel," Marion said, "can I talk to you for a moment?"

"Sure."

Their backyard featured a giant gneiss boulder, which Judy and Marion used to climb and scrape their knees on as kids. Marion had learned at school that rocks like these had been rolled into place by retreating glaciers back in the Ice Age and were known as "glacial erratics." When she'd told her father that, he'd been impressed: "Well, look at you, with the fancy scientific phrases. You sound like your sister."

The warmth of the compliment had lingered for days after.

She leaned against the rock and looked back at the house. "I guess you've heard the news?"

He nodded. "I have to say, when your father told me, I was shocked. Becoming a chorus girl seems like a rather audacious move."

"I'm not a chorus girl." Everyone was so obtuse. Could no one even bother to try to see her point of view? It was crucial to get Nathaniel on board with her decision, otherwise she stood no chance. "A student from the dance studio mentioned the auditions at Radio City, and at the last minute I decided to go as well. It was a grueling process, there were hundreds of other girls. When they called out my name, I was shocked. But now I'm a Rockette. It means I get paid to do what I love, which is dance. Isn't that incredible? I'm excited about it and I hope you can be, too."

"What about our wedding? What about all the planning you have to do this year?"

She wanted to say that he hadn't even proposed yet, so it was all still theoretical. Also, she resented the assumption that *she* would have to do all the planning, and he'd just show up the day of. But that was probably asking too much. "I can plan a wedding and work. Other women do it all the time."

"What's your schedule going to be like?"

How best to put it? "We work from eleven in the morning to ten at night, three weeks at a time."

"Eleven hours a day? What about weekends?"

"Well, today is an exception, as they had some technical issues with the show that's currently running, which meant the new girls didn't have to go in. But normally, there are no weekends off. We dance four shows a day on weekends as well. My first performance is next Thursday."

His face fell. It was an insane schedule, to be honest.

"But it's three weeks straight, but then one whole week off," she added. "I can get a lot done in a week."

"I'm finally back in Bronxville for good, and you go and get yourself a job where I'll never see you. What's going on here?"

"Isn't it only fair that I get a chance to throw myself into something, like you did with college? Not to mention touring Europe. I don't think I'm asking too much."

Nathaniel relented slightly. "I know I've asked a lot of you, waiting around for me to come home. But I was looking forward to finally being together. You have to agree, the timing is not good."

"I get that. Look, being a Rockette is the hardest thing I've ever done. I mean, the choreography is beyond difficult. But I love it. Can't you grant me this one thing?"

He pulled out a small box from his jacket pocket. He opened it and studied it for a moment before turning it to show Marion what was inside: a large square diamond set in a platinum ring, with three small round diamonds running along either side.

His grandmother's ring, the reason he'd flown to Florida.

But he kept the box close to his body. He was showing it to her, not offering it.

"It's beautiful," she said. "And so kind of her to pass it on."

"Well, your father's asked me to not propose until this peccadillo is cleared up."

Peccadillo? Is that the way they saw it? And what was it with men thinking that by withholding baubles they could control a woman? First her mother's pearls, now this. Did they think she was that simpleminded?

"I really don't understand it, Nathaniel," she finally said. "Most boyfriends would be over the moon to hear that their girlfriend is a Rockette. They'd be bragging to all their buddies."

"Sure. I mean, it's amazing." For the first time that morning she heard a hint of pride in his voice. He looked at her and started to smile, but then seemed to remember something and the smile vanished. "But your father has said that he won't let me propose unless you listen to him."

He snapped the box shut and put it back in his coat pocket. "You should go talk to your father."

※

After Nathaniel left, Marion marched back into the house and found her father in the basement, where he had his workshop. The workbench was cluttered with tools, and a large, oily lathe stood nearby. He'd made rocking horses and dollhouses for Judy and Marion when they were children, and these days he liked to design small tables and give them as gifts to friends. They were exquisitely made, of course. He always said this was how he cleared his head from the craziness of the week, by creating something tangible.

"How could you?"

"Now, Marion. Settle down and let's talk like adults." He pointed to a high stool nearby.

She took a seat and crossed her arms. "You told Nathaniel he wasn't allowed to propose until I stopped dancing?"

"That's not what I said. I told him you might need some time to really think about what you want in life, and that it would be smart of him to give you some breathing room."

He was so good at twisting things around. "He didn't take it that way, not at all. You can't control us, we're both adults."

"To be honest, this is a betrayal. You went behind my back, against my wishes. I thought we were closer than that."

He was manipulating her, but she couldn't help feeling bad for hurting him. "I can do it for a year or so, then quit. It's not the end of the world."

"I don't like the road you're heading down. It won't end well, I promise you."

"I get that you don't want me to go into the arts. That somehow it makes me flighty or a dilettante. But that's not true."

"As I've said dozens of times, the most important thing to me is that my girls are taken care of. Judy can work anywhere with her skills, so I'm not worried about her. If you get married, I trust Nathaniel will keep you safe and happy. What I don't want is you thinking that dancing is a potential career, then getting swept away by the late nights and the so-called glamour and leaving Nathaniel behind. I want you safe, living a good life. That is my priority, for both you and Judy."

She wondered if he was thinking of Lucille, the way she'd almost left him behind. "What if a good life involves dance?"

Simon's eyes blazed. "Let's say you do this, and you and Nathaniel drift apart. How many good years would you have as a dancer? Five or six? Then what?"

"There's no reason I can't dance and plan a wedding at the same time. Nathaniel and I will be fine."

Deep down, though, she knew the schedule was grueling and there was no guarantee that Nathaniel would stick around and wait for her. Yet she'd been expected to do just that.

Simon placed a piece of wood in a vise. "You've always been drawn to the arts, I understand that. Your mother loved that sort of thing as well. It was one of the things that attracted me to her. You're like her, and not only because you look like her. You've both got that same ethereal quality, like you float through the world. But she was happy as a mother and wife. She understood that as the wife of an executive, she had an important job as well."

"What was that, exactly?"

"To make sure our home life ran smoothly, to be ready to entertain at a moment's notice, and to raise you girls to be obedient and well-mannered." His finger twitched. "She was more than fulfilled doing so. Why can't you be, too?"

She had to make him understand. "You say my mother and I both floated through the world. In many ways, I have. You've given me everything a daughter could want, and I know I'm lucky in that a lot has come easy to me. But at rehearsals, I have been pushed harder than I ever have before, and it's not coming easy. In fact, I'm convinced that they'll pull me aside and tell me that I'm fired at any moment. For once in my life, I can't flash a pretty smile to get what I want. I'm having a hard time, and if I walk away, it'll mean that I'm not up to the challenge. I don't want to have to live with wondering what might have been. This is an opportunity for me, and I need to embrace it."

"No."

She waited. "That's all you have to say?"

"That's all."

During her plea, his demeanor had darkened. His eyes had grown icy, his mouth set in a grim line. Whatever she'd said had touched a nerve, although she didn't understand why. What was she missing?

"Well, I'm going to stick with it. That's what Mom would have wanted."

He picked up a scrap of wood and threw it across the room, making her jump. "How would you know what your mother would've wanted?" he yelled. "I'm telling you what I want. Marry Nathaniel and drop this business."

She'd rarely gone against his wishes. But now she had to. Even if it cost her everything. "And if I don't?"

"You'll regret throwing away the opportunities that are in front of you now. I'm warning you."

"I understand your concern, but I respectfully disagree."

"You *respectfully disagree*? What, do you think this is some court of law? No. You're in my house, and if you can't abide by what I'm saying, then you can leave. See what it's like out there when you don't have your family to take care of you. Try to go it alone and see how long you last."

"You're kicking me out?"

"That's right."

"But, Dad—"

"Enough. You have a choice to make. You decide. I have no doubt you'll come to your senses soon enough."

She didn't want to burst into tears in front of him. That would mean that he'd won. She ran back upstairs to her room.

Marion sat on her bed with its faded quilt and curled in on herself, letting the tears fall until she was spent. No one—Nathaniel, her father, even the hateful Miss Beaumont—could be bothered to see her perspective. They wanted her to behave like a good girl and please them, never mind what pleased her. Simon thought by giving her an ultimatum, he'd stop her in her tracks. But she had a stubborn streak just like he did, and she wasn't about to let him push her around.

She drew a deep breath. Her mind was made up.

She packed her Samsonite suitcase with clothes and dancing gear. In her desk was an envelope containing a hundred dollars, saved up from various Christmases and birthdays, and she tucked the bills into her purse, her hands shaking.

But where would she go?

✴

Marion's arms grew sore as she walked up Sixth Avenue. The handle of the suitcase left a dent in her palm, and although a man waiting for the light to change on Forty-Fourth Street had offered to help, she'd shaken her head. She didn't want to be asked where she was headed or what she was doing. She wasn't sure what the answer was.

Inside Radio City, the dancers filed by after finishing the noon show, laughing and gorgeous. Bunny finally appeared.

"Marion!" she yelled out. "The new girls aren't called today, you ninny. If I were you, I'd be off getting my hair done. Once you're dancing you'll be so sick of this place."

"Right. I was just—" She didn't know how to explain what she was doing. On the train on the way to the city she'd run over the conversations with Nathaniel and her father in her head, wondering what she'd done that was so egregious that she deserved to be abandoned. She had a job, for goodness' sake, one that most women would kill to get. Was that so crazy?

She burst into tears.

"Now, now," said Bunny. "What happened?"

"I had to leave home. My father is so angry, I've never seen him like that before. My boyfriend won't propose unless I quit this job. I'm fairly certain Russell is about to fire me any day now, so why I'm doubling down and coming here is beyond me. But here I am. I want to be a Rockette. I want to dance and get paid for it. I want to be part of this group, more than anything."

"I thought you said your father was okay with this."

"I lied. I didn't even tell him until a couple of days ago. I was scared."

Bunny pulled her close. "I'm sorry he was a beast. You don't deserve that. None of us do."

"But I have nowhere to go."

Bunny grabbed the suitcase with one hand and encircled Marion's waist with the other, her grip sure and strong. "I have an idea. Come with me."

CHAPTER TEN

I think we have just enough time in between shows, but we're going to have to hotfoot it," said Bunny as she and Marion dodged around tourists taking photos and businessmen in suits, heading north and then east along Fifty-Third Street.

Bunny got plenty of looks, especially from the men, as her stage makeup looked garish in the harsh daylight. But there was no point in taking it off when she had a show in a couple of hours, and then two more after that. Marion understood what it was like to be gawked at and was impressed with Bunny's imperviousness to the men's stares.

They stopped in front of a dowdy brown building, four stories high, with a steep set of stairs leading up to a pair of heavy oak doors.

"You're going to love this," said Bunny, reaching for Marion's suitcase and lugging it up the steps. Marion followed, unsure of what exactly was going on.

The door led to a large parlor where a group of girls around their age were chatting loudly, seated on couches and chairs that looked like they'd been there since the last century. Posters from Broadway shows hung on the walls, along with photos of famous stage actresses, including Ellen Terry and Sarah Bernhardt. The clatter of dishes drifted up from a lower floor.

"Where are we?" asked Marion.

"The Rehearsal Club. A boardinghouse for girls in the performing arts."

"This is where you live?"

"Sure thing. Me and four other Rockettes. Mrs. Fleming, who runs the place, loves us because we get a steady paycheck and never fall behind on rent. The other girls are actress and singer wannabes, with a couple of comedians and opera singers thrown into the mix, but we try not to hold it against them. Comes with room and board."

To live right in the middle of New York, within walking distance of the theater, was a dream. "How much?"

"Eighteen dollars a week. Leaves you with more than enough extra for fun. Speaking of fun, I'm going out with my beau tonight, along with a friend of his. You can join us, and we'll celebrate your new home."

Marion looked about. Living in a boardinghouse with actresses? Her father would have a heart attack. On the train into the city, she'd imagined finding a room at the top of a brownstone owned by an elderly lady with a cat or two. But she didn't know how to even begin to find accommodations like that. Her life had been so sheltered, she was ashamed to admit. "I'm not sure."

"Not sure about what, the Club or dinner tonight?"

"Maybe both?"

Bunny looked at her like she was crazy. "Let's go find Mrs. Fleming; she'll give you all the details, and then you can decide, all right?"

Mrs. Fleming's office was located at the back of the building, a small room that held a desk, several metal filing cabinets, and an overstuffed brown couch that overwhelmed the space. A gray-haired woman in a simple gray dress sat behind the desk, but when she looked up and smiled, her face flooded with warmth.

"What can I do for you, dear?" she asked Bunny.

"Mrs. Fleming, my friend Marion here is a new Rockette and needs a place to stay. There's an extra bed in my room, I'd be happy to share with her."

"Why don't you have a seat?" said Mrs. Fleming to Marion, gesturing to the sofa.

"I've got to get back to Radio City," said Bunny. "Meet me at the stage door at ten and we'll grab dinner." Bunny blew Marion a kiss and disappeared.

After she was gone, Mrs. Fleming picked up a clipboard and a pen. "Congratulations on becoming a Rockette. Now, what's your full name?"

"Marion Brooks."

"Is that your stage name or your real name?"

"Real name."

"Lucky you. I've heard some of the worst real names in my time, let me tell you. Edna Quattlebaum, for example, who changed her name to Angela Cadbury, which I didn't think was much of an improvement." She gave Marion a sly grin. "My full name is Mitzi Fleming, which you have to agree is a sublime stage name. My mother wanted me to be in pictures, but I'm much happier behind the scenes."

Marion was unsure how to reply, so she stayed silent.

"I insist on telling prospective boarders a little history of the place, so they appreciate what we have here. Back when actresses were considered no better than streetwalkers and often found it impossible to rent a room, two women—Daisy Greer and Jane Harriss Hall—decided to create a boardinghouse where girls like you and Bunny could stay and pursue creative careers. Have you seen the film *Stage Door* with Kate Hepburn?"

Marion nodded.

"Our locale was the inspiration for the movie, and countless stars-in-the-making have passed through our doors. Perhaps you'll be the next one. However, we have several rules in place." She checked off each one on her fingers as she spoke. "No smoking, no alcohol, no boys beyond the parlor. You must be in by midnight, the doors are locked after that. You must be between eighteen and twenty-five, neither married nor divorced."

"I'm nineteen and not married." And certainly not getting married anytime soon, after her last conversation with Nathaniel.

"Excellent. Room and board includes two home-cooked meals a day. On weekends, you're on your own. Anyone living here has to be pursuing a career on the stage, whether taking classes, looking for an agent, or auditioning. You already have a job, so that's covered. The cost is eighteen dollars a week. Let me show you around."

The tour took them to the practice room, where one girl was banging away on a scuffed upright piano while another belted out a song in a strong alto. Down in the basement was the dining room, with a dozen Formica tables crammed into the small space. They took the creaky stairs up to the second floor, where the wallpaper curled away from the ceiling in the corners. The place could do with a serious sprucing-up, but then Marion had grown up in a beautifully appointed house that Mrs. Hornsby had kept in impeccable order. She was quite spoiled in that way, she had to admit.

"This is where Bunny sleeps," said Mrs. Fleming, opening a door. The room was large, with two beds, each with a bedside table, and two dressers with mirrors. A metal wardrobe loomed in a corner and a pair of hideous orange floral curtains framed a large window that looked onto the street. To the right, Marion spied a small bathroom, where bras and stockings hung from a clothesline that draped across the ceiling.

"So, what do you think?"

Marion put her suitcase down on the sloping wood floor. She realized she didn't have much of a choice if she wanted to be able to sleep that night. "Sure. I'll take it."

"Then you're all set. Welcome to the Rehearsal Club."

After Mrs. Fleming left, Marion placed her clothes in the drawers of the empty bureau, hung her dresses in the wardrobe, then tucked the suitcase under the bed. As the din of street noise floated in through the open window, she considered what she'd done in the past twenty-four hours. Defied her father. Left home. Moved in with a girl she'd only recently met and barely knew.

She was suddenly seized with panic at what she'd put into motion. A completely different life from the one she'd envisioned. Right now, she should be getting ready for a date with Nathaniel, varnishing her nails for when she showed off his sparkling engagement ring, accepting her father's bear hug when they returned from their date, watching him shake the hand of the man who would become her husband.

Instead, she was sitting on a lumpy bed listening to the wail of a police siren on the street below, surrounded by strangers.

But underneath all the fretting and worry was something she was just starting to put a finger on, something that she knew was the driving force behind her actions over the past two days: a tiny flame of excitement at having made a decision and followed through.

She was in charge of her own life now, for better or for worse.

＊

The sound of women's laughter woke Marion up from a deep sleep. She'd lain back on the bed, just to shut her eyes, but now it was dark outside and it took a moment for her to get her bearings.

She'd defied her father and was now on her own. Alone.

This was the first time she'd been away from home since she'd attended summer camp as an eleven-year-old, and a similar wave of homesickness spread through her. That no one had her back, and no one really cared what happened to her.

But she had a job and a place to lay her head at night. It was time to grow up. Maybe her absence would place her on new footing with her father, one where he respected her choices and saw her as an adult. Same with Nathaniel. It had to.

It was nine thirty, according to the clock on Bunny's dresser. Marion turned on the light and put on a fresh dress, brushed her hair so it was presentable, and checked her reflection in the mirror. She looked older, somehow, and rather wan, like she'd been hiding in a closet for a couple of months. Some food in her stomach would help that, as would seeing Bunny.

At Radio City, Bunny flew out of the stage door and gave Marion a hug. She smelled of expensive perfume and her hair fell down her back in long waves after being held up in a tight bun the entire day. Her silk dress showed off her figure and practically glowed in the lamplight.

"Wow," said Marion. "You look amazing." She rued the dowdiness of her own choice, a teal-green cotton day dress with a pleated skirt and a bow at the neck. She looked like she was going to a church social.

"I can't wait for you to meet Dale. He's a sweetheart."

In her dazed state, Marion had completely forgotten that this wasn't just the two of them grabbing a bite after the show. She was about to tell Bunny that she simply wasn't up to a big night out and retreat to the safety of their room when a handsome man came up behind Bunny and grabbed her around the waist.

"There's my rabbit." He whirled her around and kissed her. After, Bunny threw her head back and laughed. "You big bear." She pulled out of his embrace and gestured to Marion. "Marion, meet Dale Janson. Dale, this is Marion, a fellow dancer and my new roommate."

"Pleased to meet you," said Marion, wilting a little under his intense gaze. Dale had blond hair, blue eyes, and a deep voice like an actor's. Together, he and Bunny made a smashing couple.

"And this is my buddy Peter Griggs."

A tall, rather ungainly man with curly hair turned around from where he had been staring up at one of the skyscrapers that rose into the night sky above Radio City. Marion had assumed he was one of the audience members from the show waiting for autographs outside the stage door, or a tourist.

As they shook hands, she realized that this was to be a double date. Both men were dressed formally, in black suits and ties. Even though she and Nathaniel were going through a rough patch, it was wrong to be out with some other guy so soon after their first big fight. Not that this man Peter had anything on Nathaniel. Where Nathaniel had an innate confidence, Peter seemed rather insecure and socially awkward. It was going to be a long night.

Bunny and Dale dominated the conversation on the walk to Fifty-Fifth Street, where they ducked under the awning to Le Pavillon. Marion had heard her father rave about the restaurant only a couple of weeks ago. Inside, thick carpeting muffled their footsteps. The walls were wrapped with bucolic scenes of Paris, and white roses bloomed in the center of each table. The maître d' fawned over Dale, offering winks and arm squeezes. Marion caught Peter rolling his eyes as they were led to their table in the middle of the room, although she wasn't sure if it was the stuffy restaurant or the fawning he objected to. She didn't have much experience with fancy restaurants or cocktails. When she and Nathaniel went on dates, they usually hit a movie and the local bistro, nothing this elegant.

She quickly scanned the place for her father, even though most Sunday nights he preferred to have dinner at home before settling into his favorite chair in the living room to watch television. Maybe right now he and Judy were missing Marion as much as she was missing them. Or did they figure that at any moment she'd walk in the door, contrite and obedient?

Well, she'd made it this far and was determined to enjoy the meal, not to mention the fact that she was starving. When the waiter appeared to take their order, she chose the lamb stew, while everyone else went for the fancy-sounding choices, like the chicken braised in champagne or the filet of sole bonne femme. After a round of martinis for the table, Dale ordered a bottle of white wine to go with dinner. Marion noticed that Bunny only sipped her drinks, and she did the same, knowing that it would be impossible to rehearse the next day if she were hungover.

Throughout the meal, Dale did much of the talking, ranging from his job selling newfangled office machines to the hottest club that they should hit next Saturday night. Bunny reminded him that she had to work for three weeks straight and he reassured her that would be fine. "My schedule's not much better, so I'll take whatever I can get."

As verbose as Dale was, his friend was the opposite. Peter ate his meal with a serious expression and spoke very little. Marion wondered why he'd even agreed to go out tonight and tried to not take it personally.

Finally, the waiter cleared their plates and they were given coffee and a small plate of French cookies.

"So, Marion," said Dale. "How do you like the big city?"

"I'm from Bronxville," Marion answered. "So it's not like I'm new to it. My father works here, and I took classes and taught dance on the west side."

"Well, you're in for a treat, now that you're living with Bunny. This one knows how to enjoy life, am I right?"

Bunny smiled. "What's there not to enjoy?"

"Tell that to Peter here. That man has a tendency to look on the dark side of things."

Bunny turned to Peter. "Why's that?"

Peter considered the question a moment before he answered. "Maybe because I work with schizophrenic patients who are institutionalized and have no hope of survival in the outside world."

His response left them all speechless, then Dale laughed. "Don't let this guy fool you. Back when we were at Harvard, he was the life of the party, until he got all serious junior year." He turned to Peter. "You remember the time we tossed all of Scooter's clothes in the tree outside Lowell House? He had to run out into the courtyard in his pajamas and climb up to get them, while the girls went nuts laughing. Poor sod."

Bunny leaned forward. "You really work with crazy people?"

Peter nodded. "At Creedmoor State Hospital, in Queens."

"Do you ever get attacked or anything?" asked Bunny.

Peter glanced toward the exit, and Marion wondered if he was planning to dash out and avoid the interrogation. Although he *had* opened himself up to it by his provocative answer.

"I've been attacked," said Peter. "Part of the job, unfortunately."

The words came out quietly, as if he was reluctant to admit as much.

Their conversation was interrupted by a loud bellowing that erupted behind Marion. She turned around to see a short, stout man standing face-to-face with the maître d', practically spitting as he shouted. Off to the side stood a young woman, her face shellacked with makeup, who looked like she wanted to disappear into the folds of her fur coat, her shoulders up near her ears.

"I will not be banished to Siberia!" yelled her date. "I may be from out of town, but I was warned that I'd be stuck in the back. Put me up front, with the rest of the bigwigs. Don't you know who I am?"

"Check out that guy," said Dale, thumbing in the man's direction. "If the owner, Henri, were here tonight, he'd toss him out on his behind."

They turned back to their meal, but the man would not be placated. "I want the best table you have, immediately."

"This is the best, sir," the maître d' pleaded. "I promise you."

"Who do you take me for?"

He shoved one of the chairs hard into the table next to it, sending the vase of white roses flying. A busboy with quick reflexes caught it right before it hit the floor.

Dale rose to his feet. "That's enough of that."

He stomped over and yelled for the man to "sit down and stop acting like an ass," which only made the other patron shout louder. The maître d' and the rest of the diners and waitstaff watched the scene in horror.

Peter wiped his mouth with his napkin, placed it on the table, and slowly rose and went to Dale. He took him by the arm, and Marion overheard him quietly telling his friend that their dates were quite nervous and to check that they were all right.

Dale did as he was told, placing a protective arm over Bunny's shoulders, as Peter turned to the irate man. Under the table, Marion slipped off her high heels, figuring she might have to sprint out of the way, and braced herself for the brawl that she was sure was coming. Peter was taller, but the other guy had at least thirty pounds on him.

But instead of punching him, Peter went and stood by the man's side. The woman had stepped back, ashen, as soon as Dale had rushed over. Clearly, she'd been witness to this kind of bad behavior before.

Peter turned his head and said something quietly to the man. Instead of screaming, the man replied back in a normal tone, "Is that so?"

They spoke back and forth a few times, and then the man nodded to the maître d'. "I don't want this table," he said.

"Like I said, sir, the dining room is full up—"

"I want that one."

He pointed to a table in a dark corner, right next to the kitchen doors. The absolute worst one in the room.

The maître d' didn't ask questions, quickly showing the man to the table, pulling back the chair for his date, and placing menus in their hands. A waiter came and took their drink orders, and by then Peter had made his way back to his own table. The other diners turned back to their conversations, although a few men seated nearby held up their drinks to Peter as a thanks for keeping the peace.

Peter sat in his chair and picked up his fork, as if nothing had occurred.

"That was incredible," said Bunny.

"Well done, my man," added Dale. "I think we put an end to the nonsense."

Peter shrugged.

"What did you say to him?" asked Marion.

"I de-escalated the situation is all."

"How?" Marion really wanted to know. Whatever he had done, it had worked like magic. She'd been mistaken before, thinking of Peter as insecure and awkward. He had a quiet air of authority to him, one that he kept to himself rather than broadcast around the room.

"The man is a textbook narcissist, so I used what I knew about his behavioral tendencies to get him to do what I wanted," said Peter. "It's a matter of outmanipulating the manipulator."

"Narcissist—that's someone with a huge ego, right?" said Dale.

"That's one of the traits," answered Peter.

"I'm intrigued. How does this outmanipulation work?" insisted Marion.

"I didn't confront him, which is exactly what he expected me to do. I stood side by side so that he got the impression that we were on the same team, as what he wants more than anything is to have someone to blame or lash out at for whatever perceived slight has occurred, like not getting a prime table. I told him that many people, even New Yorkers, don't know that the back room is most preferential at Le Pavillon, and that I'd seen Marilyn Monroe at that far corner table two days ago. It's all about redirection."

Marion also couldn't help noticing that by asking Dale to check on her and Bunny, Peter had redirected Dale into taking on the role of protector instead of brawler, which had made him stand down as well.

Dale gave a laugh, unaware that he'd been played as much as the other guy. "Does that mean you can look at each of us and figure out how to get us to do your bidding?"

"Everyone can be analyzed, everyone has quirks," said Peter.

"Even people you hardly know?" asked Bunny.

"Even strangers."

"Go on then, analyze one of the girls. You just met Marion, analyze her," said Dale.

"That's all right. I'm off the clock," said Peter.

Marion hoped the conversation would move on to another topic, but Dale wouldn't give up. Bunny even joined in. "Go on, give it a go."

Peter put down his utensils and took a sip of wine, looking at Marion the entire time. His gaze wasn't prurient, though, and there was a calm confidence in his expression that probably reassured his patients. She hadn't realized how blue his eyes were, or maybe it was the contrast with his pale skin.

Finally, he spoke. "You're probably the second born, and you have an innate fearlessness that you hide from other people because you don't want to come across as conceited. But there's something off, something missing. My guess is you've lost a parent, probably your mother."

Marion couldn't answer. It was too much, on top of the day that she'd just had, to think of Lucille, to have that loss tossed in her face out of the blue. She let out a small gasp.

Peter's face fell. "N-no, I'm wrong," he said quickly. "Sorry about that. You're not close with one of your siblings, that's all I mean."

He was covering up what he'd first said. The stutter gave him away. Marion quickly collected herself, appreciating that he realized that he'd cut too close and then backtracked.

Bunny clapped her hands together with delight. "Marion, I don't remember you telling me you had a sibling. Is that right? Is Peter right?"

"I do. I have an older sister."

Before Bunny could respond, Dale began complaining about his own brother, and the conversation shifted away from Marion, to her great relief.

Their waiter brought out a dessert on the house, but before they could dive in, Bunny looked at her watch and let out a gasp.

"It's almost curfew," she said. "You boys stay and enjoy, we've got to hightail it out of here. Thanks a ton for dinner."

"We'll walk you back," offered Dale, half rising.

"Nope. We can't wait another minute. Let's go, Marion. See you soon!"

They were out the door before Dale had time to protest.

"That was a strange night, right?" said Bunny once they were outside. "That Peter is an odd duck. Smart, but odd. What do you think?"

"Not my type at all," said Marion. "Besides, I'm still almost-engaged. I think."

Bunny threw back her head and laughed. "At least the dinner was yummy. Ready to go home?"

Marion was going "home" to the Rehearsal Club, not her bed in

Bronxville. Everything felt out of sorts, and it didn't help that the confrontation in the restaurant, followed by Peter's prescience, had set her anxiety surging. But she'd put this plan in motion, and, for now, she was willing to see where it would go.

Bunny linked her hand with Marion's, and they were off.

CHAPTER ELEVEN

Marion waited in the Rehearsal Club parlor the next morning as a girl with a Southern accent finished up a call on the pay phone beside the staircase. Bunny had already headed over to the theater and Marion said she'd catch up with her at rehearsal. She needed to call her father and let him know where she was, a task that had kept her tossing and turning all night with dread. The screech of cars and people on the street outside hadn't helped much, but hopefully she'd get used to the noise and learn to conk out immediately, as Bunny had after they'd returned from that strange dinner with Dale and Peter.

Marion sat in a chair that was close enough to grab the phone as soon as the other girl hung up, but not so close as to seem nosy. Still, she couldn't help overhearing her tearful plea.

"I didn't get the role, Mommy, but I have another audition for a show next week, and if I get that, I'll be all set. I only need enough money for another week. Or two. Please?"

When she finally hung up, the girl ran up the stairs before Marion could offer any sympathy. Marion was incredibly lucky to have a well-paying job as a professional dancer. She had a lot to be very grateful for, and she wasn't about to give it up because her family didn't approve.

Near the fireplace, a half dozen girls practiced lines for a play they were planning to perform later that week at the Club, talking over each other and bursting into laughter. Marion cupped the receiver with one hand as the call went through.

"Mr. Brooks's office, how may I help you?"

Judy spoke with her business voice, a register lower than her actual one, something that had always annoyed Marion. But hearing it now made her want to burst into tears like the Southern girl.

"Judy, it's me."

There was an intake of breath. "Marion, where the heck are you? You didn't come back for dinner last night and Dad tried to pretend he wasn't worried, but I heard him call Nathaniel and ask if you were there. He said you weren't. What's going on?"

"Dad told me to leave, so I left." Marion tried to rid her voice of self-pity, but it crept in anyway.

"That's crazy. I'm sure he didn't mean it. You have to come home."

Hearing her sister so concerned threw Marion off-balance; it wasn't at all what she expected. "I'm not sure that's a good idea right now. I've never seen him so angry. But I know I should talk to him."

"All right. Just say you're sorry."

"It's more complicated than that."

Judy let out a small sigh and placed Marion on hold. Her father picked up after only a few seconds.

"Marion?"

"Daddy."

She hadn't called him that in ages, but it came out automatically and she immediately regretted it. This was a negotiation, and she'd just handed him all the cards.

"Now, Marion. You gave me and Judy quite a scare. What's that racket in the background? Are you with some of your high school friends? Is that where you went?"

"I'm in the city. I called to tell you that I'm staying at a place called the Rehearsal Club, on West Fifty-Third Street. The number here is CI 7-2004. I wanted to let you know that I'm fine."

"The Rehearsal Club," her father repeated dryly. "What's that?"

"It's a boardinghouse for women dancers and actors. Like I told you yesterday, I'm going to try being a Rockette. I hope you can support me in this."

"For God's sake, you are going to ruin your life with your hardheadedness. You're making a terrible mistake."

"I disagree."

"Well, then, I suppose we have nothing more to discuss. When you've come to your senses, let me know. I simply do not have time for your histrionics."

Then he hung up.

Marion sat there, stunned. A girl from across the room let out a screech and fell to the floor, and it took a moment before Marion realized she was acting.

She hadn't expected much from the call with Simon; his stubbornness was not a surprise. Judy's concern was, though. It was as if a chink had appeared in the wall of resentments and estrangement that divided them. But there was no time to process the exchange further; she had to get to rehearsal.

They were to dance in full makeup and costume in the rehearsal hall for the producer, Mr. Leonidoff. After that, there were only three more days until they performed the cowboy number in front of an audience. Marion was terrified at the thought, but the other new girls were as well, which made her feel a little better.

Bunny had insisted Marion take the empty place next to her in the dressing room, and as soon as Marion arrived, she carefully pulled on the fringed bolero jacket and matching short skirt in a palomino pattern that had been sewn to her specific measurements. Even though

Bunny was a couple of inches shorter than Marion, their hemlines had been tailored to form a straight line when they stood side by side—a trick that added to the illusion the dancers were exactly the same height. The outfits were finished off with cowboy hats—also custom fit so they wouldn't fall off—and a holster holding a plastic gun, which sat low on her hips.

After she and Bunny finished dressing, they took the elevator up to the rehearsal hall, where Russell and Emily stood waiting along with Mr. Leonidoff, who sat in a chair against the mirrored wall. During the first run-through, with Simon's harsh words still echoing in Marion's mind, she missed a step and got left behind as the girls made their way to the front of the stage for the kick line. Russell called out for Beulah to stop playing.

"Miss Brooks, if we were onstage right now, tell me what would happen?"

"I-I'd miss the kick line?" Marion stammered.

Russell shook his head. "No. You'd be lying facedown on the floor. Can you tell me why?"

Of course, the stage elevators. Tape had been used to mark the edges of the three motorized hydraulic elevators that rose into place as they danced, forming three separate levels. If she missed her mark, she'd fall off the elevated section of the stage and, as Russell said, land on her face.

"I'm sorry. The elevators, yes. I won't make that mistake again."

"I should hope not," Mr. Leonidoff said, glaring at Marion. "May I remind you that you'll only get the opportunity to rehearse onstage the morning before the first performance? That's this Thursday, three days away. It's crucial that every dancer—particularly the new ones—stay focused so that by the time you're onstage you have the routine down cold and can handle the shock of dancing before the audience at Radio City. And it will be a shock, I assure you."

It occurred to Marion that if she messed this up, she'd have no one to call home to, unlike the girl on the phone this morning.

She hit her marks perfectly the rest of the rehearsal.

※

"I'm not sure how I'm supposed to dance when my eyes are only half open."

Bunny grabbed a Danish and a coffee from the cafeteria in the basement of Radio City, and Marion did the same, having arrived at six thirty, when the city was still draped in darkness, for the final rehearsal for the cowboy number onstage.

The movie premiering at Radio City that day, *The Wings of Eagles*, rolled out at ten. Two hours later, the Rockettes would perform *Westward Ho!*, the boot-stepping, gunslinging number they'd been working on all week. The show featured not only the Rockettes, but also the corps de ballet and the choral ensemble, who would be singing cowboy songs. Marion reminded herself that their dance number was only a small part of the show, albeit the closing one, and that she was simply a cog in a wheel. If she performed the steps in the right order and hit her marks, all would be fine.

If she made a mistake, though, everyone would notice—one of the downsides of being a cog. All night, she'd had terrible nightmares that she was running late and missed the curtain, or that she dropped her gun and tripped over the lip of the stage, falling face-first into the orchestra. Even worse, that she'd "kicked out."

Whenever any of the veteran dancers mentioned "kicking out," they did so in a whisper, as if saying the words out loud might cause it to actually happen. Bunny had explained to Marion that it was every Rockette's nightmare: when the choreography called for a certain number of kicks, say, eight, but a dancer miscounted and did nine. Besides falling, it was the one move that was sure to catch every audience member's attention and pull them out of the illusion that they were watching a magical entity that had one mind, one body.

By the time Marion had woken up, she was tired and shaky and slightly panicked.

She and Bunny slugged back their coffee on their way to the dressing room, where Marion pulled on her costume, made up her face, brushed her hair back into a tight bun that made her temples ache, and finally tightened her holster around her hips. Soon enough, she was standing in the wings in one of three lines, ready for the final rehearsal. All around her, the stagehands moved about, pulling ropes, arranging props on a table. It was a massive operation, to be sure.

Marion tried to stay as focused as she could as they trotted onstage. The lights were bright, but she could still see where Russell, Mr. Leonidoff, the designers, and the businesspeople from Radio City were sitting out in the audience. The rich sound of the orchestra was a far cry from the tinny piano in the rehearsal hall, which made it all even more distracting. But she got through the entire routine without a hitch, hitting her mark when the stage elevator rose so she didn't fall on her face, and then it was over and they remained onstage as a professional photographer took their photos for promotional materials that would be sold in the lobby during intermission.

Back in the rehearsal hall, Emily and Russell gave them their final notes, and then the girls raced upstairs to put on powder to cover their shiny faces and a new slash of lipstick before the big show.

"I don't know how on earth you do this and also dance four shows a day," said Marion to Bunny. "I mean, just doing the rehearsals this week was enough to lay me out cold." Starting tomorrow, she'd be dancing four shows a day, and very soon, Russell had warned, they'd be learning the choreography to Radio City's iconic *Christmas Spectacular* on top of the regular schedule. She wouldn't have a day off for another two weeks.

"You get used to it," said Bunny. "Before long, you'll be onstage kicking while trying to decide what to eat for lunch, or whether or not to buy that new coat at Bloomingdale's. It becomes second nature. Is there any chance your family's coming today?"

It was a tradition for the new girls to invite their families to the first show, and already several bouquets of roses had been delivered to the squealing recipients.

"No. Maybe another time."

"Well, this is for you. Happy opening day."

Bunny handed over a small box of chocolates, wrapped in a big purple bow, and Marion fought back tears. "You're so thoughtful."

"You're going to be great, don't worry so much."

At ten minutes to noon, the murmurs of the audience drifted back to where the dancers were again lined up stage right. The corps de ballet performed first, entering from the wings stage left, but Marion was barely able to watch. Instead, she ran through the steps in her head and continued doing so as the choral ensemble harmonized through their two songs. As they finished up, Marion noticed an odd series of movements in the line ahead of her. The girl closest to the stage licked her index finger, turned to the girl behind her, and tapped her under the chin. That girl turned and did the same to the dancer behind her, and so on.

"It's good luck," whispered the dancer in front of Marion when it was her turn. *Strange*, thought Marion, but she could use all the luck she could get, so she quickly licked her finger and then touched the dancer behind her under the chin, and the chain continued.

The audience applauded politely as the singers held their final note. After a couple of beats, the orchestra launched into the next number and the stage manager gave the go-ahead for the Rockettes to head on out.

Before she knew it, Marion was onstage at Radio City, smiling and dancing, counting the steps in her head. Her nerves fell away, as all her energy was directed toward staying focused and blending in, becoming one with the troupe. As they moved into the kick line for the big finale, her body tingled with anticipation and suddenly they were kicking in perfect tandem as the audience broke out into applause. Even though the dancers weren't touching, they had become a machine of precision and beauty, a single entity. Marion's heart swelled with pride as they hit the final pose, the audience clapping wildly.

She'd done it. She was a Rockette.

Backstage, the veteran dancers congratulated the new ones, and then they all charged back upstairs to the dressing rooms. Marion took off the costume and changed into street clothes. She needed to get some air if she was going to do three more shows that day, not to mention over the next two weeks.

A slew of family members was gathered outside the stage door, embracing their daughters, fathers wiping tears from their eyes. Marion couldn't help but glance around for Judy and Simon even though she knew they weren't there. She charged through the crowd, out to the street, where she took in great gulps of the October air.

"Marion."

Nathaniel stood a few feet away.

He opened his arms and she ran into them, holding back tears, hoping her mascara wouldn't run. Her heart was bursting at the very fact that he was here, that he'd made the effort to show up when none of her family members could be bothered.

"You were amazing up there," he said when they pulled back and studied each other. "That was incredible." He gave a shy smile. "And you're pretty cute as a cowgirl."

"I'm so happy you came," she said. "It means the world to me, and now you can see why I did what I did, right?"

"Sure. I get it now, it's a big deal. I'm proud of you. Do you have time to grab lunch?"

She hated to turn down his offer after he'd made such an effort. "I'm afraid I have to go back up for notes, and then we might have another rehearsal if they think we need it, and then three more shows."

"That's a lot of kicks."

"Tell me about it. There are days when I can barely make it home."

"Your father said you'd moved into some boardinghouse."

"Right. I was going to call you today and tell you. It's called the Rehearsal Club, and a few of the other Rockettes stay there, too. It's run by a lovely older lady."

"I see."

"I know this is coming fast and furious, and trust me, my head is spinning as well. But now that you've seen this, can you tell my father what I'm doing, how great it is? Maybe if he hears it from you, he'll relent and start talking to me again. It's awful, not being part of the family." All her resolve faded away; she hadn't realized how much she missed her former room with its pink wallpaper and the stability of her old life with her father, her sister, and Mrs. Hornsby. "I hate that I have to choose."

"Your father is old-fashioned, I guess."

"But can you see how it's unfair? I want to be able to do what I love and get paid for it. What's wrong with that?"

"We both know it's not the *idea* of working, it's the *type* of work."

"Please, just talk to him."

He stepped back and shoved his hands deep into his coat pockets. "I can't do that."

"Why not?"

"Your father would kill me if he knew I came here."

Whose side was Nathaniel on? The excitement at seeing him began to wane as she realized what she was dealing with. "Be your own man, Nathaniel. Are you going to be intimidated by my father for the rest of your life? You and I are supposed to be getting engaged, not you and he."

"I'm thinking of our future."

She didn't understand his logic. "How is that?"

"Your father said that he'll get me a job at Met Power, in the junior executive training program. It would be as good as going to business school, and I'd get a great salary. I don't want to derail that, it's important to me. To us, as a family."

"When did all this happen?"

"Just the other day. And get this, the associates in the training program learn not only what goes on in a big organization like Met Power, but we also get to take part in all the fun stuff, like dinners out and golf trips. Your dad even said he could see me following in his footsteps."

Her father had roped Nathaniel into his orbit. The betrayal hurt, and the fact that Nathaniel didn't see that he was being manipulated made her angry.

She stepped back. "I've got to go."

"I want to see you, though. Can I see you? Maybe tennis on Saturday?"

"I'm living in the city now. And besides, I have four shows that day."

"For goodness' sake, when do you get a day off?"

"We go three weeks on, seven days a week, then one week off. I told you that already."

"That's inhumane."

"That's discipline. That's commitment." She paused. "And that's what it means to be a Rockette."

CHAPTER TWELVE

Once Marion had that first show under her belt, the days fell into an easy rhythm. On Wednesdays during dinner break, she joined a dozen or so dancers and headed to Moriarty's, the chophouse across the street, where the stagehands gathered at the bar called out cheerful hellos as they waltzed by. They'd settle in at a long table to enjoy a steak dinner, which came out fast and hot, as the waiters knew they were short on time. Marion used up so much energy dancing and kicking that she found she could eat whatever she wanted these days, and the filet helped replenish some of the calories that had been burned up during the week. The owner of the place loved having the Radio City crew around, especially after the prop master built a fake fire hydrant to be placed out front and whisked away whenever a VIP patron needed a parking spot.

It was the eve of Marion's first week off, after twenty-one straight days of working hard enough to earn every penny of her salary. At every notes session, Emily seemed to have some nitpicky instruction specifically for Marion: her kicks were too high, her fingers overly splayed. Marion wrote them down and kept the list on her dressing room table, reviewing it carefully before the next show.

By then, Radio City had become a second home. In the morning, she'd head to the cafeteria and order a coffee and an egg sandwich on rye toast. Once, when she thought she'd pulled a muscle, she'd been seen by the nurse at the infirmary, who'd given her a cream that soothed it right away and then sent her back to the rehearsal hall, good as new. In between the afternoon shows, Marion would sometimes stop by the lounge and join in a game of hearts or help with a jigsaw puzzle, listening to the veteran dancers talk about the time Cary Grant or Lucille Ball came backstage after seeing the show. There were Hula-Hoops and shuffleboard on the roof on sunny days, and movies in the private screening room once a week after the third show.

She got used to taking catnaps in the dormitory, and a couple of nights she even stayed over when they had an early call the next morning. With its tightly placed rows of white metal beds and wool blankets, the dormitory looked a little like an orphanage for overworked dancers.

There was so much to learn and so much fun to be had, even when things went wrong, which they sometimes did. Like the time when the stage lift they were supposed to sit on in the middle of the cowboy number didn't rise in time, and they all fell on their bottoms on the floor. Russell said he was quite impressed at how quickly they all popped back up without missing a beat, a testament to their collective strength. A test of their collective stamina occurred regularly at the last show of the day, when the conductor had a habit of speeding up the orchestra's tempo in order to catch an earlier train home, leaving both the musicians and the dancers breathless.

During dinner at Moriarty's, they laughed about an earlier rehearsal where the new girls had been introduced to the choreography for the *Christmas Spectacular*'s Wooden Soldiers number, which involved a precarious and technically challenging cascading slow fall, set off by a fake cannon shot that came from stage left. They first practiced in tight groups of six, facing the cannon with their arms bent at a ninety-degree angle, with only inches in between each dancer. The first girl slowly rocked back on her heels, allowing her full body weight to lean on the girl behind her, and one by one each of the dancers would do the same, arms tucked tightly under the armpits of the girl in front of them for leverage. This was repeated, girl after girl, until the entire line was seated, legs outstretched on either side, like a line of human dominos.

If anyone moved too quickly, the line fell apart. Having one leg out of position could result in a serious injury. It took a huge leap of faith, or *lean* of faith, as Bunny put it over dinner, to let someone else support all your weight and not chicken out at the last minute. Marion dreaded the day they would have to do it in full costume, wearing stiffly starched white pants and a helmet that had to stay upright, which no doubt would distract from a move that was hard enough in rehearsal clothes.

Listening to the dancers talk and laugh, Marion considered herself lucky. She'd landed in a warm sisterhood where her ambition and drive were celebrated, not questioned. Still, she missed her real family terribly. Every time she returned to the Rehearsal Club she hoped to see a message on the bulletin board beside the pay phone letting her know that her father had called. He knew where she was staying, where she worked. Was he really so angry at her that he would cut off all communication and not be the slightest bit interested in how she was holding up? She'd spoken with Mrs. Hornsby a couple of times, checking in, but she didn't want to put their housekeeper in a difficult position, acting as the middleman between her and Simon, and kept their conversations short and light. Still, Marion detected the slightest edge of disappointment in Mrs. Hornsby's voice, a quiet weariness that left Marion feeling guilty and sad.

Nathaniel had reached out a couple of times since their discussion outside the theater, but there wasn't much to say. It appeared that he wanted a cushy job at Met Power more than he wanted her as his fiancée, and the truth stung. He'd told Marion that the ring was hers as soon as she came home, but to be honest, it was a relief to push all wedding plans aside. They were at a standoff, and for now, that was fine with Marion.

Marion plunked down some money for the tab and excused herself, saying that she needed to make a phone call before the next show. But instead of going back to the pay phones near the dressing rooms, she headed up to the eighth floor, where the infamous Roxy apartment was located. Named after the gregarious impresario who had created the Rockettes, the suite was built to his specifications. With its soaring, twenty-foot-high, gold leaf ceiling and walls in polished cherry, the enclave gleamed with class and sophistication. The sofas and tables were the epitome of Art Deco, created by industrial designer Donald Deskey specifically for the building.

When Bunny had first shown the Roxy apartment to Marion, she'd said that these days it was rarely used, making it the perfect spot if you needed some privacy to make a phone call.

Marion walked through the lounge and into a circular room with a large dining table in the center. A telephone sat on a console against the wall. She picked up the receiver and dialed her home number.

Judy picked up after several rings. "Brooks residence."

"Judy. It's me."

They'd talked every few days since Marion had been kicked out of the house, checking in with each other, Marion timing her calls for when she knew Simon would be settled in his armchair watching Walter Cronkite. For Marion, it was a lifeline to her family and she was grateful Judy hadn't shut her out as well. They'd been equally shaken by Simon's shocking edict, and one of the only good things that had come out of Marion's estrangement with her father was this burgeoning rapprochement with Judy.

There was a pause, and in the background she could hear her father asking who was on the line.

"It's Beth from work, for me," Judy answered.

Marion waited, imagining Judy perched on the straight-back chair next to the phone.

"How are you doing?" whispered Judy finally.

"Fine. We're getting ready for the Christmas show. It's crazy, with all the costumes and choreography. A little overwhelming, to be honest. Do you remember going as girls?"

"I do. It made you sad."

"What are you talking about?"

"I looked over and there were tears streaming down your face."

Funny, how they had continually misread each other. "I was crying because I was so moved by the dancing. I wasn't sad at all." Marion let out a small laugh. "How's work going?"

"Busy. But good. It's weird how different our lives are. I can't imagine doing what you do."

"Thank goodness, otherwise Dad would have a heart attack."

They both giggled at the thought.

"Can we meet?" asked Marion quickly. "I'd really like to talk to you. At the ice rink, like we used to do? You know what day it is tomorrow."

"Right. But work is crazy, I don't know if I can get away. I don't want to upset Dad."

Why was everyone so afraid of Simon Brooks? The man had far too much power over the people around him.

Suddenly, Simon's voice bellowed in the background. "What are you whispering about back there?"

"I've gotta go," said Judy in a rush.

"Don't, Judy," pleaded Marion. "Tell him to talk to me."

But it was too late. A dial tone rang in her ear.

She gently replaced the receiver. While it was wonderful to connect with Judy again, after each call her doubts came creeping back and the enormity of her decision pressed down on her. Was it worth it to lose her family for a job that, as her father had said, might only last a few years?

What would happen after she stopped being a Rockette, or got injured and couldn't dance anymore? There was no backup plan.

What if Simon was right?

She had barely set the phone receiver in its cradle when the door to the Roxy apartment burst open.

Bunny appeared, followed by Dale and his friend Peter. Marion walked out of the dining area and joined them in the lounge, still trying to shake off the truncated call with her sister.

"Guess who surprised us," said Bunny. But her smile didn't reach her eyes; something was off. "I told the boys we'd have a quick sip of Roxy liquor with them before the next show."

"Is that a good idea?" asked Marion, unsure about the idea of drinking before dancing, as well as being caught dipping into the Roxy liquor cabinet, but Bunny had already gone to the bar and was pouring the drinks.

"Bunny, let's talk, okay?" Dale said.

Bunny shook her head. "There's nothing to say."

"Sure there is."

"You promised."

"I know, but—" He took her arm and cocked his head in the direction of the door that led out to a small balcony. "Come out here, let me explain."

They withdrew and closed the balcony door behind them. Peter stood in the middle of the room, drink in hand, looking about uncomfortably.

Marion hadn't expected to see Peter again, not after that strange dinner. But here he was. She should really go and get ready for the next show, but leaving him seemed rude.

He gestured to one of the couches. "I guess we'll have to make small talk until whatever is going on is settled."

She sat, and he did as well. She placed her drink on the coffee table, and he did also. It was like they were playing a game of Simon Says.

"How's the show going?" asked Peter.

"Fine, thanks."

Peter leaned forward, elbows on his knees, hands clasped. "Look, to be honest, when Dale said we were going to stop by Radio City, I kind of hoped I'd see you again."

She plastered a vague smile on her face and braced herself for what was coming next. He'd want to take her to dinner, just the two of them, most likely. While it was true that she and Nathaniel were going through a rough patch, she certainly wasn't interested in going on a date with anyone else.

"I wanted to apologize for the way I acted at the restaurant a few weeks ago," said Peter finally. "For analyzing you without your consent. That was wrong of me."

She hadn't expected an apology. Peter was looking at her strangely, and it took her a moment to figure out what was different about his gaze.

Men tended to have three ways of reacting to Marion: In most cases, they stammered and made terrible jokes in an effort to impress. Others became cold and dismissive, as if they figured they could win her over by taking the opposite tack and throwing her off-balance.

Finally, there was a minority of men with inflated egos who had been unexpectedly spurned at one time. They were the most dangerous to interact with, as they tended to be domineering and resentful.

Peter wasn't in the first category. He wasn't affected by her beauty, not glancing from her neck to her lips to her bustline, unsure of where to look. Nor did he seem cold or resentful.

His eyes remained glued on hers—he was simply taking in her reaction to his words. In spite of herself, she blushed.

"I appreciate your apology. And yes, I wouldn't recommend doing that on future dates." Marion paused. "Even if you were right." She wasn't sure why she'd just told him that. Peter was studying her so intently, and being so unabashedly honest, she couldn't help it.

He looked pained. "Even more apologies on my part, then. It was unprofessional." He cleared his throat. "Look, I know this is awkward. I agreed to meet Dale for a drink but seem to have gotten caught up in some kind of lovers' spat. If you have to go, please do. There's no need to entertain me."

Peter intrigued Marion. There was a directness to his character and his delivery that was rare in New York, which seemed to be bursting with blowhards and poseurs. Like Dale.

"That's all right," she said. "I'm fine to stay for a little while."

The door to the balcony had opened partway—Marion spied Bunny's manicured fingers on the handle—and sounds of the argument drifted into the room.

"What's going on with them?" asked Marion.

"I have an idea, but I wouldn't want to presume," answered Peter.

"Very enigmatic."

Bunny's raised voice brought their conversation to a halt. "You promised it was over. You said you were living somewhere else."

"I had to move back home. Temporarily, that's all," said Dale.

"I don't believe you." The words were filled with anguish. This was not the Bunny Marion knew, the girl who laughed her way through a sad movie. "Don't play me, Dale Janson."

"What's all the fuss about? You know I love you best."

His hand covered hers and the door shut once again.

Marion looked at Peter, shocked. "Is Dale married?"

Peter nodded.

Marion digested the information. Bunny was dating a married man. Marion had heard some whispers that a few of the other dancers had "patrons," men of questionable marital status who bought them extravagant gifts, but she hadn't thought Dale was one of them.

Her father would be horrified to think she was living with a girl who ran around with married men.

"That's terrible," Marion said.

Peter was shaking his head, as if this kind of thing happened every day.

She turned on him. "How can you be friends with a man who cheats on his wife? Even worse, why would you agree to go on a double date with Dale, knowing that his wife was waiting for him at home?"

Peter didn't answer right away. "It's not like that. Dale was a good friend to me, back when we were in college. He stepped in when I was having trouble, helped me figure out my place in the world. To be honest, I don't think I could have made it through all four years without his friendship." Peter glanced over at the balcony doorway. "After he moved to New York, something changed, he seems to have lost his footing. I guess a part of me feels like it's my turn to step in and try to support him. Even if I don't agree with some of the decisions he's making."

The door opened, and Bunny and Dale reappeared, Bunny's face streaked with tears. "Get out of here," she said to Dale. "I don't want to see you again, not until you're really done with her."

Dale started to say something, but Bunny screeched for him to leave. He did so, and Peter followed, throwing Marion a sympathetic look as he shut the door behind him.

"Bunny? Are you okay?" Marion said softly.

Bunny shook her head, one hand going to her throat. "Sorry you had to hear all that."

"What's going on?"

"I'm sorry I haven't told you this yet, but he's married. Dale's married and he said he would leave his wife and he won't. I had no idea when I first met him. He lied to me. About everything. I hate the way you're looking at me right now." Bunny buried her face in her hands.

Marion thought of Peter. Her friend deserved her support, not her judgment. "I'm sorry, Bunny. He's a jerk. You don't need him. Let's find you someone sweet and wonderful."

"But I love him."

The idea of putting up with someone's bad behavior because you "loved" them sounded truly ridiculous to Marion; the words didn't compute. Then again, this grand passion between Bunny and Dale was nothing like the warm fondness she and Nathaniel shared.

But maybe that was because she'd never truly been in love.

※

Finally, after three weeks of working harder than she ever had in her life, it was Marion's week off. She slept late and wandered down to the parlor of the Rehearsal Club, hoping to curl up in a corner chair and read a book. But the sounds of a girl belting out a show tune from the practice room sent her fleeing back upstairs, where the blaring of horns on the street wasn't much of an improvement.

Bunny hadn't wanted to talk about the situation with Dale before bed the night before, and that morning a huge bouquet of roses had shown up. Bunny had read the card with a funny smile on her face, much to Marion's dismay. She didn't want to come off as prudish or judgmental, but she still couldn't help worrying that the man was using Bunny in a way that the girl didn't deserve.

Just before noon, Marion pulled on her wool coat and warm socks and walked up Sixth Avenue to Central Park. From there, it was a short dogleg to the ice-skating rink.

When Lucille was alive, she'd take Judy and Marion ice-skating the first day the Central Park rink opened in November, and even when they were barely talking, Judy and Marion had kept up the tradition. Judy, who tended to lumber as she walked, was a sylph on the ice, gliding as gracefully as an Olympic star, hardly ever falling. Marion wobbled and usually fell flat on her behind at least twice, and the reversal of the girls' roles was refreshing. For once, Judy got to be the queen, and Marion was the lady-in-waiting.

Marion scanned the crowd as she pulled on a pair of battered rental skates. Simon had gotten Judy her own pair for Christmas four years ago, the blades gleaming and the leather as white as snow. Not many fathers would have been thoughtful enough to pick out such a perfect, special gift. But their father always had a knack when it came to birthday or holiday presents. The next year he'd given Marion her mother's pearls and Judy her wristwatch. Pitch-perfect, once again.

After the incident with Bunny and Dale the night before, Marion realized how much she needed her family to ground her, no matter their faults or blind spots. Her life right now was a whirlwind and she barely had time to think, and she didn't want to drift too far off course and end up like Bunny, involved with a married man, making dubious choices.

She finished tying her skates and sighed. Maybe Judy had gotten tied up at work, or maybe it was simply too much for her sister to bear this year, with the family falling apart. Marion figured she'd take a couple of turns around the rink anyway, for tradition's sake, but just as she was rising, she spotted Judy at the cashier. Whether it was the surprise or the cold air, her eyes teared up.

"You came," she said, as Judy drew near.

"I did."

They drifted around the ice together, not touching but matching each other's stride. Marion stuck to safe topics, inquiring about Mrs. Hornsby's pending retirement and Judy's job. But when one of Marion's skates slid out from under her and she wobbled, Judy grasped her hand and didn't let it go.

"Nathaniel comes by the house every few days," said Judy.

"Sometimes I think Dad should just adopt him as his son and get it over with. He likes Nathaniel way better than me. They can cut me out of the picture altogether."

"Do you want to marry him?"

Marion hadn't ever been asked this by anyone; the wedding had simply been a given. "I don't know."

"I think you could do better."

She hadn't even considered that Judy might have an opinion on the matter. Never mind such a strong one. Marion's defenses rose. "What's wrong with him? He's kind and funny, and we know his family well."

"You don't mention love at all. I mean, I don't have much experience, but I would think that comes first."

"You're right. You don't know." Marion regretted snapping at her as soon as the words came out of her mouth. "Sorry. I can't think straight anymore. It feels like there are two separate tracks of my life running at the same time. The one where Dad and Nathaniel expect me to come home and become the good little wife, and the one where I'm a successful dancer."

"I wish I could do something to help. I really do."

They continued skating in slow, easy circles around the rink. "I want you to come to see the *Christmas Spectacular* at Radio City," Marion said.

"I'm not sure that's a good idea. Dad would kill me."

"Part of growing up is striking out on your own path, doing what you think is best," said Marion. "That's what I'm doing. I'm having an amazing time, I'm earning my own money, I'm surrounded by wonderful, supportive people. What I don't get is why my father and my sister are so cruel as to cut me off for doing what I love."

"I haven't cut you off," said Judy.

"But you're not standing by my side, standing up to him. You can't even come to see me dance without being scared that he'll take your watch away from you as punishment or kick you out of the house as he did me. Meanwhile, other families make the effort to see their daughters or sisters in the show and cry with happiness when they come backstage."

She could tell she'd hit home with Judy by the way she bit her lip. Judy always did that when she was unsure.

"I don't understand why you're content to do whatever he says," Marion continued. "To obey his every command. You should strike out on your own path as well. Do you really want to be working for him for the rest of your life? Don't you want more?"

"I happen to like my job. And what more should I expect? I'm not pretty like you, it's not like anyone's knocking on my door to get married."

Marion drew back, surprised. "You want to get married?"

"Of course. I want a family, kids. But it's probably not in the cards."

"Our lives aren't set in stone. You can do anything you want."

"No. *You* can do anything you want. For the rest of us, the choices are rather limited."

"That's not true." Yet Marion knew she was treated differently from her sister because of her looks. By friends, by strangers. And it wasn't fair.

Judy glided to the middle of the rink and came to a stop, facing Marion. The other skaters flew around them in a blur of brightly colored coats and hats. "Do you remember my friend Stan? We were in the math club together."

"Sure, I remember him." He was the boy who'd left suddenly one day, and Judy wouldn't tell Marion what was wrong. "I was worried he'd hurt you in some way, attacked you."

"Oh, no, there was no threat of that."

"Then what?"

"He'd made a big deal of wanting to come over and do our algebra homework together, but he was top of the class in algebra, it didn't make any sense. Then I remembered prom was coming up soon, and I started wondering if maybe he was going to ask me to it, and this way he could do so in private. As we were studying at the dining room table, I had this whole movie playing in my head: going to you for advice, shopping for a dress together, Stan and I walking arm in arm into the school gym, everyone saying what a nice couple we made. Maybe a kiss at the end of the night." She paused. "At one point, he excused himself to go to the bathroom. When he didn't come back after a while, I went upstairs and found him staring into your room through your cracked door. Watching you as you changed clothes."

Marion involuntarily crossed her arms over her chest, as if the boy were there now. "That's awful."

"He ran out of the house when I caught him, and then I resigned from the math club for good. I don't know why I even bothered."

"It's not your fault, what happened." Marion wished she could throttle Stan. At the same time, she was amazed and gratified that Judy would have asked for her advice on a prom gown. "He's the one who should have resigned, not you."

"For a long time, I thought it was your fault."

"He was a creep. There are plenty of them out there." She was thinking of Dale. "But they're not all like that. Dad's not like that."

Judy looked up at the city skyline to the south, which rose high above the tree branches. "There's something going on with him."

"With Dad? What do you mean?"

"I know what he does every second of every day, practically, but sometimes he goes off to these appointments that aren't in the calendar. Hours that are not accounted for. He's slipping off to do something, and I'm not sure what it is."

How strange. "Do you think he's seeing someone?"

While their father had been pursued by several women he'd encountered over the years—at the tennis club, or when they were all out to dinner, ladies who were obviously smitten by his mix of charm and gruffness—he'd never followed up.

"It's the only thing I can think of. But why would he hide it?" Judy checked her watch. "I have to go."

"Already?"

"I have to get back downtown."

"Well, I loved seeing you," said Marion, and she meant it. Something about Judy brought her back to earth, reminded her that she was solid and safe.

To her surprise, Judy leaned in and gave her a hug. Marion remembered when they were little girls and would fling themselves into each other's arms over the silliest things: the promise of ice cream after dinner, the radio announcing a snow day for the school district. They stood there, embracing in the cold wind, and Judy murmured in her ear, "I'll come to see you."

"You will?" Marion almost fell in her surprise, her skate sliding out from under her, but Judy caught her right in time and they both laughed. "Next Thursday is the opening day for the *Christmas Spectacular.* I'll leave a ticket for you for the six-o'clock show. Is that all right? You'll come?"

Judy gave a quick nod. "I'll be there."

CHAPTER THIRTEEN

The first two shows of the *Christmas Spectacular* went by in a whirlwind for Marion, and while she adored the applause and the smiling faces of the children who waited for autographs outside the stage door, she blew past them, apologizing profusely, in order to meet Judy at the Rehearsal Club. She'd convinced her sister—over a rushed call—to come early so she could properly show her around her new life. Once Judy saw how well she was doing, she would report back to Simon and his curiosity might get the best of him, and he'd overcome his stubbornness.

Judy was waiting near the steps to the Rehearsal Club's front door, clutching her purse tightly to her side. She'd dressed up for the occasion, wearing her camel hair coat instead of her work trench, her hair tied back in a red bow. The fact that she'd made an effort moved Marion almost to tears.

"You look marvelous," she said. "The bow's a nice touch. Do you remember Mom dressed us up in gorgeous red velvet dresses when we went to the *Christmas Spectacular*? We looked like a couple of princesses."

"I remember the collar being very itchy and wanting to throw it on the floor," said Judy.

Some things would never change. "Well, why don't you come on up and I can show you my new digs?"

Inside, a couple of the actresses screeched with laughter in the parlor while another boarder trying to use the telephone yelled for them to quiet down.

"It's not usually so crazy," said Marion over the din. "The woman who runs it, Mrs. Fleming, is very strict about things like curfews and not letting boys up. Sort of like the Barbizon Hotel for Women, but for creative types. Noisy creative types," she joked.

Judy gave a wan smile.

Upstairs, Marion threw open the door to her room, which she'd spent a couple of hours that morning dusting and straightening up. The lumpy beds were a far cry from the sturdy cast-iron ones in Bronxville, and the orange curtains were just as ugly as they had ever been, but she'd done the best she could.

To her dismay, Bunny's side of the room looked like a cyclone had hit. Her dresser drawers were open, clothes tossed on the bed as well as the floor. From the bathroom, Bunny's voice rang out. "I cannot find my good garter belt and bra. I know they're here somewhere, but you have to help me look."

"Bunny, I—"

"Don't tell Mrs. Fleming, but I'm going to stay at a hotel with Dale tonight. His wife is off visiting relatives . . ." Her words trailed off as she stepped out of the bathroom, a pair of black stockings draped over one arm, and caught sight of Judy.

Marion made introductions through gritted teeth.

"What a pleasure to meet you," said Bunny with forced cheer. "I hope you enjoy the show!"

Judy didn't respond, and Marion quickly ushered her out.

During the walk to the theater, Judy was subdued. Marion went into overdrive, telling her about how when one of the residents at the Rehearsal Club had landed a role in a Broadway musical, everyone had chipped in for a cake to celebrate. "They're quite lovely, once you get to know them. Bunny as well. She was the very first Rockette I met."

"She's dating a married man," said Judy. "How can you room with someone like that?"

"It doesn't mean I'll do the same. It's a big world, and people do all kinds of things."

"They certainly do."

Judy's reserve began to dissipate as Marion gave her the grand tour of the backstage area of Radio City. How could it not, as they backed out of the way for a camel being brought down to the animal room, as glee club singers and ballerinas flew up and down the stairs? It was madness, but a joyous, wondrous madness.

For the first time that day, Judy's mouth showed a hint of a smile.

Marion brought Judy into the dressing room and showed her the rack labeled with Marion's name. "Here are my costumes. The pants for the Wooden Soldiers number are so stiff we have to stand on a chair in order to slide into them. It's crazy! And here's where I sit and do my makeup and hair before each show."

Judy picked up a lipstick. "Awfully red, this is." She pointed to a small photograph tucked into the edge of the mirror. "I love that photo of Mom."

Marion had taken it with her the day she left home. She liked being able to see her mother's smiling face before each show, as if she were giving Marion her blessing. "Me too. She looks so glamorous, with her hair all done up." She paused. "Sometimes in my dreams I hear her calling out to me."

"After she'd gone to Boston but before she died, I could have sworn I caught a glimpse of her across the street from our school, like an apparition."

A chill traveled down Marion's spine. "Same here. It's like we knew she wouldn't be coming back or something."

Things were getting maudlin. Marion carried on. She had enough time to show Judy the rehearsal hall and then the roof deck, where a couple of girls were lounging in Adirondack chairs, the city skyline rising around them in every direction.

"So do you see why I couldn't pass up this opportunity?" Marion struggled to find the words to explain it so Judy could understand. "I'm part of something bigger than myself. It's like you working with Dad. You're accomplishing something together, you're part of a team."

"The way Dad would see it is that we're part of a major corporation that provides electricity to an entire city, while you're tap-dancing in between matinees. I'm not trying to be harsh, just explaining his point of view. Besides, it's not in your nature to be part of a team."

"What does that mean?"

"You outshine everyone around you. You can't help it, you just do. You're always the star of the show, wherever you go."

"The whole point of the Rockettes is there is no star, we're a single unit. Just wait until you see. Wait until you see the kids' faces and hear the applause."

"I understand why you're enthralled with all this. But is it worth the cost of losing your family?"

"Have I lost you, Judy? If anything, I feel like we're closer than we have been in ages."

"I want you to come home, I want to have everyone together again. Poor Dad, think of it from his point of view. He lost Mom, and now he'll lose you as well?"

Judy turned her face away to look out at the city skyline, but Marion could tell she was near tears.

✳

"That was awful, does your sister think I'm a tramp?"

Bunny stood behind Marion where she sat at her dressing table, looking at her in the mirror.

Marion reassured her, mainly because she didn't want to deal with that right now. She needed to sit and think for a moment, recover from her talk with her sister. They'd separated at the stage door, promising to meet there right after the show was over so Marion could say goodbye before Judy took the train back to Bronxville.

Judy's words—that Marion was always outshining everyone around her—hit hard. These days, she was just trying to fit in, to manage the best she could. In fact, Marion's time with the Rockettes had showed her the value of pulling back, figuratively as well as physically. When a number called for an arabesque, with one leg up in the air behind her, Marion knew that stepping into her natural, full extension would be too much. If she did that, it wouldn't match the other dancers and she'd get an earful from Russell. Instead, she had to activate the muscles that countered the position in order to conform, even though it hurt. It was a small price to pay.

The stage manager called places. Backstage, Marion licked her finger and touched the underside of the chin of the girl behind her and tried to settle her nerves. She was no stranger to the Radio City stage anymore and she knew the *Christmas Spectacular* routines cold, but today she was dancing for her sister and wanted to be perfect. The organists at the two Wurlitzers flanking the stage played Christmas carols as the audience settled into their seats. Once they finished, the orchestra appeared as if by magic, rising up from the pit for the overture, then slowly sinking back down as the audience applauded.

First up for the Rockettes was a fierce tap number that required serious concentration. Then they ran into the wings to change into their Wooden Soldiers costumes. Assisted by her dresser, Marion slid on the starched pants and secured the clasp of the helmet tightly under her chin. In the last show, her helmet had slid off to the side during the fall. Luckily, the girl right behind her had quickly pushed it upright, but Russell, of course, had noticed. Nothing ever got past him.

The most difficult section of that number, other than the fall, was when they formed a long line and rotated in a large circle. In order to keep the line straight, the tall dancers near the center had to take baby steps, legs stiff, arms down at their sides, as the shorter girls on the ends of the line trucked along as fast as they could, all while maintaining the illusion of soldierlike rigidity.

Marion breathed a sigh of relief when all the dancers managed to keep their rotating line perfectly straight without any wobbles and her helmet stayed put during the long fall, which felt like it took ages. As they headed offstage Marion glanced over to the section where she knew her sister was seated. The expression on Judy's face matched that of the young girl to her left—wide-eyed and smiling—and her hands were clasped together as if in prayer. She had fallen under the spell of the *Christmas Spectacular* just as Marion had hoped she would. The seat to Judy's right was empty, and next to that was a man in a trench coat. Marion wouldn't have noticed him except that he reached down and lifted something bulky into his lap that gave off a brief flash of reflected light.

In the wings, Marion did a quick costume change for the nativity scene, pleased that Judy seemed to be letting down her guard. Their conversation on the roof had been eye-opening but also wonderful in its honesty. Maybe now they could enter a new stage in their relationship. It couldn't have been easy for Judy, growing up in a house with two large personalities when her own was more subdued, and Marion was glad she'd confided in her about the terrible incident with the math kid. Now they could move on from their messy teenaged years and grow together into women. That was what their mother would have wanted, to be sure.

One of the camels tried to eat the hay during the nativity scene, and a sheep erupted in a series of baas, but it worked well enough. Marion glanced into the audience again as the lights went down, thrilled to see Judy still staring happily up at the stage. Both seats to her right were now empty; the man had probably headed to the men's lounge for a smoke.

The Rockettes entered for the final number, dressed in green-and-red sequined leotards. A riser lifted them slowly up into the air as they kicked and pranced, every movement of their limbs tight and sharp, exactly the way Russell had choreographed. Marion's kicks were perfectly eye height, her smile unforced. For the first time she wasn't faking it or worried about getting something wrong. She knew these moves in her bones, and the controlled freedom and pure joy of standing in a long line of dancers doing exactly the same thing sent a zing through her body. This was her best show yet, perfectly timed for impressing one of the most important people in her life. The audience clapped and cheered wildly in response.

But then a strange thundering—like a firecracker but deeper and much louder—erupted out of nowhere, almost bursting her eardrums. In her confusion, she wondered if the fake cannon they used for the Wooden Soldiers number had been replaced with a real one and a stagehand had accidentally set it off backstage. But no, the sound had come from the audience, the echo reverberating around the cavernous space. Through the ringing in her ears, Marion heard people down at the orchestra level shouting for help. The conductor had turned his back to the stage and was trying to see into the audience, shielding the stage lights with his hand.

The music came to a halt as the smell of smoke hit Marion's nostrils. The house lights rose and she searched for Judy. Her seat was empty, thank goodness. Maybe she'd gone out to get a candy bar from the concession stand.

But as the smoke cleared, Marion realized that the seat where her sister had been sitting was blackened, the red velvet charred. Only then did she hear screams coming from the next seat over, where the young girl was now buried under a pile of coats.

But no, it was only one coat. A camel hair coat. Judy's coat, with a bloody hand sticking out from a sleeve.

Marion stepped forward, yelling for help, pointing down to where Judy's inert body, the red ribbon still in her hair, lay across the lap of the screaming young girl.

CHAPTER FOURTEEN

The sedan slices through the canyons of midtown, but north of Times Square a couple of roads are blocked off and we are rerouted, first east, then back west. I can tell Piper is getting more anxious, checking her watch every thirty seconds and letting out a few sighs. On Fifty-Third Street, the traffic comes to a dead halt.

I look out the window. The terrain is completely unfamiliar, but I know where I am. The ghosts of buildings past hover over the minimalist architecture of the museum on one side of the street and the hulking black skyscraper on the other, like mirages. I can almost hear Mrs. Fleming's throaty laugh and the cacophony of over-stimulated boardinghouse girls as they tumble down the steep front steps.

"I have to get out of the car," I say.

"What?" Piper says, startled. She and the driver exchange a worried look.

"Open the door," I demand.

He pulls over as much as is possible in standstill traffic, and I open the door and let myself out before he has a chance to do it for me. Piper gets out as well and hurries to my side. The rain has eased, become more of a mist. I can feel droplets on my cheeks and nose, but they're light, like kisses.

I point across the street to the museum. "I used to stay at a girls' boardinghouse right there," I say.

"When was this?" asks Piper, although I can tell she's just placating me, hoping I'll get back in the car.

"When I was a Rockette." As the sweet memories keep popping up, I need to breathe in the acrid air of New York as a counterpoint.

"Let the car go," I tell Piper.

"Go where?"

"Wherever. We can walk the rest of the way."

"Can you?"

Her concern only makes me more stubborn. "Of course."

She and the driver speak quietly off to the side, and then he withdraws a large umbrella from his trunk and hands it over to her before getting back into the sedan.

We head to Sixth Avenue. The sidewalks are crowded and for a few seconds I wonder if I've made a mistake, letting the car go. Then Piper offers me her arm. I take it, and the umbrella as well, holding it in my free hand as a cane.

"Tell me more about this boardinghouse," Piper says.

"It was called the Rehearsal Club and was for women who were in show business."

"What a wonderful idea," says Piper. "I wish they had something like that now. I live in the East Village and it's always a little scary when I come home late at night. How much was your rent when you lived there?"

I think back. "Something like eighteen dollars a week."

Piper calculates the math in her head. "That's seventy-two bucks a month! I pay five hundred."

"And that included two meals a day."

"I wish I lived back then. You had the world at your fingertips."

"It was just as difficult to break in. Especially if you wanted a career in the arts."

"But the city was different, I bet. More welcoming."

We wait at the corner for the light to change. "Manhattan's never been welcoming. It's our perception that changes. In fact, it seems to me that whenever a person comes to New York, the year that they arrive gets coated in amber, in a way. Frozen for perpetuity. You walk around memorizing every block, every corner, because it's all new and that's how you navigate the neighborhoods. *That's* the year everything is perfect. From then on, as the city changes—and of course, the city has always been changing—we yearn for the past and fight against anything new. For example, the Rehearsal Club was in a brownstone, which has since been torn down and replaced by a museum. I wish I could walk down the street and see the original building, look up at the window where I used to sit and stare at all the people walking by. But it's gone. *Poof.*"

The light changes and we step off the curb. "Doesn't that make you sad?" asks Piper. "That there's very little left of the New York you knew back then?"

"When I do get nostalgic, I think back on the farmer who had a clapboard house on that same spot back in the early 1800s, which was demolished to put up an ugly brownstone. How he must have rued the day his farmland was buried under concrete and pavement."

"Or the Native Americans who camped on that spot of forest before the farmer."

I like this girl. "Exactly."

"So I guess I'll remember the time that I worked in Radio City

Music Hall, before it was torn down to become a super-tall office tower or something."

I look up and see the neon marquee on the next block, shining in the dark sky like a beacon.

"This one will never come down," I say. "No one messes with Radio City."

CHAPTER FIFTEEN

NOVEMBER 1956

Marion was dragged into the wings by two of her fellow Rockettes as the audience members scrambled to get out of the theater, everyone running away from the site of the explosion. It was as if a giant boulder had been dropped into a lake, the waves rippling out in a circle, but the waves were people, climbing over rows of seats, escaping any way they could.

Marion didn't want to ripple away from the center. That was where Judy was. She turned away from the girls who were crying and comforting each other and ran back onstage, jumping down into the aisle. By then the ushers were on the scene, doing their best to guide the throng to the exits. The young girl who'd been sitting next to Judy was wrapped in her mother's arms, the house manager leading them up the aisle, away from where Judy had been laid on her back. She was surrounded by people, and Marion could only see her stockinged feet, with one shoe missing. She had the crazy thought that she must find that shoe or Judy would be very upset.

Her ears still ringing, Marion fought her way through the crowd, shouting that it was her sister.

Judy's face was serene, unharmed. She was sleeping, and all that was needed was for Marion to shake her awake. She knelt by her side, urging her to wake up, before feeling something strange on her legs.

Blood—Judy's blood—was staining Marion's flesh-colored tights.

The ringing in her ears was replaced by the sound of sirens. A pair of medics crouched over Judy and began examining her. Marion cried out for them to be gentle, stepping back to give them room and realizing that Mr. Leonidoff and Russell were right beside her. Bunny hovered nearby.

Marion waited as Judy was lifted onto a stretcher, her eyes closed, face white. Bunny conferred with the medics.

"What happened?" Marion said to no one in particular. "What was that?"

No one answered, but Marion already knew the answer. A bomb had exploded. Where Judy had been sitting.

Bunny came over and gently put her arms around Marion. "Let's get your things and I'll come with you."

"Where?" Marion asked.

"To Roosevelt Hospital. Where they're taking her. We'll meet them there."

They ran backstage and Marion threw a trench coat over her costume, not bothering to wipe the blood off her legs. Then they were in a taxi—Mr. Leonidoff had personally hailed it—and heading west. Marion couldn't speak. For the first time in her life, she understood why people prayed and bargained and asked for favors from an unseen entity. Anything to make her sister whole again.

They were directed to a waiting room, where Marion picked up the pay phone and called her father. She tried the home number, but there was no answer, so she tried him at work.

"Yes."

His voice was gruff. She pictured him in his office, only the desk lamp on, the rest of the room blanketed in darkness.

"Dad. It's me." A sob erupted from her throat. "It's Marion. There's been another bomb."

"What?"

"At Radio City. Judy is in the hospital. You have to come."

"Wait a minute. You're not making any sense. Judy's at home."

Marion wished that she were. She wished that it hadn't been Judy, just someone who looked like her. That Judy had been so offended by Bunny's dalliances and Marion's new life that she'd given her ticket to someone else and taken the train home. She would be back in Bronxville making scrambled eggs for dinner, the way she always did when their father worked late.

But no. That wasn't what had happened.

"Judy came to see me at Radio City," Marion explained. "Something exploded. She's been taken to Roosevelt Hospital. You should come right away."

She caught his strangled cry right before the line went dead.

Ten minutes later, her father flew through the hospital doors and ran right up to the receptionist. Now that he was here, everything would be fixed. That was what her father did. He had the power to make everything all right.

He said something to the woman behind the desk. She nodded and then pointed to Marion.

Her father turned and looked at her. For a moment, she thought that he'd open his arms wide, gather her to him. But he turned to the receptionist and said something else and then was ushered back to wherever Judy was.

Marion sat back down, hating the weight of Bunny's arm over her shoulders but unable to shrug it off.

When her father emerged through the doors again, it was in the company of a doctor with a long face. The muscles around his mouth were tight. Carefully, Marion approached.

"How is she?"

The doctor addressed Marion. Her father had already heard what he was about to say. "Your sister suffered serious injuries from some kind of explosive device, to her hip and legs. I'm afraid she didn't make it. The blood loss was too severe. I'm so sorry."

Marion let out a cry as the doctor's words echoed in her head. Judy had been by Marion's side less than two hours ago, but now she was dead. How could both things be true?

Beside her, Simon crumpled and Marion wrapped her arms around him. He let her, and she murmured into his ear, "I'm here. I'm here."

As the doctor departed, her father pulled away, wiping his eyes with a handkerchief. "I don't understand. Why was Judy at Radio City?"

"She came to see me."

"How could you have done such a thing?"

"I invited her, that's all."

"What were you thinking? How could you?" His face was stricken, his eyes wild. She'd never seen him like this and it scared her. He straightened. "I've got to go."

"Let me come with you," she said. "Please, Dad."

"No. Not right now. There are arrangements to be made, I have to take care of things."

"I can help."

He lumbered down the hall and out the doors before she could stop him.

Marion numbly watched him go. Before she let herself fall apart, there was one more thing she needed to do, and so she insisted that she and Bunny return to the theater. She was grateful to her friend for staying with her through the ordeal, but it wasn't over yet. She needed answers.

The policeman standing outside the lobby took one look at Marion's bloody legs and let Bunny and her through. The auditorium looked strangely ordinary, like a crowd might begin filing in for the next show any moment now, other than the fact that several policemen were making their way slowly through each row, one by one, scanning for clues. Another had a camera and was taking photographs with a bright flash down near the bomb site.

Russell stood near the stage, speaking with a detective who was taking notes. He spotted Marion and Bunny and headed over to them, the detective trailing behind.

Russell hugged them both. "You shouldn't be here. Go home and rest. Marion, take off as much time as you need."

She didn't want to discuss the future. "Did they catch who did this?"

"This is Detective Ogden," Russell said. "He'll be looking into it. Detective Ogden, Marion here is one of our Rockettes, and the victim is her sister."

"Was. Was my sister."

Tears came to Russell's eyes. "I'm so sorry."

She turned to the detective, a tall man with a thin mustache. An oversized black overcoat hung from his skinny frame like bat wings. "Was anyone else hurt?" She was thinking of the young girl next to Judy.

"Shrapnel from the bomb hurt two other people, but not seriously."

"Was it the Big Apple Bomber?"

"We don't know. It'll take time to figure that out." He stared openly at Marion before his features settled into a guarded, wary expression. She braced herself, guessing that he was the angry, spurned type.

"It must be him," said Bunny. "I mean, who else would do this?"

Marion spoke up. "I think I saw the guy. I can give you a description."

Detective Ogden rubbed his mouth with the back of his hand. "We'll reach out to you tomorrow, after we've done the legwork here. Where do you live?"

"The Rehearsal Club." She waited while he wrote the address down on his notepad. "Shouldn't I come down to the station or something tonight? Don't you want to know what I saw?"

"One thing at a time. We'll reach out when we're ready."

Russell motioned to Bunny. "Take her home. For now, you need to get some rest."

As they walked up the aisle to the lobby, Marion turned around one last time, then let Bunny guide her outside into the cold night air.

⁕

Marion lay on her bed in the Rehearsal Club listening to the sounds of the other girls who lived on her floor laughing, shouting, getting ready for class or an audition. Girls whose families were safely back at home, wherever home was.

Her father had been right. It was all her fault for inviting Judy in the first place. She'd put her sister in harm's way and would never forgive herself, and she was certain that her father would never forgive her, either. It was exactly what Judy had told her that day on the roof of Radio City—Marion was always putting herself in the spotlight—and if she hadn't asked Judy to come watch her dance, she'd still be alive.

Right now, she'd be arriving at her desk in the Met Power headquarters for another typical workday, putting her purse in a drawer and then scooping their father's telephone messages into a neat stack. Marion preferred to imagine that alternative universe, where things were still going along like they had before. It was better than dealing with the real one.

The door opened and Bunny came in with a bowl of oatmeal and put it down on Marion's bedside table.

"You should eat a little something," urged Bunny. "The cook sprinkled this with brown sugar, exactly the way you like it."

Marion sat upright but didn't even look at the oatmeal. The thought of spooning it into her mouth made her feel ill. "Is there water?" she asked hoarsely.

Bunny went into the bathroom and ran the faucet, coming back with a glass of water. Marion took a sip and placed it down beside the bowl.

"You sure you don't want even a bite?" said Bunny. "You haven't eaten since lunch yesterday."

"I'm not hungry."

"I'm so sorry, Marion. What can I do to help? I can call your father, try to talk to him if you like."

"No. Absolutely not."

"Is there anyone else I can call?"

Nathaniel came to mind, but Marion summarily dismissed the idea. He wouldn't know what to say at a time like this. He'd never had to deal with a sudden tragedy. The few times she'd brought up her mother's death, he'd nodded and then changed the subject, unable to handle Marion's complicated mix of emotions.

She had no one, except Bunny. "Thank you for taking care of me," she said.

Bunny squeezed her arm. "Of course. And Russell says to take all the time you need."

"What are they telling you about the performances?"

"They said they need a couple of days and then we'll be back on schedule."

"Even with a mad bomber on the loose?"

Bunny shook her head. "He's hit Radio City twice before, you know."

Of course. Marion did know that. The bomber had struck so many sites, some multiple times, that she had completely forgotten that Radio City had been a target before. In a bustling city like New York, the news made headlines for a day before everyone moved on to the next crisis. On top of that, many of the madman's bombs either hadn't gone off or had been found before they'd detonated, so the perceived threat level wasn't exactly high. Until now. "What happened before this one?"

"A cleaner found one bomb, which hadn't gone off. The other went off but didn't cause any injuries."

A light knock sounded at the door. Mrs. Fleming peered in, looking worried. "Marion, there are a couple of policemen here. They'd like to talk to you. I said I'd check and make sure you were up to it."

Marion nodded. She wanted to find out what was going on with the investigation, figure out who had done this to her family. She threw off the covers. "I'll be right down."

Detective Ogden, whom she'd met the night before, was waiting in the practice room with another man, whom he introduced as Captain Somers. Where Ogden was wiry, Somers was portly and clean-cut. He also had about fifteen years on Ogden, judging by his gray hair and heavy jowls. They stood as she entered and motioned for her to take a seat. Somers yanked out a notepad and a pen from the inside pocket of his coat, leaning forward in his chair.

"We're so sorry for your loss," he said.

"Thank you." Marion had to make this right. Part of her knew that nothing could be done to replace her sister, but another part wanted action, something that would prove to her father that it wasn't her fault. "We have to find out who did this."

"We've had a team searching the entire theater, tagging and bagging evidence," said Somers. "I'm the head of the crime lab, and I assure you we'll do everything we can to find him."

"Where was the bomb located? Under the seat?"

Somers shook his head. "We can't divulge that information at this time."

Marion became incensed. "My sister lost her life in a horrible, horrible way. Right in front of my eyes. And you can't tell me the most basic detail? And why am I the one asking all the questions?"

The two men exchanged glances, and Somers gave Ogden a slight nod.

Ogden looked back at Marion. "It was planted inside the seat next to her. The bomber used a knife to cut into the upholstery and slid the pipe bomb inside."

"Under the little girl?"

"No. On the other side."

"In the empty seat between her and the man in the overcoat, then."

Somers snapped to attention. "You saw the man on the other side of your sister?"

"I did. I told Detective Ogden so last night."

A vein in Ogden's forehead pulsed. His eyes stayed on Marion.

"Tell me what he looked like," said Somers.

Marion closed her eyes, trying to remember every detail. "It was when the lights onstage went down, and only briefly. But there was a man, in his forties or fifties, or thereabouts, wearing a light-brown trench coat. He was there early in the show but gone later."

Somers was scribbling wildly on his pad. "Anything else you remember about him?"

"He had a round face, not much hair. I think he wore glasses. It was quick and it was dark, and I was mainly looking to see what my sister's reaction was."

"What was your sister's reaction?" asked Ogden.

"She was smiling, clapping. She was happy." Marion swallowed hard. Her sister's body had been torn apart by this madman. The men waited her out as the tears fell, Somers reaching over to offer her his handkerchief. They'd probably dealt with shock and grief many times before and knew to give Marion time to collect herself, sensing that any more empty words of sympathy would only send her into a rage.

"Why don't they check the patrons for bombs before they come in?" she finally asked when she could speak without crying. "This happened twice before at Radio City."

Ogden answered, "The theater seats around six thousand people. It's simply not possible. Is there anyone who might have wanted to hurt your sister?"

"My father is an executive at Met Power, which the bomber mentioned a number of times in his notes, including the most recent. Do you think there could be a connection?"

"Perhaps," said Somers. "Would anyone else have known where she was going?"

"I doubt she told a soul. She knew my father didn't approve of this job, so she would have kept her plan to attend secret."

"Your father doesn't approve of you dancing?"

"No. We've been estranged for the past month."

"I'm sorry to hear that." They asked her a few more questions and then Somers rose to go. "Thank you for your time today, we'll be in touch."

Marion's voice rose. "What about going to the press, asking them for help? Maybe someone else saw him as well. Someone might be able to describe him better than I can."

"We don't know for sure that man is the bomber, first of all." Somers's tone was gentle but firm. "He may have placed it a day or two ago. And by going to the press, we risk angering the bomber more, or encouraging him. Neither of which we want to do at this point."

Marion shook her head. "There must be a better way. I mean, it's been sixteen years. Do you think maybe it's time to try another tack?"

Somers handed Marion a card with his name and phone number on it.

"If you remember anything else, please let us know."

CHAPTER SIXTEEN

Please come home."

Marion never thought she'd be so happy to hear those words. After her father's rejection at the hospital, she'd wondered if he'd ever speak to her again. But he'd called the Rehearsal Club not long after the police had left, and she'd raced downstairs and breathlessly picked up the receiver. His normally booming voice seemed weak and far away.

"I will," she answered. "I'm on my way." Her father needed her, and she missed her connection to her old life, to her family.

What was left of her family.

At home, she fell first into Mrs. Hornsby's arms, then her father's. Mrs. Hornsby's eyes glistened with tears and her father's were puffy, like he'd been crying all morning. They both looked worn, older than their years, and Marion quickly stepped up to help. Her father had already lived through the torturous process of planning a funeral after Lucille was killed, and Marion wanted to take as much of the burden off him as she could. Making phone calls, drawing up lists, and organizing the wake gave her something to focus on, instead of the raw truth of Judy's death.

The funeral was set for the following Wednesday, and after, Judy would be laid to rest in the same Bronxville cemetery as her mother.

When Marion came down the morning of the funeral, Mrs. Hornsby pulled her close. Marion inhaled the scent of sugar cookies and mint.

"Your father's locked in his study," said Mrs. Hornsby. "He said to be ready when the car comes at eleven. Let me know if you need help with your hair."

"Thank you, Mrs. Hornsby. I know this is as hard for you as it is for the rest of us."

After drinking a cup of coffee, Marion changed into a black dress. The pearls were back in her jewelry box, and she clasped them around her neck before dissolving into tears. It was probably better that Lucille wasn't around to have to bear the pain of this day and all the days to come. Would her mother also have considered Marion complicit in the death of her sister? Even though her father hadn't mentioned that terrible accusation he'd made that night at the hospital, Marion couldn't help but sense that it simmered just below the surface of their every interaction.

Because Judy would never be back. Several times in the past few days, Marion had considered asking Judy's advice about something, only to remember that she was gone. She'd also realized that with Judy's death, her sister's memories of their mother had vanished as well. Being older, Judy had more stored up, and every so often she would offhandedly reveal something about Lucille that Marion didn't know, like the fact that she adored strawberry milkshakes or that she was scared of horses.

Now all that was lost.

Marion stared at herself in the mirror. Here she was again, selfishly thinking of herself first. Thinking of the memories she would be denied by Judy's death, instead of all the things Judy might have done with her own life that were now impossible. Maybe she would've met a nice boy and married. Maybe she would've been the one with a family while Marion stayed a single girl until her last days.

How was it that Judy, who'd never been much of a risk-taker when she was alive, was the sister who had died? She'd never rode in fast cars with boys the way Marion had, or moved to New York, where she might get mugged. Or bombed.

No, Marion had put Judy in harm's way, and deep down, she was certain Simon must still hate her for it.

There had to be something she could do to avenge her sister's death, to honor her memory. She had to find out who did this to her sister and then maybe her father would forgive her. To have lost both of them was too much to bear, especially since she and Judy had finally broached their great divide over the past month and found a common ground.

An article in the newspaper echoed what the detectives had already told Marion, with a few added details. The crude homemade bomb had been buried in the upholstery of a seat in the fifteenth row on the right side facing the stage. The mechanism, according to the article, was a one-inch-wide pipe about four inches long, with a simple timer and battery. A seat-by-seat search by the bomb squad produced no other suspicious objects. Marion had cut the article out of the newspaper and saved it.

Mrs. Hornsby called to Marion from downstairs. She glanced out the window and saw a black car waiting by the curb, her father walking toward it with a briefcase in hand, as if it were a normal day and he was off to work. Marion flew down to the landing, grabbed her coat, and raced along the footpath.

Inside the car, her father patted her hand. "You look beautiful."

Marion hadn't slept in days and knew better. She pointed to the briefcase at his feet. "What's inside?" For some reason, its presence made her ill at ease.

He regarded it as if it were a foreign object. "I don't know why I brought it. Habit, I suppose. How silly of me."

"I'm sure you can leave it in the car."

His face was drawn, his normally bright eyes red with grief. "I tried to keep our family together after your mother died, and I failed."

"We appreciate everything you've done for us. I mean, Judy and I both love you—loved you—and we know how tough it was to raise two young daughters."

He blew his nose and looked over at Marion. "I should've taken better care of her."

"Look, we both have regrets. I should have made more of an effort to reach out to her as we grew older. I don't know what happened, why we drifted apart. But we'd reached a deeper understanding recently."

"You girls were always very different. Your mother used to say she wished Judy had a dash of your verve and you had a pinch of Judy's restraint."

How true that was. And how she missed Lucille. Marion bit the inside of her mouth to keep from crying. "I know no matter where I go, I'll take part of Judy with me."

Simon's tone grew stern. "You can't go away again. I want you to marry Nathaniel, settle down in Bronxville. You need a man to take care of you, and Nathaniel is a good choice. I've lost one daughter and I can't afford to lose you as well."

Marion wasn't sure where her future lay. Part of her ached to take care of her father and devote herself to making him whole, even though she knew deep down there was no hope of ever achieving that. Yet the thought of turning her back on her budding career as a professional dancer sent her into a panic. How could she blithely abandon the one thing that gave her joy?

But did she deserve to feel joy, after what happened to Judy?

Before she could respond, the car pulled into the church driveway.

It seemed like practically the entire town had turned out; the stone steps leading up to the church's entrance were clogged with a bottle-neck of black-clad mourners. Simon got out of the car, but Marion waited a moment, staring down at the briefcase he'd left behind. The lock gleamed in the sunlight and she was transported back to the stage, looking down at her sister, where a similar flash of light caught her eye not long before the explosion.

She shook it away and let the driver help her out of the car, then followed the stream of mourners along the narrow pathway to the church, where her sister's coffin lay waiting.

Back at the house for the reception, Nathaniel said hello and kissed Marion gently on the lips. He tried to pull her close but she resisted, saying she had work to do. She couldn't cope with him right then and instead spent most of her time in the kitchen helping Mrs. Hornsby with the food and drinks. In doing so she was able to successfully put off the pastor, who wanted to offer her private grief counseling, as well as Nathaniel's mother, who suggested they go out the next day for lunch for "girl talk." Marion had politely declined.

Eventually, she escaped upstairs, where the door to Judy's room was open. Everything was exactly as her sister had left it, her books piled up neatly on the bedside table, her sweaters stacked carefully on the shelves, coordinated by color.

Simon had made it clear he wanted Marion to stay there with him, but the taste of independence she'd experienced—of making enough money, of being in charge of her own life—was intoxicating. Yet how could she leave her father on his own? The decision tore at her heart.

A knock on the doorframe pulled her out of her thoughts.

Nathaniel stood there holding a glass of wine. "I thought you might need a drink."

She accepted it and he sat on the bed beside her, rubbing his hands along his thighs.

"Marion, I know you've been through hell and back, and I want you to know that I'm here for you. We've had our ups and downs lately, and I'm fine to give you all the space you need. When you're ready, I'm ready. Even if it's in six months or a year from now. I won't desert you in your time of trouble, and if there's anything I can do to help in the meantime, just let me know."

He took a deep breath when he'd finished, looking over at her like a student who'd just finished a big test. He must've practiced it in the mirror several times. Dear Nathaniel. She'd been dodging him for the past month and felt ashamed of her behavior.

"I appreciate it, Nathaniel, I really do." He'd sensed exactly what she needed right then, which was less pressure, more support. "I'm sorry I've been standoffish. It's so overwhelming."

She began to cry, and he put his arm around her. She nestled into his shoulder, like she used to when life seemed so simple and their future clear. After a moment, she glanced up at him. "So much has changed since you came home from Europe, I feel like I'm a completely different person."

He kissed the top of her head. "There's no need to discuss it now, not at your sister's funeral. I love you, I'm here for you."

From the stairs, Mrs. Hornsby called out for Marion, and the moment was broken. In any event, Nathaniel was right: she shouldn't make any major life decisions right now.

＊

Two days later, she was eating breakfast when Simon came barreling downstairs in a suit and tie, briefcase in hand.

"I'm off, have a good day," he said.

"To where?"

"Work, of course."

Marion stared at him, confused. "Don't you want to take some time off? I'm sure they'd understand."

"They need me, and it will keep me occupied. I'll be back by six." He paused, taking in the expression on her face. "What?"

"I figured you'd at least wait until next week."

"I'm busy, there's a lot to be done. And it'll take my mind off what happened."

What happened. After Simon's tearful breakdown in the car on the way to the funeral, now he couldn't even say Judy's name. Then again, he'd gone right back to work after Lucille died, so why should Judy's death be any different? Marion knew it was a coping mechanism, but it seemed unfair. "So you get to go out and live your life, but you want me to put everything on hold?" The words came out harsher than she expected.

"Not this again. You can talk to Nathaniel, get started on the wedding plans."

"We spoke after the funeral. He said he wants to give me some breathing room, and I appreciate that."

Simon rested the briefcase on the table and began lecturing her, telling her what was best for her and why as her father she should obey him. But Marion didn't listen; she was too busy staring at the briefcase.

A memory from the night of the bombing pierced its way into her consciousness. She was back at the theater, looking down at Judy in the audience as the man in the trench coat lifted a black briefcase to his lap.

She could picture it perfectly: black leather, with two buckles on either side of a large silver lock. The lock had caught the lights and reflected it.

She should tell the cops. Maybe it would help them figure out who the Big Apple Bomber was. If that was how he was transporting the bombs, they would know to look out for it.

Mrs. Hornsby's arrival interrupted her father's harangue, and after he'd left, Marion went upstairs and rifled through her purse. The card that Captain Somers had given her was at the very bottom.

The secretary who answered Marion's phone call said she'd have to take a message. The address was in downtown Manhattan, and rather than waiting around all day for him to call back, Marion decided to go in person, despite her father's wishes. She'd take the train in and right back out and no one would be the wiser.

⁂

An hour later, she found herself standing in front of New York City's Police Headquarters, a massive Beaux Arts building with a dome that rose out of the crooked alleys of Little Italy, a study in power and intimidation. She made her way to the third floor and was told by a secretary to wait, that Captain Somers was in a meeting. But his office door was cracked and Marion could overhear the conversation from where she sat in a metal chair right outside.

"It's time to go to the press." She recognized the voice as that of Captain Somers.

An unfamiliar deep bass answered. "I'll tell you when you can go to the press. And it's not now. There's more work to do."

"Yes, Chief. We understand," said Somers. "But it's been sixteen years. It's imperative that we crack this open."

"I'm with you, Chief." This man spoke in a higher register, a tenor. Detective Ogden, the one with the mustache. "We have other avenues to pursue."

Somers began to speak, but the chief cut him off. "Tell me what you know about this madman so far."

"He might be from Westchester," said Ogden. "That's where his letters are mailed from."

"Or maybe he's from somewhere else, and he's putting you off the trail. And why do you assume it's a 'he'?"

"He's left bombs in men's rooms, in Grand Central and Penn Station," said Somers. "A woman would draw too much attention to do that."

That was the best they could do? They sounded pathetic, even to Marion.

"Find the guy, now. If there's another death, it's on your head." The chief blustered out of the room without giving Marion a glance. Without waiting for the secretary to announce her, Marion slipped in.

"Miss Brooks," Somers said. "What can we do for you?" He glared briefly at Ogden before turning his attention back to her. The two men didn't like each other, that much was evident. Maybe that was why the investigation was stuck in the mire.

"I remembered something."

Somers offered her a seat across from his desk, while Ogden remained standing.

Marion smoothed her skirt. "I remembered that the man sitting next to my sister held a briefcase in his lap. It must've been right before he left."

Somers lifted his chin. "Is that right?"

"It was black leather. And it had two black buckles and a big silver lock."

She sat back and clasped her hands in her lap.

"That's it?" Ogden said.

"I thought it might help. I mean, can't you have the police look for a man with a trench coat and a black briefcase with a big silver lock?"

She flushed with embarrassment. Even to her own ears, she sounded ridiculous.

"There are thousands of men fitting that description in New York City," said Ogden, an edge to his voice.

Somers held his hand up. "Thank you very much, Miss Brooks. That is a great help. We'll let you know if we learn anything more."

She'd come all this way. "There has to be something more you can do."

"We're doing everything we can, I assure you," answered Somers. "We're very sorry for your loss."

She didn't want their pity. She rose to go but turned back at the doorway. "Is that it? I mean, what, are you waiting for the man to come up and introduce himself? There has to be a way to figure out who this guy is. Sure, there are a ton of guys with trench coats and briefcases, but there must be something about this guy that's different from the rest."

Everyone can be analyzed. Everyone has quirks. Even strangers.

At the dinner with Bunny and Dale, Dale's friend Peter had said that. He'd handled the crazy bully using psychiatry.

He'd been able to deduce impressively accurate facts about Marion's life and personality not long after they were introduced. Maybe he could work his magic here as well.

"I met someone who can analyze people and pinpoint some of their deepest secrets after barely meeting them," she said. "You should talk to him. He's doing a psychiatric residency at Creedmoor State Hospital."

"When we catch this guy," said Somers, stepping around his desk, joining Marion in the doorway, "and I promise you we'll catch this guy, all the shrinks in the city will be lined up to analyze him. I don't care about that. I want him caught."

"What if instead you figure out what type of madman would commit these kinds of acts?" She had to make them understand. "Solve the puzzle in reverse."

"He's crazy, that's why he does it," said Ogden. "That's all there is to it."

"So what, you wait until the next bombing? Hope you catch him in the act?"

Neither man responded. That was exactly what their plan was. Unbelievable.

"Thanks for coming by, Miss Brooks." Somers motioned to the secretary to escort her out. He offered his condolences once more before shutting the door behind her.

※

"I'll have a cheeseburger with fries and a side of broccoli."

Marion couldn't help but smile. Nathaniel had called earlier in the day to see if she'd meet him at the diner in town. Unlike the other times he'd asked, when she'd been working at Radio City, today she had no reason to say no.

"I can't believe you still eat broccoli at every meal." She shook her head at the memory of him ordering it alongside a stack of waffles the summer of her junior year. They'd played tennis at the club all morning and then grabbed a quick brunch before she'd headed into the city for her dance class. How long ago that all seemed now.

"Of course," he said proudly. "It's the key to longevity. Or so my grandfather says."

"I saw him the other day driving around in that convertible of his. Maybe he's onto something."

"Pushing ninety and a terror behind the wheel." Nathaniel went to reach for her hand but then tucked both of his under the table instead, in his lap. They were on uncertain footing these days, and neither knew how to behave.

"Do you remember the time Judy tried to parallel park on Pondfield Road and ended up with the entire car on the sidewalk?" she said. "She called the house in an absolute tizzy, and we had to go and rescue her."

Nathaniel laughed. "I'm still not sure how she lodged the car the way she did. It was right after she'd gotten her license, and she was mortified." He paused. "You don't mind talking about her?"

"I'd rather talk about her than do what my father's doing, which is pretend like nothing happened. It's a relief to say her name out loud."

Until their food came, Nathaniel and Marion traded "remember whens," about Judy, their classmates, and each other, of graduation parties, and the time that Mr. Gibbs had blown up something in his chemistry lab and they all ditched school for the day and headed to the beach instead. They could have gone on like this forever, Marion knew, but she was more interested in looking to the future these days, not the past. Or she had been, until Judy had been killed. Now, she didn't know quite where to look.

Nathaniel noticed she'd become distracted and put down his burger. "I know we have a big transition to make, from high school sweethearts to grown-up people. Adults."

"Eek. I'm not sure I'm ready for that."

He remained serious. "I think I am. I know I am."

"Do you really want to work for my dad at Met Power? I somehow can't imagine you enjoying that kind of work."

"What do you see me as instead?"

"An advertising executive, a pilot."

"Not all of us have big dreams like you do. Not that there's anything wrong with dreaming, I'm not saying that. But for me, I'd be happy if I can go into work every day and earn a steady paycheck and then come home to you."

She imagined being married and living in a house with Nathaniel. Cooking dinner before going upstairs and replacing her housedress with something pretty. Sitting in the living room, idly waiting for him to come back from the city. That didn't sound appealing at all. "How do you know that will make you happy? How can you be sure that after one month or one year you won't be ready to chuck everything in and head to California?"

"I know because I've lived it. I want to have a family like the one I grew up in. A house full of kids, chaos, and craziness. I've seen my father's face when he gets home and my younger brothers race to the door."

Marion's homelife, by contrast, had been eerily quiet most of the time, as she and Judy maneuvered around each other as best they could. Her father worked long hours, and once they hit high school Mrs. Hornsby was only there during the weekdays. It was a lonely existence.

"You deserve that, Nathaniel."

"I think, once you've had time to deal with the shock of what happened, you'll see that you deserve it, too."

Marion wasn't so sure.

By Sunday, Marion was fidgety and irritable. She had absolutely nothing to do other than wander the rooms of the Bronxville house, and her father had holed up in his study most of the weekend. Meanwhile, she had no doubt the police were doddering about, doing nothing to move the investigation forward.

Late in the afternoon, Mrs. Hornsby stopped by unexpectedly, mumbling something about moving some casseroles that folks had dropped off from the freezer to the fridge, but Marion had a sense she was worried about the two of them alone in their big house. Marion offered to make her coffee and she accepted, but then insisted she brew it instead, saying Marion always made it too strong.

"Sit down," said Mrs. Hornsby. "Keep me company while I figure out which of these two dozen dishes you'll have for dinner this coming week."

"We have enough to feed an army," said Marion. "You should take some home with you. Give them to Tommy and his family." Tommy lived just down the street from his mother in the next town over.

"I may do just that." She lifted the tinfoil from the corner of a dish and sniffed. "Your father hates lasagna. Might as well not let it go to waste. I'll pack that one up."

Marion was flooded with warmth for this woman, who'd nurtured her and Judy as if they were her own. She'd trundled Marion to and from dance class and took Judy out for sundaes whenever she came home with straight As, which was often. "Mrs. Hornsby, I don't think any of us have ever thanked you enough for taking care of us for so many years, especially after Mom died."

Mrs. Hornsby gave a slight smile but shook off the sentiment. "It was what had to be done. Besides, the two of you were a dream to raise after having dealt with Tommy's hellion streak. I swear that boy took years off my life with his antics."

"Were you happy when he joined the police force, then?"

"God, no. While my husband may not have been killed on the job, the job killed him, that much is certain. The stress of being a cop is unending. I thought my heart would break when Tommy announced that he'd applied to the police academy. But I knew there was nothing much I could do about it. He's his own person."

"I wish my father saw things your way," complained Marion.

Mrs. Hornsby put down the casserole dish and picked up her coffee. She leaned against the counter and took a sip. "I have to say, like your father, I had my trepidations about you becoming a Rockette, but you've changed since you started dancing there. You have a confidence in your bearing, a sparkle. I know what happened to Judy is terrible, but I don't want you to punish yourself for that. It wasn't your fault."

Marion disagreed, but she stayed quiet. It was rare for Mrs. Hornsby to talk like this. "You think I should continue? What about Nathaniel?"

"If it is meant to be, he'll still be around when you're ready to settle down. Your mother would have wanted you to dance, I know that much."

"How? How do you know that?"

"She could've sent you to the local ballet school right here in town, but from the very beginning she insisted you take classes at one of the top studios in the city. She knew you had talent and wanted to make sure it was nurtured and encouraged by the best."

Marion had never thought of it that way, the endless train rides back and forth, first with her mother, then with Mrs. Hornsby, until she was old enough to take the train herself.

She stood and kissed Mrs. Hornsby on the cheek and helped her sort through the rest of the meals; then she went upstairs and packed up her bag.

It was time to go back to the Rehearsal Club. Simon had the best of intentions, but she'd lose her mind if she stayed in Bronxville any longer. Her trip into Manhattan a couple of days earlier had gone fine, and that, along with her conversation with Mrs. Hornsby, helped to solidify her decision to return.

Simon gave out a grumpy "come in" when she knocked on the study door not long after Mrs. Hornsby had left. "Is it dinnertime yet?"

"Dad, I'm going," she said.

"Are you going out with Nathaniel?"

"No. I'm going to Manhattan. I've considered what you've said, but I need to have my life back. Just like you find working helps you move forward, I need to do the same." Simon tried to interrupt, but she held firm. "I didn't tell you this, but I went in on Friday and met with the police. I'd remembered something that I thought might help and they were utterly useless. I want to stay on top of them, for Judy's sake, and it will be easier if I'm in Manhattan. I'll be careful, I promise."

"There's a madman out there, and you're going to be wandering around the city? I thought we talked about this already."

"I have to do everything I can to help solve this. And I know you don't approve, but I'd like to start dancing again with the Rockettes. I'll go mad if I don't have something to focus on, and before you say it, I'm not interested in getting engaged and spending my days picking out linens and tableware. Not yet, anyway. I hope you can support me."

"Why should I do that? You're perfectly capable of supporting yourself. Not to mention catching a criminal who's been on the loose for sixteen years." His sarcasm stung.

"Don't be like that, please."

"Like what? Like a father who's worried sick about his child?"

They were at an impasse. Again. Marion had hoped that the past week might have brought them together, but Simon still refused to view Marion as a woman with a will of her own instead of as a possession to be protected at all costs. Just like her pearls, locked away in a safe.

Simon had already turned back to his work. She shut the door with a quiet click and gathered her things.

* * *

Bunny was in their room in the Rehearsal Club, along with two of the other Rockettes, Sylvia and Rhonda, who were both from Minnesota.

They rose from where they'd been sitting on Marion's bed, drinking water glasses filled with forbidden red wine, and apologized profusely.

"No, no. Please stay," Marion said. "And pour me one as well."

"How are you?" asked Bunny.

Marion sat on the floor, her back against the bureau, and took a long swallow of wine. "I've been better. How's the show going?"

"We're dancing to a full house again," said Bunny. "But we miss you. Russell asks after you every day."

Russell had sent an enormous flower arrangement to the funeral and had left a note for Marion at the Rehearsal Club saying that she should take all the time she needed. *I understand if you don't want to return, but if you do, I'll be there for you in every way necessary*, he'd written.

"Will you go back to Radio City?" asked Sylvia. "I'm sorry, I'm sure it's too early to even think about anything like that."

"No, it's okay." The wine warmed Marion up. "You can ask. And the answer is I have to go back. I have to support myself from now on."

"Your father still disapproves?" asked Bunny.

"He refuses to understand. I get it, he's afraid something will happen to me, too, and wants to keep me on a tight leash. But I can't live the life he wants for me. Why do I have to give up everything I love?"

"You'll reconcile with your dad," said Bunny. "He just needs some time."

But neither Rhonda nor Bunny knew Simon Brooks the way Marion did. He was a man from the Lower East Side, where insults were met with fists and grudges were long-lasting. "Sure. Maybe."

"In any event, it's good to be independent," said Bunny. "Here's to making our own money and standing on our own two feet."

They all took a drink except Sylvia. "Look who's talking. Dale gives you gifts and dinners and who knows what else."

Marion thought Bunny might be offended, but she just laughed. "I need to dump him, I admit that. Did you know the place he took me and Marion to dinner is notorious for being the restaurant where men bring their mistresses? I mean, what an insult."

"But you *are* his mistress," said Rhonda.

"Maybe not for long. He's boring. I need someone creative and fun. Like an artist, say."

"Artists are notoriously poor, Bunny," said Rhonda.

"And troubled," added Sylvia.

"And heavy drinkers," said Marion. It felt good to hear laughter and conversation, a welcome distraction from her own troubles.

"How about a nice doctor, then?" said Bunny. "Or a magician?"

"A doctor who does magic tricks," added Rhonda.

The girls continued shouting out occupations, doubling over in laughter after each one. Marion joined in but stopped drinking.

She suddenly knew exactly what she needed to do the next day, and she'd need a clear head to do it.

CHAPTER SEVENTEEN

The journey to Queens required a subway followed by a city bus, which rolled past dank-looking tenements under a gray sky. Marion walked the final leg, which brought her to the entrance of Creedmoor State Hospital, a campus of drab brick buildings surrounded by a tall fence.

It looked like the kind of place that once you stepped inside, you might not be able to escape. Maybe she'd made a terrible mistake by coming here. After all, she was wracked with grief and had hardly slept the night before; surely she looked a fright. Maybe they would sense that her mind was spinning out of control and make her stay.

But she had to do something, try to learn all she could about this person who had killed Judy. First thing that morning, Marion had called Russell to say she wanted to start dancing again, and he'd said she could return that very day if she liked. She'd asked Bunny to call Dale and find out Peter's last name, which neither of them could remember. Bunny was supposed to break up with the guy at the same time, but after she'd whispered "Griggs" from the phone in the parlor, Marion had heard Bunny's giggly laugh. Dale had some kind of hold on her, unfortunately.

That morning an article had appeared in the *Times* that set

Marion's teeth on edge. A reporter had gotten wise to the fact that the victim's sister was a Rockette and her father a Met Power executive and speculated that Judy might have been targeted specifically. The press had been calling the phone at the Rehearsal Club nonstop since then, trying to get a statement from Marion. The residents had been instructed by Mrs. Fleming to hang up on any inquiries for Marion, and she was grateful for the screening. It was all too much, especially when she considered that her father must be experiencing a similar invasion of privacy.

Even so, if the choice was between going out to take action or sitting around the Bronxville house and listening to the phone ring nonstop, she'd take the first choice any day.

At Creedmoor, a receptionist in the lobby barely looked up when Marion entered. After Marion gave her Dr. Griggs's name, she directed Marion to building number eleven, outside and around the back. "Tony here will escort you," she said, pointing to a rather large man in a uniform who guarded the front door.

She followed the man back outside, past a large vegetable garden where several inmates were spreading mulch under the watchful eye of a matron. A series of pens with livestock—chickens, several pigs—stood in the distance. Finally they reached building number eleven, which was a twin of the first building. The receptionist told Marion to wait.

A buzzer sounded and a door opened. Peter wore a white coat with the words *Creedmoor State Hospital* embroidered above the pocket. He looked slightly annoyed, as if he'd been called away from something important, but when he caught sight of Marion his eyes widened with surprise. "Miss Brooks?"

She rose and held out her hand. "Yes. Nice to see you again."

He gave a brief shake of her hand. "What are you doing here?"

"I'd like to speak with you in private, if I may."

The receptionist regarded them with an open stare. Marion realized how out of place she must look, in her tweed coat with its nipped waist and fur collar, the shiny leather pumps on her feet. Peter motioned for Marion to follow him.

They went through several locked doors and down a long hall, where the moans of the inmates echoed against the bare walls. Some of the doors were open, and Marion peered inside one to see a man sitting on his bed, rocking back and forth and humming to himself. In the hallway, an old man with a gray beard sat in a metal chair, his mottled hands gripping his knees. Peter patted his shoulder as they walked by.

His office had room enough for a desk, a couple of chairs, and a wooden file cabinet overflowing with paper. Files were piled up precariously on the windowsill. By comparison, the top of his desk was quite organized, with several neat stacks of books and folders, a leather blotter lined up perfectly against the edge of the desk.

He waited for her to sit before he did the same.

Dale said that they'd met at Harvard. Why would Peter choose to do his residency at a place like this when he'd gone to one of the top medical schools in the country? Perhaps he was at the bottom of his class, and this was all he had been offered.

Peter surveyed his office; the expression on her face must've given her away. "Sorry it's such a mess."

"How many inmates are there here?"

"We call them patients."

"Right, sorry. Patients."

"Six thousand."

Enough to fill up Radio City. Out in the hallway, a patient howled.

"How can I help you?"

Marion detected an air of irritation in Peter's voice, which was a surprise. Everyone she'd spoken to in the past week had treated her differently since the bombing. Yet with Peter, there was no added note of concern in his voice, no pity in his eyes.

He didn't know.

Which was refreshing.

"How long have you worked here?" she asked.

"I'm in the second year of my residency."

"It seems nice, with the garden and all." Her words sounded weak even to her own ears.

"The idea behind it is laudable. Not sure about the execution. Creedmoor is modeled on the asylums of the last century, where patients were able to work, to participate in activities. We have an orchestra, a theater company. I applied because I thought it would be a place where I could possibly make a difference in the lives of the mentally ill."

"That's very admirable of you."

He waved off the compliment. "Unfortunately, these days, when a patient arrives, they're prescribed Thorazine, which is hailed as a wonder drug but, in fact, turns them into zombies, roaming the halls, useless and unhappy."

"They can't be helped?"

"It's an easy way out, especially with those prone to violence. Instead of being analyzed and studied so that we can get to the bottom of their illnesses, they're written off as lost causes, left to waste away."

Another howl erupted from the hallway, making Marion jump. She thought of the bomber. "What about someone who's hurt someone? Or killed someone? Isn't it better that way, so they can't harm anyone else?"

"There is something to be learned from every patient. The entire field of psychiatry will come to a halt if we simply overmedicate the troubled. In my spare time, I'm working on my own project, trying to figure out a way to predict whether a mental patient will be docile or dangerous when they're committed to an institution like Creedmoor."

She leaned forward. This was what she was looking for; this was why she'd come. "How do you do that?"

"I do an interview with each new patient. Ask them specific questions about their past and their current state of mind, then six months later, I compare their behavior to their answers, see if I can come up with a pattern. I call it 'profiling.'"

Profiling. That was exactly what was needed when it came to the bomber. He had certain patterns, and maybe the police could identify him that way. "Your bosses must be quite pleased with this project. It sounds unique. And important." She hoped she wasn't putting it on too thick.

"They think I'm as crazy as my patients."

Not exactly what she wanted to hear. "Are you able to find any patterns?"

He pushed the sleeves of his doctor's coat back, revealing his forearms, his skin pale. "Miss Brooks?"

Marion looked up, embarrassed that he'd caught her staring. "Yes?"

"You've been asking me questions since you arrived, but I still have no idea why you're here."

"Right. You're probably wondering."

"I am. And I'm afraid I don't have much more time. I have rounds at eleven."

How much to tell him? She didn't want to have to deal with his pity. "Of course, sorry. I need your help in identifying the Big Apple Bomber."

Peter let out a sharp laugh. "Wow. Not the answer I expected. I figured you had a relative you thought needed to be committed, which is usually why anyone takes the time to come all the way out here in person."

She shook her head. "No. Did you hear about the latest bombing?"

"I know something happened a week or so ago, but it was while I was doing a forty-eight-hour shift and I haven't had time to catch up on the news."

"He hit Radio City. It's the third time he's done so."

That caught his attention. "I'm so sorry. Were you there?"

"I was." She blinked away the horrific image of her sister and the screaming girl. "The Rockettes were onstage when the bomb went off. The police are stymied, and it's been sixteen years, which is more than long enough for this man to terrorize the city. I thought you might be able to help."

He looked at her like she was nuts, which really made perfect sense. She was a Rockette, kicking and dancing for her weekly wage. Not the typical pursuer of sociopaths.

She continued. "When you were at the restaurant, you were able to analyze that man who was abusing the staff and put him straight. I thought you might have some insights into who this bomber is."

"Without having met him?"

"Why not? I mean, I'm sure they have notes he's left—that sort of thing—that you can look at. Maybe there's a pattern, like with the project you're doing."

He leaned forward, picked up a pen, and then put it back down. "Because it's more involved than that. What I do is science, not some parlor trick."

"That's exactly what the investigation needs: science. The police are stuck, and maybe you can help them out of it, give them some ideas to go on. You have to."

"Why?" He looked genuinely confused. "Why are you here?"

"I am here because . . ." She couldn't finish the sentence.

"Look, if the police want help with their investigation, they're going to approach a doctor with a long history in psychoanalysis, not me. Is there something else you're not telling me?"

She couldn't answer his question honestly. If she did, she'd end up bursting into tears and he'd dismiss her as some hysterical, grieving relative.

"I saw the bomber," she finally said. "That day."

He looked at her, eyes wide. "You did? Have you told the police?"

"Yes. Not that it did much good."

"What did he look like?"

"A balding man in his forties, with glasses, wearing a trench coat and carrying a black leather briefcase." She was pleased with how many details she'd come up with.

But Peter didn't seem impressed at all. He sat back in his chair. "That describes thousands of men in the city."

"That's what the police said."

"And they're right." He checked his watch. "I'm sure you are very upset by what happened. It must've been quite frightening. But it's not your job to figure out who the Big Apple Bomber is. You stick with what you do best, and let the police do their job."

His patronizing tone sent her over the edge; her entire body sizzled with rage. "Just because I dance doesn't mean I'm an idiot."

"I didn't say that, not at all."

"I'm a citizen of this city, as you are, and my taxes help pay for the police. If they can't figure out who this guy is, after sixteen years, then maybe they should be looking outside the box. I plan on making them do that. There cannot be another death. There simply cannot."

He put his hands up. "I didn't know there was a death. I thought most of these bombs didn't go off, or if they did, the injuries were slight."

"That's not true. And furthermore, I resent you telling me what I can and cannot do with my life."

He sat back, a stunned look on his face. "I apologize."

If he only knew. But at least he was listening to her again.

"That's why I thought you might be able to help, with your profiling." But the words sounded ridiculous, even to her own ears. Maybe he was right, and she was flailing around, trying to fix something that was completely unfixable.

She'd come all this way for nothing.

He checked his watch again. "Thanks for coming by. I-I'll think about it, all right?"

But she knew he was lying.

※

Marion lay on her bed at the Rehearsal Club, staring up at the ceiling, lost in a black fog of hopelessness. Yesterday after she'd talked with Peter, she'd headed to Radio City to rejoin the troupe. While initially the other Rockettes had fussed over her, after the first of four shows that day it was back to business, which in many ways was a huge relief. When she was onstage, she focused on the steps and on her technique and avoided looking at the section of the audience where Judy had last been. The seats had been quickly replaced, eradicating any signs of violence. In between shows she mainly kept to herself, heading up to the roof bundled in a coat and reading in one of the faded Adirondack chairs.

Down in the front parlor, the girls were doing things that normal girls did: waiting for dates, practicing lines together, playing checkers near the fireplace. Marion was no longer a normal girl. In fact, ever since Marion had taken the job at Radio City, her life had been upended. And she'd done it all to herself. Cast off her father, put her sister in terrible jeopardy, and invited tragedy into their small family, which had seen enough pain already.

"Marion?" Bunny called to her from where she stood by the telephone, holding the receiver over her shoulder. "There's a call for you."

Marion shook her head. "No phone calls. It's probably another stupid reporter."

"It's not. It's Peter Griggs."

Marion took the receiver from Bunny and lifted it to her ear. "This is Marion."

"Marion, it's Peter."

She waited.

"I didn't know. I'm so sorry. I did some research, and it was your sister who was killed, wasn't it?"

"Yes. Her name was Judy."

"Why didn't you tell me when we met? I came off like an ass. I'm sorry."

"I wanted you to take my request seriously. Not as a grieving sister."

"I will, if you like."

"What do you mean?"

"I'll offer to help with the investigation."

"You will?"

"Keep in mind I'm only a resident, so I doubt they'll even give me the time of day. But I think you're onto something. If there's a way to figure out the kind of man the bomber is, I would like to help."

The gloom that had surrounded Marion lifted a little. She had Peter on her side, and maybe that would make a difference. "That's great."

"But again, there's no reason why they'd bother to listen to me. I have no credentials, other than a medical degree."

"I'll figure that part out." Marion paused. "I may have a way in."

CHAPTER EIGHTEEN

Marion paced outside police headquarters. She had very little time to spare if she was going to make it back up to Radio City for her eleven-o'clock call. She imagined that Peter was the type of person for whom punctuality was important, but maybe he'd changed his mind and wouldn't show up after all.

"Marion."

She turned to see a tall, baby-faced man in a police uniform approaching. He had the same dimple in the middle of his chin as his mother, Mrs. Hornsby, and Marion smiled with relief that he'd come. He held out his arms and she ran into them, not minding as the cold metal of his badge pressed against her cheek.

"Tommy. You're so kind to do this."

"You know I'm a momma's boy deep down. If she told me to jump off a bridge, I'd have to do it, so meeting you downtown's a breeze."

After Marion had hung up from her call with Peter, she'd rung the house in Bronxville, knowing her father would be at work. When Mrs. Hornsby answered, Marion had asked her to reach out to her son. Tommy came from a long line of cops that went all the way back to his great-grandfather, and he had been on the police force for over twenty years. Marion hoped that legacy might be able to smooth the way that day.

"Thanks, Tommy. I wouldn't have bothered you if it wasn't important."

"I'm sorry about your sister. I was at the funeral, but there were so many people, I didn't get a chance to offer my condolences in person." Unlike Marion's father, who'd toned down his accent, Tommy spoke like a true born-and-bred New Yorker.

"It's okay, I saw you there, and I'm so glad you—and your mom— have been there for my father."

"Of course. Now, what do you need from me?"

Marion explained about Peter's offer to help with the investigation. "He's got a gift with this sort of thing; I saw it myself. I need to get him in there to meet with the detectives."

Tommy cocked his head. "Why don't you make an appointment yourself? You don't need me to make introductions."

"I tried that already. They figure I'm some crazy grieving relative and refuse to take me seriously."

His expression was guarded. "What do you want me to do exactly?"

"Get me in there, with Peter—I mean, Dr. Griggs—and we'll take it from there."

"What are the cops' names?"

"It's a Detective Ogden and a Captain Somers."

"Yikes. You gotta realize I'm just a beat cop. They outrank me and may not respond well to any meddling on my part."

Marion's heart sank. "I'm sorry. I don't want to get you into any trouble. I was only hoping . . ." She trailed off.

"I'll do it, don't worry your head about that. But I can't promise anything."

"Of course. I can't thank you enough." Out of the corner of her eye she caught sight of Peter loping along the sidewalk. Without his white doctor's coat, he looked very young and very uncertain, almost bumping into a young woman because he was too busy staring up at the grand copper dome of headquarters.

Tommy turned to see what she was looking at. "Is that him?"

"It is."

"Huh. Okay."

Marion made the introductions, restraining herself from reaching up and straightening Peter's tie. "Tommy—I mean Officer Hornsby—is a dear friend of the family," she said to Peter.

"I'd do anything for the Brooks family," said Tommy as he shook Peter's hand. "They've taken good care of my mother all these years."

"More like she's taken good care of us," said Marion.

"No, your pop has done more for my family than you'll ever know. He's a stand-up guy, your dad. You ready to storm the battlements?"

Peter looked a little woozy at the idea, his lips red against his pale skin. Maybe this was a total mistake. But it was the only thing she could think of. It had to work.

Tommy led the way into the building and up to the third floor.

Ogden and Somers were standing right outside Somers's office, coffee cups in hand, deep in conversation.

Tommy headed straight to them, and they both smiled widely at first, but then caught sight of Marion and exchanged a quick glance.

"Tommy, shouldn't you be out finding pickpockets or whatever you do these days?" said Somers. Even though he was teasing, there was a warmth in his voice. Everyone loved Tommy.

"I've caught them all, if you can believe it."

"I certainly can. Nice to see you downtown. And I see you have an entourage this morning."

Tommy stood tall. "That's right. Can I have a minute of your time?"

Somers gestured for him to come into his office, and Tommy indicated that Marion and Peter should wait outside. The door didn't close completely behind them, so Tommy's words carried out into the hallway.

"I know you've already met Marion Brooks," said Tommy. "She's like family to me. I was hoping you could give her a little more of your time although I know you have your hands full. Can you do that for me?"

A moment later, Tommy came out and pointed with his thumb back to where Somers and Ogden waited. "They're all yours. I love ya, kid. Reach out if there's anything else I can do."

"Thank you, Tommy." She squeezed his arm and headed in. "I owe you one."

She and Peter entered, and each took a seat opposite the desk. Ogden stood near the windowsill, a coffee cup in one hand.

"It's good to see you, Miss Brooks," said Somers, leaning back in his chair. "And I see you brought a friend."

"That's right. You're kind to see us."

"I assume this is the shrink you were talking about last week?"

"I'm a resident doctor at Creedmoor, in Queens," interjected Peter.

"You look like you recently graduated from high school, if you don't mind me saying," said Somers.

"I'm in the second year of my residency."

"Right."

This wasn't off to a great start. "He went to Harvard," added Marion. "He's been profiling people who are insane, and I really think he could help us figure out who the Big Apple Bomber is."

"Profiling?" asked Somers. "What's that?" At least he hadn't dismissed them outright.

Peter cleared his throat. "I ask patients questions about their past, their upbringing, what sort of experiences were seminal in their childhoods and early adulthood. At Creedmoor I have access to thousands of patients—"

"Six thousand," interrupted Marion.

"Six thousand. So yes, I'm able to compare patterns. From that, I can tell to a fairly accurate degree whether a patient will be a danger to others during his stay at Creedmoor, or if he can be provided certain freedoms. I try to predict how someone who's mentally unfit might react to a certain situation, like a conflict with his doctor or an argument with another patient. Whether he'll lash out in anger or not."

"Well, I can tell you right now that our guy likes to lash out in anger," said Ogden. "Case closed."

"But it's not closed, is it?" Peter's sudden assertiveness surprised Marion. "You have a physical description, which is vague from what I understand. While I'm not promising anything, I might be able to give you an emotional description, a personality road map of someone who is capable of this distinct type of violent behavior."

Ogden finished his coffee and tossed the paper cup in the garbage. "And what would we do with that, exactly? We work with facts. Concrete facts. What you're describing is theoretical, and that's why police work and psychiatry don't mix. Never been done before. Never gonna happen. Can you imagine, bringing in a shrink?" He looked over at Somers, who was leaning forward, elbows on his desk, staring at Peter.

"Maybe that's why it's been sixteen years and you still don't have your man," said Marion. "Perhaps it's time to consider a different tactic."

"Wait a minute." Somers held out one hand. "What is it exactly that you would want from us?" he asked Peter.

"Let me see the police file. Also, any letters he's written. Whatever you have, really."

"That is confidential information," said Somers. "No one except the police are privy. The top brass don't want it going public."

Even though Marion felt strongly that going public was the exact right thing to do after sixteen futile years, this wasn't the time to fight that fight.

"We understand," she said. "Captain Somers, do you have a sister?"

He gave the slightest nod.

"If something happened to her, wouldn't you do everything you could to find out who hurt her?"

He didn't have to answer; the grave look on his face said it all.

"What do you have to lose?" she continued. "If Dr. Griggs can help, that's great. If not, you haven't lost any ground."

"If it weren't for Tommy, I wouldn't even consider this," said Somers. It was obvious he was teetering right on the edge of a decision.

Marion didn't dare stir.

Finally, Somers sighed. "Fine. We'll give you an hour." He looked up at Ogden. "Show him the files."

"What about her?" Ogden pointed his thumb in Marion's direction.

"I'm not going anywhere," said Marion. "It was my idea in the first place, remember?"

"You can stay, but only he gets to look at the files," said Somers. "Okay?"

Marion looked at the clock. Nine A.M. There wasn't much time if she was going to make it to Radio City by eleven.

But they were in.

※

They were shown to a large table outside Somers's office, where the clatter of typewriters and the shriek of ringing phones echoed off the walls. Peter took out a pad of paper and a pen from his briefcase and set them down, lined up perfectly parallel with each other, then cleared his throat.

"I've never done this before. We may be in over our heads."

"It'll be fine," Marion answered. "I'm right here with you."

Ogden showed up, pushing a cart filled with files and photographs. He lifted them out and unceremoniously dumped them on the table.

"Miss Brooks, you can sit over there." He pointed to a chair against a wall.

Marion moved to her appointed seat and nodded demurely. "Thank you, Detective Ogden."

For the next hour, she watched as Peter worked his way through photographs, police files, and what seemed to be letters that the bomber had sent. It was unbearable being so close to the evidence on hand and unable to look at it, but she knew if she scooted her chair closer to Peter, which she was tempted to do, Ogden would toss them both out. The thought of coming across any crime scene photos also kept her glued to her chair. She didn't need to see those.

Peter stayed focused on the evidence, writing something down on his notepad every so often as Marion watched the clock tick on. She didn't want to have to leave and miss whatever Peter said to the detectives.

At one point, all the policemen in the room, including Ogden, were called away for some kind of meeting. Marion slid her chair a little closer.

"Anything yet?" she whispered to Peter.

He looked up in surprise, as if he'd forgotten where he was. "Maybe. It's fascinating, for sure. He's mailed out a number of letters, to Met Power, to the newspapers, to the police. The guy's a regular pen pal."

"There's something to work with?"

"I think there is. Over the years he's become more and more angry. The letters become more taunting, the threats escalate. They have to catch this guy, and fast." He turned to meet her eyes. "Of course, it's too late for that, for you. I'm sorry."

"I want him caught before he kills someone else."

The sound of the policemen returning drove Marion back to her appointed spot.

At ten o'clock exactly, Ogden gestured for them to follow him back to Somers's office. Peter closed his notepad and pushed back his chair. "I'm ready."

They knocked on Somers's door and entered, Ogden trailing close behind. This time Peter stood at the window while she and Ogden took the seats. Somers sat back in his chair, arms crossed. "So. What did you discover, Dr. Griggs?"

"As I mentioned before, usually a psychiatrist studies the patient and then predicts the behavior. In this case, I'm working backward, examining the behavior and then trying to figure out what type of person would act this way, looking at all the factors that come into play with this kind of unstable conduct. I tried to use that to determine his identity. Reverse psychology, if you will."

So far, so good. Both policemen were listening closely, and even the sarcastic look on Ogden's face was smoothed over, replaced with interest.

"Determine his identity?" asked Somers.

"Not anything as specific as his name, but other factors that aren't insignificant, like his race, what kind of work he might do. Keep in mind, to this guy, his behavior makes perfect sense. He sees the world with a warped point of view, and if I can get into his head, I can figure out what sort of man might see the world that way. The letters are very helpful, in that regard. The early ones are typed, the later ones handwritten. That handwriting will help identify him, eventually. He's becoming bolder, but also possibly more likely to make a mistake."

"That's pretty obvious, even to us, Dr. Griggs," said Ogden. "That's the best you can do?"

"My diagnosis is your bomber is a paranoid schizophrenic. He might hear voices that aren't real, and he can hold a grudge for years, if necessary."

"So we're looking for someone who talks to himself?" Ogden said. "Again, that's half the city, right, Captain?"

"Let him finish," said Somers.

Peter took a deep breath. "Most paranoid schizophrenics don't develop their illness until after age thirty, so your guy, if he's been at this for sixteen years, is probably in his mid-forties or early fifties. They also tend to be neither fat nor skinny, in my experience, so he's of medium build. The phrases he uses in his letters are not quite American. *Dastardly deeds*, for example, or writing *The Metropolitan Power Company* when anyone in New York would refer to the company as *Met Power*. He's been mailing the letters from multiple locations in Westchester, which leads me to believe he lives just beyond that county, in southwest Connecticut, say, and mails them on his way into the city. That area has a lot of industrial towns where Slav immigrants settled, which indicates he's a Slav, and probably Roman Catholic."

"A Slav?" said Somers. "That's a pretty big leap."

"He used a knife to insert the bomb into the seat when he could have just placed it underneath. The fact that he utilizes both bombs and knives adds to my case. Both are very Slavic in terms of weaponry."

"You learn that at medical school?" said Ogden.

"I studied European history at Harvard." Peter flipped the page on his notepad and continued, as if that answered the question. "In general, paranoid schizophrenics are fastidious, so he probably presents very well, neatly dressed, closely shaved, takes care with his appearance but nothing too flashy. The block lettering in his correspondence is impeccable, which suggests he's a perfectionist. Because of this, he probably has problems with authority and hasn't been able to hold down any job for very long. He isn't rich, by any means, probably even struggling to pay the bills, but you wouldn't know it by looking at him."

Somers interrupted. "He signs the letters *F.P.* Do you think those are his initials?"

"No. I'm sure those initials have some kind of meaning to him, something that makes him feel superior to us. He wouldn't use his own name or initials. He's too smart for that. As for his childhood, I would venture to say that an Oedipus complex turned him against his father as a child. He hasn't had many, if any, sexual relationships and probably lives with a female relative. A sister, or an aunt, perhaps. Unfortunately, paranoid schizophrenics, because they're so outwardly normal seeming, are the hardest to catch in a case like this. He's unlikely to make any mistakes, he's too fastidious for that, and his egotism is fed by the fact that he hasn't been caught yet. Which makes him even more destructive. It's a terrible cycle that will only be stopped when he's apprehended."

It was like watching the conductor of an orchestra, the way Peter was presenting his case. Marion listened raptly, awed by his specificity and his passionate delivery.

"Something bad happened to him, probably while he was working at Met Power, which I strongly believe he did at one time or another. My guess is he was an excellent employee—never late to work, meticulous at his job—and then was snubbed or disregarded in some way and it snowballed into a vicious grudge. Some kind of injustice turned him into this monster, feeding his paranoid beliefs. He feels morally superior to everyone around him and has a desperate desire to be praised for his intelligence."

Marion sat back in her chair, stunned. This was beyond what she'd imagined Peter might do. The very specifics of his analysis were undeniably helpful in the case. The bomber's religion, where he lived. The fact that he'd worked for Met Power.

Somers and Ogden exchanged a look.

"Anything else?" asked Somers.

"Yes. This is more of a conjecture, but my guess is when you arrest him, he'll be wearing a double-breasted suit. And it will be buttoned."

Ogden let out a sharp laugh. "Oh man, that's a good one. Right, Captain?"

Somers rose to his feet. "Well, thank you, Dr. Griggs, for your time. We'll take it from here."

Peter looked back and forth between the two men. "Do you want my notes? I can type them up for you."

"That's fine. We'll reach out if we need further information."

Marion stood as well. "Are you not going to use this information? I mean, Dr. Griggs has pretty much handed you the guy on a platter."

"Right," said Somers. "In his forties or fifties, nice dresser, foreigner, hates his father, in love with his mother. I've heard enough about this psychoanalysis mumbo jumbo from my wife." Somers looked over at Ogden. "Did you know she goes three times a week? Costs me a fortune."

Peter closed his notebook and jammed it into his briefcase, his cheeks flushed red. "Fine. Good luck with the case."

How could he give up so easily when what he'd said was brilliant?

"That's it, then?" Marion said to the policemen, her cheeks burning with fury.

"That's it," answered Somers. "We're very sorry for everything you've gone through, Miss Brooks, truly. But we'll take it from here. Thanks for coming by."

Peter barged out of the office headfirst, shoulders curved, as if he were fighting a headwind. Marion followed but couldn't help overhearing Ogden addressing his superior on her way out.

"Guess we should start rounding up all the guys in double-breasted suits, right, Captain?"

The door closed before she could hear his reply.

※

"Well, that was a disaster."

Peter's fists were clenched. He and Marion stood on the sidewalk outside police headquarters as pedestrians hurried by, serving as a reminder to Marion that she only had a half hour to get uptown.

"What you came up with was marvelous," she said. "They're idiots for not taking it seriously."

"They laughed me out of the room. To be honest, I don't get much more respect at Creedmoor for my supposedly 'radical' ideas."

This morning had eroded Peter's confidence in himself, and Marion hated that she'd been the cause. Especially when what he said had made so much sense.

"I can't thank you enough for coming down here and trying."

Peter ran a hand through his hair so that his curls stood up on end. "Maybe they're right."

"About what?"

"We're out of our league. You should be off dancing, I should be handing out sedatives to mental patients."

She resented being reduced to her occupation. "I can't help but take the opposite tack. Especially now that we know the extent of the ineptitude of the men running the investigation."

"Well, I think we're done here. They had absolutely no interest in what I had to say."

Marion couldn't stop now, not when they had learned so much about the bomber from Peter's analysis. But she'd need him by her side. "There's more we can do."

"Like what?"

"I'll talk to Tommy and we'll approach their supervisors. We'll go to the chief of police if we have to. Or even the press."

"I'm sorry for your loss, I really am. But these guys couldn't care less about my approach. And they'll never be convinced otherwise. Look, I've got to go."

Tears pricked Marion's eyes as Peter disappeared into the crowd. She'd lost her mother and sister, alienated her father, and now the one person who could help find the bomber resented her. It was as if she'd internalized the idea that people would find her disappointing and abandon her and then made it happen in real life.

She was thinking like a psychiatrist, she realized. Peter's words had seeped into her brain and now she was thinking like he did.

Which only further proved to her what an expert he was, even if the idiots at police headquarters didn't feel the same.

CHAPTER NINETEEN

Marion wiped off the last of her eye makeup and tossed the cotton ball on her dressing table. Without the heavy liner and the bright-red lipstick, her face was wan in the harsh light. Her feet ached and her shoulders were stiff. The next day couldn't come fast enough.

"What are you doing for your week off?" asked Bunny, pulling the bobby pins from her hair.

"I'm planning on crawling into bed and not coming out until next week's call time."

Bunny slid off her character shoes. "My feet are killing me. But Dale wants to go out dancing tonight. Can you believe it?"

Dale was still in the picture, and Marion knew better than to ask if he was still married. Of course he was. Bunny wasn't the only Rockette who'd taken up with a "patron," if Marion could call him that, and while at first she hadn't been able to understand it, her views had softened over time. A couple of days earlier, when they were both lying in the darkness of their bedroom at the Rehearsal Club, Bunny had confessed that until she'd turned sixteen, she'd been a skinny thing, all pointy elbows and knobby knees, ignored by the boys at her school and mocked by the girls, which made her desperate for atten- tion. "I find myself drawn to bad boys," she'd admitted.

Peter had figured that out right off, probably, the psychological model that explained why Dale and Bunny were attracted to each other. Marion still felt terrible for getting him involved with the police and letting them humiliate him. She wished there was a way to make it right. She'd tried calling him soon after last week's disastrous meeting with the police, but the secretary at Creedmoor had taken a message and he'd never called back.

Bunny gently elbowed Marion. "You should come with us. It's a new club downtown."

"That's fine. I'll take a rain check."

"You haven't been anywhere other than the theater or the Rehearsal Club all this week. I know it's been less than a month since Judy passed away, but it's okay to live your life. I hate to see you punishing yourself like this."

"I simply don't have the energy. Sorry, Bunny." She was in a slump for sure, but she was still showing up to work on time and getting through four shows a day while grieving her sister. There was no energy for anything else. She'd talked to her father a few times on the phone, and each time he'd asked her to move home. Each time, she'd refused. They were at an impasse.

"Marion, Russell wants to see you when you're done here." Emily jangled her bracelets as she passed by.

Marion looked over at Bunny, who shrugged. "He probably wants to check on you, see how you're holding up."

Marion pulled on her street clothes and walked to Russell's office, where every inch of wall space was covered with press photos of the Rockettes taken through the years, performing for the troops during World War II, at the New York World's Fair in 1939, winning the grand prize at the 1937 Paris Exposition. Russell came around from his desk and gave her a hug the moment she was in the door.

"How are you doing, Marion?" he asked.

"I'm fine."

"Are you sure?"

He held her by the shoulders. The concern Marion saw in his eyes almost made her burst into tears, but she couldn't do that, it wouldn't be professional. "Yes, I'm doing okay." She waited, but he didn't respond right away. "Is something wrong?"

He gestured for her to take a seat. "I'm wondering if we should have insisted you take more time off, after what happened."

"It was my decision to come back, I wanted to come back. I want to dance." She didn't mention that she had to dance if she wanted to continue supporting herself, to afford her room and board at the Rehearsal Club.

"We're worried about you. I don't blame you, after what you experienced. But it appears that you're struggling to fit in with the rest of the dancers onstage. I hate having to say this—I feel awful—but Mr. Leonidoff asked me to talk to you, and I promised I would."

"Okay." She felt queasy. Mr. Leonidoff tended to let Russell handle the day-to-day business of the Rockettes. The fact that he was the impetus behind this conversation didn't bode well.

"Sometimes new Rockettes have a hard time adjusting to the role. The restrictions of this style of dance can feel stifling for some. You're a terrific dancer, don't get me wrong, but there are times you stand out from the crowd. I think you know what I'm talking about."

"I know I'm getting more notes than any of the other dancers. I'm sorry for letting you down. I want to be better, I do."

If she lost this job, she'd have to completely start over: find an agent who would send her out on auditions, try to please producers and casting directors. She'd seen enough of her fellow residents at the Rehearsal Club go through the cycle of audition and rejection to know that it took serious resilience to tread the boards of Broadway. There was no way she'd be up to it right now.

Or, of course, she could take the easy way out and move home, agree to marry Nathaniel. But the image of Lucille's stash of boxes in the attic was never far from Marion's thoughts: Lucille, who'd been so eager to have a career in the theater and then had to give it all up. Marion was forging ahead as a way of carrying on Lucille's legacy, and most of the time that made all the heartache worthwhile.

"I'm sorry, Russell. I hate to disappoint you, and I promise I'll pull it together. I have a week off, so that will give me more than enough time to refocus and tighten up my dancing. Please, give me another chance."

Russell smiled. "Of course, my dear. Go home and rest, and I'll see you in a week. I want to make sure we're not pushing you too fast, that's all."

"I truly appreciate it. And I won't disappoint you."

The theater was practically empty by the time she made it to the stage door; the security guard gave her a nod as she passed by. Outside, the air was cold and a few flurries skittered under the streetlights.

"Marion."

She turned to see Peter leaning against the building a few feet away. He wore a navy peacoat and a woolen cap over his head, and some of his curls peeked out from the sides. His eyes were blue and bright; he looked like some handsome sailor who'd just arrived in town. Something about him was different, and it took her a moment to realize it was because he was smiling. Usually, he was such a serious man.

"What are you doing here?"

"I got a call today. Somers wants to see me again, first thing tomorrow."

"Why? What's happened?" She shivered and pulled her scarf closer around her neck.

"It's cold out here. What do you say we grab a bite? I haven't had a chance to eat all day and I'm starved."

They crossed the street to Moriarty's and took a seat in one of the booths. The place was empty this late, and quiet.

He ordered a hamburger and she did the same, unable to bear the thought of looking at a menu and deciding what she wanted. Food had become unappealing recently, and between doing over six hundred kicks a day and not eating much, she worried she was losing her muscle tone.

"How are you doing?" Peter asked, placing his napkin on his lap.

"I'm fine. I guess. What do the police want?"

"Well, unfortunately, there was another bombing today."

She felt the blood drain from her face. "Where?"

"The Paramount Theatre."

The Paramount, located in Times Square, showed films as well as live music events, much like Radio City. "Was anyone hurt?"

"Somers said no. But he didn't say more than that, other than the fact that he wants me downtown at nine tomorrow morning and asked me to bring my notes. I told him you had to come as well and he agreed."

"Why?"

"I knew you'd want to be there. I think they've realized we are onto something."

That was the best news she'd heard in a long time. Maybe they were finally making headway, and her idea of dragging Peter into the investigation hadn't been as crazy as everyone else made it seem. "That's kind of you. I do want to be there."

"Also, I wanted to apologize for the way I behaved the last time I saw you."

"You were frustrated, I understand that."

"I shouldn't have taken it out on you."

"I appreciate that. And it's fine, really. We're all under a lot of stress."

The waiter came by with a glass of wine for Marion and a beer for Peter.

"I find I'm doing a lot of apologizing to you these days," Peter said, after the waiter left. "I'm sorry for that."

"There you go again."

They both laughed.

Marion picked up her glass. "I felt terrible about pulling you into the case in the first place. Let's say right now we both apologize for everything that's happened, as well as everything that might possibly happen, and move on. Sound good?"

He lifted his beer. "In that case, my deepest apologies."

"I humbly beg your forgiveness as well."

Laughing, they clinked glasses.

Marion took a sip of her wine. "Did you grow up around here?"

"My family's from Vermont. Small town, quiet. My dad drives a truck, my mom was a housewife."

She noticed he used the past tense in describing his mother, but she didn't want to pry, as they were just getting to know each other. "And you ended up at Harvard, and a doctor."

"I had a high school teacher who told me I was smart enough to apply, which I have to say surprised me at the time. I'd never known anyone who went to Harvard."

"Have you always been interested in psychiatry?"

"Not at all. I figured I'd major in history and go to law school or something like that. But then my mother got sick."

"Oh, no, I'm sorry to hear it."

"Not sick physically."

Marion waited for him to explain.

"When I was a sophomore, I got a call from my father saying that my mom had been found screaming in the grocery store that she was being followed, that someone was after her. She'd had a psychotic break. She was admitted to a psychiatric hospital and never made it home. She died there, killed herself."

"That's terrible. I'm so sorry, Peter."

A touch of anger had crept into his voice and his neck turned red. "I was stunned that that was the way the mind worked, that a switch could go off and change your personality and behavior so suddenly. My father was crushed, and no one in our town looked at us the same way again. We were the crazy family, not to be trusted. Keep in mind that if she'd died of cancer or a heart attack, they would've been at our doorstep in a minute with casseroles and words of comfort. Not for a mental illness, unfortunately."

Marion thought of the outpouring at Judy's funeral. He had a point. "It must've been awful."

"She was a good mom. Not openly affectionate, not one to offer up a hug or even a pat on the head, but she made sure I was fed and warm." He paused. "As a kid, I had a horse named Rusty, who was pretty much my best friend growing up. When Rusty came down with colic one freezing winter night, my mother walked him around and around for hours until the emergency had passed. She knew I'd have been devastated if something had happened to him." He paused and looked up at Marion. "Sorry. I haven't talked about it in a while."

"Remember, no more apologies. And I understand. As I mentioned when we talked in the Roxy apartment, you were correct in your analysis of me. I did lose my mother, when I was seven. We have that in common."

"I was rude to bring that up without any warning."

"I appreciate that you walked it back so fast. But I've been wondering ever since, how did you know?"

"The way you looked to Bunny for guidance. You tended to echo what she was doing, which made me think you hadn't had a female role model growing up." He paused. "How did it happen?"

"She went up to Boston to take care of a sick friend. She was always doing things like that, baking muffins for the family down the block who'd just had a baby or sitting with someone's grandparent who was ailing. My sister and I didn't think twice about it, just carried on with our lives. Then one morning our dad sat us down and said that she'd been killed the night before. A driver hadn't seen her as she was crossing the street."

They stared at each other a moment without talking, members of the same tragic club.

Their food came, and Marion welcomed the interruption, the bustle of setting down plates and refilling water glasses. Enough talk of the past.

For once Marion was hungry. She had to consciously slow down in order to not inhale the burger too quickly.

"When did you decide to study premed?" asked Marion in between bites.

"After my sophomore year. I wanted to see if I could help people who had the same kinds of illnesses as my mother."

"And do you find you're able to do that?" She was fairly certain she already knew the answer.

"Not at the moment, no. Not at Creedmoor. There, it's all about medicating patients."

"Would that have worked for your mom?" she asked, wiping her hands on her napkin.

"It might have helped. At least she would have stabilized, but it shouldn't be a long-term solution."

Marion had been so young when her mother died that she hadn't understood exactly what was happening. For weeks after, she expected Lucille to be waiting for her at home after school. Peter had been older, but that hadn't made the loss any easier. "What do you want to do after your residency is over?"

He let out a long breath. "There's so much. I'd like to research and eventually publish articles about the role of mental illness in people who are considered indigent. Eventually I'd like to have my own practice, working with patients who are difficult to treat, like narcissists and sociopaths."

"Like Captain Somers's wife, who goes for psychoanalysis three times a week?"

Peter laughed. "That's not my kind of patient, I'm afraid. Although that is where the money is these days."

"You're going to do bigger things than analyze unhappy wives," said Marion. "I'm sure of it."

Their reception at police headquarters was quite different this time around. Ogden showed them to a large conference room, where Somers sat at the head of the table, surrounded by a dozen men in a mix of plain clothes and uniform. Peter was directed to sit at the opposite end of the table, and Marion took the chair to his right.

"Can we get you anything? Coffee?" asked Somers.

They both declined, eager to find out what was going on.

"Like I said on the phone last night, there was an attempted bombing at the Paramount Theatre yesterday," said Somers.

Marion had read about it in the newspaper this morning. As Peter had mentioned, no one had been injured or killed, thank goodness. The pipe bomb had been discovered before it exploded, and the bomb squad had taken it away in a special wagon called Big Bertha, which was basically a flatbed truck covered by a steel enclosure. A photo of the truck heading down Broadway, trailed by police cruisers, had appeared next to the article.

Somers continued. "I was wondering if Dr. Griggs could repeat what he hypothesized after examining the evidence last week."

Peter did so, and Marion couldn't help but notice the change in response as compared to their previous meeting. All the men took notes, including Somers, and no one interrupted with snarky comments. Peter summed up by stressing the importance of looking into any disgruntled former employees of Met Power who fit his description. "He would have worked there in the 1930s. That's where you're going to find him, I'm sure of it."

Ogden spoke up. "We've been through all the files they have, but they only date from 1940 on."

"Nothing earlier?" asked the chief.

"Afraid not."

"We need to go through the ones they do have again, then," said Somers. "Any other questions?"

Marion thought of her father and all the work that was headed his way once more. How frustrating it must be to not be able to provide an answer.

"I have a question," said Peter. "What exactly happened that made you decide to bring me back in?"

Marion was shocked at his audacity, although she had to admit she'd wondered the very same thing.

"The latest bomb was discovered by an usher who was sweeping up in between shows," answered Somers. "A pipe bomb was found partly sticking out of a seat. Luckily, the usher remembered the man who'd sat nearby during the previous showing of the film. He was alone, wearing a trench coat with glasses and carrying a black briefcase."

A perfect match to Marion's description.

"It turns out the usher is Slav, and he recognized a similar accent when he took the man's ticket in the lobby. He asked where he was from and the man lied, said he was German. That stood out in the usher's mind when he was questioned by the police."

Peter had been right. Marion wanted to raise her arms in the air in victory but stayed mum as the men peppered him with more questions. Eventually, Somers motioned to Marion. "We have a police sketch of the guy, from the usher's memory. Would you take a look at it, Miss Brooks?"

Marion was tempted to ask why they hadn't bothered doing a police sketch three weeks ago, after the Radio City bombing, but she already suspected the answer. She was a woman—a dancer, no less—so her recollection was valued less than a man's.

Ogden carried the sketch to where she was sitting, and she gave him a hard look before studying it.

It was the same man she'd seen next to Judy. The same round glasses, a slightly bulbous nose, the large forehead.

"Yes," she said. "It's him."

CHAPTER TWENTY

Tavern on the Green shimmered with holiday sparkle as Marion walked in. The place was packed with a mix of tourists and New Yorkers—the former usually arriving by horse-drawn carriage after a romantic trip through Central Park, the latter slamming the doors of taxis as they sprinted inside. Located on the western edge of Central Park, the one-story brick building had been a sheepfold in the late 1800s before being converted into one of the city's toniest destinations for dinner and dancing.

It was the last place Marion would expect to see her father, but there he was, at a table not far off the dance floor, sitting with three men and their wives. She'd called the Bronxville house earlier, hoping that if she told him the latest development in the case he might begin to thaw toward her, but Mrs. Hornsby had answered the phone. She'd said that Simon was in the city at a work dinner, not expected home until late, so Marion decided to try to catch him in person.

Simon lifted his wineglass in a toast, a wide smile on his face, regaling his guests with some tale that made them all laugh, the women demurely covering their mouths as they did so. But then the orchestra returned from a break and the couples got up to dance, leaving him alone at the table. He lifted his wineglass to his lips but put it down before taking a sip, his hand shaking. He was only pretending to be part of the giddy energy in the room and it was costing him. Marion's heart broke, but instead of going to him she retreated to a seat at the bar.

A half hour later, she heard her father's raucous laugh before she saw him. She leaped off her barstool so that she was directly in his way as the party headed to the front doors. One of the men noticed her first—she recognized him as a vice president who'd been at Met Power almost as long as her father had—and called out her name.

Her father looked up in surprise. Their eyes met, and for a moment Marion froze, wondering if she'd made a terrible mistake. Would he openly snub her in front of his dinner guests? He walked over and placed his hands on her arms, leaned in to give her a kiss on the forehead. "Everyone, this is my daughter Marion."

Introductions were made, hands were shaken, and the vice president asked if she had dined there as well.

"I met a friend for a drink and was just going home," she lied. "Dad, can I have a word?"

"Of course." He said his goodbyes and shuffled the group out the front entrance, then turned back to her. "Follow me," he said.

They stepped out onto a terrace that during the summer was used for dining and dancing under the stars. The night was unseasonably warm and Marion let her coat settle loosely around her shoulders as they took seats at one of the empty tables. The lack of honking horns or general street noise made it feel as if they were out in the country, although the city skyline twinkled through the bare-branched trees.

"How are you doing?" she asked.

"I'm managing." He looked at her squarely. "And you?"

"Same."

"It's almost a month since Judy's been gone," he said. "All this time I've been rambling around in that big house, only Mrs. Hornsby for company, surrounded by the reminders of my elder daughter. Then I go to work, where her desk is still planted in front of my office door, the chair where my beloved girl worked now filled by someone else. She's everywhere."

For Marion, the only physical reminder of Judy was a photo of the two of them as girls that sat on her bedside table. Between that and her intense focus on the investigation, she'd sometimes been able to shove her mourning to the side, to push it down. It didn't hurt that she worked herself into a sweat dancing four shows a day, so that when she went to bed she fell fast asleep and didn't dream.

"I'm so sorry, Dad."

He looked over at her. "And now I feel as if I've lost you as well. You're too hard on your old man, Marion. You don't understand what it's like to have your family disappear, one by one. What if I lose you next?"

"I'm not going anywhere. But at the same time, you can't keep me safe by locking me up. Not when I'm finally finding my way in the world."

"I miss you."

Her eyes burned. "I miss you, too."

"Nathaniel comes over every few days, we have a drink together," said Simon. "He's a good man."

A better son than she was a daughter. "Listen, I've been working with the police on the case, trying to help them catch the bomber. A friend of mine who's a doctor is consulting as well."

Simon's eyes registered surprise. "A Rockette and a doctor consulting with the police? I would say that's the least likely duo to crack the mystery of the Big Apple Bomber if ever I saw one."

Her defenses rose, but she kept her voice even. "Well, the doctor is good at understanding people's motivations, figuring out what kind of person would do such a thing. And I saw the man sitting next to

Judy, so I'm helpful in that capacity. Recently, an usher from the Paramount actually spoke with the bomber, right before the last incident. The police made a sketch and ran it by me. It's definitely the same guy."

"Well, I suppose that's progress. Although I really don't like you meddling in the investigation. Not one bit."

"I'm helping, not meddling. The police are saying that they believe the bomber might have worked for Met Power in the 1930s, something about his age and when the bombings started. I thought maybe your office could help them narrow down the suspect list."

"We've given them access to all the employee files we have. Unfortunately, they only go back as far as 1940." He was trembling, even though the night air was warm and there wasn't even a hint of wind.

"Why is that?"

"There was a warehouse fire that destroyed some of the records." He shoved his hands into the pockets of his cashmere overcoat. "I'm amazed we have as many as we do, to be honest. Judy and I had been working hard to create a system where employee information could be easily accessed, but it's not easy when Met Power has been supplying electricity to New York since—"

She finished the sentence for him. "Since 1882, when they served fifty-nine customers in a square-mile area in lower Manhattan."

Simon laughed. "I guess I've said that before?"

"A few times."

"Did you know the Rockettes began in 1925 in Missouri?"

His smile vanished. "That's a new one for me."

"I love how proud you are of what you do," said Marion. "And I feel the same way about being a Rockette."

"I understand your point. But it's not safe. I've been getting all kinds of calls from reporters, from kooks, since it happened. They know who Judy was, who I am. I have no doubt they know who you are. Yet you're out there on a stage in front of thousands of people, putting yourself completely at risk."

"I'm being careful. Hopefully there will be a break in the case soon."

"I hope so, Marion. I truly do."

"And I'm sorry for everything, I'm sorry for what we're going through."

How insufficient the words were.

Marion slipped into the dining room of the Rehearsal Club right after the breakfast shift had ended and sweet-talked the cook into making her some scrambled eggs. Someone had left a *New York Times* on one of the tables, and Marion browsed the arts section while she ate, enjoying the quiet. The Rehearsal Club was rarely tranquil. Mornings were filled with the chatter of girls who worked day jobs rushing out the door, evenings with the revved-up howls of the actresses bursting with energy after taking their final bows on Broadway. It was the same at Radio City, where she was constantly surrounded by movement and sound, the high-flying energy of women who danced for thousands of people every day. The sisterhood was splendid when you were looking for a fun time, but these days Marion was more subdued, her thoughts haunted by the loss of Judy, the memories of their brief time together flashing in her brain when she least expected it. Like the fact that Judy would only eat scrambled eggs with ketchup, the sight of which always made Marion queasy.

These days, small memories, inconsequential ones, could send her into tears.

An article in the paper about the bombings pulled her back to the present. After a long list of the past incidents and a recap of the police investigation, Peter's name caught her eye:

Dr. Peter Griggs, a doctor at Creedmoor State Hospital, was enlisted to assist the police. After an extensive examination of the evidence, he reported the bomber may be "single, in his forties or fifties, may get angry when criticized, and feels superior to others. He's a skilled mechanic, unsocial but not antisocial, most likely suffering from a case of progressive paranoia, and may have worked or currently works for Met Power."

A surge of excitement ran through her. After sixteen years, the police had finally shared information with the public, which might help to bring down her sister's killer. Maybe someone out there reading Peter's profile would recognize, in the sketch or the psychological workup, the man who had terrorized the city for so long.

She finished breakfast and was heading back to her room when she noticed a single letter in her mail cubby.

The white envelope had no return address, but the postmark caught her eye: *Mt. Kisco, NY.* She opened it and gasped at the typed message inside.

To the Dancing Doll:

Tell your father that Met Power will get what's coming to it. They deserve to suffer, after what I went through.

The Big Apple Bomber

Fingers shaking, she replaced the letter back in the envelope and slipped it into the pocket of her cardigan, trying not to get any more of her fingerprints on it.

This was exactly what her father had warned her about. While she knew she should go to the police right away, first she wanted to talk to Peter.

She called his office at Creedmoor, but the secretary said Dr. Griggs wasn't in that day, that he was down at the Bowery.

"The Bowery?" asked Marion. That part of town was considered seedy and dangerous. "What does he do there?"

"Not sure. Something to do with the Salvation Army, I think."

"Is there a number I can reach him at?"

"I'm afraid not."

Marion left a message for him to call and went up to her room. She couldn't sit around and wait for him to call her back. There was no time.

She threw on a plain wool coat, put a scarf over her head, and took the subway downtown to Eighth Street. The streets were crowded, and at first Marion became panicked at the noise and crush of bodies, imagining that every man in a trench coat might be the bomber. She hurried past the handsome Italianate brownstone building that housed Cooper Union, a tuition-free college where Abraham Lincoln had once given an address. After that, her surroundings changed rapidly. The raised tracks of the Third Avenue El snaked over the street traffic, casting everything beneath them in shadow. Low tenements that lined either side were grimy and dark, the sidewalks littered with torn newspapers and broken glass.

And men. So many men. Men with hollow cheeks and thick stubble, the older ones with lips curled around toothless gums. They lay sleeping in doorways, over grates, a few lying half off the curb, oblivious to the trucks and cars whizzing within feet of their dirty, unlaced boots. Some had no coats, even in the cold weather, and the ones on the few who did were torn and filthy. She was about to give up and head back uptown when she spied the sign for the Salvation Army ahead. She'd come this far.

Inside, a man carrying a box of canned soup directed her to a large open room filled with tables, where she noticed Peter off in a corner.

He sat across from a disheveled gentleman who seemed to be ranting about something, one finger pointed at the ceiling, as Peter scribbled something in a notebook and nodded. A long counter ran along one wall, where a line of men held white ceramic bowls and patiently waited to be served the day's fare. The place was noisy and smelled of unwashed necks and cabbage, but she ventured in, ignoring the whistles and catcalls, until she was close enough to Peter to get his attention.

He looked up. The surprise in his expression was quickly replaced with concern. He excused himself from the man he was talking with and guided Marion by the elbow into a small alcove.

"What are you doing here?" he asked.

"Your secretary said you'd be here. I got a letter, and I think it's from the bomber."

"A letter? Where did he send it?"

"The Rehearsal Club. It arrived this morning. The postmark is Westchester."

"You should go to the police."

"I know. That's my next stop, but I figured you'd want to see it first."

He brought her down a hall and into a small office area, closing the door behind them.

"Do you come here every week?" Marion asked.

"I do."

"As part of your job at Creedmoor?"

"No, it's outside of that. I'm considering writing a research paper on what goes on down here and trying to get it published."

"I can't believe how many men there are like this."

"Neither could I, at first. They do what they can to make money during the day, stealing, begging, doing odd jobs, and then many of them drink themselves into oblivion at night at the flophouses."

"What a terrible life."

"They don't choose it. Many of them, I'm discovering, have some kind of mental illness like paranoia or schizophrenia and use alcohol to cope. I'm trying to figure out if there's a better way to help them besides giving them food and a bed for a night and preaching abstinence."

Peter was doing so much good in the world, while Marion wore silly costumes and tap shoes in order to earn her weekly paycheck. She thought back to Peter's recent pitch at police headquarters. When he spoke, his voice had a resonance that made Marion's stomach flip. He was smarter than pretty much anyone else in whatever room he was in, but he stayed focused on getting things accomplished, not one-upping those who'd doubted him or showing off how brilliant he was.

Marion carefully pulled out the letter from her cardigan using her gloved hand.

She laid it on the table, where Peter examined the postal code. "Mount Kisco," he said. "Halfway between the city and the towns in Connecticut where I think he must live. Consistent with the others the police have."

She pulled out the note inside, opening it up on the desk as carefully as she could without smoothing out the wrinkles.

"It's not him." Peter straightened and crossed his arms.

Marion looked up, surprised. "What? Why do you think so?"

"The real Big Apple Bomber refers to the company as *Metropolitan Power* in the other letters. And it's typed."

"But the early letters were typed as well."

"He hasn't sent a typed one in a few years. Also, the name 'Big Apple Bomber' was created by the press; it's not what he calls himself. Our guy signs his *F.P.*"

"Maybe he's embracing it these days, getting cocky."

"Maybe." But he didn't look convinced. "Still, it's alarming that this man sent it to where you live, and I don't like the dancing doll reference. The police need to know about it."

"I'll head there right now."

"And I'm coming with you."

CHAPTER TWENTY-ONE

The third floor of police headquarters was buzzing with activity when Marion and Peter arrived. Somers's office was empty, but Ogden was at his desk eating a pastrami sandwich. He reluctantly wrapped it up as they explained why they'd come.

"You were contacted by the bomber?" he asked.

"Not exactly," said Marion.

"I don't think it's him," added Peter.

"After being on the case for, what, a few days, you think you can make that call?" Ogden countered.

Marion didn't like the way this was going already. "Is Captain Somers around?"

Ogden regarded her with a glower. "No. He's out trying to put out the fire you two set off with your 'profile.' We've been slammed ever since we fed the information to the press. Everyone and their mother are calling with tips, either turning in some neighbor who kicks his dog or a co-worker who rubbed them the wrong way."

This was a man who was determined to be unhappy no matter what, it seemed. "Isn't it a good thing that you have something to work with, after sixteen years?" Marion asked.

"Define 'good.'"

Peter touched Marion on the arm. "Show him the letter."

She placed it on the table. Ogden reached into his desk and put on a pair of rubber gloves. "You got this today?"

Marion nodded.

"It's fairly obvious it's not him," repeated Peter.

Marion stopped herself from nudging Peter in the ribs. Ogden disliked them both, and tossing out his opinion before the man even had a chance to study the letter was sure to put him off.

"Why don't you think it's the Big Apple Bomber?" asked Ogden, measuring out the words.

"It's not signed *F.P.* like the others; he uses *Met Power* instead of *Metropolitan Power*. And the fact that it's typed."

"He's typed letters before." Ogden examined the postmark. "Westchester again. Well, that's consistent."

"But as I've said before, I don't think he lives in Westchester," said Peter. "He's smarter than that; he wouldn't mail the letters from where he lives."

"You can't know that for sure." Ogden sat back in his chair, arms folded. "In fact, I've already ordered our team to get handwriting samples from every Met Power employee who lives in Westchester County. They're checking driver's license applications, jury lists, pistol permits, judgments, court files. It's a huge undertaking, but we're getting close." He rose and picked up the letter from his desk. "I'm going to get this fingerprinted."

"None of the other letters had fingerprints," said Peter.

"Maybe he's getting lazy."

"Do you mind if we wait?" asked Marion. Since it was her week off from Radio City, she didn't have to worry about the time.

"Whatever suits you."

After he left, Marion turned to Peter. "I know he's a jerk, but maybe you could ease up a bit."

"Ease up? The sheer stupidity of this investigation is maddening."

"But if you push too hard he'll exclude us entirely. He's already resentful of all the tips your profile is bringing in."

"Somers seems to have a good head on his shoulders, but this Ogden is a pill. The tips are a gold mine. Why Ogden's wasting time scouring Westchester is beyond me."

"I couldn't agree more. But we need him to keep us in the loop with what's going on with the case, so for now, try not to sock him in the nose."

"Was it that obvious?"

Marion couldn't help but laugh. "Somewhat."

Eventually, Ogden returned, a triumphant smile on his face. "We got him!" he said with a shout from the far side of the room. Everyone stopped what they were doing. "This letter came today. It bears the prints of the Big Apple Bomber." He seemed to have forgotten that Marion and Peter were even there. "We're looking for a Vincent Hardenby, of Mount Kisco, New York. He's a former Met Power worker with a record—used to steal from jobsites, apparently." As he began shouting orders, the other detectives and policemen rose from their desks, ready for action.

Marion and Peter remained where they were.

"It's not him," said Peter, to no one in particular.

"Maybe it is." Marion wanted it to be. She desperately wanted this to end. For her father's sake, for the sake of the city.

"If I'm right, what do you think the real bomber will do when they announce they've made an arrest?"

"Set off another bomb, to prove them wrong," said Marion glumly. "They're desperate to catch him. Desperation makes people do stupid things. I shouldn't have brought the letter in."

"You had no choice. We'll just have to wait until they figure it out themselves." Peter surveyed the empty room. "Say, I'm starving. Do you want to get something to eat?"

Marion had no plans, and the day stretched ahead. Any diversion from the fact that the police were out hunting the wrong guy while the actual bomber continued on his merry way was welcome. "Sure thing."

"There's not much around here, in terms of restaurants," said Peter. "It's all Irish pubs for cops. But I live close by and can make us lunch there, if that's not too forward."

The Rockettes were regularly sent invitations for private dinners, usually by older men looking for something else on the side, and while some of them accepted—that was how Bunny had met Dale— most of them knew better. Of course, Peter was as far from Dale as could be, and Marion trusted him enough to know this wasn't a trick or a ruse.

She was overthinking it. He considered her a friend, as she did him. This wasn't a date; it was a police investigation.

"Are you okay?" Peter asked.

She nodded. "Of course. Lunch at your place. Lead the way."

※

Marion and Peter stepped into a freight elevator in an ugly industrial building on Crosby Street. He yanked the lever that sent it upward, pulling it back as they reached the fifth floor. It was strange to think that Peter chose to live in this dingy, seemingly abandoned ware-house, but Marion kept a smile on her face and tried not to show her discomfort as he unlocked a door at the end of a grungy hallway.

He pushed open the door and stepped back to let her inside. The glare of light threw her at first after the darkness of the hallway, but as her eyes adjusted, she looked around in wonder. The space was big and bright, with steel casement windows that extended along the en-tire street side of the building. It had bare plaster walls and the floors were clearly the original wood, which over the decades had acquired a rich patina. One corner held a large stainless steel sink, an oven, shelves with a mix of pans and dishes, and a rustic dining room table with two benches. In another corner, a screen partly hid a bed on a low platform. Near the windows sat a pair of comfy-looking leather armchairs and a deep-blue velvet sofa.

It was a far cry from Marion's cramped bedroom at the Rehearsal Club or the overdecorated house in Bronxville with its heavy drapes and knickknacks. This was a place where you could come back and find peace after a crazy day. The air felt light and pure. It was a place where you could breathe easy.

"It's marvelous," she said. "How long have you lived here?"

"Two years. An artist friend passed it on to me," said Peter. "He moved to San Francisco right as I finished med school. It's something of a hike from Creedmoor, but I won't be working there forever."

He went to the kitchen and lit the stove, then began filling up a large pot with water. From the refrigerator, he took out a jar of tomato sauce and poured it into a saucepan to heat up.

Marion sat on a stool next to the counter. "What do you want to do after Creedmoor?"

"I'm still figuring that out. First off, I need to write and publish the research paper I was telling you about."

"About mental illness among the men in the Bowery?"

"Yes."

"And you're working on that on top of what you're doing at Creedmoor?"

"Sure. I figure I should attack from all sides."

"Attack what? Or who?"

"The conventional medical approach to mental illness. That people who crack up should be locked away and sedated. Unfortunately, anyone who deviates from society's idea of sane is often blamed for being mentally ill, considered somehow morally deficient, when, in fact, I'm certain there's a physiological reason for it. Have you heard of Phineas Gage?"

Marion shook her head.

"He was a railroad construction foreman in the 1840s and had a terrible accident. An explosion drove a steel rod up from beneath his cheek, behind his eye, and then out the top of his head, obliterating the frontal lobe."

Marion avoided looking at the tomato sauce as he stirred it.

"He lived. In fact, went on to live for another twelve years, thanks to the doctor who saved him. But his personality changed drastically. Where he once was an even-keeled, decent man, after his recovery he was prone to swearing, quick to anger, and impulsive."

"Because that particular part of his brain was damaged?"

"Exactly."

"It's amazing he lived at all."

Peter added pasta to the water once it was boiling, and when it was ready, he spooned it into two bowls, followed by tomato sauce and a sprinkle of basil. Marion carried the bowls over to the dining room table. She had to move some papers to make room, and a familiar grid caught her eye.

"You do crosswords?" she asked.

He joined her at the table and nodded. "That's one I'm working on from the *Times.*"

"I do the Sunday one, but only in pencil." Marion's father worked religiously on that crossword every Sunday morning after breakfast. Marion had only taken it up since she'd started dancing as a Rockette. There was something comforting about knowing they were probably working on it at the same moment, Simon in his easy chair and Marion at her dressing table. "I always have to erase and it ends up being a mess, but so far I've been able to finish." She was quite proud of that fact.

Peter wiped his mouth with his napkin. "I actually create the puzzle, then send it to the *Times* and hope they use it. So far, they've published three of mine."

Was there anything this guy couldn't do? "You are multitalented, clearly. When do you sleep?"

"I don't need much, and there's so much work to be done."

"And here I am thinking four shows a day is tough. You're putting the rest of us to shame, you know. You're basically doing two full-time jobs as well as a side hobby."

Peter refused to meet her eyes as he twirled the pasta on his fork. The compliment had upset him in some way, which was not what she'd intended. She replayed the conversation in her head, trying to figure out what she'd said that might have offended him.

"My dad does the crossword," she said, trying to fill the space. "I'll have to tell him that I know one of the creators. He'll be very impressed."

"How is your dad doing?" asked Peter. "It must be hard, with everything that's going on."

The sudden intimacy of the question made her choke up inside. She couldn't get a read on Peter at all. The more she got to know him, the more she realized how complex he was, something of an enigma. Nathaniel had always been an open book in many ways, his life unfolding smoothly out in front of him: wife, children, a nine-to-five job. Marion couldn't picture him chopping basil in a kitchen or attempting a crossword puzzle. Or stepping foot in the Bowery.

"To be honest, I'm not sure," she said. "I think my father still blames me for Judy's death. Meanwhile, he wants me to move home and lock myself away so he doesn't lose another daughter. Part of me wants to find out who killed my sister, and another feels bad for disobeying my father." It began raining outside and the sound reminded her of her childhood, of watching from the old swing seat on the back patio as a summer rain drenched the garden. She was so tired and wanted more than anything to curl up and sleep for days.

"You're living your life. There's nothing wrong with that."

"You don't know my father."

"I get it, more than you know. My dad couldn't imagine why I'd go into this field. He hated to talk about my mom after she died, refused to discuss it. These days, we hardly talk at all, about anything."

"My father doesn't bring up my mother, either, it was always only Judy or me who would talk about her." Their shared experiences made her feel less lonely. "Do you miss your father?"

"I'm busy. I try not to think about him."

"Maybe you should reach out to him. After all this time—"

Peter interrupted. "No."

Marion sat back, stunned at the curtness of his answer. "Sorry. I didn't mean anything." But she couldn't help but think of the détente that had occurred between Judy and her before her sister died. "People can change."

"Not my father. He's the one who allowed my mother to be sent away to a place that was ill-equipped to take care of her. He didn't even visit her once."

"Right, of course. I'm sorry, I overstepped."

She stared down at a knot in the wooden table, trying to keep her composure. But it was too much, this talk of dead mothers and distant fathers. Marion burst into tears.

Peter came around to her side of the table and sat next to her on the bench. He put his arm around her shoulders as she sobbed into her napkin. "I'm sorry, Marion. It's still a tough thing for me to talk about."

"That's okay. I get it."

He pulled her close and kissed the top of her head. It was a brotherly kiss, comforting. "I shouldn't have been so short with you.

When I think about what you're going through, between your sister and your dad, that letter. What can I do to help?"

She pulled back slightly and studied him.

What can I do to help? Such a simple phrase, yet somehow Peter knew exactly the right thing to say to her at this moment. He didn't offer judgment or advice, just his presence and his solidity and his kindness of spirit. The hope that he could help her out of her pain and the reassurance that not all was lost. Marion's skin began to prickle. She felt the same way she did when a thunderstorm was looming, the electric anticipation that a powerful, unseen force would soon be making itself known.

They stayed like that, frozen, for a moment, and then at the exact same time, they leaned in and kissed and a splendid heat traveled through Marion's body. Peter's hands gently cupped either side of her face, and they kissed deeper, his breath and the taste of him sweet and tangy. Kissing Nathaniel hadn't been anything like this. Not even close. Nathaniel's approach was still that of a teenaged boy—even if he was twenty-one—eager and slightly clumsy, with a focus on his own pleasure. Peter's energy radiated out, toward Marion.

Slowly, they both drew back and Peter dropped his hands to his lap. "I'm sorry. I sh-shouldn't have done that."

That stutter again. He'd done it at the restaurant when analyzing Marion, taking back what he'd said about her mother. It meant he wasn't telling the truth, and Marion felt a frisson of satisfaction that she knew him so well. And that he actually didn't regret kissing her, even if he denied it now.

"It was nice," said Marion. "Really nice."

He raised his eyebrows, as if he was surprised to hear her say that, before scrambling to his feet. He picked the bowls up off the table, placed them in the sink, and wiped his hands on a dish towel, looking around the room, anywhere but at Marion. "I should get back to the Bowery."

Had she said or done something wrong? Maybe he didn't like the way she kissed. Maybe he regretted inviting her to lunch.

"We've both got so much going on," Peter said. "I don't want to distract you."

Marion wasn't sure what he meant by not distracting her. She didn't have much experience with men, only Nathaniel, who'd made it clear that they would be a couple from their very first date. Peter, however, seemed drawn to her one moment and then pushed her away the next. They barely knew each other, and she wasn't quite sure how she felt about him, but at the same time she couldn't get a clear read on the guy.

For the rest of the day, her lips burned with the memory of their kiss.

CHAPTER TWENTY-TWO

On the final day of her week off, Marion's father left a message for her at the Rehearsal Club, asking her to come to dinner in Bronxville that evening. She called back and breathlessly told Mrs. Hornsby she'd be there.

Simon had just needed time, and maybe now they could make some headway in repairing their relationship. It would be another chance for him to see that she was an independent woman out in the world, yet still very much his daughter. That morning, the papers had heralded the arrest of a man suspected to be the Big Apple Bomber, the same Vincent Hardenby of Mount Kisco whose fingerprints were on the letter sent to Marion. While Marion and Peter knew it wasn't the bomber, at least the creep who'd mailed it was off the streets.

Snow fell softly as Marion walked from the train station to the house. It seemed so long ago that she'd done this trek five days a week after teaching dance at the studio, when her thoughts were full of a very different future from the one she'd now made for herself. When Judy was alive and her father happy.

She felt guilty about how eager she was to get back to work at Radio City the next day. There was nothing that lifted her spirits more than dancing onstage in front of thousands of people, not to mention the camaraderie of the girls backstage. The weekly paycheck didn't hurt, either. If only this new world hadn't come at the expense of her old one.

"Your father's not back yet," said Mrs. Hornsby when Marion arrived and let herself in the front door. "I've made a meat loaf and it's in the oven; there are some peas on the stove."

Marion gave her a hug. "Thank you, I'll take it from here. You go home."

The silence of the house made Marion shiver even though it was warm enough inside. She went up to her bedroom and grabbed a cardigan that she wanted to take back to the city with her. The door to Judy's room was closed. She pushed it open and gasped. It had been completely stripped of anything to do with her sister. The old teddy bear that used to sit on the chair by the window was gone, as were the knickknacks on her bureau. The closet was bare, besides a dozen or so hangers that clanged against each other when Marion ran her hand along them. She'd considered looking for something of Judy's that she could take with her, some keepsake to have close. But it had all been swept clean.

A memory came back to her, of her father stripping the master bedroom closet of all of Lucille's clothes not long after her funeral. Marion had asked what he was doing and he'd snapped at her, which had made her run to her room and cry. She waited for him to come and comfort her, but he never did.

The sound of the front door opening startled her. Downstairs, she greeted Simon as he brushed the snow off his coat and hat.

"Mrs. Hornsby left us dinner, it'll take only a second to get it together."

She headed to the dining room to set the table, but Simon called her back. "Let's eat in the kitchen; there's no need to go to any trouble."

No doubt he didn't want to have to look at Judy's empty chair in the dining room, where they used to talk over work night after night. She hated the thought of him eating dinner alone in the kitchen while Mrs. Hornsby hovered nearby.

Marion plated the food and joined him at the small table. "Well, this is quite an improvement," she said, taking a bite of the meat loaf. "At the Rehearsal Club, we joke that it's like army rations. But luckily there's a great cafeteria at Radio City where I usually grab a bite in between shows."

Simon grunted and kept on eating.

She changed the subject. "Is Mrs. Hornsby still due to retire at the end of the year?"

"Apparently so. I suppose I should get her a gold watch or something to commemorate her years of service. That's what they do at Met Power."

"How about a nice brooch?" offered Marion. "I can help you pick it out."

"Sure. If you like."

"Who will be taking her place?"

"I'm not sure."

His hesitancy was out of character; he was being cagey for some reason. She remembered Judy talking about the secret appointments he kept during work hours. Could it be a woman friend, perhaps? Maybe he was biding his time, knowing that he'd be bringing in a new wife soon enough. But why would he have kept that a secret from her and Judy? They were both grown women and would've been pleased to hear he'd found a partner.

She asked him about his work, and he talked about new hires, issues with the board of directors, all safe topics. Not once did he ask her about her own life.

The doorbell sounded as she was washing up the last of the dishes and her father was in the living room pouring out his nightly scotch.

The rumble of hellos made her spine stiffen.

Nathaniel.

Her father had invited him, knowing she'd be here. Irritated at his presumption, she almost dropped the plate she was holding. This was supposed to be *their* night together.

The two men stood close together, each with a scotch in hand, watching the television as she entered the living room. She said hello to Nathaniel and took the chair by the fireplace, her arms crossed. On the screen, a man with a thick head of black hair and a hawkish nose was being led by uniformed policemen up the stairs of police headquarters, as the newscaster gleefully reported an arrest in the case of the Big Apple Bomber.

"Thank God," said Simon, as Nathaniel nodded. "They've got him."

Just as she and Peter had predicted, this man looked nothing like the one she'd seen at Radio City. Or the one the usher at the Paramount had described. Why weren't the police taking that into account?

She knew the answer: Because they were eager to close the case. Any criminal would do, after sixteen years.

"It's not him," said Marion.

"They seem pretty sure," said Simon. "Let's hope they put him away for life. I'd like to see to that myself."

Marion didn't bother to explain. The one silver lining was that at least the man who'd sent the threatening letter to the Rehearsal Club was now otherwise engaged.

As the evening drew on, Nathaniel and her father talked of people they knew, of the new hardware store that was opening downtown. Her father asked about Nathaniel's parents and siblings. He had so many questions for this man who wasn't even family, yet none for Marion. At the same time, this was the world she'd been brought up in, where men talked and women listened. The way Simon went about things was so irksome and backhanded. It made her want to run even further away.

He's a grieving man, she reminded herself. *He needs time.*

"Nathaniel starts work at Met Power next month, lucky for us," said her father.

She congratulated Nathaniel, but he'd already asked her father a question about the junior executive training program, and her words faded away.

Finally, they finished their drinks and Nathaniel rose. "It was nice seeing you, Marion. I thought maybe we could have dinner one night next week."

"I'm back to work tomorrow. Three weeks straight."

"Oh well. Good luck with that."

They were like robots, saying absolutely nothing to each other that was meaningful.

After he left, Simon lashed out at Marion. "You were quite rude, young lady."

"What were you thinking, inviting him over without telling me? I thought we were spending the evening together, just the two of us."

"We were. It just so happens Nathaniel stops by every so often, to check on me."

The fact that Marion did not hung in the air. "That's nice of him," she conceded. "He's a good man."

"Then why don't you come home and marry him? I've been thinking about it, and you and Nathaniel can live here, if you like."

Had it come to this? He was trying to bribe her with a gift of the house? "What are you talking about? If we did that, where would you go?"

"I'd stay here as well."

He had to be kidding. But then again, maybe that was why he was reluctant to replace Mrs. Hornsby. He figured Marion would take her place, cooking and cleaning and looking after the men of the house. Which was simply not going to happen.

"I have a job, remember?" she said. "I live in the city. Honestly, why don't you and Nathaniel just move in together, if that's what you want so badly?"

He ignored her sarcasm. "I've said this before and I'll say it again: dancing is not a career, it's a hobby that will fade out and then you'll be all alone."

She'd had enough of his dire predictions. Marion turned off the television and whirled around to face him. Dancing onstage at Radio City, laughing with Bunny at the antics of the girls at the Rehearsal Club, even working with Peter these last few weeks, had kept Marion engaged and moving through the world with purpose. She wasn't about to give that up. "I know you mean well, but I want to be free to live my life the way I want to. Mom wanted to act, that was her dream, and she gave it all up to take care of you, me, and Judy. Yet she kept all her playbills and scripts in a box in the attic because that time in her life meant something to her. I'm proud that I take after her in that way, in pursuing a career in the arts. Let me follow my dream, since you didn't let Mom follow hers."

"What did you say?" Simon's upper lip lifted, like a growling dog.

"Mom sacrificed doing what she loved in order to raise me and Judy. I want to honor her legacy by dancing."

"You want to honor her legacy?"

"Yes."

"Give me a goddamn break."

Marion winced. Her father rarely swore unless someone pushed him to the limit.

"Right. I'll tell you what she sacrificed," he said. "You want to know the truth?"

"Yes, I do."

"Is that right? You want to know what really happened, when your mother went off to take care of her sick friend in Boston?"

Marion waited, petrified at what he was about to unveil. The story of Lucille's passing had always seemed devoid of details, the same words repeated with little embellishment. Like something was missing.

When Simon finally spoke, his voice was filled with derision.

"Your mother gave up her acting dreams, sure. For a while. She had Judy and you, and for ten years or so that was fine. Or so I thought. Until one day when I came home from work and she told me that she'd been asked to take a role in a play that was previewing up in Boston. The star had dropped out, and the director—the same one who'd directed the Broadway show she was cast in before we were married—wanted Lucille to step in and take over. And she wanted to do it. A month in Boston, and then it would be coming to Broadway. She said that now that you and Judy were older you were more independent, and she wanted to be more than a mother and a wife."

Simon stared off into the distance. "I was stunned. I begged her to reconsider, to stay. For a few hours I thought we'd smoothed things over. But then, that evening, she put you to bed and came down to this room with her suitcase packed. In no uncertain terms, she told me that she was going and Mrs. Hornsby would take over while she was away."

What her father was saying couldn't be true. Nothing made sense. Marion still remembered inhaling Mrs. Hornsby's clean, lemony scent when she tucked Marion and Judy into their beds. It was pleasant enough, but it was far from the rich floral that wafted off their mother, a perfume that Marion searched for whenever she was in a department store but had yet to find.

He continued. "We argued some more, and she said she'd be filing for divorce when she got back to New York. After everything I'd done for her, everything I'd worked so hard to provide, she was walking out on it all. Apparently, we were not enough. Her acting career was more important than her husband and children."

Marion grew dizzy. Her chest tightened and she thought she might faint. No wonder her father had been so angry at her earlier speech. Her mother wasn't a martyr who'd given up her dreams for her family. In fact, the opposite was true. She had embraced her dreams and left them all behind in the dust.

"I told everyone that she was visiting a sick friend," said Simon, "as I was certain that after a week away from you girls she'd come running back, that she'd miss you too much. But that never happened."

"She left us?"

"You, me, Judy. Left us all." He eyed Marion. "You say you want to be exactly like her? You're right on track, as far as I can see. Rejecting your family in pursuit of some silly dream. Not caring who you hurt while you do so. Well done, then, Marion. Well done."

He paused. "Your mother would be proud."

CHAPTER TWENTY-THREE

Rehearsals at Radio City typically started on time, so today it was strange that the dancers were still waiting for Russell and Emily at five minutes past the hour. Beulah sat behind her piano, patient as always, and over near the door stood a man and a woman Marion didn't recognize. Probably a couple of VIPs who were getting a backstage tour.

She hadn't slept at all the night before, mulling over her father's devastating revelations. Had Lucille been so bored with her life as a mother that she had been willing to leave Judy and Marion behind? Or maybe her passion for theater was so overwhelming that she was prepared to abandon the two daughters who loved her. Or even worse, perhaps Marion and Judy weren't good enough, smart enough, or entertaining enough to make her stick around? The image of Lucille that Marion had nurtured all these years—a kind, patient, loving woman who laughed at her daughters' antics and held them when they cried—had not been that at all. It had all been an act. Which meant all those times that Marion had come into the kitchen to find her mother staring into space, a cup of tea cooling on the table in front of her, and assumed she was content and peaceful, enjoying a quiet moment while her children played upstairs, may, in fact, have been something completely different: a bored, angry woman making plans to escape the dreary life around her.

In a way, Marion was glad Judy had never known the truth, that she had died thinking the Brooks family was a happy one. Although it would have been nice to be able to share the pain of Lucille's rejection with her sister.

Before she'd come to rehearsal, Marion had called the house and burst into tears the minute Mrs. Hornsby picked up.

"Is it true?" she'd asked.

Mrs. Hornsby had patiently waited until Marion was able to repeat what her father had told her. Marion had prayed he had been lying as a way to break Lucille's hold on her.

But Mrs. Hornsby didn't deny it. "She loved you both," she said right off. "After Judy was born, your mother did some local community theater—she tried to keep her hand in acting—but once you came along, your father insisted she give it all up. He's a fine man, Mr. Brooks, but he has certain way of looking at the world. It comes from his upbringing, where women remained in the home their entire lives."

Marion understood that. The streets her father grew up on were dangerous; women didn't dare venture out alone after dark. It was a different era. "What happened? Why did she leave when she did?"

"When your mother came to me, she was at her wit's end. As far as I remember, she'd been asked to take the leading role in a play. Your father wouldn't have it, but she was determined to go anyway. She asked if I'd step up and be ready to take care of you both while she was in Boston. It was temporary, as far as I understood it."

Temporary. Was that true, or had Lucille said that as a way of making a quick escape? They'd never know.

Mrs. Hornsby continued. "Your father told everyone that Lucille was visiting a sick friend and insisted I do the same. Then one morning we heard the awful news. A terrible tragedy, and a terrible loss. Your mother was a beauty, inside and out."

"But it was temporary, her moving away?"

"I can't say for certain what was in her heart. But that's what she told me." Mrs. Hornsby sighed into the phone. "I'm sorry for withholding this from you, but I didn't think it was my story to tell."

"I appreciate it, Mrs. Hornsby. That and everything else you've done for us over the years. You're like a mother to me, I hope you know that."

There were tears in Marion's eyes when she hung up.

In the rehearsal hall, she joined Bunny where she was stretching on the floor, one leg out to the side. When they first moved in together, Bunny had told her about growing up in the Midwest, where her father was a car salesman and her mother a painter.

"Bunny, what was it like to have an artist mother when you were growing up?" Marion folded over her legs until she felt the familiar resistance in her hamstrings.

"Annoying. I'd come home from school and she'd be locked in her studio, painting away. Or I'd bring friends over and she'd eventually emerge with a dot of blue paint at the end of her nose. I always thought it was embarrassing."

"Did she ever seem like she resented having a family?"

"Sometimes. But it was more like she would become detached, as opposed to resentful. Which was fine with me. Less nagging."

"And your father was okay with what she did?"

Bunny shrugged. "Sure. I mean, why not? Your father giving you trouble again?"

Marion didn't want to talk about her own family. "How's Dale?" she asked, deflecting.

"He's taking me to see Martha Graham."

Marion really wished Bunny would free herself of this guy, but no luck yet. "Martha Graham! Maybe you can invite her to come see the Rockettes."

Bunny chuckled. "She can help us modernize the 'Babes in Toyland' number." She jumped to her feet. "We can add some of her signature moves."

Bunny executed a series of Graham-esque upper body contractions and releases, while her feet tapped away at the familiar choreography. Beulah, who'd been watching, put her hands on the keyboard and layered in the music, which made it even more ridiculous. The other dancers laughed and clapped and demanded more.

"Go on," said Bunny, holding out a hand to Marion. "Your turn."

Marion needed to shake off the manic energy coursing through her veins before rehearsals began or she'd overdo it and further frustrate Russell. She rose and thought for a moment. She began with the stiff, regimented moves of the wooden soldiers, but then, without warning, broke into a loose, Gwen Verdon–style slink. Beulah picked up the melody right away, giving it an extra kick as Marion snapped back and forth between the steps they knew so well and an improvised movement that came out of nowhere. She allowed her body to go wherever it wanted instead of submitting to Russell's strict choreography. She shimmied and let her hips shake as the other dancers cried out with glee.

Out of the corner of her eye, she noticed that the two strangers were watching her intently. Probably not what they expected when they arranged to see a Rockettes rehearsal, but Marion was tired of caring what everyone else thought. She finished up with a mash-up of movements, going from Fosse to Balanchine to Jerome Robbins, drawing on everything she'd learned during her years of training and the performances she'd seen in New York. By then, even the normally straight-faced Beulah was having a hard time keeping up, practically doubled over in laughter.

For the grand finale, Bunny joined Marion and they broke out into the kick line from the opening number.

"What's going on in here?"

With a crash, Bunny went down hard onto the floor.

Russell and Emily stood in the doorway, Russell looking as angry as Marion had ever seen him, his eyes dark with fury. But she didn't have time to answer. She knelt next to where Bunny sat cradling her ankle. "Well, that was silly of me," said Bunny, grimacing with pain.

"Oh, no," Marion cried. "Are you all right?"

Russell rushed over and leaned down to gently grasp Bunny's ankle. After a quick examination, he motioned for Emily to help her up, then enlisted one of the assistants to take Bunny's other side. "Take her to the infirmary. I think it's just a sprain, but you're not dancing today." He glared at Marion. "You two should know better. I'm very disappointed."

The thought of disappointing the sweet man who'd given her the greatest chance in her life was almost worse than disappointing her father. "I'll go with her to the infirmary," offered Marion.

"That's not necessary. Step outside with me for a moment, Marion, please."

Marion followed him into the hallway like a schoolgirl who'd been caught cheating. Certainly, this was the last straw, he was going to fire her on the spot.

"Marion, I know you're struggling," Russell said once he'd closed the door to the rehearsal hall behind them. "My job is to keep everyone safe from harm, and number one in that regard is making sure everyone respects the level of difficulty involved in dancing on that stage. I love what I do, except for when I have to place a call to a dancer's parents and tell them that she has a serious injury. I prefer to avoid that at all costs."

"Of course. I'm sorry. It won't happen again."

"The last thing I want is for one of my dancers to get hurt."

"I understand."

"Very well, then. Let's get the show on the road." He held the door open for her and waved her through with a flourish of his arm, always the gentleman.

Back inside the rehearsal hall, he instructed an assistant to phone one of the dancers on her week off to fill in Bunny's spot and called for the troupe to take their positions. Then he went to the corner where the man and woman stood and greeted them warmly, shaking their hands. He turned back to the assembled dancers. "Now that you've had your fun at the expense of one of your own, I hope we can take this rehearsal seriously."

For the next hour, Marion stayed focused and didn't make any mistakes, although her mind kept drifting off to Bunny and how badly she might be hurt. She'd head up to see her the first chance she could, but for now, she had to get into costume and perform in her first show in a week.

There'd be no more fooling around.

Marion was desperate to check in on Bunny, but she was stymied by a long notes session from Emily and then a last-minute costume fix on the broken zipper on her wooden soldier's uniform. The notes session was especially dispiriting, as Emily took her to task on a number of issues, moments where her kicks were an inch too high or the extension of her arms exaggerated.

Even worse, Marion had kicked out in the grand finale.

They had been lined up on the riser, the crowd cheering. There was so much adrenaline coursing through Marion's veins, her thoughts bouncing between her mother's last days, Bunny's injury, her father's wrath, and the fact that the bomber was still on the loose, and all that energy had to find an outlet. As the other girls came to a stop for the last beat of the show, arms high in the air, Marion had continued kicking.

The girls nearby had gasped, as had some members of the audience. She'd wanted to curl into a ball, face in her hands, but she'd plastered a smile on her face and joined the others in the correct pose as the curtain dropped.

None of the dancers mentioned it after the show was over, but they all avoided her eyes. She'd done the unthinkable. By kicking out, Marion had exposed the truth about the troupe: they were human, fallible, and utterly individual.

Marion slunk off to the infirmary, where Bunny lay on an examination table. A nurse had just finished reexamining her ankle and was wrapping it up; an ice pack lay nearby.

"How's it feeling?" asked Marion.

"The swelling's gone down. I think I'll live, right, Nurse?" said Bunny.

The nurse smiled and patted her leg gently. "We'll have you back on your feet in a day or two. But I'd like you to stay in the dormitory overnight. The more you keep off it, the faster we'll get you back onstage. I'm going to get you some crutches."

After the nurse left, Marion lifted a stack of fashion magazines from a nearby chair and sat.

"I think I've read every issue of *Mademoiselle* from the past two years," said Bunny. "Not a bad way to pass the time. How did the shows go?"

The first day back was always exhausting, as the fresh dancers readjusted to the schedule. But Marion's fatigue was more than that. She was completely spent. "They were long and hard. Especially the last one." She couldn't mention kicking out, it was too embarrassing.

"You'll be good as gold tomorrow," Bunny reassured her. "Don't let it get to you."

"I should be saying that to you. I'm so sorry that you're hurt."

Bunny smiled. "I'll be fine. It was fun, and we deserve a little fun, don't we? And the way you improvised an entire dance, going back and forth the way you did? It was amazing."

"Not according to Russell and Emily."

"They want to keep everything the same year after year, but sometimes I can't help but think we should jazz it up. I bet the other girls do as well."

"You're looking to stage a mutiny? I don't think the audience would approve. They come here for the comfort of the familiar."

Bunny crossed her arms. "You're probably right. But you're too good for us, you know."

"Stop that right now. I'm a mess. I hurt everyone I come into contact with."

She hadn't meant to cry, but she couldn't help it.

"I want you to go back to the Rehearsal Club and get some rest," said Bunny. "You've been running around the city nonstop, you're exhausted. But before you go, I heard something that I wanted to share with you. It's rather distressing."

Marion froze. "What's that?"

"The nurse told me there was another bombing."

The memory of the night Judy died threatened to overwhelm Marion. She reminded herself to breathe. "Another one? Where?"

"In a phone booth in Macy's. No one was hurt, she said."

"Thank goodness."

"Yes. But that means the man they arrested yesterday wasn't the Big Apple Bomber. He's still on the loose."

By now, Somers and Ogden knew Peter had been right: they'd arrested the wrong man. If only the police had listened to him, they wouldn't have wasted two days when they could have been following up on more tips, looking for the actual bomber.

At least no one had been hurt. She gave Bunny a long hug and promised to bring her coffee and a Danish in the morning. The halls of the building were empty at this late hour, so Marion was surprised to hear her name spoken out loud as she passed by the administrative offices.

She turned, thinking someone had called out to her, but no, the conversation was coming from the open door to Russell's office; he was talking to Emily. Even though she knew she shouldn't, Marion edged a little closer.

"Marion reminds me of another dancer we had back in the late thirties," said Russell. "Vera-Ellen was her name."

"Vera-Ellen, the movie star?" answered Emily.

Marion had seen Vera-Ellen in *White Christmas* with Bing Crosby a couple of years ago; she was captivating. Maybe things weren't so bad if Russell was comparing her to Vera-Ellen. Maybe she'd read this all wrong.

"That's her," said Russell. "Both beautiful and talented, a formidable combination. Unfortunately, she only lasted a couple of weeks at Radio City because she simply couldn't do what we asked of her. There was too much life in her, and she stood out every time she walked onstage."

Lasted only a couple of weeks? What they were saying didn't bode well for Marion's future as a Rockette. Russell was considering letting her go, and probably only hadn't acted on it yet because he felt sorry for her, after Judy's death.

"Do you want to follow up with her about kicking out?" asked Emily. "I mentioned it in the notes session, but Leon noticed and pretty much went through the roof."

Russell's sigh was audible. "I'll speak with her tomorrow. What's crazy is even when she kicks out, it's a beautiful sight. Some girls just shine. Not what we want, but still."

Marion's breath caught in her throat.

Instead of going back to her room at the Rehearsal Club, she took the stairs up to the roof. She needed fresh air.

Even on a moonless night, the roof was gently lit by the city around it. On warm days it swarmed with employees from the theater below, but now it was eerily empty, the paddle tennis court abandoned, the patio swings stilled. Marion walked to the balustrade and looked out over the edge, where even this late at night she could see people down on the sidewalk going about their business, jumping into taxis, leaving restaurants, heading to the subway with their collars pulled up against the cold.

How many were wondering whether they'd make it through Grand Central or Penn Station safely that evening, or avoiding phone booths in case a bomb had been planted inside? The idea that one man could hold the entire city in his sway, terrorizing, injuring, and killing, infuriated Marion. She wanted him caught, and no one seemed up to the job.

Then again, who did Marion think she was? She couldn't do anything right. Just that day she'd drawn Bunny into her recklessness and disappointed Russell and Emily yet again.

Maybe she'd disappointed her mother in some way as well. Marion still couldn't quite wrap her head around the fact that Lucille had chosen to abandon Marion and Judy, unable to shove her artistic life in a box and conform for the good of the family. Yet how different was that from what Marion was doing at this very moment, by choosing her love of dance over her father's wishes?

No matter how much she loved to dance, Marion didn't want to be that type of person. Maybe she didn't want to take after her mother after all. That legacy was not one she wished to carry forward. What if, by going after her own dream, Marion was on the road to ruin as well? Just as her father had predicted.

Behind her, the door to the roof slammed shut. Marion whirled around. It was a still night, no wind, and she was sure she'd closed it properly behind her. "Is someone there?"

In the semidarkness, a dozen shadows loomed. A person could easily hide behind the many planters arranged around the perimeter of the roof. A movement near the backstop of the handball court caught her attention, but then all was silent and still again.

Too silent, and too still.

Someone else was up there with her, she was certain of it.

She was eight stories high, and the door was the only way out. To reach the exit, she'd have to make a run for it across the open roof deck. Panic gripped her; she thought she might be sick.

For about a minute there was no other movement, no other sounds.

Maybe it had been a pigeon and this was all in her head. The sound of the door might have actually been the slam of a taxicab door on the street below, the noise echoing off the limestone skyscrapers of Rockefeller Center. She shook her head, annoyed at herself for being so silly. After four shows, she needed to get some rest.

Marion shoved off from the balustrade, which she'd been gripping as if it were an anchor, and moved as silently as possible across the roof deck toward the exit.

She moved fast and had almost made it to the exit when she heard a distinct scuffling noise to her right. That was no pigeon. Someone was hiding behind the backboard—she'd been right.

If she could make it inside the building and call for help, she might stand a chance. She was just about to grab hold of the doorknob when an arm suddenly wrapped around her neck, yanking her back from the doorway, further onto the rooftop. She clutched at the arm with both hands, trying to free her windpipe and scream, but the more she fought back, the tighter he squeezed. Together they spun around in a grisly pas de deux.

Marion was trapped on the roof of Radio City with a madman.

CHAPTER TWENTY-FOUR

When Marion and Judy were in their early teens, their father brought them into the backyard on a warm spring day and insisted they learn how to fight, in case they were ever mugged. Marion rolled her eyes and Judy gave a nervous laugh, but Simon insisted. "Where I grew up, you had to know how to stand up for yourself, not just with words, but with fists, too, if it came to that."

"You're going to teach us to be street fighters?" asked Marion. "I don't think there's much call for that in Bronxville."

"You're going to be dealing with boys soon." He looked at Marion, not Judy, as he spoke. "And boys can be stupid. You have to be able to get free if you're ever attacked. Marion. Turn around."

She did so, and before she knew it her father was behind her, his arms wrapping around her in a bear hug. She squirmed but couldn't get free, and burst out laughing at the ridiculousness of it. She was supposed to be getting ready for a school mixer that night, not wrestling with her dad.

"Stop squirming, that's lesson number one," said her father. She couldn't see his face, but she felt his breath in her hair.

"Okay." She went still.

"By not squirming, you'll catch him by surprise. That's what he's going to be expecting. Now, lift your right foot and jam it hard down on mine."

She strained to look back at him. "I'll break your toe if I do that."

"Trust me, I'll be fine."

She did as instructed, and her father moved his foot just in time.

"Your attacker won't be expecting that, and it'll hurt like the dickens. He'll loosen his grip even more, and the minute you feel that loosening, drop to the ground, like a sack of potatoes."

"Really?"

"Yes, really. Like you're fainting, but straight down."

She paused for a moment, and then let her knees buckle. Before she knew it, she was on the ground.

"Roll! Roll away!" her father yelled.

She rolled, crossing her arms over her chest. Thank goodness she was wearing her old jeans and a tee shirt that day. Poor Mrs. Hornsby would have a fit at the grass stains.

"Good, Marion. That's good. Now run to safety!"

She ran, giggling, onto the back porch.

She watched as he put Judy through the same paces. Judy didn't have the same body awareness that Marion did, so her moves were clumsy, but Simon didn't mind. "You do whatever you have to do to escape. It's not about style, it's about self-defense."

Simon's words came back to Marion as she stood on the roof of Radio City, pinned in a stranger's arms. A stranger who wanted to hurt her.

Even though it went against every natural instinct she had, she forced herself to relax. Her shoulders dropped and she leaned slightly against him instead of trying to pull away. The attacker shifted his own balance to adjust, which gave her the opportunity to lift one leg and jam the heel of her shoe into the man's foot. She could tell she'd hit the soft, vulnerable part of his foot by the howl that erupted behind her left ear. It was followed by a strange clattering sound, as if something heavy had been dropped.

Fall, roll. Her father's commands echoed in her head. The man's grip loosened and she collapsed to the ground before rolling away. As she scrambled to her feet, he half-heartedly tried to lunge at her again, but he'd lost his momentum. She dodged around him, yanked the door open, and ran inside.

Marion flew down the stairs as fast as she could. At the fifth-floor landing she looked back and didn't see him, but by the sound of his footsteps, he wasn't far behind. One flight down, she ditched the stairs and went straight for the door marked *Fly Floor*, hoping he'd continue down.

A couple of times Marion and some of the other Rockettes had accepted the stagehands' invitation to view the other acts from the fly rail, which ran high above the stage, along the very back wall of the theater. They'd plant themselves on the catwalk and watch the corps de ballet or glee club perform far below their dangling feet. The flymen were in charge of switching out the scenery and backdrops in between acts, which involved a complicated system of ropes, pulleys, and counterweights. The catwalk was a frighteningly narrow passageway, but the flymen traversed it as if it were an ordinary street sidewalk.

Marion kicked off her heels before entering the catwalk; they were only slowing her down. She walked as fast as she could, sliding her hand along the handrail for support.

About halfway across, she heard a clattering sound far below her. She paused and looked down; one of her shoes had fallen to the stage. Her attacker was still on her trail and had either purposely or accidentally kicked it. It was a long way down.

She strained to see behind her. Even though the only light came from the ghost bulb on the stage below, she got a quick glimpse of her pursuer. It wasn't the man from the television who had sent her the threatening letter, the one who'd been wrongly accused of being the bomber.

It was the same man who'd sat next to her sister. Same round face, small eyes, and red nose, like a ground mole.

This was F.P.

The Big Apple Bomber.

She took off at a run, hoping she wouldn't lose her balance and tumble over the side. The catwalk vibrated from the heavy steps of the bomber as he followed, making it even harder to stay on track. But she made it to the end and kept on, across the landing and out the door to the hallway. There, she called wildly for help but was met with silence. No one was around at this hour. She continued her descent down the main stairway, tears blurring her vision. From the sound of his footsteps, he was practically on top of her now. With one shove, he could send her flying, break every bone in her body. She dug deep and willed herself to move, to keep moving. Her body was the one thing she could control, and these days she was stronger than she'd ever been. She sped up, taking the stairs as fast as she could go, her leg muscles straining. The sound of his panting and huffing grew fainter.

She'd reached the basement level, which offered a view of the thick pistons that drove the four elevated stages up and down. Directly in front of her, on top of the pit elevator, was the band car, which held the orchestra.

Unlike the other three elevators, the pit elevator supporting the band car had the ability to move back and forth as well as up and down. Before each show, a stagehand crawled on his stomach into a narrow space at the bottom of the band car, which was padded with a thin foam mattress to keep him comfortable while he waited for his cue. As soon as the pit elevator rose to the stage level, the stagehand would unplug the connector that supplied the band car's power and get handed a different one, which then took over as the pit elevator slid upstage.

It was the perfect hiding spot, and she dove inside, trying to quiet her breathing in the airless, tight confines.

Not long after, she heard footsteps. The bomber's ankles and shoes passed by, and she heard him open the door to the stairs stage right. After a moment, it slammed closed, but she knew better than to crawl out just yet. He hadn't left. She could still hear his raspy, wet breath. He paced back and forth a couple of times and then let out a string of swearwords.

Finally, he retreated to where they'd come from, stage left.

She scrambled out and fled the opposite way. On the first floor, she found two security guards and explained what was going on, describing the attacker in a rush of words. They radioed the other guards to be on the lookout for an intruder in the building.

What if the man found Bunny, who was staying overnight?

One of the security guards' radios squawked in response a few seconds later: "A man in a trench coat left via the Fiftieth Street stage door about thirty seconds ago. Flew by in a rush and jumped in a cab."

He'd escaped.

※

After giving the Radio City security guards the names of Captain Somers and Detective Ogden, Marion waited in the greenroom near the stage door. The guards assured her they would be right outside and that she was safe, but her body still twitched with fear. Only one person would understand.

Hands shaking, she picked up the phone and asked to be connected to Peter Griggs on Crosby Street. The phone rang three times before a groggy voice answered.

"Hello?"

She looked at the time. It was after midnight.

"Peter, it's Marion. I'm sorry to wake you. I didn't know who else to call." And then she dissolved into tears. She did her best to explain what had happened, but he cut her off as soon as she said the word *attacked*.

"I'm on my way. You're still at Radio City?" he asked.

"Yes."

"Don't go anywhere."

Not long after she hung up, a swarm of policemen arrived at the stage door. Detective Ogden showed up about fifteen minutes later. When she asked if Captain Somers was on his way, Ogden shook his head. "He's got other things to deal with."

"Really? When the bomber is still on the loose?" Her nerves had worn off in the waiting, and she'd never liked Ogden.

Before the detective could respond, the door to the greenroom opened and Peter appeared. His hair was tousled and his shirt buttoned wrong. She'd never been so glad to see someone, and she rushed into his arms. Despite all the weirdness between them two days earlier, he was the one who understood her best right now. Who knew what she was going through.

"Ah, the good doctor," said Ogden.

They both ignored him. "You okay?" Peter asked.

"Shaken up, but otherwise unhurt."

Detective Ogden took out a notebook. "All right, then. Describe what happened to you tonight."

"I'd much rather walk you through it."

"Please do." He snapped the book shut, and she led the way up to the roof, where a half dozen police officers were canvassing the area. She pointed out the spot where she was attacked, showed where she'd run down the stairs and across the catwalk. One of her shoes still lay on the landing, the other on the stage floor. Marion couldn't imagine ever wearing them again.

"I had made it to the other side of the theater when I turned around and saw him," said Marion. "He was standing where we are now."

"And you saw his face clearly?"

"Yes. It was the same man who was in Radio City right before the bomb went off."

Ogden pointed to the ghost light on the stage. "That doesn't give off much light. How can you be sure? How do we know it wasn't some crazed Rockette fan?"

"Because I know. I saw him."

Peter stood tall. "What's with all the resistance? Here you have someone who's seen the bomber not once, but twice, and who was nearly—" He stopped, catching himself. "Who he went after, and you're still pushing back?"

Marion knew why. Peter had humiliated Ogden and Somers by being right about the fact that they had the wrong guy in custody. On top of that, she'd brought them the letter from the imitator, which had sent them off on the wild-goose chase, even though she and Peter had warned otherwise. Ogden didn't like being upstaged.

Ogden moved back into the hallway, but Marion and Peter stayed on his tail. He wasn't going to get out of this so easily.

"What about Hardenby?" asked Marion. "Is he still in jail?"

Ogden shook his head. "No. We couldn't hold him after the latest bomb went off. It'll be in the news tomorrow, I'm sure. The press will go wild with this."

"So he gets to walk away?"

"He'll be charged with making a criminal threat, but not with setting the bombs. Apparently, he hates Met Power as much as the Big Apple Bomber does and decided to join in on the fun. He sent it to you because he'd seen the Rockettes when he was a kid, heard about your connection to the Radio City bombing in the papers and all, and figured you'd be an easy target. We don't think he's a further threat to you."

Marion looked over at Peter. "What do you think?"

"I think he's a bomber wannabe and was probably shocked at being tossed in jail. I don't see him as a threat."

"Well, I'm glad you cleared that up, Doctor," said Ogden, not bothering to hide the sarcasm in his voice.

The dark energy that had been coursing through Marion's body since the attack surged again. "If you'd been out hunting for the right guy maybe this wouldn't have happened. You might have had him by now. Do you even care one bit that I was almost killed tonight? That my sister was killed, due to your incompetence? F.P. has been around for sixteen years now." She pointed a finger right in Ogden's face. "How many more people have to get killed or injured before you get your act together and do your job?"

"What's going on here?"

Captain Somers strode toward them.

Marion stepped back, breathing heavily. Peter answered for her. "We were expressing our concern about the way this case is being handled. The bomber went after Marion tonight, and meanwhile your man Ogden here doesn't seem to understand the seriousness of the situation."

Somers glared at Ogden. "That's enough. Go back to headquarters."

Once Ogden had slunk away, Somers placed a hand on Marion's shoulder. "I'm sorry we got sidetracked with the letter you brought to us."

"The letter that I told you was not from the bomber," interjected Peter.

Somers accepted the criticism with a mild nod.

"What about the other witness, the usher at the Paramount?" said

Marion. "If the bomber came after me, there's a good chance he's coming after him as well."

Somers rubbed his mouth with the back of his hand. "Right. About that. That's why I was late getting here. I'm afraid he's already been targeted."

"Targeted?" asked Peter. "What does that mean?"

"We sent a team to his apartment in the Bronx after we got Marion's call. His apartment had been broken into, and he'd been attacked."

"Is he all right?" asked Marion.

"No. He was killed."

"Killed?" Marion shuddered. "By the bomber?"

"He was hit on the head with something, possibly a hammer, and then strangled. We believe the bomber came here right after, to try to neutralize the second witness."

"'Neutralize the second witness'?" repeated Marion. "You mean kill me."

"Captain!"

One of the policemen working the scene approached. He carried a hammer in his gloved hand. That was what had made the clattering noise when Marion had stomped hard on the attacker's foot. He'd dropped it and left it behind.

The reality that she could have been murdered finally hit her full force. Her father would have gotten another call in the night saying his daughter had been killed. He would've never recovered from the shock, and it would have been all her fault for being selfish and petty-minded, pursuing her dreams at the cost of her own life.

He'd been right about everything after all.

The room twirled around her as she fainted to the ground.

CHAPTER TWENTY-FIVE

DECEMBER 1992

As Piper and I approach the theater, the wet street glistens red and blue from the lights of Radio City's marquee. *Special Christmas Spectacular—Celebrating the 60th Anniversary of the Rockettes*, it reads.

In spite of myself, my heart lifts into my throat. This was the place that in many ways defined who I am today. Where I learned the value of good friends and hard work. I can still summon up the crazy mix of skittishness and hyper-focus that would settle upon me backstage as we waited for our cue. It falls over me now, like a shower of pinpricks.

The crowd outside is delirious with excitement, a mix of gaping tourists and assured city slickers, along with dozens of children in their best outfits. Black cars wait in line for their turn to pull up to the curb.

Piper picks up on my energy and begins rattling off the schedule of the evening. "It starts with a show by the dancers, followed by an homage to those injured or killed by the Big Apple Bomber. Then, after—"

I cut her off. "What homage?"

"It was mentioned in the invitation we sent you."

"I never read the silly invitation. I assume this homage would include Judy?"

Piper gives the slightest of nods.

Bile rises in my throat. "I am adamant that her name not be sullied by some maudlin nonsense. She will not be relegated to some footnote to history, nor elevated to sainthood by those who never knew her. I want to know right now what's going to be said about Judy."

"It's simply a moment of silence." Piper looks like she's been slapped.

"That's all? No one will be extolling the virtues of my long-lost sister or using her in any way?"

"Absolutely not. Ms. Burris put me in charge of the homage, and I would never have allowed that. It's a list of the people who were affected and then a request for a moment to remember their pain and loss." Piper's expression is serious. "Ms. Brooks, I read the book and I couldn't believe what happened back then, how all that has been forgotten. What you and your family went through is a part of the legacy of this building, even if it doesn't fit with the snappy Christmas show that it's most famous for."

I'm relieved to know I won't have my heart wrenched in two by some dancing elves singing about bombs just because of that damn book. "Well, then, I suppose that's all right," I concede.

Piper ducks her head and tucks an errant curl behind one ear. "It's not long until curtain."

I notice that her carefully arranged updo has wilted in the humidity, and the fancy high heels she's chosen to wear are water stained.

I feel bad about making her get out of the car, as well as my overreaction.

This one-hour journey to the place where I lost and learned so much has turned me into a witch, making me sharp and edgy with my escort, who's simply trying to do her job.

"Do you really like what you do?" I ask. "It seems awfully stressful."

"Sure." But her heart isn't in the answer. I realize why I'm being so cross with her. It's because she reminds me of myself, back when I was just starting out. Frightened and overwhelmed. Not for the first time I give thanks that Russell saw something in me the day I auditioned.

"You're a good dancer, I can tell that just from looking at you."

"You can?"

"Yes. You're passionate and smart, a powerful combination for the stage. You feel things more deeply than most people." Piper's eyes well up with tears, proving my point. "You like modern, you said?"

"I do. I like the freedom involved."

"There's a choreographer you should meet. I'll get you his contact information and I want you to call him."

"You'd do that for me?"

"I'll make the introduction, but you'll have to take it from there."

"I will. I can't tell you how much I appreciate that, and I promise I won't disappoint you."

"The key, my dear, is to make sure you don't disappoint yourself."

We come to a stop, facing the long line of brass doors tucked under the marquee. They resemble a golden mouth, luring the public inside before swallowing them whole.

"Very well, then," I say. "I'm ready. It's time."

CHAPTER TWENTY-SIX

DECEMBER 1956

Marion opened her eyes, confused that she wasn't in her room at the Rehearsal Club. With a rush, the evening's events came back to her. The roof, the man, the hammer.

"She's awake."

Peter's face loomed over her. She looked around and realized she was on the couch in the greenroom. Somers was talking to a policeman near the door. Peter handed her a glass of water and she sat upright to take a sip.

"How did I get down here?"

"I carried you after you fainted," said Peter. "You didn't hit your head or anything, I caught you on the way down."

Embarrassment ran through her. Peter patted her arm; it was as if he knew exactly what she was thinking. "It was very ladylike, I assure you. Only a dancer could faint that gracefully. Most people sink like a bag of bricks."

Somers came over. "How are you doing?"

"I'm fine," she said. "It was just the shock of it all."

"I'll have one of our patrol cars take you home. I'd recommend you not be alone for the next few days."

She knew exactly where she wanted to go.

248

"I'd like to go to Bronxville."

Somers nodded and left the room to arrange it.

"Are you sure?" said Peter. "You can come to my place, if you like. I can sleep on the couch."

"No, that's kind of you. But I'm sure you have enough to deal with right now. I have a lot to think about, a lot to sort out."

Peter studied her. "Is there something else going on? I mean, beyond the fact that you were attacked by a madman."

She thought of the painful conversation she'd overheard between Russell and Emily and involuntarily grimaced at the memory of kicking out earlier that evening. Mr. Leonidoff was no doubt calling for her head. She'd let Russell and Emily down, as well as the other dancers. It was over.

"I'm going to quit the Rockettes."

There, she'd said it.

Peter nodded. "I understand why, at least temporarily. It's not safe for you, not until they catch the bomber. But I think they're close. He's making mistakes, getting desperate. You can always go back, right?"

"No. I'm done. I love being a Rockette, but I'm not a good fit, as much as I hate to admit that. Not to mention the fact that my presence lured the bomber backstage, where anyone else could've been attacked or worse. I need to stop thinking of myself and what I want. Stop being so selfish."

Peter looked like he wanted to say more, but they were interrupted by Somers's return.

"Your ride is here," he said, holding out one arm. "I'll escort you to the vehicle myself."

❋

It was long after midnight when she rang the doorbell to her Bronxville home. She could have let herself in, but she didn't want her father to mistake her for an intruder. When he opened the door and saw her standing next to a police officer, his bleary-eyed demeanor was quickly replaced with one of concern.

"What's going on? Are you all right?" he asked, reaching out for her.

She nodded, and the police officer explained what had happened. She was grateful that he provided the narrative, as she would have had a hard time finding the right words. *Bomber, attacked, escaped.* The right words, but not the whole story.

Simon put his arm around her and gingerly led her into the living room, as if she were a feral cat who might bolt at any minute. "You're trembling. Come with me, you're safe now. Would you like a warm drink? Some hot chocolate?"

She was exhausted but wired, and drinking something might help her sleep. "That would be great."

In many ways it was a relief to be back home. Her father would protect her from the crazy world outside. She told herself that she'd made the right decision, to return, and now they could start their relationship on new footing.

Simon guided her to the couch and, not long after, returned from the kitchen with two mugs, handing one to her. Instead of easing into his armchair, he took a seat beside her, and she leaned into his solid torso.

"Are you really okay?" he asked. "That must have been terrifying. Are you hurt?"

"I'm fine, I suppose. It all happened so fast. I didn't have any time to think." She told him how his earlier lesson in self-defense had helped her escape, and he nodded solemnly.

"That's my girl. I just wish you hadn't been there in the first place. If I'd have been there, he wouldn't have made it out alive. The thought of losing you as well—"

"I'm sorry for putting you through this, but I'm okay. And I'm home now." She wasn't quite sure what she'd do with herself, but for tonight she wouldn't worry about it. Having made the decision was enough.

"Thank God you're safe. Do not under any circumstance open a window or a door, do you understand? And no going outside, not even in the backyard. Not until they find this guy."

She shook off a whisper of claustrophobia. "I won't, I promise."

"I saw there was something in the newspaper about the madman, that they think they know what kind of person he is. Is that what your doctor friend figured out?"

"Yes." Simon listened intently as Marion explained in more detail about the work she and Peter had done to help move the investigation forward. "I hope that Dr. Griggs's contribution will help find Judy's killer soon."

"I do as well." He frowned. "But I don't think it's a good idea, you being involved in the case. This is a man's job. Besides, you're too close to it to think straight."

For once, she didn't object to his decrees, although his crack about it being a man's job stung. "I'm done with it all. Done with dancing, done with being a sleuth. Judy would have wanted me here with you, I realize that now. And I'm sorry for putting you through what I did." She did have one last question, though. "Are you absolutely sure that Met Power doesn't have the files from before 1940? That's the key, Peter thinks. All the destruction the bomber's caused comes from something that happened in the 1930s."

Her father's right hand shook ever so slightly. Exactly as it had when she'd brought up the subject at Tavern on the Green. He put down his mug and rubbed his other hand over his stubbly cheeks, shoving the right one into the pocket of his robe.

"Those files are dead. They were lost ages ago. We've scoured everything we have, trust me." He patted her knee. "But this is exactly what you need to let go of. It's too stressful, and not for you to figure out."

She yawned.

"It's time for your bed, Miss Marion."

He hadn't called her that in years. They both rose.

"Before you go, I want to say something." He put his hand under her chin and lifted it. This was a different gaze from what Marion was used to. He was looking at her not as a child but as a grown-up. "It was wrong, the way I told you about your mother, full of anger. I shouldn't have done that. I'd kept it a secret for so long because I never wanted you to think badly of her. If I could erase everything I told you, I would."

"I pushed you, it's not your fault," answered Marion.

It was good to clear the air. Yet there was something else, something wrong that nagged at Marion's brain, but she couldn't wrestle her thoughts into submission to figure it out.

It was impossible to think straight, with exhaustion setting in. For now, she sought solace in her childhood bedroom, in her childhood bed, and slept without dreaming.

❄

Marion didn't wake until the early afternoon. In all her life, she'd never slept so late, but maybe it was the aftereffects of the attack, her mind and body trying to work out the trauma of what had happened. Her muscles were sore, but she wasn't sure if that was from her harrowing escape or from doing four shows a day; aching muscles were just part of a Rockette's job.

Downstairs, Marion could hear Mrs. Hornsby puttering around, and she vaguely remembered waking up long enough to hear her father going off to work. A part of her was disappointed he hadn't stayed home to be with her, but he probably wanted to stay on top of any news of the bomber, to be ready in case there was any way Met Power could assist the police.

The night before had been terrible, but she tried to focus on the talk she'd had with her father afterward instead, where it felt as if they had really listened to each other for the first time in ages.

But still. Something was off.

The door to her father's study was ajar. Normally it was kept shut, from the time when they were little girls and she and Judy would sneak in and play Secretary and Boss, which involved Marion sitting in her father's chair and dictating some kind of gibberish to Judy, who'd scribble it all down with one of his fancy fountain pens. After they spilled ink everywhere trying to refill it, they were banned from the room and the door was kept closed.

Marion went to her father's desk and glanced at the papers laid on top.

Nothing of interest, only memos and letters.

But Simon was hiding something. Whenever she brought up Met Power and the bomber, his hands shook. Just like with Peter's stutter, the shaking gave him away.

Her throat was tight as she opened the desk drawers. Even though she knew Simon was at work, her heart pounded as she sifted through boring meeting notes and accounting forms. She didn't know what anything meant, if any of it was important.

She was a good daughter and they were on their way to repairing their relationship. Then why did she have this burning need to snoop around? She closed the door behind her and went downstairs, where Mrs. Hornsby fussed over her and made her a late lunch. Russell had called and left a message a few hours earlier, asking after Marion and sending his love and concern. As she was finishing up lunch, Bunny called and they spoke briefly, Marion assuring her friend that she was fine, and Bunny reassuring Marion that her ankle was fully healed.

Marion dressed and wandered around the house, feeling adrift, trying to figure out what the rest of her life would entail. The thought of getting married and having kids, as some of her friends had already done, felt like something of a letdown after the whirlwind of her life at Radio City.

She wondered what Peter was doing right then. Seeing patients, most likely; she shouldn't disturb him with a call. Maybe she and Peter could stay friends, although with his schedule she doubted he had much time for friends. He was so devoted to his work, and she saw that in herself as well. What he felt for psychiatric medicine, she had felt for dance.

She had to talk to Russell, explain that she was leaving the Rockettes, and that was not something she could do over the phone.

That evening, when her father returned home, she told him that she needed to go to Radio City the next day and tell Russell in person that she was quitting. "Then I'll go to the Rehearsal Club, pack up, and you can pick me up Sunday morning."

"You cannot go back into the city," said Simon. "I won't allow it."

They were back to square one. "If I'm going to live at home, I'm going to need to have some independence, some freedom of movement."

"You were attacked by a madman. Why would you want to go back to the city where he might still be looking for you?"

While Marion had to admit he had a point, she had to finish off her short career as a Rockette in the right way. "Russell deserves as much. It's good manners."

Simon had always been a stickler for proper professional conduct. To her surprise, he softened. "How about this? Let's ask Nathaniel to escort you. I'll feel better if he's with you. He can pick you up in the morning as well, drive you home. As long as you promise you will not venture out. You are either in Nathaniel's company or you are at your boardinghouse, do you understand?"

If that was what it took, she didn't see how she could object.

※

Early the next day, Nathaniel picked her up, full of questions. She filled him in on the bomber's attack, playing it down as much as she could. He immediately went into outraged boyfriend mode, banging on the steering wheel as he listed the things he would do if he ever got into the same room as her attacker. By the time they arrived in midtown, her head was aching from having to calm him down. She asked him to wait outside in the car when they got to Radio City, imagining him scowling at Russell the whole time if she brought him inside.

Russell leaped up from his desk when she walked into his office. "My darling. I heard what happened. Are you all right? I called your house yesterday, but they said you were asleep." He put his hands on her shoulders, holding her at arm's length and studying her closely.

"I wanted to talk to you in person. First of all, I'm fine. But I can't be a Rockette anymore." She blinked hard, trying not to cry. "It's too dangerous, for me and for the other girls if I'm around. I'm so sorry."

"You take all the time you need, hopefully they'll find this madman soon."

"No, I'm leaving for good." Her voice cracked, as if her own body were trying to stop her from throwing away the one thing that had given her the most joy in her life so far. "I haven't been dancing well, we both know that. I'm pulling everyone down with me."

His brows furrowed. "You have a unique style, there's no question about that. But you've been under terrible stress. Why don't you take some time off and think about things? No one is pushing you out the door, I want to make that clear."

But Marion knew the truth from having overheard his earlier conversation with Emily, comparing her to Vera-Ellen. She didn't blame him for speaking honestly about her own limitations as a Rockette—he was like a favorite uncle and could do no harm—but she understood deep down that she didn't belong.

"No. You should find someone else to replace me." She hugged him hard, knowing she only had a few seconds before she broke down in tears. "I'll come by later to pick up my things."

"There's no rush, no rush at all."

Marion whispered a thank-you and ran out of the building.

She was a failure. While it would be easy to tell anyone who asked that she'd pulled out of the Rockettes of her own volition, she knew she didn't really belong with the troupe. She didn't belong anywhere.

Nathaniel apologized as soon as she got back into the car.

"I'm sorry if I got out of control, Marion." He placed a hand on her cheek. "You and I are making a fresh start, okay?"

A fresh start. She could sure use one.

He eased the car into gear for the few short blocks to the Rehearsal Club. "I've been thinking about the proposal, and I really want it to be special. How about on Christmas Eve we take a carriage ride in Central Park?"

Marion winced. She didn't want to think that far ahead just yet.

Nathaniel kept on. "Once we're married, your father said that we can move into the house. And here's a thought: if we have a girl, we could name her Judy." He paused. "Well, maybe her middle name can be Judy." He flashed a confident smile. "Just think, I'll be coming home at the end of the day to you, and I gotta say, there's nothing else a man could want in the world. Married to a former Rockette, no less."

Marion stared out the window of the car, miserable. "I was a Rockette for less than two months. I don't think it counts."

Two months, when her life had cracked open with possibilities and also been wracked with pain and guilt. She'd felt more love and loss in those weeks than at any other time in her nineteen years.

It was back to Bronxville and her old life. Yet Nathaniel's image of her future was haunting. She'd be stepping right into Lucille's uncomfortable shoes. By dancing, she was following the carefree, selfish Lucille who would abandon her family, but if she chose the opposite path and ended up with a husband and kids, she had a sinking feeling that she'd eventually be climbing the walls, just like Lucille before she skipped town. Was Marion destined to turn into her mother, no matter what choice she made?

They pulled up to the steps of the Rehearsal Club.

Nathaniel leaned over to kiss her.

She turned and grabbed the door handle, yanking it open. "I have to go. Thank you for driving me. I'll see you later."

"Wait a minute, what time should I pick you up tomorrow?"

"I don't know. I'll figure that out later."

She flew up the steps of the Rehearsal Club but stopped in her tracks when she realized a man was standing in the doorway, blocking the way in.

Her gaze traveled from a pair of black Oxford shoes up to a tan trench coat, and she took a deep breath, ready to scream. But instead of seeing the puffy pink face of the bomber, she was looking into the deep-blue eyes of Peter Griggs.

"Peter? What are you doing here?" Marion glanced back into the street. Nathaniel was easing his Chevy Bel Air out into traffic, on his way back to Bronxville.

"I thought I'd leave a message, or that maybe Bunny would know how to reach you. I was wondering how you are doing."

"That's nice of you."

Her foot slipped on the step and he reached out to steady her. "Who was that who dropped you off?"

"A friend." She didn't know why she was lying. It was too much to explain right now. "I'm staying here for a night so I can pack up."

"You were serious when you said you were quitting?"

"I just left Russell at Radio City, told him the news. So, yes." Tears pricked her eyes. She didn't want to go inside to the din of the lobby of the Rehearsal Club. But she'd promised her father. She took a deep breath, but it was as if her chest was constricted, like she was wearing a tight girdle.

"Are you okay?" asked Peter.

He was probably worried she was going to pass out again. "I'm fine, I just feel like I need air."

"Let's take a walk," he said. "I know exactly what will help."

She'd promised Simon that she'd remain inside the Rehearsal Club. But Peter would protect her if anyone tried to attack again. It wasn't as if she was alone, and a walk might revive her.

They walked south a few blocks and turned left, heading into the Rockefeller complex, which spanned three blocks between Fifth and Sixth Avenues. Marion loved walking through the maze of buildings of varying heights and shapes that all shared the same Art Deco architecture, decorated with murals, bas-reliefs, sculptures, and mosaics. The ice rink sat in the very center, surrounded by wide plazas with lush gardens. Peter led her to the entrance of 30 Rockefeller Center—the tallest of the buildings—and she smiled when they stepped into the elevator and he pushed the button for the very top floor.

The observation deck. She knew it was a popular tourist destination but had never ventured there herself. When the elevator opened, they walked out of the small foyer to a wraparound deck seventy stories up, overlooking the entire city. The air was fresh and clean, the view cast out at least fifty miles. They walked slowly around, and at the south side, where the Empire State Building towered over downtown Manhattan, Marion stopped and leaned against the railing.

"This was a good idea," she said. "Nothing like being up this high to get some perspective on things. Thank you."

"How did it go with your father?"

"He's relieved I'm home, that I'm no longer dancing."

"I know I asked you this before, but what if they find the bomber? Would you want to go back to Radio City then?"

"It's more complicated than that." She didn't want to have to explain Russell's comment to Emily that she simply didn't make a good Rockette. "In any event, my father confided something to me a few days ago. He said that my mother wasn't happy being home and raising us, that she'd decided to go back to acting. She was in Boston, performing in a play, when she died, not visiting a sick friend, as Judy and I were told."

Peter stayed silent, listening.

"Mrs. Hornsby told me that the separation may have been only temporary, she was going to come back to New York with the show eventually, but I wonder if my mother told her that in order to soften the blow, make a clean getaway. I don't know what to think anymore, or how to behave."

"Why is that?"

"Because no matter what I do now, I might turn into her. If I continue dancing, I'm rejecting my father and—" She was about say "Nathaniel." "And a quiet, ordinary life. If I marry and have kids and do all that, I give up a creative life."

"Is the man who dropped you off part of that quiet, ordinary life?" Peter's jaw stiffened.

"He's an old family friend, we started dating in high school, and my father wants me to settle down with him."

"Do you want that, I mean, to have kids eventually?"

How to explain? The thought of having a child with Nathaniel made her feel slightly queasy. But with someone else, someone smart and ambitious and kind, she would.

Someone like Peter.

She couldn't meet his eyes as she answered. "I guess so. That would be great, if it works out, I always imagined I would. But what if I end up deserting them?"

Peter looked away, studying a couple of tourists who were fiddling with a camera. "With the discovery of the double helix a few years ago, we're learning more and more about genetic traits that are passed down generation to generation. I'm talking about traits that are truly malignant, like Huntington's disease, or hemophilia, or sickle cell disease. But what you're talking about are aspects of your mom that are more amorphous."

"You've lost me. What are you saying?"

"What I'm saying is your mother's decisions are not your destiny. The outcome, luckily, is in your hands, not your DNA."

"How so?"

"You can decide to emulate the parts of your mother that you admire and ignore the others. You loved her, right? She was a good mom?"

"She was charming and attentive. I had no idea she wasn't happy, she never let on."

"Maybe you can be both nurturing and creative. As opposed to stifled and impulsive."

Marion let out a small exhale. "I hadn't thought about it like that."

"It helps to get some perspective."

They smiled at each other, then looked back out at the view.

"It doesn't seem fair," ventured Peter. "I wouldn't give up my career for a family. No man I know would. Why do you have to?"

"Do you want to have a family?"

"No. So I suppose it's a moot point."

His decisiveness surprised her. "Really? You don't want kids or a wife?"

"Absolutely not."

"Why not?"

"The more important question is, how will you feel if you give up dance?"

He hadn't answered her question. He was probably deflecting in order to make it clear to Marion that he wasn't interested in her in that way. And, of course, that was what he would say, having just seen her with her high school sweetheart.

She deflected right back. "When I was talking to my dad, there was something going on. I can't explain it, but I think he knows something about those missing files. Whenever I've mentioned them, his hand shakes and he hides it in a pocket. It's strange."

"Like a tell in poker."

"Yes."

"But you didn't answer my question, about giving up your dancing."

"You dodged mine as well."

"Touché."

They stared at each other for a moment, at a standoff. Peter's face was inches from her own. Lately, with Nathaniel, Marion felt herself withdrawing whenever she encountered him—on the drive to the city she was practically hugging the passenger-side door—but with Peter, it was the opposite, as if there were a magnetic field between them, pulling them together.

Finally, Marion spoke. "What will it be like not to dance? It'll be like a piece of my heart has been removed from my body. I'm sure that's what my mother felt as well, that's why she hid everything away up in the attic, out of sight. I've danced practically my whole life. Walking wasn't good enough, I wanted to run. Jumping wasn't enough, I had to leap. It's the way I move in the world. Without it, I'll feel like I'm dead inside."

"There are people who actually do feel like they are dead. It's a psychiatric condition called Cotard's delusion."

Leave it to Peter to go off on a random tangent. Even though she'd answered his question, he still was avoiding hers. She wouldn't press it. "What's Cotard's delusion?"

"People with it think that they're dead, or are rotting away, or have lost their internal organs."

In spite of herself, she laughed. "Sorry. It's just the last thing I expected to hear. How awful. Can you help them?"

"Drugs and electric shock have been known to help. It's believed to be caused by damage to a certain part of the brain, as it can occur after a blow to the head or brain damage."

"Well, I guess that puts things into perspective. Thank you, Dr. Griggs. I do understand logically that I am not dead." She paused. "Wait a minute." A dim memory popped into her head.

Peter began to speak, but she cut him off.

"Dead inside. They're dead. The dead files." She scrunched her eyes shut, trying to summon whatever image was floating around in the recesses of her brain. "The night after I auditioned for the Rockettes, I had dinner at home with Judy and my dad. They were talking about work stuff, which I found completely boring, but at some point she said something about moving some files, and my dad referred to them as 'dead files.' Last night, he used that phrase again, when I pressed him about the missing employee files from the 1930s. He said that they were dead, that they were lost ages ago."

"Yet your sister said they were moved?"

"Yes. In fact, he told her to keep them on the same floor as his office." She looked at Peter, astonished at the connection. "They exist. That's why he shakes."

"Do you think he'll admit he has them if you confront him?"

"No way."

"Wait a minute. Why would he keep the files hidden when they could lead to the person who killed his daughter?"

It didn't make sense.

"We have to go," she said.

"Where?"

She pointed south to the Met Power skyscraper on Irving Place, with the clock at the very top. "To his offices. To find those files."

"When, now? It's a Saturday morning."

"That's right. Now."

CHAPTER TWENTY-SEVEN

his is a really bad idea."

Peter stood inside the marble lobby of the Met Power building, shaking his head, as he and Marion waited for the elevator.

Marion and Judy had been up to her father's office throughout their entire lives, visiting with their mother on trips to the city while she was alive or coming with Mrs. Hornsby for the annual Christmas party that was held for the employees' families each December. Simon had played Santa several times when they were teenagers, which they teased him about endlessly.

Back when they were a family, back when Judy was still alive.

Marion had to admit that her own adrenaline was beginning to spike. She'd never been here without her father present, on a weekend, when all was eerily quiet.

They stayed silent as the elevator rose. At the eighteenth floor the doors opened onto a large reception area.

Marion led the way to her father's corner office only to find the door locked. She was rifling through Judy's old desk looking for the key when a deep voice startled them.

"Can I help you?"

Marion turned to see a burly man in a security guard uniform walking toward them.

"Dennis?" said Marion. "Is that you?"

The man gave her a wide smile. "Is that Miss Marion Brooks?"

"Sure is!" She prayed he didn't sense the fear in her voice. This might be their only hope. "It's been ages. I hope you and the family are doing well."

"We certainly are." He glanced over at Peter. "Are you meeting your dad here?"

She made quick introductions. What she was about to say was terrible, but it was the only way in. "My father's asked me to pick up the last of Judy's things. My friend Peter here is helping me, but I forgot to bring the key Dad gave me."

Dennis gave a solemn nod. "I was so sorry when I heard the news. She was a lovely girl."

"She was. She is missed." The truth of the statement almost brought her to tears.

Dennis pulled out a set of keys and unlocked the door. "Go right on in and let me know if I can help you with anything. I'll check back in a half hour or so and lock up once you're done."

Once the door was open and Dennis had wandered off, Marion avoided Peter's eyes. "That was a terrible thing to do, I'm aware of it. Using Judy's death to get in here."

"You did what you had to. If you're right, you'll prevent further deaths."

She pulled out a drawer of the secretary's desk. That was the place to start, as Judy would have a record of every file, including hopefully the "dead" ones. While Peter watched, Marion ran her fingers along the tabs, not sure exactly what she was looking for. She tried the other drawers and struck gold on the last one, a file marked *Archives*. Thank goodness for Judy's impeccable organizational skills.

Marion laid it open on the desk. Inside were ten single-spaced pages of file listings: human resources, payroll, cross-referenced with room and shelf numbers. She gave half the pages to Peter and motioned for him to follow her into her father's office. If Dennis came by again, he'd see that they were inside with the light on but not what they were actually doing.

Peter looked around the room, with its Art Deco furnishings and the expansive view, and let out a low whistle.

They each began reading through the pages. On the last page of her sheaf, Marion found it. "'Dead Files/Troublesome Employees 1930–1939.' That's it!"

"Where are they kept?"

"Room 1870, Shelf 16. This floor. Exactly what Judy said."

She peeked out of her father's office, making sure that Dennis wasn't around to check on them. Room 1870 was right around the corner from her father's office.

But the door was locked.

They were so close, but she couldn't come up with any reason to ask Dennis for the key. It wasn't as if any of Judy's personal effects would be in there.

"Let me try to pick it," suggested Peter. "Do you have a hairpin?"

She plucked one from her purse and handed it over. Two minutes passed, with no luck. After another couple of interminable minutes, Marion told him she'd be right back. She ran to her father's office and looked around. If these files were valuable enough to keep away from the police, he might keep the key close at hand.

She rummaged through his desk drawers and found nothing. Straightening up, she scanned the room. On one bookshelf sat three of his "Employee of the Year" awards, identical to the one he kept in his home office.

At home, that was where he hid the key to his safe, where Marion's pearls were tucked away whenever she "misbehaved."

It was worth a try. She lifted the first one. Nothing. Same with the second.

But under the very last one lay a silver key.

She let out a strangled cry of triumph and ran back to Peter, hoping that it would be the right one. It had to be.

"Look, I think I found it!" She handed him the key.

He slipped it into the lock and turned.

They were in.

She flipped on the light and her heart dropped. The room was overflowing with boxes of files. If Dennis came back to check on them, they'd be caught red-handed. "Shelf 16, where is it?"

Four banker's boxes stood on Shelf 16. They couldn't possibly have enough time to go through them all before Dennis returned.

Peter pulled them down and placed them on a small table in the center of the room. Each file related to a former Met Power employee from the 1930s. Most were complaints about unfair dismissals or medical claims regarding injuries that occurred on the job; others mentioned respiratory troubles that the employees believed were attributed to air-quality issues at the company's plants.

No wonder Met Power kept these from the police. In case after case, Met Power had either offered a paltry amount of money to the employee or sent legal notices saying their cases were moot. Maybe these were all justified. In a company with so many thousands of employees, there were bound to be complaints and injuries.

But then why tell the police that the files didn't exist?

Marion prayed they had enough time to get through them all. They wouldn't get an opportunity like this again.

Fifteen minutes passed.

Twenty.

Nothing she read struck a chord as having to do with the bomber. But then, she wasn't really sure what she was looking for.

After twenty-five minutes, Peter spoke so quietly she didn't make out what he'd said.

"What?"

"I think we've found him."

She dropped the file she was looking at and went to Peter's side. The name on the folder read *George Martinek*.

"It says that George Martinek was hired in 1929 as a generator wiper in the Bronx," said Peter. "Two years later, in 1931, there was some kind of boiler explosion and he was badly hurt. It looks like Met Power stopped paying him a year later, and then in '34 there's a compensation claim."

"How old is he now?" asked Marion.

Peter checked. "He's fifty-three."

"It's been almost twenty-five years since he was hurt."

"Plenty of time to build up a murderous rage."

Marion paused. "What makes you think this is our guy?"

"There are dozens of typed letters from him in here." He pulled them out and laid them on the table. "They begin around 1936, after the appeals board rejected his request for compensation. The sentences are similar in structure and phrasing to the letters from the bomber: 'I'm planning on taking justice into my own hands,' 'dastardly deeds,' 'Metropolitan Power' instead of 'Met Power.'"

"That's him! You found it!"

"*We* found it." He was looking at her like no one ever had before. Like she was worthy and smart. Capable. She threw her arms around his neck.

He wrapped his arms around her waist and lifted her off her feet for a split second. If they hadn't been surrounded by files and shelves, she was sure he would have swung her around in victory, like the photos of the sailors and the girls in Times Square on V-J Day. She felt a crazy jubilation, of having accomplished something that seemed impossible.

Peter pulled back slightly and looked down at her. His hands stayed wrapped around her waist. "Now what?"

"Now we take this file and bring it to the police, show them what we've discovered. What time is it?"

He stepped back and checked his watch. "We've been here twenty-five minutes. Your friend Dennis will probably be showing up any moment now."

There was no time to waste. Marion grabbed an empty banker's box that sat near the door. She placed Martinek's file inside and directed Peter to put the box with the rest of the files back exactly where he'd found it.

"Are you sure this is a good idea?" asked Peter as they hightailed it back to Marion's father's office. "Maybe you should call your father and ask him to meet you here, show him what we've found."

"He either knows or suspects that he had the answer in those files. Why else would they be marked *Troublesome* and locked away?"

"Because the people were troublesome. They had an issue with Met Power in some way or another."

"But then why did they tell the police that they didn't have any files before 1940? He and Judy were talking about them not two months ago. They knew." The seriousness of the omission crushed down on her. Could Judy have known as well?

"You need to talk to your father. Not jump to conclusions."

Part of her didn't want to know the answer. Would Simon really choose his company over doing what was right? It didn't make sense, but all the facts pointed in that direction.

As they entered her father's office, a whistling noise startled them both. It was Dennis, returning.

There was no time. She pointed to a shelf nearby. "Quick, grab those books and put them in the box."

As Peter did so, Marion tore off the cardigan she was wearing. She stuffed the books into the box, to give it some weight, and then draped her cardigan on top, covering up whatever was underneath. She was buttoning up her coat when the door to her father's office opened and Dennis peeked his head inside.

"Did you find everything you needed?" he asked.

She lifted the box. "We did. Thank you for helping us out."

"Let me get that for you," offered Dennis.

Peter stepped forward. "That's all right, I've got it." He took the box out of Marion's hands.

Dennis seemed unsure. "What do you have there?"

"A pair of shoes she left behind, this sweater," answered Marion. "I don't want Dad to have to deal with it, it's easier this way."

"Of course. I understand."

Out in the harsh sunlight of the street, Marion led Peter to the nearest telephone booth. She slid a dime into the slot and pulled out the card with Captain Somers's phone number on it from her purse. It rang a few times and then a familiar voice picked up.

"Ogden here."

She wished Somers had picked up the phone, not the eternally recalcitrant Ogden. "Is Captain Somers there?"

"Who's calling?"

"This is Marion Brooks."

"Right. How can we help you?"

"Peter—Dr. Griggs—and I have uncovered a former Met Power employee who fits the profile of the Big Apple Bomber perfectly. We can be there in a half hour."

"Take your time. We're in the middle of something else right now, a shooting on the Upper East Side."

"But we have the guy."

"Right. Give me his name and I'll look into it when I get a chance."

"But you don't understand, it's the Big Apple Bomber. We're certain."

"Sure. Just like your letter writer was the guy."

She tried not to let her exasperation creep into her voice even though she wanted to scream. "His name is George Martinek. His last known residence was the Bronx."

"That's not Connecticut. I thought the good doctor said he'd be in Connecticut."

"That's the last address on his file, from back in the thirties. He's probably in Connecticut now."

"Sure thing. Right. Got it, I gotta go."

The phone went dead.

"He doesn't believe us. He's not even going to check on it, I can tell."

"That was Ogden?" asked Peter.

"Yup. I think we would've stood a chance if it was Somers, but not Ogden. He's mad at us for making him look like an idiot."

"Then I'll go down myself and get it into Somers's hands."

"Apparently he's out, there was a shooting uptown." After all their hard work, they weren't being taken seriously. And they were so close.

"Let's go back to my place and go through the file closely," said Peter. "Maybe we can uncover something that will get the cops to stand up and take notice."

CHAPTER TWENTY-EIGHT

B ack at Peter's loft, Marion and Peter pored over the contents of Met Power's employee file for George Martinek.

According to the company's own reports, on September 5, 1931, a malfunctioning boiler blew up as Martinek was walking by. Toxic fumes entered his airway and lungs, leaving him in a heap on the floor, hacking up blood, where two co-workers found him. He tried to go back to work but collapsed after twenty minutes and was sent home to his boardinghouse on the Upper West Side of Manhattan. There, blood spewed out of his mouth as he lay in bed, vomiting over and over. He eventually was moved to a hospital.

"That accident sounds ghastly," said Marion. "I almost feel bad for the guy."

"That's not all," said Peter, pulling out the next document. "Not long after, he was admitted to a sanatorium in Arizona, where he received injections into his stomach. But they didn't help, and he was unable to work anymore. That's when he started writing his letters. Did Met Power help at all?"

Marion sifted through the papers. "At first. He got a small insurance settlement, and then part of his salary, and later they suggested he apply for disability through the Workmen's Comp Board of New

York State." She turned the page over. "However, it looks like Met Power waited to suggest that until it was too late, and the statute of limitations had already expired."

"That way Met Power wouldn't have to pay his claim. Did Martinek have any recourse?"

"He appealed the Workmen's Comp Board's ruling three times and was denied three times."

They were quiet for a moment as they continued reading through the notes. After Martinek ran out of money, he left the sanatorium and went to live with his two older, unmarried sisters at 14 Brick Street in Waterbury, Connecticut.

"An industrial town in southwestern Connecticut with a large Slavic population," said Peter.

"Exactly where you said he'd be. Living with female relatives, as you said he would be." Marion pulled out the transcripts from the Workmen's Comp hearings and studied them. When she was done, she looked up at Peter. "His co-workers testified against him, saying that he was lying."

"Why would they do that?"

"Maybe they didn't like him. Didn't you say that this type of person could be smug and self-righteous?"

"That's true. At some point, his letters to Met Power change in tone, become delusional," said Peter. "My guess is that he had a psychotic break in his thirties that sent him down this path of sociopathic revenge."

"This has to be the guy. Are there any photos of him?"

"Unfortunately, no." Peter paused. "I suppose now we take everything we have to police headquarters and fight like hell until someone takes this file seriously."

"You know they'll just stash it in some box. They think we're the enemy. Especially after Hardenby's arrest and release."

"There's no other choice."

"Sure there is." She pointed to the address he'd written down in his notebook: *14 Brick Street, Waterbury, Connecticut.* "We go there."

※

For a good hour, Marion worked on convincing Peter to join her on a road trip to Waterbury.

"We'll get up early and drive out, get a look at the place," she said.

"That's crazy. That's for the police to handle, not us."

"I'm the one who was attacked. I think I have every right to track him down, just the way he tracked me. See if he likes it." She hoped she sounded braver than she felt.

"You are not getting anywhere near him. Can you imagine what your father would say if he knew what we were even contemplating?"

Marion had assured Simon she'd stay put at the Rehearsal Club and had already blown that promise. "I don't think my father has any right to tell me what to do at this point, if these files mean what I think they do." She eyed Peter sideways. "Did you just admit that you're contemplating it?"

Peter lifted one eyebrow but otherwise ignored her teasing. "Tomorrow's Sunday. If the Martineks fit the profile, they'll be going to church."

"We wait outside the house and watch them leave for church. At that point we'll know for sure if he's the bomber and can tell the police so."

Peter frowned. "How do you plan on getting up there? A yellow taxi in Waterbury would draw some notice. Not to mention it would be an expensive ride."

"Bunny said Dale has a car. Can you call him and borrow it?"

"I'll ask. But if not, then we stay put and go to the police, all right?"

She promised, feeling a thrill when Dale picked up after the second ring and agreed to lend Peter his car the next day.

Marion hadn't even noticed that it had gotten dark out, she'd been so engrossed in the contents of Martinek's file and the details of their plan. "Shoot."

"What?" asked Peter.

"It's past curfew at the Rehearsal Club. The doors will be locked."

"You could stay here. You can take my bed. I'll sleep on the couch."

"I couldn't impose." She could only imagine what Nathaniel or her father would think.

"Look at it this way. The bomber knows about the Rehearsal Club, but he doesn't know about this place. You'll be safe, and I'll sleep better."

She agreed. It made sense. And she did feel safer with him.

He loaned her a pair of pajamas that were way too big but soft and comfy, and laughed when she walked out of the bathroom wearing them.

"What?" she said.

"Those are enormous on you. Yet you still look like a fashion model. Not sure how you pull that off."

She gave him a shy smile. This was the first time he'd made any mention of the way she looked, and she felt a rush of exhilaration at that fact. All day, she'd been keenly aware of every move he made, of when his arm brushed hers or when they reached for a document at the same time and their hands touched. She was sure he felt the connection as well. Her first impression of him, as a gangling boy, had been replaced by something else entirely over the past few weeks. Peter was smart, funny, very sensitive but in a good way, and he had the bluest eyes she'd ever seen. She didn't know what she would've done without him, and certainly the investigation wouldn't have been as far along as it was.

He was wearing a white tee shirt that showed off his wide shoulders and accentuated the way his torso tapered down to his narrow waist. They stared at each other a moment, but then Peter retreated to the couch, where he'd laid a quilt and a pillow, and she climbed into the bed.

The apartment was an open loft, with only a folded screen separating the bed from the rest of the space, which meant she was basically lying in the same room as a man. Peter was right there, not twenty feet away, and she could hear him turning over, trying to get comfortable. He was having as difficult a time nodding off as she was. Finally, the muffled purr of the street noise outside lulled her into a dreamless sleep.

The next thing she knew, Peter's alarm was going off. The sky was still dark as they scrambled out the door to pick up Dale's car from the parking garage. There was no time to waste if they were going to get to Waterbury and stake out Martinek's home while he was at church. She couldn't go on like this much longer, she knew, every day rife with danger and chaos. Her brain would melt away from sheer exhaustion. Peter looked haggard as well, and they didn't speak much on the drive. That early, the roads were clear, and they flew past town after town, eventually reaching Waterbury, where a sign read *Welcome to Brass City!*

The town was set in a narrow valley, cut through by a wide river lined with boxy redbrick factories.

"There are a number of Lithuanian immigrants here, like Martinek," said Peter. "Most of them work in the factories making buttons, buckles, that kind of thing."

He turned off the main street and Marion guided him using the atlas. Brick Street was a narrow road with a steep incline. The mailbox outside number 14 read *Martinek.*

"That's it," said Marion.

"We're pretty conspicuous here." Peter backed the car up the hill and parked so they had a decent view of Martinek's residence without being right on top of it.

The house was three stories, the top floor painted a sickly pink that was peeling in places. Railed porches ran all the way across the first and second floors, and a small balcony sagged dangerously on the third. An unpaved driveway on the side of the house led to a small garage set far back from the road, while a couple of leafless shrubs decorated the tiny patch of lawn out front.

They had hardly settled in when the front door opened.

"Here they come!" Marion slid low in her seat and pulled her hat brim down. Peter held a newspaper right below his eyeline and pretended to read.

Two women in their sixties walked out first, clutching their handbags as they maneuvered down the rickety front steps. They wore their Sunday best, although their wool coats were shabby in places and their hats twenty years out of date. Soon after, a man in a trench coat appeared.

Marion held her breath. In profile, it looked like him: same jowls, same pear-shaped silhouette. For a brief moment, he looked their way, then one of the sisters spoke and he hurried to catch up as they walked down the hill, away from the car.

"That was him." Marion was sure of it. Those eyes, the glasses. "That's the man who attacked me and who was sitting next to Judy at Radio City. That's our man."

"Did he see us?" asked Peter.

"I don't think so."

The trio turned right at the end of the street. Peter took Marion's hand. "Are you okay?"

She nodded and squeezed it, grateful for the gesture. "I'm glad we found him, thanks to your sleuthing skills. You might want to join the police when this is all over. They sure could use you."

Peter stiffened, his eyes on the rearview mirror. "A family is walking down the street toward us. We should probably get out of here."

"Hold on. I have an idea."

Marion opened the passenger door.

"What are you doing?" said Peter with alarm.

"We've come all this way, why waste the opportunity?"

She waited as the family neared the car, a wide smile on her face.
"Good morning!"

The couple were around thirty, and the son seemed to be around
seven or eight. All were dressed in their Sunday best, like the Martinek's. The boy's hair had been slicked down, but an errant cowlick
flicked up at the crown of his head.

Marion spoke quickly. "My husband and I are thinking about
moving to this area. We were wondering what it's like to live here, if
you like it."

By then Peter had gotten out of the car and nodded warily.

"Are you looking at the old Samuels place?" asked the woman in
an accent that Marion couldn't place.

Marion nodded. "Considering it. Would you say this is a quiet
street?"

"Well, we live around the corner, but this whole area is fairly quiet,"
answered the man. "Nice people, everyone looks out for each other."

"Except for them." The boy was pointing at number 14.

"Now, Lukas," said the woman. "That's not kind."

"It's true," Lukas insisted. "All the kids call that the crazy house.
Once our ball ended up going down their driveway, and the man
came out of the garage and screamed at us."

"Now, now," said the wife. "They have had a tough time of it. The
sisters, Anna and Mae, have had to take care of their baby brother for
ages now. He's not in good health." She lowered her voice, as if someone
might overhear. "They work in the brass mill and there's never enough

278

money to go around. That's why the house looks like it does. I feel bad for them."

"Whole family has a nasty streak, as far as I'm concerned," said her husband.

"Waterbury's a fine town," said the woman. "A nice place to raise a family."

"He's building a monster in his garage," interjected the boy. "You can hear him banging on it all day."

His mother scolded him in another language.

"Well, thank you very much," said Marion. Peter tipped his hat at them as the family walked away.

Marion walked around to his side of the car. "Well, that seals it."

"I'm thinking *you* should consider joining the police force after that interrogation," said Peter. "Nicely done. Now let's get back to the city so we can pass this all on to Captain Somers."

"I want to see one more thing." Marion started walking toward the house.

"Where are you going? This is crazy!" Peter caught up with her.

"We'll just peek in the windows of the garage." She checked her watch. "They won't be back for at least an hour."

The windows, unfortunately, were of smoked glass. She tried the door, but it was locked.

"We're going to get thrown in jail for trespassing," countered Peter. "Let's go."

But Marion couldn't help herself. They'd come this far. Who was this man who had the entire city under his spell? They had plenty of time, and she had to know more. If they found some concrete evidence, then Somers and Ogden would have to step up.

The backyard was strewn with old car tires and rusting cans. A small set of steps led to the back door. Marion crept closer and pointed. "It's open. The back door, look."

The door seemed to have gotten stuck before fully closing, the frame around it rotted in places.

Peter muttered something behind her, but she didn't respond. Up on the porch, she pulled the door open. It squeaked uneasily.

Inside was a dingy kitchen with a cracked linoleum floor. A stack of dishes filled the sink, and the air smelled of onions and grease. Through another door was a parlor with several pictures of Jesus nailed into the faded floral wallpaper. Lace curtains had turned a disagreeable shade of light brown, almost an oatmeal, and hung stiffly.

"We can't be here, Marion," said Peter in a loud whisper. "What if there are tenants upstairs?"

"Look, through there." She pointed to the room on the other side of the vestibule. "That's his bedroom, I bet."

"Hold on." Peter crept up to the front door and pushed aside the curtain so he could see out. Satisfied no one was coming, he followed Marion. "A quick look around and then we're out of here."

The room was small but clean. On a dresser sat a couple of subway tokens and a typewriter.

"Oh my God." Peter was staring down at a small bedside table, where something had been tucked under the base of a lamp. "It's two tickets for a show at Radio City."

"What?" Marion leaned down to study them. He was right. Two tickets, seats HH 601 and 602, to see the one-o'clock movie at Radio City on Monday, December 17.

Today was the sixteenth.

Marion felt the blood drain from her face. Tomorrow, the Rockettes would be performing the *Christmas Spectacular* at noon, right before the one-o'clock showing.

"Radio City's his next target." Marion's body began to shake as the memory of that terrible night came flooding back. "What do we do? Should we take them and bring them to the police?" she asked.

Peter shook his head. "That will only tip our hand. He'll know someone was here, that we're onto him. He might decide to show up the next day, or who knows when?"

A noise outside on the street caught their attention. Peter and Marion carefully peered out the window.

A couple of kids were circling their bikes in the middle of the street. It took a second for Marion to understand what was going on. In the center of the circle was Martinek, trying to cross the road toward his house. The kids were taunting him, and he shook his fists in rage.

"It's the bomber." Peter looked at Marion, his face white. "He's back."

CHAPTER TWENTY-NINE

W e have to get out of here, now!"
Peter grabbed Marion and together they ran through the vestibule and parlor, crouching low so as not to be seen through the windows at the front of the house. In the kitchen Marion bumped into a chair, knocking it over. She stopped to right it, but Peter grabbed her hand. "There's no time."

She followed him out the door and down the back steps.

They froze as the sound of coughing echoed in the air. It was a wretched noise, like Martinek's lungs were straining to expel some kind of poison. That was what he lived with, every day, the chronic pain that had made him turn violent.

"He's on the front porch," said Marion. A door slammed. He was inside the house.

They crept carefully through weeds and up a cracked pathway that ran along the far side of the house, crouching low under Martinek's bedroom windows. All was silent.

They had to somehow get back to the car, which involved crossing in front of the house and possibly exposing themselves to Martinek's view if he was near a window.

Another slam of a door. This time it came from the back of the house. He was following their trail.

"He's seen the chair," said Peter. "Quick, run!"

They couldn't risk passing in front of the house, so instead Marion and Peter sprinted down the street and around the block, where a man picking up the paper at the end of his driveway gave them a sharp look. They slowed to a more reasonable pace and sauntered by, Peter lifting his hat in greeting as they did so.

"We're a married couple, inspecting the neighborhood," murmured Peter. "Put your arm in mine."

She did so, and he held it firmly against his body, the two of them breathing hard, walking in lockstep almost as if they were one. Up the hill, across, and then back down Brick Street, where there was no sign of Martinek.

At the car, Peter opened the door for Marion and then jumped in the driver's seat. He put it into reverse and backed all the way up the street until he reached the intersection.

It was only once they were back on the highway that Marion remembered to breathe.

They'd made it, but just barely.

⁂

They drove straight to police headquarters in downtown Manhattan. Peter parked across the street and the two of them ran inside.

At the reception desk on the first floor, Peter explained who they were and that they had something to report about the Big Apple Bomber. "Captain Somers knows us."

"The captain is off today," said the receptionist. "Is there anyone else I can call?"

Just their luck.

"Detective Ogden," said Marion reluctantly.

The woman picked up the receiver and dialed an extension. "I see . . . Yes . . . Will do." She hung up and Marion could tell from the sour look on her face that they weren't welcome.

"I'm afraid he can't see you now. I can take a message." She picked up a pen.

"No, it's vital that he see us," said Peter. "We know where the Big Apple Bomber lives. We've located him."

"You and every other Tom, Dick, and Harry in the city," said the woman. "Trust me, I've been fielding calls nonstop the past week. You can leave a message, or Detective Ogden said you can come back tomorrow after three, when he'll have time."

Peter looked at Marion. "Can we storm up there?"

Marion shook her head. "Not if we don't want to end up in a jail cell. Ogden hates us, thinks we made him look like an ass." She paused. "Which we did, because he is."

The woman behind the desk clucked her tongue. Marion didn't care that she could hear. "We're so close. This is insane."

Together, they walked back outside.

"If Martinek is set on planting another bomb tomorrow, there's no time to waste," said Marion. "We have to figure out another plan, try to catch him in the act."

"The two of us?" Peter looked ill.

If they had the right guy, and she was certain they did, it meant that her father shared the blame in Judy's death, for not turning over the documents to the police right away. She couldn't bear the thought. Turning in the bomber meant turning in her father.

But if they waited for the police to come to their senses and listen to what she and Peter had to say, it would give the bomber a chance to set yet another bomb and possibly kill or injure more people.

"I have a plan," said Marion finally. "I know what we should do."

Marion couldn't go back to Bronxville and look Simon in the eye, knowing what he and his fellow employees at Met Power had done. After she and Peter got back to the loft, she called the house and was relieved when Mrs. Hornsby answered.

"Can you tell Dad I'll be staying in the city one more night?" she said.

"Oh, my dear, I was planning on making your favorite dish tonight, chicken and dumplings." A muffled noise in the background pulled away her attention. "Oh, hold on, your father just walked in the door. Here he is."

Marion grimaced. Her father was not the man she'd thought he was, and she didn't want to have to face that truth just yet.

"Marion?" Simon said. "Are you ready to get picked up? I'll come myself if Nathaniel isn't available."

"I'm not ready," she said.

Peter had moved to the other side of the loft, where a desk sat near the window, trying to give her some privacy, but he could still hear everything.

"I need another night," she said.

Her father let out a disappointed sigh. "Marion. That's not what we agreed on."

"I can't explain why, but I have to stay."

"I'm driving to the Rehearsal Club right now, then. I'll drag you out if I have to."

"You won't find me there."

"Is this some kind of riddle? Please, Marion, I have to know that you're safe. How can you do this to me?"

"I think that's a question for both of us."

"I have no idea what you're talking about." He paused. "Did you go to my office yesterday to collect Judy's things? I stopped by this afternoon to catch up on some work, and Dennis said he ran into you."

"I was there, yes."

"What's going on?" But the words didn't have the vehemence of his earlier questions.

"I have to go. I'll be in touch when I can. I'm safe, but I can't see you right now."

Marion hung up.

With nowhere else to go, Marion stayed at Peter's apartment again, where they solidified their plan well into the night. Even then, she couldn't sleep, knowing that her father had an inkling of what was coming, knowing that she would be betraying the man who'd raised her and loved her dearly. She cried silently into her pillow—or thought she was silent—until Peter got up and knelt by the side of the bed. He stroked her hair and spoke in a low, soothing voice, telling her that it would all be okay.

"Thank you," she whispered once she was able to speak without crying.

She moved over and he lay down on his back and allowed her to curl up into him. She pulled herself closer, letting the warmth of his body calm her own, breathing in the scent of him, and only then did she finally fall asleep.

The next morning, Peter was already up as Marion emerged from a deep sleep. They didn't speak of the fact that they had slept in the same bed all night. Instead, Marion made pancakes on the stove while Peter brewed the coffee, each one weaving around the other with an easy grace, as if they'd done this all their lives. Marion was too nervous to be hungry, but Peter insisted, saying that they needed to have energy and be at the top of their game. "And that requires fuel."

"Yes, Dr. Griggs," she said.

At the Radio City box office, Peter asked for a ticket to the one-o'clock matinee. "Seat II 514, if it's available."

It was. He tucked it into his jacket pocket and turned to Marion. "This is it. Are you going to be okay?" he asked.

"I have to be. This has to work."

"Be careful."

"You too."

He reached out and touched her cheek. She thought he might lean in for a kiss, but then a tourist jostled into her and the moment passed. Peter disappeared inside.

Marion went around to the stage door and greeted the security guards, telling them she was stopping by to pick up her belongings. She passed the rehearsal hall as the troupe was leaving the notes session, and Bunny ran over and gave her arm a squeeze. They'd talked the night before on the phone, and Marion was grateful she'd agreed to their crazy plan.

"Are you ready?" whispered Bunny.

"You bet," she answered. Then, in a louder voice, she said how excited she was to have one last visit with the troupe. Emily and Russell came over and gave her a hug.

"We'll miss you," said Russell. "I have no doubt you're going to do great things."

If he only knew.

In the dressing room, Marion slunk over to the clothes rack with her name on it, which luckily hadn't been taken away yet. She grabbed the costume for the first number and made her way through the noise and excitement of the dressing room before tucking herself into a bathroom near the right wing of the stage. There, she pulled on the fitted velvet leggings and matching jacket and quickly plastered her face with pancake makeup, mascara, lipstick, and rouge. After so many performances, she had the routine down pat.

She'd been a Rockette for a little less than two months, and this would be her final show, no matter what happened out there. Her final time stepping into the spotlight. So much had changed. What if she'd never auditioned in the first place? Her sister would be alive, Marion would probably be engaged to Nathaniel. Her father would be happy and all would be well.

But if she'd never auditioned, she wouldn't have met Bunny and the other Rockettes or been able to experience what it was like to have a sublime passion driving her life. Passion for dance, for her own independence. She would have never met Peter, nor would they have figured out together who the bomber was. Considering the incompetence of the police, more people would be killed or injured, with the investigators no closer to figuring out the identity of the Big Apple Bomber than they were before.

She had to get this guy off the streets, it was the only way to honor her sister's memory. No matter what it cost her.

On the intercom, the stage manager called out for the dancers to take their places.

Marion listened as they assembled in the wings, ready for their entrance. At the last moment, she slipped out of the bathroom and, in the dark, stepped behind Bunny.

Bunny deftly switched places with her and disappeared.

As the Rockette in front of Marion turned around to do the traditional finger–chin lick, her eyes opened wide at the sight of Marion. But then the music started and they were all moving forward, into the glare of the stage lights. Onstage, Marion's heart pounded with fear. The Big Apple Bomber, whose bedroom she'd been in a little more than twenty-four hours ago, was sitting out there in the audience, not thirty feet away.

Holding a bomb ready to be detonated.

CHAPTER THIRTY

M arion tried her best to stay focused on the show, on what steps
came next and where she had to move when. She reminded herself that Peter was out in the audience as well. Besides, George Martinek was not going to set off the bomb while he was still in the
theater, which was another reason not to panic. His modus operandi
was to slide the bomb into the upholstery of the seat next to him
while the audience's attention was on the stage and then slip away
unnoticed. As long as he was in his seat, the bomb would not be
detonated. At least not intentionally.

Peter was sitting directly across the aisle from Martinek, one row
back, so he could keep a close eye on the bomber's actions.

And Tommy Hornsby was just up the aisle, standing right near
the closest exit.

Peter and Marion had called Tommy the night before and asked
him to meet them at Peter's. Once he'd arrived, Marion had explained
what she and Peter knew, how they knew it, and that they had no
doubt in their minds that the Big Apple Bomber was going to strike
Radio City the next day.

At first Tommy had been wary and encouraged them to go back
to Captain Somers to make a formal report.

"We can't even get past the receptionist," said Peter. "They don't want our help, they've made that clear enough."

As the night wore on, Tommy began to understand the seriousness of the situation, and before he left, he agreed to their plan: to catch Martinek in the act. It was the only way. Tommy told them that he wouldn't be wearing his uniform, which might scare off Martinek, but he would be armed and ready to block Martinek's escape as soon as he tried to leave the theater.

Marion was dancing in Bunny's place, knowing that to the audience, all the girls onstage looked alike, although no doubt Russell and Emily up in the viewing room had caught on quickly that something was amiss. The *Christmas Spectacular* was like a train, though: once it began, there was no stopping it. Bunny had immediately agreed to do the switch when Marion called the night before, even though it might put her job in jeopardy. "Hey, you're putting your *life* in jeopardy," she'd said to Marion. "It's the least I can do."

Before the Wooden Soldiers number, Marion caught a glimpse out into the audience. There was Peter, right where he was supposed to be. And there was Martinek, his face puffy and red, wearing his trench coat. Marion imagined the sharp knife he must carry with him in order to slit the upholstery of the seat next to him cleanly and quickly. Not to mention the bomb, which was probably in the briefcase at his feet.

Their plan seemed paltry now. Marion was stuck onstage, useless. Peter was in a terrible position—what if the bomb accidentally exploded?

The soldiers' fall went well. Knowing that any lack of concentration could hurt not only herself but also the other dancers, Marion steeled her mind and her body as she fell backward, ever so slowly, to the floor. At the final beat they all turned their heads out to the audience to give the salute.

As the lights went down, Marion's attention was drawn to where Peter was sitting.

A man in an usher's uniform stood right next to him, whispering and gesturing. Peter said something back, shook his head, but then the usher took his arm. Marion had to get backstage to change costumes for the next number, but she got one more look back before she disappeared into the wings.

Peter's seat was empty.

The usher had forced him out.

That only left Tommy, who was all the way at the back of the theater. Unless he, too, had been removed.

Marion's mind raced as she changed backstage into a long robe with a hood for the nativity scene. What was she going to do now? Her breathing became strained. It was as if she couldn't pull in enough oxygen to keep her heart pumping.

The Rockette standing next to her looked over, worried. "Are you okay?" So far, none of the other dancers had said anything about Marion taking Bunny's place. Replacements happened all the time, and most of the girls probably didn't even know she'd left the troupe.

Marion panted, one hand on her hip. "I can't breathe."

This was no time to be keeling over. The dancer who was in charge of leading out the camel—a good-natured creature called Cornelius—moved closer. "Is everything all right?" she asked. Cornelius nudged his way over as well, as if interested in the answer.

Marion shook her head. No, everything was quite wrong, in fact.

Just then, the camel sneezed, spraying Marion directly in the face with wet strands of mucus.

She straightened up, stunned, and wiped her face with her robe while the dancers around her erupted in giggles.

While unwelcome, the shower of slime pulled her right out of her panic attack. She silently thanked the camel as the music swelled and they all marched back onstage.

From her position far stage right, Marion got a good look at Martinek.

He was still there. She was supposed to be facing upstage, gazing up at the manger where the baby Jesus lay, like all the other dancers. But since the hood kept her face in shadow, she cheated out, keeping her eyes on their target.

Martinek slowly leaned down and fumbled with something at his feet, then straightened back up. He'd removed the bomb from the briefcase.

Marion held her breath as he reached into his coat. Everyone around Martinek was gazing up at the stage, at the animals and the nativity tableau. Having live animals onstage hypnotized the Radio City audiences, as one never knew if a sheep might balk or a donkey might decide to do his business right as the baby Jesus was lifted into the air. The latter had happened during a couple of shows, and while the kids in the audience had loved it, their parents probably not so much. They hadn't brought the whole family to Radio City for poop jokes.

A flash, a reflection, caught Marion's eye. It was Martinek's knife. While his gaze stayed on the stage, she could see his left arm working, cutting through the velvet of the seat next to him.

Once that was done, he'd pull out the bomb and slide it inside. She couldn't let him do that.

But Peter wasn't there to tackle him. Peter wasn't there to stop him. And Tommy had never seen Martinek in the flesh, only the police drawing.

It was up to Marion.

She took a deep breath. What if she was wrong?

But no, she'd seen the flash of the knife. That was him. That was the man who'd killed her sister.

Marion drifted slowly downstage, toward the set of steps that led into the aisle.

She desperately wanted to point down at Martinek and scream

that the Big Apple Bomber was in the house, but that would only end in chaos, with audience members caught in a stampede, and give him a chance to get away. She had to get closer.

The conductor took notice of Marion, a confused look on his face. She was now two feet away from the steps, completely out of position for the tableau.

One foot away.

And then she was on the top stair. The moment had come. She was about to throw the entire *Christmas Spectacular* into disarray; kicking out would seem like a minor stumble in comparison.

She took a deep breath and threw off her robe. Underneath, she was wearing the costume for the finale, a leotard decorated with bright red and green sequins. A jarring contrast to the current number, but that couldn't be helped. The robe would only get in her way. She heard the other dancers onstage murmur as the audience seated nearby gasped.

The whole time she'd been creeping to the edge of the stage, Martinek had been looking down, fiddling with something out of view, most likely the bomb. But now, distracted by the noises of concern from the people around him, he looked up.

Their eyes met. Martinek froze.

"Stop the music!" yelled Marion, her arms spread out, fingers wide. The sound of her voice echoed to the highest reaches of the balcony, and the orchestra sputtered to a halt.

Marion heard a strange clanking, then a long, rolling sound. A small boy in the first row looked down and lifted his feet as a silver metal object rolled under them.

Before Marion could stop him, the boy picked up the pipe and showed it to the woman who sat next to him. "Look, Mom."

The man sitting on the other side of the boy, clearly his father, took one look at the object and yelled, "It's a bomb!"

As the crowd around screamed and tried to scatter, the father grabbed the pipe bomb from his son and lobbed it high into the air.

Up, over Marion's head.

Right toward the other Rockettes, standing helplessly onstage.

＊

When Marion was a young dancer, she impatiently tolerated the barre section that began each ballet class, hating being stuck in one place, and reveled in the allegro, when the dancers were allowed to take turns traveling across the room, incorporating livelier steps and finally jumps. Her favorite was the grand jeté, which was as close to flying as a dancer could possibly get. It required a dancer to leap off one leg, fly high in the air, legs extended into a full split, toes pointed, and land lightly and with grace. The execution demanded both strength and flexibility, and the first time Marion performed one perfectly Miss Stanwich broke out into applause. Soon, Marion could leap higher and stay airborne longer than any of the other students. Soaring across the studio floor, she understood what it was to be weightless and free.

As the pipe bomb arced over Marion's head and toward her fellow dancers, she instinctively went after it, taking four or five running steps before pushing off as hard as she could. She rose high into the air, the result of years of training, and with her legs long and her arms and fingers fully outstretched she was just able to grasp the pipe bomb as it began its descent. She closed her fingers around it and landed, skidding to a stop.

By then, the audience was in full panic mode, screaming and trying to scatter, falling over each other as they tried to get to the exits, their hands filled with coats and purses. The high-pitched wails of children rose into the air.

"Go!" shouted Marion to the dancers onstage. The dancer playing

Mary nodded and began directing everyone off stage left, away from the bomb.

Marion was holding a bomb in her hand, the same kind that had killed Judy and injured dozens. She had no idea when Martinek had set the timer for, or if, having been manhandled, it was more likely to explode at any moment. She stifled the impulse to drop it and run.

A hay bale, part of the nativity scene, sat on the stage a few feet away from where Marion had landed. She thrust the pipe bomb deep inside. She had no idea if that would make any difference if it went off, but right then she had to stop Martinek from leaving. That had been Peter's job, but he was gone.

It was up to her.

She ran back to the edge of the stage, to the stairs. Martinek was heading up the aisle with the rest of the crowd. She shouted and pointed at him, hoping someone in the crowd would help, but the members of the audience were too busy fighting their way out of the theater and her voice was lost among their panicked cries. She might be able to catch up to him and cut him off if she took the aisle just to the right, one that ran parallel but was shorter.

She edged out into the crowd, watching him the best she could. He was caught in the scrum as well, but she was gaining on him. Suddenly, he turned right, heading to the aisle that ran along the Fifty-First Street side of the theater, with the lobby at one end and the stairs to the mezzanine at the other. She did the same. There, the audience members were all heading left toward the lobby, to safety, but she didn't see Martinek in that group. She looked to her right. He wasn't climbing the stairs.

But then a movement to the right of the stairway caught her eye.

He was only five or six feet away from her, reaching for the knob of a narrow door wedged between the stairs and the wall. The door that led backstage.

She took another leap and threw all her body weight onto him, hands on his shoulders, her torso slamming into his. He smashed face-first into the doorway, letting out a grunt. She may have had the element of surprise, but he was burlier and twisted around, easily shoving her off. Her right knee connected with the ground hard. They were both panting as they scrambled to their feet, crouching low, sussing each other out. Martinek's glasses had come off and his face was beet red, his head shiny.

Slowly, he slid the knife out of his coat pocket.

Caught up in the madness, she'd forgotten he had it.

She had no defense against him whatsoever. Except what she knew about the man. Marion remembered what Peter had said about the bomber needing to feel superior to everyone around him.

"Look, sir, you don't have to do this," she said, trying to sound polite, subservient.

Martinek lifted his chin. "You bet I do." His voice was high-pitched, with a thick accent. "And I'm not afraid. This is what I wanted all along. I wanted to show them, and thanks to you, I have."

"What do you mean? Show them how?"

"This will be in all the papers. I'll finally get what's due to me. Now they'll have to listen. Now I'll finally get what I want."

"Which is what?"

"Justice."

A movement behind him caught her eye. Tommy and Peter had broken through the crowd and were about thirty feet away. The Big Apple Bomber didn't know it, but he was trapped.

Unfortunately, he was the one with the knife.

"That's right," Marion said. "You'll finally get justice. I know what happened to you. I know what they did to you."

"What your father's company did to me. I ought to kill you right now; your father cannot suffer enough."

"He wasn't in charge of your case."

"But look where he is now, living the good life off my misery. Any of those executives could have made this right, but they chose not to."

Peter and Tommy were getting closer, gaining ground. She had to keep Martinek focused on her.

"Did you target my sister on purpose? Did you know she was the daughter of a Met Power executive?"

He laughed. "Nah. That was a lucky break."

Marion winced. "That's a terrible thing to say."

"You know what's terrible? Having your lungs seared with toxins. Waking up every morning, year after year, feeling like you've swallowed glass and hacking out your insides. There were times when I wished I was dead."

"I'm sorry for what you went through."

"No, you're not. I saw you and that man snooping around my house. I will kill you, and then kill him, and no one will be the wiser. Like with the other witness. I'm invincible."

"The police know about you." She was telling the truth, even if only one policeman knew. She silently cursed Somers and Ogden for ignoring their pleas. Thank goodness for Tommy. "They'll find you. It's better to give up now."

"I'll never give up."

Peter and Tommy were only ten feet away. But from their vantage point, they weren't able to see that he had a weapon.

"Put down the knife," she said loudly. "Don't hurt anyone else, there's no point to it."

Peter and Tommy stopped in their tracks.

"I don't like people telling me what to do," said Martinek. "You're exactly like my sisters, yammering on and on and on."

She had to keep him talking, keep him focused on her. "Then you tell me. Why did you do it?"

"Metropolitan Power ruined my life. I did my best to get back at them, but the newspapers and press never wrote about it, there were no consequences."

"So you ramped up your approach."

"That's right. I picked the biggest New York City landmarks I could think of: Penn Station, the public library, Radio City. This city almost put me in the grave, and I figured I'd make it a graveyard of destruction in return. I want payback, and I will get it."

"Why did you sign the letters *F.P.*? What does that mean?"

He laughed. "Fair Play. What I was doing was fair play."

From the corner of her eye, she noticed Peter and Tommy exchange a look. Tommy drew his gun, but the sound caught Martinek's attention and he whirled around.

"Backup has arrived, I see," he said.

Audience members were still streaming out of the theater. Tommy's gun was useless; the sound of gunfire would cause even more of a stampede than there currently was now, not to mention the danger of firing in such a tight space.

Martinek had the upper hand.

Without warning, Martinek whirled back around and ran toward Marion. He grabbed her around the neck and pulled her to him, holding the knife out in front of her face, and she was brought immediately back to that night on the roof of the theater. She could feel his hot breath in her ear as she unsuccessfully tried to pull his arm away from her throat. As they started inching toward the stage door, she realized that he was going to try to take her hostage, use her to get safely out of the building. She couldn't let that happen.

Peter's face was white with panic.

She had to disable Martinek in some way. She tried to stomp on his foot and drop to the ground, but Martinek was ready for her this time and only tightened his grip.

He dragged her closer to the backstage door, the knife dancing wildly a few inches from her face. She didn't have a choice but to go along with him, but if he got her out of sight of Peter and Tommy, she'd be doomed.

They were almost to the door; Marion's windpipe was being crushed. As she struggled to breathe, the image of the kids on bikes circling Martinek in Waterbury came into her head.

How he'd yelled so hard he'd given himself a coughing fit. That was his weakness, one she might be able to exploit. If she got it wrong, though, she'd be as good as dead.

She took a deep breath, cocked her arm, and elbowed him, as hard as she could, right in the solar plexus.

He let out an "oomph" and fell against the stage door, coughing so hard he was unable to catch a breath. As he slid to the ground, the knife fell out of his hand and Marion quickly kicked it away.

Within seconds, Tommy was on him, handcuffs out, pulling his hands behind his back, reading him his rights.

Peter ran to Marion and took her in his arms. She fell into them gladly.

"Are you all right?" he asked. "You're not hurt?"

"I'm fine. But we've got to get out of here. The bomb's still on the stage."

Beside them, Tommy hoisted Martinek onto his feet. The bomber's coat had fallen open in the struggle. Marion and Peter exchanged a look.

The Big Apple Bomber was wearing a double-breasted suit, buttoned up all the way.

CHAPTER THIRTY-ONE

The police rushed down the aisle not long after Tommy handcuffed Martinek, and hustled him out of the theater. Meanwhile, the bomb unit had arrived and carefully extracted the bomb from the hay bale where Marion had shoved it. Outside Radio City, ambulances were lined up, handling any injuries that had occurred in the scramble to escape.

Marion and Peter were brought up to the Roxy apartment, where they were told to wait until the police were ready to speak with them. Marion went to the bar and took out a bottle of scotch.

"How about a drink, Dr. Griggs?" she asked. "I think we deserve it."

"You deserve two drinks, at least."

She poured them out and walked over to him, handed him a glass.

"Are you sure you're all right?" He gestured to her right leg.

She hadn't realized she was limping. "It was something of a hard landing when I tackled him. But I'm sure it's nothing."

Peter guided her over to a striped couch and helped her sit down. He knelt in front of her, placed her foot on his leg, and began palpitating her knee gently.

His touch set every nerve in her body on fire. Probably an aftereffect of the ordeal, she told herself. She imagined him sliding his hand further up her thigh and squirmed.

"Does that hurt?" he asked, looking up at her.

"It's just tender. That's all."

"You're shivering."

"It's cold."

He removed his hands and guided her leg down to the floor. With an easy gesture, he took off his suit jacket and placed it around her shoulders, taking a seat next to her.

"What happened during the performance? Where did you go?" she asked.

"Martinek got up right before the show began, spoke to one of the ushers, and then sat back down. Not long after, the head usher approached me and demanded I come with him. I tried to put him off, but he insisted and I didn't want to draw any more attention to myself than I already had. He took me through the lobby and to the office of the head of security, where I was told that there had been a complaint."

"What kind of complaint?"

"That the father of one of the Rockettes believed I was stalking his daughter and had demanded I be thrown out."

"Now, that's rich."

"Martinek had obviously recognized me and was trying to get rid of me. I tried to explain, but, of course, I ended up sounding like a madman, and then we heard screams and I knew it was too late. I'm so sorry."

"He knew we were onto him. That was why he returned from church early in Waterbury, and his suspicions were confirmed after he noticed the chair in the kitchen that I knocked over. It's my fault, for insisting we break in the way we did. He knew we were snooping around his house."

"If you hadn't insisted on going into the house, we would have never found the tickets."

"You've got a point."

The door opened and Captain Somers and Detective Ogden blew into the room, Tommy trailing close behind them.

"What's going on?" asked Marion. "Has he been taken away?"

Somers nodded. "Martinek confessed right away to being the Big Apple Bomber. He seemed eager to tell his side of the story. Tommy told us all about the documentation you found from Met Power, from the dead files. We'll admit that into evidence."

Marion spoke up. "We tried to get it to you directly, Captain, but no one was interested."

"I apologize for that." He glared at Ogden. "It appears there was a lapse in communication, one that will be addressed."

Ogden looked like he'd eaten a sour pickle. Good. He deserved to be punished for hamstringing the investigation the way he had.

"What about Met Power?" Marion had to ask. "Are they in trouble? For having the missing files but not telling the police about it?"

"I can't say anything for sure at this point. There will be an investigation. You're free to go home. We'll be in touch, though." Captain Somers turned to Peter and reached out his hand. "Dr. Griggs, I owe you an apology. Your description of the Big Apple Bomber, as far as I can tell, was right on target. Right down to the double-breasted suit."

Marion shot a look at Ogden, who avoided her gaze.

"I had to give a statement to the press," said Somers. "I hope you don't mind, but I mentioned that your assistance was crucial in breaking the case."

"I don't mind at all," said Peter. "As was Marion's, of course."

"Of course." He turned and shook Marion's hand as well.

A policeman and Peter accompanied Marion to the dressing room, where she changed into her street clothes. On the way to the stage door, they ran into Russell, who gave Marion a huge hug.

"You saved the day, Marion," said Russell. "That leap, that catch! I have to say, it was the most exciting nativity scene we've had in years."

She smiled. "Sorry for sneaking in. It was the only way, and I hope Bunny's not in trouble."

"Not one bit. Look, why don't you come in tomorrow at ten and we'll have a chat. Does that sound good?"

Maybe he was going to ask her to come back as a Rockette? If so, she wasn't sure what her answer would be. "All right. I'll see you tomorrow."

Outside the stage door, the street was quiet. Over on Sixth Avenue, the reflection of the police car lights bounced off the nearby buildings, but the sidewalks of Fifty-First Street were empty. The dancers and crew had all departed. Marion turned to Peter and took a deep breath, letting it out with a whoosh. "I didn't realize how much I was holding in these past few days. He's caught. We did it."

"We sure did."

They were standing so close, it was only natural that Peter would lift his hands to her waist and that she'd place hers on his shoulders. Only natural that he'd lean in and kiss her, slowly and deeply. She wanted nothing more than to lose herself in this wonderful man and not have to think about what the next day might bring.

A soft snow began to fall around them.

"These past two days have been crazy," said Peter when they finally pulled apart. "But good crazy, if that makes any sense."

"Because we caught the Big Apple Bomber?"

"Because I was with you."

Marion smiled and placed her hands on each side of his face. "You make a very good detective, Dr. Griggs."

Her heart hammered in her chest as their lips touched again briefly, softly.

"Dr. Griggs!"

Marion and Peter turned in the direction of the yelling. A half dozen men in overcoats and suits, some holding notebooks, others wielding cameras, had rounded the corner from Sixth Avenue and were headed their way. They surrounded them, yelling out questions, flashbulbs popping with blinding fury.

"Dr. Griggs, how did you know the bomber would be wearing a double-breasted suit?"

"Dr. Griggs, where are you from? How long have you worked for the police? Will you be helping to solve more cases?"

Marion was shoved out of the way. Peter reached for her, but she let herself drift off to the sidelines as he answered question after question, explaining who he was, how he'd approached the investigation.

Eventually, exhausted but happy, she turned and walked away.

※

The girls at the Rehearsal Club didn't let Marion go to bed until after two in the morning. The other Rockettes who lived there, including Bunny, had returned from Radio City bursting with the news of the bomber's capture and how Marion had saved them from certain death. By the time Marion walked through the heavy oak doors, the parlor was mobbed with girls wanting to know more. She did her best to fill them in, and finally Mrs. Fleming came out in her robe and curlers, clapping her hands and telling them all to disperse and let Marion get some rest. She was grateful for the interruption. And grateful that she had paid through the month and still had a place to rest her head.

As she and Bunny settled into their twin beds, Bunny paused a moment before turning off the light. "I've made a decision," she said.

"What's that?" Marion stifled a yawn.

"I'm going to break up with Dale. For good."

Marion had heard Bunny say so before, but there was a gravitas to her voice that was different this time around. "What made you decide that?"

"After watching you today, and seeing what you did, I realize that life's too short to wait around for a fool like him."

"Good for you!"

But Bunny still hadn't turned out the lights. "Besides, one of the cops on the scene was awfully handsome. He asked for my number. Do you think he'll call?"

Some things would never change. But Marion was relieved for Bunny's sake. Ditching Dale was a smart move, no question.

The next morning, Marion's thoughts were consumed with what would happen to her father. The police knew Met Power executives had concealed files from their investigation. What kind of trouble would he be in? While she was relieved that George Martinek could no longer wreak havoc on the city and that she and Peter had caught her sister's killer, Simon was the only family she had left. Would he hate her for what she'd done?

And at the same time, how could he have kept the police from looking at those files? Had Judy known as well? If so, what had they been thinking?

Marion also couldn't help wondering how Peter had fared with the press after she'd left. That kiss. Whenever she thought of it her face grew warm.

It was probably nothing, a rash act prompted by the relief that the worst was over and no one had gotten hurt. Peter hadn't called the Rehearsal Club that morning, although she'd checked the message board twice before she headed out.

He was probably back at Creedmoor, working away. On to the next thing. There was no point in wondering what their time together had meant. Besides, she had to get back to Radio City and meet with Russell.

When she showed up at ten, Russell wasn't alone in his office. A well-dressed couple who looked strangely familiar sat on the couch and smiled as she walked in.

Russell welcomed Marion warmly and asked how she was after the events of the previous night.

She reassured him she was fine. "I'm glad that it's all over."

"As are we," said Russell. "Please, take a seat. I'd like to introduce you to Mr. and Mrs. Hoag. They were watching the show with me and Emily last night."

"Ivan and Amanda Hoag?" said Marion. The Hoags produced some of the best musicals on Broadway. Marion had seen an article in one of the trade magazines that called them the Golden Couple of the Great White Way. "Of the Hoag Organization?"

The Hoags nodded in tandem.

"We're pleased to meet you, Marion," said Mrs. Hoag. "The theaters around the city owe you a serious debt for getting this madman off the streets."

"It was mainly Dr. Griggs," Marion said. "He's the one who figured out who the culprit was in the first place."

As she spoke, she realized where she'd seen the Hoags before. They'd been the strangers at the rehearsal where Bunny had gotten injured. Marion flushed with embarrassment at the thought that they'd seen her acting like an idiot and encouraging her friend to do the same. Mocking the Rockettes, of all things.

Hopefully they would be leaving soon, and she and Russell could speak in private.

Mr. Hoag sat forward on the couch and looked at Marion. "We noticed what you were doing at the rehearsal last week."

Had it only been last week? It seemed like eons ago. "Right, about that—"

He didn't let her finish. "My wife and I are putting together a new musical that we hope to bring to Broadway next season. It's about the Missouri Rockets."

Of course, Marion knew the Missouri Rockets were the dance troupe Russell put together in 1925, and after becoming a big hit on Broadway and performing at Radio City's opening night seven years later, they were rechristened the Rockettes. Every dancer in Radio City knew the origin story, as Russell loved recounting it.

"What a good idea," said Marion. "I can't wait to see it."

"Well, we were hoping you might do more than that. We need someone to help with the choreography, someone who understands what it's like to do a kick line but can translate it into something more interesting, more dynamic." Mr. Hoag gave an easy smile to Russell. "Not that there's anything wrong with what's done here."

"No offense taken," said Russell, clearly enjoying himself.

Mrs. Hoag nudged her husband. "Get to the point. Oh, never mind, I'll get to it myself. We want you to come on board as an assistant choreographer for the show. You'll be involved in casting the dancers, developing the show."

Marion wasn't sure she was hearing correctly. "You want me to be an assistant choreographer?"

"Yes. Russell here says that you're the right person for the job," said Mr. Hoag, "and he clearly knows what he's talking about."

She looked over at Russell. "Really?"

Russell placed both hands on his desk. "Now, I want to make it clear, you don't have to leave Radio City, Marion. You have a place here if you want it. But I thought your affinity for self-expression, shall we say, might be better suited to the Broadway stage. Might be ideal for it, really."

Marion didn't know what to think, what to say. She had never choreographed before. But then again, at the dance studio she'd created combinations for her advanced students every week. And she wouldn't be the choreographer, just the assistant. Maybe Russell was right, maybe this would be a good fit.

But it would mean giving up dancing, giving up being onstage, in front of a crowd.

Mrs. Hoag named the director and choreographer they were considering. "We'd like you to meet with the director first, if that's all right with you. He's in town today, if you're free."

Marion almost jumped out of her chair. "I'm sorry, who is the director?"

"Mr. Darren Noble. Do you know him?"

She recognized his name immediately. "I don't know him. But I'd like to meet with him right away, if that's possible."

"I like your enthusiasm," said Mr. Hoag. "We can set that up, no problem at all. He's staying at the Edison Hotel."

Marion grabbed her purse and rose. "Tell him I'm on my way."

CHAPTER THIRTY-TWO

Marion asked the concierge at the Edison Hotel to direct her to where Mr. Noble was waiting in the opulent lobby. He pointed to a wide-shouldered man with a thick head of gray hair reading the newspaper, seated on one of the plush sofas across the way.

She hurried over and held out her hand. "Mr. Noble, I'm Marion Brooks. I was sent by the Hoags."

He folded up the newspaper and rose, taking her hand in his. "It's a pleasure. I know they were just speaking with you this morning. I appreciate you coming by so quickly." He spoke with a Southern drawl and moved with an easy grace.

"I didn't want to miss the opportunity."

"Glad to hear it." He began speaking of his vision for the show, and Marion nodded encouragingly, said all the right things, but inside she was just waiting for this part of the interview to be over.

She threw out a couple of questions that she hoped were pertinent. He seemed to think they were and followed up by asking her about her experience working with the Rockettes. She was gracious and sang Russell's praises, and then Mr. Noble was offering her the position of assistant choreographer, adding that the full team was set to meet next week.

She had the job. But that was only part of the reason she was there. Marion steadied herself, wondering if she was about to dash it all with her next request.

"Mr. Noble, do you mind if I ask you some questions? Not about the show. About something else."

He blinked a couple of times. "Sure. What's that?"

"I believe you knew my mother, Lucille Brooks. Well, she was Lucille Chandler before she got married."

He broke out into a huge smile. "I *knew* you looked familiar! You have her profile. Lucille Chandler, of course. What an amazing co-incidence."

"You knew her before she was married, and then later, when she was up in Boston, right? Where she died."

At the memory, Mr. Noble grew serious. "I'm so sorry. Yes, of course. That was a terrible time, just terrible. I'm so sorry for your loss. Your mother was a visionary on the stage, no one came close. I only wish she'd lived long enough for others to see her work."

"I was quite young when it all happened, and I was wondering if you could share anything you remember about her back then. It would mean a lot to me."

He crossed his legs and settled into the sofa. "Of course. As I said, your mother was a great talent, and I was upset when she didn't join the play I was doing back in '33, but, of course, I quickly understood why."

Because she had to get married. A shotgun wedding to Simon. Marion didn't say so out loud, just nodded. "I understand that later she went up to Boston to take over for someone who dropped out at the last minute?"

"She did. It was tough to convince her, and she agreed only after we included a clause in her contract that she could return to New York every Sunday after the matinee, so she could see you and your sister on her day off."

"That was in her contract? But we never saw her."

He rubbed his mustache, avoiding Marion's eyes. "Right. I'm not surprised."

He knew something. And he was questioning whether to tell Marion what it was.

"Look," she said, "I'm aware that my parents were having difficulties back then. My father said that she left us behind, hardly looked back."

"No. That's not the truth." He leaned forward. "I don't want to speak ill of your father, but you should know that he warned Lucille that if she tried to see you or your sister while she was away, he'd fight for full custody. He hoped by cutting her off completely, she'd be forced to return to him. However, I know for a fact she went back to New York every Monday, even if you didn't see her."

But they had. Both Marion and Judy had seen their mother watching them from afar during their school recess; she hadn't been an apparition. It was Lucille, doing her best to check on her daughters, even if she blended back into the crowd the minute she thought they'd spotted her.

"How do you know all this?" Marion was putting her new job at risk by being so bold, but she couldn't help it. "Were you close?"

"My dear, we were very close."

Marion's face must have given away her surprise, as Mr. Noble quickly held out his hand, palm facing Marion. "But not in the way that you think. My preference isn't for the ladies, if you know what I mean."

"Oh, I'm sorry. I didn't mean to assume—"

"I loved your mother for her talent and her kindness. And I didn't like to see her upset. As soon as the show came to Broadway, she was going to find an apartment in New York City for the three of you and bring you with her. She felt like your father treated her more like a doll than a person, and she was worried he'd be just as controlling with you and your sister."

So it *had* been temporary. Lucille hadn't abandoned them. If only their father had told her the truth from the beginning. But that would've reflected badly on him, as a husband and father, and to Simon, appearance was everything. "What happened on the night she died? My father never said much about it. Was she hurt badly? Did she suffer?" These were terrible questions to ask. Just saying them out loud made her feel sick. But she had to know.

Mr. Noble took Marion's hands in his. "Your father called the theater that night and they got into a bad row. Lucille wasn't coming back to him, and he knew it by then. When she hung up, she was upset and one of the other actresses offered to walk her back to the hotel where we were all staying. The car came flying down the street but your mother was distracted and stepped off the curb without looking. She died instantly, I was told. A terrible loss for the theater, and a terrible loss for you." He paused. "I'm sorry, this isn't the typical job interview, by any means. Can I get you a drink? I could sure use one."

"You're so kind, and I'm sorry if I'm going off the rails here."

"I understand. You are allowed to go off the rails. This is the theater, after all."

Marion wiped away her tears. "I'm glad she had you as a friend. And thank you for telling me all this. It's an enormous relief, to know the truth."

"As for that drink?" Mr. Noble had a hand raised, calling for the waiter.

As much as she could have used one, she needed time to think about this sudden right turn in her career, as well as the revelations about Lucille.

And there was only one person she wanted to confide in.

"I'm sorry, but it's just not going to work out," said Marion.

Nathaniel sat forlornly in an armchair in a corner of the Rehearsal Club's sitting room. For once, it was devoid of residents, and when he'd shown up with a bouquet of red roses just as she was getting ready to meet Peter for dinner downtown, she knew it was time to make her intentions—or lack of intentions—clear.

"Why not?" asked Nathaniel. "What about everything we talked about? Living in your house with your dad, having kids, our life together."

"*You* talked about that, I listened. I'm going to be working here in New York from now on, living here as well. Our paths are going in different directions, and I think it's best we part ways amicably, don't you think?"

"But I have the ring." He patted his jacket pocket. "Now that the bomber has been caught and it's safe, I thought we could take a carriage ride, like we talked about."

"Like *you* talked about. The life you want, it's not for me, and I'm sorry if it took me so long to figure that out."

A trio of girls walked in, giggling, and went up the stairs.

Nathaniel stared at the bouquet. "Well, now I feel like an idiot."

Marion's heart went out to him. This rejection must sting, as Nathaniel tended to get whatever he was after. "I'm sorry, and I have no doubt you'll find your dream girl. It's just not me. If you're about to get engaged, you should feel like you're on the exact same page with that person. And we don't have that, not really. I'll always treasure the past few years, even when I had to watch you eat broccoli and waffles, and I hope you'll always be a part of my life."

The side of his mouth turned up in a half smile. "I hope for that as well. Can I ask a question?"

"Sure."

"Is it all right if I still take the junior executive position? If you're not comfortable with that, I'll find something else."

Marion reached over and squeezed his hand. "There may be news coming out in the next week or so that changes your plans, I'm afraid. I don't know for sure. You might want to investigate other options."

She'd been fretting about her father all day, bouncing back and forth between worry and rage. She'd tried to reach Simon at work, but the woman who answered had sounded flustered, saying that he was no longer employed there, then practically hung up on Marion. She'd rung him at home, but there had been no answer.

After Nathaniel left, Marion gave the roses to Mrs. Fleming to liven up the parlor and went back upstairs to get dressed. When Marion told Bunny she was having dinner with Peter at the Coach House, Bunny practically swooned.

"He's taking you to the Coach House? That's one of the most romantic spots in the city. Get ready for some wooing, my girl."

Marion dismissed her silliness with a wave of her hand, but then put on her nicest dress—a sapphire-blue frock that swept down her body like a wave—and took extra time with her hair and makeup. She had planned on ending things with Nathaniel the next day, after visiting her father at home, but by coming here to the city Nathaniel had pushed that particular discussion forward. Which was even better.

She had a lot to say to Peter and was now free and clear to do so.

The Coach House was just that, a nineteenth-century former carriage stable off Washington Square, known for its sophisticated fare and beautiful decor. The walls were brick and mahogany, with brass chandeliers hanging from the ceiling, the patrons well-dressed and poised, a far cry from the rowdy crowd at Moriarty's.

Peter was already sitting at the table. He rose as she approached and gave her a light kiss on the cheek. She sat down, feeling awkward, and at first the conversation was stilted. Peter adjusted his tie several times and she knew he was as nervous as she was. Which was ridiculous. They'd been through hell and back together, yet after that kiss on the steps of the stage door, the world had tilted and she wasn't sure what way was up.

"This is a lovely place," said Marion after the waiter had taken their orders.

Peter looked around like he'd only just noticed. "Right. I asked one of the doctors at Creedmoor for a recommendation. I thought it would be nice to celebrate. I hope it's not too much."

"No, of course not. It's perfect."

She recounted what had happened in Russell's office, including the Hoags' offer to start work in two weeks' time, right after the New Year. "To be honest, I'm relieved. With the Rockettes, I never really fit in in terms of the precise technique and execution required. I'm too much. And now, with the notoriety from the case, I really stand out. That's not what the troupe is all about, and I respect that."

"What about dancing?" asked Peter. "Will you miss it?"

"I guess in my wildest dreams I imagined being another Gwen Verdon, bringing people to their feet night after night with my dancing. But is it better to be the dancer who brings a crowd to its feet with the flick of the wrist or to be the one who invents the flick? Being a choreographer opens so many other windows. If it all works out, of course. I could fail terribly."

"I doubt that very much."

"I'm grateful for having been a Rockette. It was a crash course in handling the grind of performing in show after show. Of how hard that is on the body. You can't do it forever, and then what?"

She sounded like her father.

"Well," said Peter, "you can always become a professional baseball player, with your ability to leap and catch."

The newspapers had gone wild over the news of Marion's heroism, but she'd ignored any entreaties to tell her story. It would all die down soon enough, she hoped.

"You think the Yankees would have me?"

"They'd be crazy not to."

He held her gaze.

"I learned something else," said Marion. "The director of the show I've been hired for is the same one who hired my mother all those years ago." She ran through her conversation with Mr. Noble and how it had completely changed her opinion of her mother, not to mention that of her father. "It's such a relief to know she was planning on coming back to us. It changes everything."

"You're still the same person. A courageous, bright, and generous woman who lights up any room she's in. That doesn't change, no matter who your parents are. But I'm glad you know the truth."

Impulsively, Marion leaned over and gave him a quick kiss on the lips.

He pulled back, looking surprised, and ran a hand through his hair so that his curls stood on end.

The sound of the waiter clearing his throat brought her to her senses. She blushed as the dinner was served, embarrassed at her rash act.

"Any news from the police on the case?" she asked, collecting herself enough to eat. She hadn't had a bite all day and was starving. The roast duck was superb.

"The first step is for them to determine Martinek's fitness to stand trial. That will take some time."

"Do you think he should stand trial?"

"I think he's mentally ill. But I guess the question is, was he unfit when all this began, sixteen years ago? It's a fascinating case, really."

"As long as he's off the streets, I don't care if he's in a prison or an asylum." She paused. "Oh my gosh, what if he ends up at Creedmoor? And you're his doctor? Now, that would be a strange twist."

Peter stiffened slightly. "Right, in fact, there's been a development there."

"What kind?"

"Like you, I was offered a new job today."

"Really?" She could easily picture him working with the police, advising them on cases. In an exhilarating rush, she imagined them taking the city by storm together, meeting up over dinner in his loft at the end of the day to exchange stories. She remembered the way he'd gently stroked her hair when she was lying in his bed, and a shiver of desire ran through her.

"It's with the FBI," Peter said. "They want me to start up a new department that studies cases like the Big Apple Bomber and come up with criminal profiles. We'd handle cases across the country, not only in New York."

"That is incredible, Peter. Congratulations. It sounds like we may have found jobs that are the perfect fit." She lifted her glass and he did the same and they clinked them gently together. "If you ever need an assistant, you know where to find me. I'm sure I can run downtown from Times Square to advise you, when called for."

Peter took a sip of his wine and put down his glass. "Actually, it's in Virginia. Where the FBI headquarters are."

"Virginia?"

"Yes."

She couldn't hide her disappointment. "You'll be moving there?"

"It's an opportunity that's too good to pass up."

The room blurred. He was moving all the way to Virginia. She'd never see him again. That explained his reaction to her kiss tonight. This was a breakup dinner.

After breaking up with Nathaniel, she was now on the receiving end.

"They sure reached out fast," she finally said. "I mean, we only solved the case one day ago." But the news had traveled far and wide, with a big headline in the *New York Times* this morning. It was no surprise he'd been snapped up.

"Apparently Captain Somers gave me a glowing recommendation when they called him this morning."

"As he should."

Visions of creating a life together evaporated. Had she imagined their connection all this time? No. The way he'd looked at her last night—*hungrily* came to mind—was completely different from his countenance now. What had happened to change things? Peter was the first man who'd taken the time to get to know her, who wasn't either cowed or overexcited by the way she looked. She couldn't lose him now.

The roast duck suddenly tasted dry. She wouldn't be able to swallow another bite. "Oh. Well, maybe we could see each other when we're both free. I mean, I'd have times that I'm not working, in between jobs. I could come to visit then."

"Mounting a Broadway show has to be a huge undertaking. Who knows what the future holds, right? Besides, you have someone waiting for you back home, right? The guy with the flashy car?"

Was that a touch of jealousy in Peter's question? Or was he relieved that it appeared she was already taken? She couldn't tell what he was thinking. "No. I broke it off with him."

"You did?" He looked at her with wide eyes.

Marion nodded, trying to add a cheery, breezy note to her voice. "Of course, like you said, who knows what's ahead, right?"

"That's true."

The waiter came by, asking about dessert. They both declined. Later, outside, Marion stepped in front of him as he tried to hail a cab.

"Peter, what's going on? I thought that we—"

He let his hand fall to his side. "We do, but—"

She didn't want to hear what else was coming. Instead, she reached up and took his face in her hands and kissed him. He pulled her close, wrapping his arms around her waist, and they stayed like that for what seemed like minutes, lips on fire, pressed against each other. She hadn't imagined it. And she didn't want to let go.

She let her mind empty of everything but the heat of his breath and the strength of his embrace.

He pulled back first, looking at her as if he were memorizing her face. "I can't, I'm so sorry."

He didn't love her. A panicked numbness swept over her as she absorbed his words, and she swayed a little on her feet. She thought she might be sick.

"Why not?"

"It's hard to say. I want to tell you, but—"

She couldn't bear his bumbling. She'd thrown herself at him—literally—and he had declined her invitation. They were nothing to each other, not even friends. Marion raised her arm up again and a cab raced to the curb. She avoided Peter's eyes as she opened the door.

"I want to explain," said Peter.

But Marion's humiliation was complete. "No. I don't want to hear it. I've had enough."

She rolled down the taxi window all the way as she zoomed uptown, the sting of the cold air adding to the sting of her tears.

※

Marion woke with a throbbing headache. She was still confused about why her relationship with Peter had suddenly nose-dived. Maybe, because they had both lived through the roller-coaster ride of the past few weeks, it was destined to turn sour. He knew her at her worst, when she was grief-stricken and wild. That wasn't what a man wanted in a partner. She'd hoped Peter would be different from most men.

She pushed him from her mind. That day, she was determined to track down her father. It was time to deal with the consequences of what she'd done, of what he'd done. First, though, she went to the Hoags' office in Times Square to sign the contract for her new job. The salary was even more than she expected, and she'd be able to afford her own apartment, which was truly exciting. She'd miss Bunny and the girls at the Rehearsal Club, but it would be nice to come home to peace and quiet, not wake up to the ghastly vocal warm-ups of the musical theater actresses first thing in the morning.

The contract lasted a year, including an out-of-town tryout in Chicago. But it didn't really make a difference whether she was in New York or Chicago, not when Peter would be far off in Virginia.

She'd be starting fresh, learning as she went along from one of the best choreographers in the theater.

But without Peter by her side. Why had he seemed so warm one minute, and then cold the next? She still couldn't figure it out.

After an interminable train ride and a very cold walk from the station, she stepped up to the front door of her childhood home. No one answered her knock, so she pulled her key from her purse and unlocked it with a shaky hand. She was fearful for her father and angry at him all at the same time. Her insides roiled as she stepped inside and called out his name.

Nothing. The house was silent.

She moved through the rooms, going to the study first. His briefcase was on the couch and a bottle of whisky sat opened on the desk.

He wasn't in the kitchen or upstairs. Only when she glanced out the window of her bedroom did she spot him. He was out back in one of the porch chairs, wearing his bathrobe, seemingly oblivious to the cold wind.

She opened the door to the backyard slowly so as not to surprise him.

His eyes were red, shoulders curved over. He'd lost weight recently and his cheeks were sunken. One hand held a glass of whisky, and the other was clenched in a tight fist. He looked up and straightened.

"Marion." His voice was scratchy, as if it was the first time he'd spoken in a week. Dark stubble peppered his cheeks and chin.

"Dad. It's freezing. You should come inside."

"I'm fine."

She drew her coat around her and took a seat on the other porch chair. It was strange how different the garden was in winter versus summer. May through September, the small lawn was enclosed in a bubble of green, the tall trees and shrubs forming a giant wall of flickering leaves. This time of year, the bare branches exposed the neighboring houses, the illusion of privacy completely gone.

Not that anyone with a sound mind would be out in their backyard today.

"It was you, right?" he said.

The time had come. "Yes. I found the file for George Martinek."

"Stole it, from what I can gather. Dennis said you were with a man when you came to my office. Was that the police?"

"No. I was with the man who helped figure out who the bomber was, the doctor I told you about. Peter Griggs. And yes, I lied to Dennis. I'm sorry I had to do that."

"You didn't have to do anything."

She couldn't believe what she was hearing. "If I didn't do something, Martinek would have kept on setting bombs until he killed someone else. Is that what you wanted?"

Instead of answering, Simon took a swig of his drink.

She went on the offensive. "Why didn't you give the police the file in the first place?"

"I was ordered not to. Of course, that's not what the top brass are saying now. Now, all the blame rests right on me."

"I called your office and they said you're no longer there. I'm sorry about that, I really am."

He looked at her for the first time since she'd arrived. "How did you know? About the file?"

"I heard you and Judy talking about 'dead files' at the table one night. About moving them. That was before everything happened, so I didn't put two and two together. Not at first."

She expected him to lash out at her, but instead his eyes filled with tears.

"I'm sorry."

"Oh, Dad." She waited a beat before asking the question she most dreaded. "You knew, even before Judy's death, that you might have the answer to who was setting the bombs in your archives, didn't you?"

He closed his eyes for a moment. "We were told the police were grasping at straws and that if the files became public, Met Power would be liable to some serious lawsuits. It was a different time, back in the twenties and thirties, they told me. It could bankrupt the company if everyone who got hurt on the job back then got a chance to relitigate. Better to cover it up. And who knew if the killer even worked for Met Power in the past? There was nothing to prove that. We have disgruntled customers, of course, any big company does, so they figured it was one of them, not our problem."

Marion thought of all the other blue-collar workers, the ones whose stories filled those boxes of files. The ones who didn't go out and plant bombs but instead suffered in silence. From what she and Peter had read, Martinek's injuries had been substantial and incredibly painful. Not that that gave him an excuse to do what he did, but how many others had been hoodwinked into missing deadlines and became destitute, lost everything?

"What if you'd been the one who had the accident?" she asked. "When you first got a job at Met Power, they had you out dealing with dangerous equipment, right? What if it had been you? Did you even bother to read through the files?"

Simon shook his head. "Some, not all."

As if that excused him. "What about Judy? Did she know what the files contained?"

"Absolutely not. I told her they were employees who'd died. She had no idea. I would never have put her in that position."

"What if she'd looked at them?"

"We have warehouses full of files, it wouldn't have crossed her mind. She was a good secretary, did exactly what she was told, no more."

Dear Judy. Thank goodness. But there was one question that bothered Marion most of all.

"What about after Judy's death? Why didn't you go through them then? Why wouldn't you want to catch her killer?"

He seemed to shrink into the porch chair even more. His right hand, the one holding the glass, trembled, and he switched it to his left and put that one in his pocket. She could tell it was still shaking. Whether from cold or fear, she didn't know.

Finally, he spoke. "After her death, and especially after you were attacked, you became my sole focus. I had to save you, keep you from harm. You were my priority, not some old files." He cleared his throat. "But I suppose, if I'm being completely honest, I didn't want to know. If we had a file on the killer the entire time, and I hadn't come forward with it, then Judy's death was my fault. How could I live with that? So I buried my head in the sand, and I was wrong. I know that now. It could have been stopped, but I didn't do anything about it." Tears welled up in his eyes.

"I still can't believe you initially blamed me for luring her there in the first place. For putting her in danger."

"It was the heat of the moment, and I'm so sorry. Please, Marion, I hate myself for what I said. I love you so much." He winced, as if he were in terrible pain.

"If you'd had any kind of conscience at all, you would have gone through the files and handed them right over to the police, long before I became a Rockette, long before Judy sat in that theater seat."

He wiped his eyes with the meaty part of his hand like a child. "I know that now. But I did this for you."

"How?"

"If I didn't do what they asked of me, I would have been out of a job. And it wouldn't have been easy to get another. The corporate world doesn't like whistleblowers. I had the two of you to support, and I wanted to make sure you were happy, especially after Lucille left us. That's all I was thinking about, my two darling girls. Please believe me."

"I know the truth about Mom's time in Boston. You told her she couldn't see us, threatened her with full custody. All because she wanted to follow her dream."

"I shouldn't have done that. But we had a perfect family, why did she have to abandon us? I tried my best, after she left. You were happy as a child, right?" He gestured with his right hand and then let it fall on his lap.

His fingers began to tremble in a rolling motion, as if he were rubbing something between his index finger and his thumb. As Marion watched, the rest of the arm joined in, flapping slightly, like a chicken wing.

"What's going on?"

Simon looked down at his arm with an odd detachment, as if it didn't belong to him. "One of the reasons I wanted you to marry Nathaniel was that it was important you be settled down. I knew I wouldn't be able to care for you."

"What are you talking about?"

"I have Parkinson's disease," he said. "I'm stiff and sore all over, and it's only going to get worse. My balance is off, I've fallen twice already. Some days I can't think straight."

That explained the shaking she'd noticed at Tavern on the Green, when she'd thought he was hiding something. Her father was ill. Parkinson's disease. She'd heard of it, but she thought it was something that old people got, and her father wasn't old. "How long have you known?"

"Since the summer."

In spite of everything, it made her heart ache that he'd felt the need to keep his diagnosis from her and Judy and lived with such terrible news in silence. "Are you sure? Maybe you should get a second opinion."

"I've done that. I've seen every specialist I can. They all say the same thing. There's no cure."

That explained all his mysterious appointments and why he was so adamant that she and Nathaniel move in with him. His behavior of the past few months began to make some sense. He was desperate to know that Judy and Marion would be all right. "How fast will it progress?"

"They can't predict. Eventually I'll need full-time care. If I hadn't gotten fired, I would have received it as part of my benefits. Now I'm on my own. Another reason to be sorry. I've mucked up everything."

"Why didn't you tell me or Judy? Why keep it a secret?"

"Denial, I suppose. Seems to be a theme here, right?" He let out a raspy laugh. "Judy knew something was wrong, but I always told her I'd had too much coffee or that I had a touch of vertigo. If I told you both, if I came out with it, then it would be real. I didn't want it to be real. I saw doctor after doctor, hoping they were wrong."

"Judy told me she thought you were having an affair, with all your mysterious appointments that weren't in the calendar."

A weak smile crept onto his face. "Now, that's grand. I couldn't keep anything from that girl. And I shouldn't have kept all this from you."

His shaking grew worse. "I'm sorry, Marion. I hope you can forgive me."

CHAPTER THIRTY-THREE

After Simon's confession, Marion sat with him in silence for some time.

Her father shivered. His tremor was growing worse the colder he got. "Come inside," she said, rising. "I'm making tea."

Her father had made mistakes, justifying them by saying he was protecting his livelihood and, by extension, his family. Doing so had ended up destroying what they had and killing Judy. It was convenient for him to insist that the directives he'd been given by his superiors were nonnegotiable and that he hadn't overseen the personnel administration department when George Martinek and the other workers were ignored or tricked into losing their deserved compensation. But he knew about it later and should have acted, even if it had cost him his job. As soon as he realized the police were looking for the dead files, he should have supplied them to the investigators, not hidden them away in a locked room.

He chose to protect the company at the cost of everything he held most dear. But at the same time, Marion knew, deep down, that Simon had wanted more than anything for Judy and Marion to have happy childhoods, filled with pleasant memories to replace the worst one of all: the tragic loss of their mother.

How much of a part he played in her death was unknowable. If only he'd been able to shake his old-fashioned view of women and mothers and let Lucille have both a career and a family. Times had changed but he'd refused, digging in even deeper when it came to Judy and Marion. And then there was the Parkinson's. It was all twisted together in one big, tragic knot.

Simon asked to her stay the night, but she kissed him goodbye and took the train back to the city. She had a lot to digest but promised that she'd see him on Christmas, in six days' time.

Later, on the train ride home, it occurred to Marion that she and her father had faced disparate struggles. While Simon had no problem adapting to the corporate culture, sublimating his individuality for the good of the team, she'd grappled with the opposite problem. She'd tried hard to channel her own impulsive energy and style into the techniques required of a good Rockette, but unlike Bunny and the others, Marion's individuality tended to burst out when she least expected it. Kicking too high, smiling too widely. Russell was right, there was some intrinsic part of her that couldn't be restrained, which made her a terrible choice as a Rockette, although she appreciated that he'd taken a chance on her.

Now that she'd accepted the Hoags' offer to be an assistant choreographer, she hoped the job would be a good fit. Marion could channel all that energy into a dance for others to perform. She'd be able to let her individuality roar, yet still be part of a team. She couldn't wait to begin.

✳

The afternoon of Christmas Eve, Marion sat in the parlor of the Rehearsal Club, leafing through some of Bunny's fashion magazines. Most of the girls had gone home to their families, and the Rockettes who remained, including Bunny, were onstage right about now, doing their second show of the day.

The doorbell rang and she went to answer it.

Outside, Peter stood on the landing, holding a letter. He looked up in surprise when she opened the door.

"Marion, I came by to leave you a note. I didn't realize you'd be here."

She couldn't tell if he was dismayed or just nervous.

The past few days, he'd left several messages, all of which had gone unanswered. Marion's talk with her father had turned everything upside down, and she didn't want to rehash her conversation with Peter, not after she'd blissfully imagined a future together and been quickly put in her place. It was all too much.

"Can we talk, maybe take a walk?" he asked.

She nodded and went to fetch her coat and hat. It was a bright day, warmer than expected, and they headed down Sixth Avenue before turning east toward Rockefeller Center.

They spoke of the case as they walked—more details had been made public in the newspapers—eventually reaching the ice-skating rink in the very center of the Rockefeller complex, where several children glided along the ice, yelling to their parents to watch and laughing whenever someone took a fall. The skyscrapers soared high above, solid and immobile, while across the way taxis and buses charged down Fifth Avenue. They were in the very heart of the city, amid Rockefeller Center's television studios, theater, corporations, and stores, not to mention several cafés tucked underground and a fancy restaurant called the Rainbow Room up in the clouds.

"Rockefeller had quite a vision," said Peter, as if he were reading her mind. "I often think about the men who built this from nothing, and what it's like to stroll by with their families twenty years later and point out the stones they laid and the buildings they worked on."

"And Radio City Music Hall is truly magnificent. I'm glad I'm able to say that I danced there," said Marion. "The beginning and end of my career as a performer."

"You're on to something even more exciting."

"I hope." She wondered why Peter had stopped by, what he wanted from her. But she wasn't about to put herself out there, not after what had happened last time. Also, her father's illness made her view the world differently these days. There was so much that was outside of one's control. "When do you leave for Virginia?"

"January second. When do you start the new show?"

"Same day."

"Will you still be living at the Rehearsal Club?"

"No. I'm moving home."

Peter's jaw dropped. "What?"

She'd decided to do so only the day before. Giving up the dream of her own New York apartment and a life of independence had been difficult, but it was the right thing to do. Simon was her father, and he had no one else. She'd figured if she moved in with him, the money that she would have spent toward an apartment could go instead to their living expenses, as well as hiring help. They'd have to live frugally, but the house was fully paid for and they'd manage.

Simon had broken down in tears on the phone when she'd told him and would be picking her up in a couple of hours, driving her to Bronxville. When she'd told Bunny, her friend had promised that they would always be close, no matter where Marion ended up, and Marion hoped so.

"Why would you move back home?" asked Peter. "When you spent so much time trying to extricate yourself from your father?"

"He has Parkinson's disease."

Peter nodded slowly, taking in the news. "I'm sorry."

"I haven't had a chance to do much research yet, but I plan on hitting the library once I'm home, to find out more about it. He says it's progressive, and there's no cure."

"He's right. I'm afraid it's a debilitating disease."

"How bad?"

"Do you want to know?"

She nodded but stared down at the ice rink as he spoke.

"It usually starts with a tremor, and then there's stiffness and gait issues, like trouble walking, trouble balancing. The patient tends to fall frequently and ends up confined to a wheelchair. In the later stages, there's difficulty swallowing, which can lead to pneumonia, and dementia can set in. But every patient's journey is different. Some have slower progressions than others. I'm so sorry, Marion."

"There are moments I truly hate him. I'm still angry for what he did to my mother, but I understand that her death cemented his view that if the women in his life weren't completely under his control, then we were in danger. He didn't realize that my mother, Judy, and I deserved the same freedom to move in the world as he did. That we had dreams, just as he did, and by keeping us locked down he forced us, or at least me and my mother, to find ways to escape. Ironically, now there's a chance he may go to jail." She paused. "I don't know how much time he has left. But in the end, he's my dad."

The sadness and pity in Peter's eyes almost undid her. She was giving up so much to stay home and take care of her father, and suddenly the thought of giving up Peter as well seemed intolerable.

"We were good together, weren't we?" Her voice rose like a little girl's, but she didn't care. She desperately needed reassurance that she hadn't imagined it.

"We were amazing. You are amazing."

"Then why do we have to part ways? Maybe I can visit, or when you come back to New York—"

Peter opened his mouth like he was about to say something, but then he stopped and gave a quick shake of his head. "I wish it could be different. B-but maybe it's better this way. You deserve someone who can give you their full attention. I won't be able to do that."

"I don't need your full attention. I want to be able to be a partner with someone who is kind, smart, and who I love."

"You do?" His breath caught in his throat, and he let out a sweet, small hiccup.

"Yes, Peter, I do. Why can't this work?"

His eyes became guarded again. She was pushing too hard. But if she didn't push now, when would she ever get the chance?

"It's not possible, what you want," he finally said.

"Why?"

She waited. He didn't reply right away. He loved her as much as she did him, she was sure of it. Yet there was something stopping him, a fear of some kind. The answer came to her in a rush.

"It's because of my father, right? If you're working for the FBI, then you can't be seen with the girl whose father prevented the Big Apple Bomber from being caught years before he actually was. I've seen the articles in the paper, how my father's been singled out. Well, it's not fair. It wasn't all his fault."

She couldn't believe she was defending him.

"No, that's not what I—"

Her indignation grew. "How could you? We are separate people, me and my father. I have to take care of him or he'll be destitute and sick."

"That's not it," he said.

"Just admit it, please. That you don't want to be with me because the association will hurt your career with the FBI. It's the same thing my father went through. Wanting to please everyone at the top instead of standing up for what's right. You and I are good together, I know we are. Why can't you stand up for us? I mean, I helped apprehend the Big Apple Bomber. Don't my father and I cancel each other out, in that way?"

"It's better that we go our separate ways," he said in a tight voice.

"I'm sorry to do it, I truly am. You're one of the best people in the world."

Then why do it at all? "Admit to me that's the reason, then. Tell me that."

He paused, as if gathering up his courage. "Y-yes. That's why." He looked away.

She stared hard at him. Something was off.

That first night out at the restaurant with Bunny and Dale, Peter had stuttered when he'd lied about Marion's profile, to make up for her discomfort. He'd done it again at his loft, when he'd apologized for kissing her. Because he hadn't been sorry for kissing her. He'd been lying, and stuttering was his tell. He was lying now.

But why? Why couldn't he tell her what was really going on?

"I do love you, Marion. I do. And I'm sorry."

She checked her watch. She had to finish packing before her father arrived at the Rehearsal Club. There was no more time.

She turned and walked away.

CHAPTER THIRTY-FOUR

Piper and I sweep through the front doors of Radio City Music Hall and into the lobby, which seems to gleam even brighter than it did when I was last here, thirty-six years ago. My heart starts to pound. I'm overwhelmed by the noise and the crush of people, and I'm not sure if I'll be able to step into the cavernous theater. It's all too much. I want to get back into the close quarters of the sedan, let the windows fog up, and sink deep into the back seat. To disappear.

I tell Piper I need to go to the ladies' room. We take the elevator up and I go inside, but instead of going to the toilet I head into the adjoining powder room, where several half-backed leather chairs face oversized round mirrors, with a small glass shelf perched underneath where a woman can set her purse. *Quite civilized*, I think to myself. I sit there, watching the other patrons come and go through the mirror's reflection. The murals on the powder room's walls soothe me, large flowers and ferns drifting from floor to ceiling, making the space feel like a secret garden. Out of the blue I remember that Georgia O'Keeffe had been originally commissioned to paint this room, but her husband had interfered, and she'd eventually not only lost the commission but also suffered a nervous breakdown. Instead, a Japanese American artist named Yasuo Kuniyoshi won the commission. He did a fine job. Still, I wonder about what might have been.

I try not to think of the past much these days, but I'm suddenly struck by the memory of the afternoon my father came to pick up me and my belongings from the Rehearsal Club on Christmas Eve 1956. Not long after I had fled from Peter in tears.

The city was quiet, everyone either far away with family and friends or holed up in apartments, wrapping presents and stuffing stockings.

Simon helped me get all my things into the trunk and back seat of the car—I'd acquired so much the months that I'd lived in the city, lots of hand-me-downs from the other girls, a couple of fancy dresses I bought with my salary as a Rockette—and then we climbed inside and drove in silence to Bronxville. That was back when he could still drive. His hand shook slightly on the steering wheel, but other than that, you'd never know what was to come.

After I'd moved back home, Simon didn't go out much, as there was nowhere to go and every one of his friends dropped him once the news of his role in the bombing case came to light. There were no criminal charges, thank goodness, but he became a social pariah. For a man who lived on laughter and camaraderie, known for his enthusiastic handshakes when he bumped into a casual acquaintance, a man who remembered everyone's wives' and kids' names, the toll was steep. He withdrew into himself, literally: his hands turned into fists, his shoulders caved in toward his chest, his head tilted forward. Then there were the constant falls, because he refused to use a cane or a walker. Eventually, he was too weak to stand and, although he railed against the idea, finally settled into a wheelchair.

All of this took time, of course. That's the nature of the disease. A slow erosion of independence and freedom of movement. While he wasted away, I found steady work as a choreographer, which helped pay for aides to stay and care for him. One thing I wasn't going to do was let him get in the way of my career.

The show about the early days of Russell's dance troupe—called *Rise of the Rockettes*—was a big hit, and I found myself working for other directors, eventually dropping the *assistant* before *choreographer*, and getting nominated for my first Tony in 1959. I lost to Bob Fosse but then went on to win three after that. While I officially retired from choreographing five years ago, at the age of fifty, I'm still involved in various projects that bring me into the city and feed my need for movement and grace.

Simon passed away after a series of strokes in the late sixties. At that point, I could have moved into the city, but it had changed, and not for the better. New York was more dangerous; there was litter on the streets and graffiti in the subways. By comparison, Bronxville was a paradise, and it remained my home base, even as I worked and traveled the world.

With this new book out about the hunt for the Big Apple Bomber, my phone rings with requests for interviews constantly. Everyone had forgotten the terror that one man brought to the city over the course of sixteen years. It had receded into the city's collective memory, and if you mentioned the name "George Martinek," you'd get a blank look. I'd allowed the author to interview me for the book, knowing that it was up to me to provide nuance to my father's decisions as well as the police's ineptitude. Once it was published, I found it to be quite well-written, to my surprise.

The author included, in the end, an update on the various characters in the story. Martinek was eventually sent to a psychiatric hospital for the "isolation of the dangerous and vicious" and is a model patient at the age of eighty-nine. His only act of rebellion is that he insists on wearing his double-breasted suits instead of the striped uniform.

Tommy Hornsby was honored in a special ceremony for his brav-
ery, and Mrs. Hornsby was there, beaming with pride. I know because I was sitting right beside her. She retired as expected at the end
of 1956 and passed away several years later in her sleep. Tommy and
I still stay in touch. He's a good man.

According to the book, Peter worked his way up in the FBI, es-
tablishing an entirely new department that created criminal profiles
in order to help solve terrible murders. Several high-profile cases—
where the perpetrator was a stranger to the victims and the local
police had no leads whatsoever—were solved due to Peter's genius.

All in all, a happy ending for the two of us.

A separate ending for the two of us.

I almost married once but thought better of it and backed out. I'd
spent much of my adult life taking care of a sick man and couldn't
imagine going through that again as we grew old. The idea of playing
nursemaid didn't appeal, and on top of that, working in the theater is
an all-consuming task, where every ounce of your being is devoted to
connecting with the close circle of people around you. Then, once
that show is up and running, you move on to the next circle. My
guess is Peter's work is like that as well. Throwing yourself into an
investigation at the cost of everything else.

We couldn't have made it work, I understand that now.

Although—and there's always an *although* lurking in the recesses
of my mind—I would have loved to share the journey with him. Even
ten, twenty, years after we parted, I would hear something said at a
party and think, *Now, that would make Peter laugh.* I suppose your first
love is the one that stays with you, especially when it was never con-
summated. How easy it is to idealize someone when your time together was fraught and short. We were never bored together, never
grated on each other's nerves. It wasn't real.

My own tremor began ten years ago. I was holding the television remote in my right hand when it began moving back and forth. I knew immediately what was going on. After the doctor confirmed that I had Parkinson's, I spiraled down into a depression. I was a dancer, for God's sake; my life was about movement, my identity and sense of self were wrapped up in being able to move my limbs and body at will, to have perfect control over my muscles and tendons. I felt such shame at letting myself down. My body was always something that I could depend on, and with Parkinson's I lost a part of myself. I thought my life was over.

The prevailing advice at the time my father was diagnosed was to be careful, that someone with Parkinson's must move slowly and cautiously to avoid falling.

Instead, I fought back with every ounce of my being. I always felt my best when I was training. Even as a choreographer, I made sure to attend regular dance classes to stay in shape and remind myself of the physical demands I was making on my dancers. Doing so made it easier for me to not get frustrated or angry when they couldn't replicate what I saw in my head.

Soon after the diagnosis, I took even more classes. I discovered that when the music began, the Parkinson's faded away. That was when I knew I was on the right track. I began telling people what was going on, and to my surprise, I was asked to share what I'd learned with others with the disease. I'm in the city at least twice a week now, running workshops, teaching others how to handle their gait and balance issues, how to look at their bodies in a new way. I take the mechanics and format of a ballet class—beginning by standing at the barre and focusing on small movements, eventually building up so the students are striding across the floor, arms pumping, heads upright, smiles on their faces, some crying with surprise at the sense of freedom. It's the equivalent of a grand jeté, and just as beautiful to watch. Even if it's temporary.

I dread most the day that I wake up and can no longer smile. That I will be struck with hypomimia, where the muscles of the face no longer respond. No one will be able to tell if I'm pleased or filled with joy. No silly grins, no raised eyebrows at a bad joke. I don't want that. Every morning I check my face in the mirror and make sure that I can grin. So far, so good.

An outlier. That's what I plan to be. Someone who lives with this disease and stays fully functioning. My doctor is impressed with the slow progression. But I take nothing for granted. The hardest is to live in the moment and not worry about what's coming five or ten years from now. What happens when I can't take care of myself?

The day my father died, he was mute, riddled with dementia, choking whenever he tried to eat. All because a small section in the midbrain had stopped producing a vital chemical messenger called dopamine.

Enough with the self-pity. I've gotten this far, and I don't want to let Piper down. I push myself up to standing and find her in the lobby. My arm flaps about—the tremor gets worse whenever I'm stressed or nervous. I'd make a terrible poker player these days. I allow her to take my good arm.

Inside the theater, I'm led all the way down the aisle to the second row. I avoid looking at the seat my sister sat in on the day she died. I don't want to think about that, and luckily, before the maudlin thoughts take hold, Bunny is in my arms and the air is filled with her giddy laughter.

"You're here!" she says, her eyes wide with surprise.

"Of course. I wouldn't miss it for the world." Back in Bronxville, I had noticed in my quick glance through the program that Bunny is being honored for her work with the Rockettes alumni group. Typical of Bunny, she didn't mention it to me the last time we chatted on the phone. She knows how hard it is for me to be here, to sit in one of the red velvet seats, like Judy had done, and wonder what my sister went through that terrible night, the mixture of pain and panic she must have experienced in her final moments.

But I couldn't let Bunny down.

She'd kept her word and broken up with Dale that New Year's Eve back in 1956, and after dancing a few more seasons with the Rockettes, she married a man who owns shopping malls and moved to California. She taught dance for a while, raised three kids, and now is a grandmother of seven. Whenever she comes to town we meet and laugh about old times. We don't talk about the bad ones. We don't talk about my sister. Yet, for me, Judy's ghost is everywhere. After all, I live in the house where we grew up together. I keep her photo on my mantel. She would be fifty-eight years old, and right here by my side, if she were still alive.

The theater is filled with former Rockettes. You can spot them by their regal bearing and loose-limbed walks. Bunny looks vibrant in a slinky, sparkly gown.

"Can you believe it?" says Bunny. "It's amazing what a sisterhood this is."

"We share an experience that no one else will understand."

"Do you know I still dream about being in a kick line? Every so often, there I am, onstage, as if it was yesterday. Then I wake up with creaky joints."

"As long as you don't kick out in your dreams, you might as well enjoy them," I assure her.

The lights go down and we take our seats. The organists stop playing, take their bows, and the orchestra rises from below the stage. As the show begins, all focus turns to the marvelous, leggy dancers onstage, who are even better than we were. The choreography is sharper, tighter, and more efficient. I straighten up in my seat, watching them. Shoulders back, chin slightly lifted. I remember it well.

What happened in the fall and winter of 1956 was just one story, part of the rough-and-tumble city of New York, crammed with both love and cruelty. And quite a few gray areas, where people made terrible decisions that aren't easily summed up in a historical account of the times. People like my father.

The events coordinator for the Rockettes organization, the same Ms. Burris who'd hounded me to attend, emerges from the wings as a podium is wheeled out. She makes a lovely speech about Bunny's role in keeping all the Rockettes connected with each other, long after they've left Radio City, and when Bunny is called to the stage, she practically floats up the steps, gliding across the floor like we did in the old days and smiling just as Russell told us to. I clap hard and long, happy for my friend.

After, Ms. Burris talks about Russell, who died two years ago, and his legacy. I brace myself as she segues into the "dark times" of Radio City's history, when a madman planted bombs in this very theater. But Piper was right—she names Judy as well as the others who were injured—before asking for a moment of silence. Nothing tawdry. I needn't have worried.

When it's over, she lifts her head and says she also wants to present an award to "a special Rockette, one who helped catch the Big Apple Bomber back in 1956."

I look around, wondering what on earth she's talking about. This isn't in the program.

She speaks about the night of the madman's capture, when one Rockette sacrificed everything to bring him to justice.

This can't be happening. My stomach drops.

Then my name is called and Ann Burris looks right at me, one hand out in welcome. As if I'm supposed to somehow materialize onstage.

Slowly, I rise to my feet. The tremor in my arm has gone rogue and

I feel my face go red with embarrassment. There's a wide set of stairs at the end of the aisle, leading up to the stage, but it might as well be a steep cliff. The combination of no handrail and my untrustworthy balance means that I'll either career off the edge or fall flat on my face. I'll end up crawling up the stairs, a pitiful middle-aged lady in a blue dress. Still, I take a few steps into the aisle. What choice do I have? But at the foot of the staircase I'm stuck, frozen in place. Yet another delightful symptom of Parkinson's. Usually if I hum a tune I can get my legs going again, but my thoughts are muddled and I can't think straight.

The clapping continues, but I can't do what Bunny did, I can't make my body effortlessly leap onto the stage. I'm weak, crippled, and my eyes fill with tears of self-pity and embarrassment.

Then, out of the blue, two young women appear on either side of me. They have their hair pulled back in tight buns and are in costume, Rockettes from the show. I hadn't even noticed that they'd made their way over to me.

The women wrap their arms around my lower back, and I instinctively do the same, our arms crisscrossing at the elbows. It's the same position every Rockette over the decades has executed as they prepare for the kick line. An illusion of support, but with absolutely no contact, each dancer's arm floating in space a good two inches away from their neighbor's back.

But not this time. They hold me firmly in place, and I rest my hands on their shoulders for added leverage. The three of us take one stair at a time, pausing on each step, our toes beveled, as if this were one of Russell's routines instead of a way of helping me save face. My right arm shakes, but that doesn't matter. My gait falters, but with these two young, healthy bodies flanking my wretched one, that doesn't matter, either.

A lone sob rises from deep in my gut, but it's one of relief, and then I'm onstage, the audience jumping to its feet. The two Rockettes stay with me as Ms. Burris talks and I try to focus, to listen.

"The theaters of New York City have two people to thank for making our performance spaces safe in that dark time. Marion Brooks, as well as Dr. Peter Griggs, who I'm happy to say is with us tonight as well."

I look wildly about. He's here?

And then a figure appears on the other side of the stage.

It's Peter.

CHAPTER THIRTY-FIVE

The man walks with a lope I recognize from over thirty-five years ago, as if the length of his legs is a surprise, each step ending with a slight plod. He has the same curly hair, slightly thinning and gray. His eyes are dead set on mine, as if the thousands of people out in the audience don't even exist, even though they're clapping eagerly, pleased at having an esteemed criminologist in their midst.

Ms. Burris begins talking again, but I don't hear a word. We are standing slightly behind her, not more than three feet apart, staring at each other. He smiles and it's as if the stage lift has kicked in, pulling me high up into the air. I feel like I'm floating, like my broken body has healed and I'm a dancer once again, strong and agile.

The rest of the speech goes by in a blur. We're each handed a heavy glass award and then escorted offstage. It's such a familiar sight: the ropes and pulleys rising up the white brick walls, wicker baskets of tap shoes in one corner, the stagehands moving about with purpose. I'm surrounded by people, but the one I most want to see isn't there anymore. Peter's been pulled off in another direction. Or maybe he ran for the hills after seeing me.

Piper appears. "That was wonderful," she gushes. "I can escort you to the reception in the Rainbow Room now."

I acquiesce. I could use a little support.

The Rainbow Room was too expensive for our tastes back when I lived at the Rehearsal Club, and even today it's an elegant, breathtaking restaurant. High up on the sixty-fifth floor, featuring twenty-four-foot-high windows that look out on the city below, it's popular with tourists but also for galas like this one. A band plays on a small raised stage and the rotating dance floor is already crowded. Piper and I are edging toward the bar when someone taps me on the shoulder.

It's Peter, with two champagne glasses in his hands. He holds one out to me warily, like he's worried I might slap it away.

I take it. "Thank you, that will do nicely."

How silly of me. *That will do nicely.* Like I'm some grande dame. But I don't know what to say to him, or how to say it, after so many years apart.

"It's packed in here—how about we go on the balcony?" he says.

I tell Piper that I'm perfectly fine and she should go off and have a good time, and then follow Peter as he leads the way through the horde. We pass through a set of glass doors and suddenly the sounds of the party recede, replaced by the gentle hum of New York below us. The lights of the buildings shine with a crispness that you only find in the cooler months, and the slight breeze is refreshing.

I reach into my purse and take out my pill box. It's time for my next dose. I swallow the pill down with champagne and wait, relieved that the tremors will subside in the next thirty minutes or so.

Peter leans one arm on the balcony and watches me. He is still trim and looks quite good in his suit. He was a boy when we met, in many ways, and has matured into a very good-looking man.

"I hear you've done well for yourself," I say, wanting to take the focus off my pill-taking.

"Yes. It was a good job, I traveled all over the country. I still do some consulting work. I hear you've been traveling quite a bit as well. Not to mention winning Tony Awards. Three, right?"

I nod, pleased he knows. "What do you plan on doing with the heavy paperweight they gave us tonight?" I left mine with the coat check and am not sure if I'll pick it up at the end of the night. It's a lovely gesture, but I don't want to be awarded for anything to do with Judy's death. I still miss her after all these years.

"Doorstop."

I smile.

He ducks his head and looks at me strangely. "Marion, I've been wanting to apologize for years about the terrible way I left it with us."

"No need." I look up at the crescent moon, unable to meet his gaze. "You couldn't have achieved what you did, not with my father in the picture."

"I saw the notice when he passed away. I'm sorry."

Dad's obituary appeared in a couple of newspapers that were eager to rehash the story. "Yes, he lived another dozen years after all that."

Simon had spent his last minutes holding my hand in his, unable to speak, his eyes asking for forgiveness, which I'd already given him years before.

"You were a good daughter."

The night is turning maudlin. I don't want to hash out the past anymore. For years I wondered what I'd say if I saw Peter again. And now here we are, and it's strained and uncomfortable. I look back at the partygoers inside.

"Did you ever marry?" he asks me.

"Almost, but no. You?"

"Almost, but no."

"What made you call it off?" I say, curious.

"She wasn't you." To my surprise, Dr. Peter Griggs, the infamous killer hunter, turns bright red. "I want to tell you the truth about why

I refused to even try to make it work. Even though I had fallen madly in love with you."

I hadn't imagined it. I wait.

"I was a coward, I guess that's one way to put it. My mother, as I mentioned, became a schizophrenic at the age of thirty-seven. But that's not the whole picture. Her father did, too, at thirty-five. I knew that there was a good chance it would affect me as well." He let out a small laugh. "There I was, working at a psychiatric hospital, knowing that I might very well be committed to a similar place within the next decade."

I think back. That explains why he worked so hard, both at Creedmoor and down at the Bowery. He thought his time was running out. I could only imagine what it was like living your life in a compressed timeline, when at any moment all might be lost. "I didn't know."

"You couldn't have. That day, at the ice rink, I realized I couldn't put you through all that, knowing that you already had your father to take care of. I couldn't put you through watching as I lost my faculties as well, probably at the very same time."

That day long ago, standing at the ice rink, he'd stuttered as he reluctantly admitted that having my father as an in-law would damage his career prospects. He'd stuttered because he had been lying. That hadn't been the reason at all. He had been trying to save me from future heartache. "It wasn't your decision to make," I say. "Why weren't you honest with me? Didn't I deserve that, after everything we'd been through?"

"It wasn't only that. At our last dinner together, I wanted so desperately to tell you I was falling in love with you, but I also knew it was wrong of me to do so."

"Why?"

"Remember when we were up on the observation deck? I asked if you wanted to be a mother, and you said you did. There was even a boyfriend in the picture, the one who dropped you off that day."

"I remember."

"Well, I knew I could never be a father. There was no way I could pass my genes on to a child, it wouldn't be fair. If we went ahead and pursued a relationship, there was a chance you'd say that you really didn't want children after all. I would have hated myself if you had given that up for me and then eventually regretted it."

That same afternoon he'd talked of illnesses that were passed down from generation to generation. I hadn't put it together until now that he was talking about us, our future.

He was trying to protect me.

What a terrible waste, to have given each other up for some future tragedy that never even happened. When I speak, there's a chill in my voice. "I never had children. My life was too peripatetic for that. But I suppose I appreciate the sentiment. You seem to have made it through your thirties unscathed."

"I have."

"I'm glad. Very glad."

"I considered reaching out, once I knew I was in the clear, but at that point I was with someone. After we broke up, I was on a work trip in Los Angeles when I saw that one of your shows was doing an out-of-town tryout there. I went to the opening—it was marvelous, by the way—but as I was buying my ticket I saw you with someone . . ."

He trails off, but I know exactly who he's referring to.

It was a whirlwind romance with the assistant director, all glitter but no substance, one that fizzled out before we even got back to New York. I remember that night, though, when I was still in the midst of the initial heady spell of finding oneself in love. I hate that Peter witnessed it and walked away. "It wasn't anything, just an on-the-road romance with an assistant director. You were there?"

He nods and flinches a little, as if remembering the moment. My heart goes out to him then. My heart has always been with him. What terrible timing we've had.

"The important thing is that you're healthy," I say. "I can only imagine what it was like waking up day after day, wondering if this was it, wondering if what you were thinking and feeling was reality or something else."

"That's exactly what it was like."

"I'm afraid I didn't escape the family curse so easily. You saw me earlier, I can't even walk up to the stage without help. Like father, like daughter."

"I'm sorry, Marion. You seem better now."

"The medicine helps. For a time. I'm doing fine, actually. Better than expected."

He moves toward me. "I was excited that you'd be here tonight, that we'd see each other. I wanted a chance to explain, finally." He pauses. "Although I admit I was worried that there was some assistant director in the picture."

I laugh, and he does as well. But he's still looking at me like he's serious. Good Lord. The man is caught up in the moment, not thinking straight. "No, no assistant director. But it's too late, Peter, although I appreciate the sentiment." My heart is thudding in my chest.

"Come with me. We need a do-over."

"What?"

Back inside we grab our coats and awards at the coat check—he refuses to allow me to leave mine behind—and take a long elevator ride to the lobby. He leads me out into the plaza and then we're standing on the edge of the ice rink. Exactly the spot where we parted thirty-six years ago.

So much has changed.

And so little.

He turns to me and puts his hands gently on my shoulders. "Ask me again."

"Ask you what?"

"What you did last time we were here."

"I don't remember."

But I do.

He waits.

"Why do we have to go our separate ways?" I say finally.

"We don't. As a matter of fact, I'm free for the next however-many years, and I want to be by your side for them all. Will that do?"

"I don't want you to do this out of pity," I say. "I'm not my father. I'm going to have a different trajectory and I don't plan on needing anyone. My doc says I'll die of something else before the Parkinson's gets to me."

"We were a good team, Marion. You and me. There's no pity in this face." He points to his head. "Do you see any pity in this face?"

"No."

"My guess is there's some unsolved murder out here in the Big Apple that could use a crack team of middle-aged sleuths to break it wide open. What do you think? Shall we give it a go?"

Taking a leap this late in life is crazy, I think to myself.

Don't let yourself get hurt again, I warn myself.

But the answer is obvious.

As the skaters glide across the ice below us, I lean into him and we kiss, his lips tasting of champagne.

The answer is yes.

AUTHOR'S NOTE

All my books are set in iconic New York City landmarks, but choosing the building is only the first step in the process. I also do a wide search for seminal events that were going on in the city during the building's history, keeping an eye out for a "hook" that will hopefully help ground the story in whatever decade (or decades) I end up focusing on.

As I was researching the 1950s for *The Spectacular*, a news item caught my attention. In January 1957, a man named George Metesky was arrested and charged with planting thirty-two bombs over sixteen years around New York City. Known in the press as the "Mad Bomber," Metesky left explosives in some of the Big Apple's busiest locations, including Radio City Music Hall, Grand Central Terminal, the Paramount Theatre, the New York Public Library, and Pennsylvania Station, to name just a few. Although there were no deaths, the bombs injured fifteen people, some seriously.

I was shocked. A madman had terrorized the city for almost two decades? Very few people I spoke with had even heard of him. The inspiration behind the plot of *The Spectacular* is drawn from the Mad Bomber's story, in particular a vivid, detailed account of it written by Michael Cannell called *Incendiary: The Psychiatrist, the Mad Bomber, and the Invention of Criminal Profiling*. However, my story differs significantly from the true events (which is why I've changed the fictional perpetrator's surname, as well as his nickname and other names and details), and I want to take this opportunity to elucidate what actually did happen and give credit where it is due with respect to the expert who helped crack the case.

In 1956, with no leads and public outcry mounting, the police turned to James A. Brussel, a psychiatrist and criminologist and the assistant commissioner of the New York State Department of Mental Hygiene, who lived with his wife on the grounds of Creedmoor State Hospital in Queens. Brussel examined the letters from the bomber and the crime scene photos and came up with a "portrait" of the bomber—the very first case of criminal profiling ever. Among his many predictions: that when he was found, the bomber would be wearing a double-breasted suit, buttoned.

When Metesky was finally detained, Brussel's profile proved eerily correct. Metesky had worked for a local electrical power company from 1929 to 1931, when he was injured in a boiler explosion while on the job. In 1956, when asked for access to its old personnel records, the power company told police investigators that records of employees terminated prior to 1940 no longer existed, effectively stymieing the capture of the bomber. In fact, the files had been stored away, with police and Metesky's attorney later claiming that the company had intentionally hidden files that contained embarrassing information about some employees' workers' compensation claims. It wasn't until mid-January 1957 that the power company initiated an internal review of those files. One of the clerks found letters from Metesky with similar menacing phrases as had been published in the papers, and soon after, Metesky was arrested in his Waterbury, Connecticut, home. The power company denied any wrongdoing concerning those old records.

Brussel went on to great career success, working with FBI agents and police around the country and becoming a "folk hero of crimi-nology," according to *Smithsonian Magazine.*

In my book, Radio City Music Hall is hit three times by the bomber. In actuality, he struck twice. One bomb prematurely ex-ploded in 1953 just as Metesky was heading to the exit. A patron was tossed into the air by the blast, landing a few rows away, but only suffered superficial injuries. The second explosion, in 1954 during a showing of the movie *White Christmas,* caused deep puncture wounds in two women and contusions in two boys.

Metesky served seventeen years in a mental institution and was released in 1973. He returned to his home in Waterbury and died in 1994 at the age of ninety.

As I was researching *The Spectacular,* I was lucky enough to inter-view a number of Rockettes who danced at Radio City Music Hall over the decades, and I've taken some liberties in the novel in order to present a broader picture of what it was like to be a Rockette. For example, in 1956 the Christmas stage show included far fewer Rock-ette dance numbers than are performed today. The one described in the novel more closely reflects today's *Christmas Spectacular,* involv-ing multiple numbers and costume changes. I've also included some dances (like the "Cowboy" number) that, in fact, were performed in later years, as well as traditions like the preshow finger lick that were practiced in an earlier era.

Several books were helpful in terms of research, including *The Mad Bomber of New York: The Extraordinary True Story of the Manhunt That Paralyzed a City* by Michael M. Greenburg, *And She Danced for the King: Memoirs of a Rockette* by Ro Trent Vaselaar, *The Brownstone on West 53rd Street: Rehearsal Club Memoir* by Lora Mitchell, *Apollo's Angels: A History of Ballet* by Jennifer Homans, *Gwen Verdon: A Life on Stage and Screen* by Peter Shelley, *Radio City Musical Hall: An*

Affectionate History of the World's Greatest Theater by Charles Francisco, and *The Art of Rockefeller Center* by Christine Roussel.

For more information on Parkinson's disease, I recommend the Michael J. Fox Foundation, which I found to be a valuable resource after being diagnosed in 2020.

One final note: you may have noticed the Rockettes are referred to as girls, not women, throughout the novel. That's the term Russell Markert used for the individual members of his troupe, and as historically dancers have been called "girls" (showgirl, chorus girl, Ziegfeld girls), I chose to stay true to the period.

ACKNOWLEDGMENTS

Nine years and seven books ago, Stefanie Lieberman pulled my manuscript out of the slush pile and gave it a read and changed the course of my life with one phone call. Stefanie, I can't thank you enough for your wise counsel and friendship. I'm also grateful to Molly Steinblatt and Adam Hobbins for diving into the heart of each new novel and setting me up for success with their insights and support.

I am truly indebted to Lindsey Rose for her vision and skill as an editor, and the entire team at Dutton, who deserve a standing ovation: Christine Ball, John Parsley, Madeline McIntosh, Ivan Held, Allison Dobson, Amanda Walker, Alice Dalrymple, Sarah Thegeby, Nicole Jarvis, Caroline Payne, and Charlotte Peters. A big shout-out goes to Christopher Lin, who's responsible for the dazzling book covers; and to Kathleen Carter of Kathleen Carter Communications, for everything you do behind the scenes.

A huge thanks to Sandra Lachenauer, who gave me the idea for this book and shared archival material from her days as a Rockette—without Sandy, this story would never have been written. Thanks as well to her husband, Bob, for sharing his detailed technical knowledge of Radio City with me. I had the joy of interviewing a number of professional dancers and former Rockettes for this story, including

Sara Sessions, Margaret Pearsall, Patti DeCarlo Grantham, Rhonda Kaufman Malkin, Sandell Morse, Melissa Stern, Nancy Kaplan, and Pamela Quinn. A special thanks to Christine Roussel of the Rockefeller Archive Center for her assistance and the splendid tour of the Radio City Music Hall roof. I'm also indebted to Andrew Alpern, Florie Seery, Jim Claffey, Ruth Stanley, Nikki Slota-Terry, Olivia Fanaro, Orly Greenberg, and the team at Authors Unbound, helmed by Christie Hinrichs.

I'm lucky to be part of a warm and wonderful author community, both in real life and online. The list is far too long to include here, but thanks to the Thursday authors—Lynda Cohen Loigman, Jamie Brenner, Susie Orman Schnall, Nicola Harrison, Amy Poeppel, and Suzanne Leopold—as well as Sarah Penner, Wendy Walker, Julie Satow, Laurie Albanese, and Jenny Quinlan for helping me shape this book in the early days.

I can't thank enough the booksellers, librarians, book influencers, bookstagrammers, and reviewers who keep the literary world buzzing with your recommendations. Your enthusiasm and hard work are very much treasured.

Thanks to the readers who donated their names as characters in this book, in return for an auction donation to charity. Your generosity is truly appreciated.

A special shout-out to my dear friends who've been there from the beginning: Cynthia Besteman, Linda Powell, Angela Nevard, Madeline Rispoli, Christine Radman, Maria Radman, and Dede Pochos.

I'm so grateful to my family, immediate and extended, for their enthusiastic support and for sending me hilarious texts right when I need them. And finally, thanks to Greg Wands for knowing exactly what it is like to turn a vague notion into a book, including all the hard work in between, and for making our life bright, joyful, and full of love.

ABOUT THE AUTHOR

Fiona Davis is the *New York Times* bestselling author of several novels, including *The Dollhouse, The Address, The Masterpiece, The Chelsea Girls, The Lions of Fifth Avenue,* and *The Magnolia Palace.* She lives in New York City and is a graduate of the Columbia Journalism School.